THE ANALYST

Brandon Rolfe

ISBN 978-1-909204-03-4

Printed by Dolman Scott

www.dolmanscott.com

CHAPTER 1

London, September, 1887

The rain finally stopped. Then a coy sun dared peek through a torn patch in the brooding sky. Invitation enough for the twisting rivers of shiny black umbrellas and mackintoshes to dry up into brighter colours of coats and jackets. One such explosion of colour caught Adam Balchard's eye, at the corner of Billingsgate Market on Thames Street. It was the brown and yellow check suit of Sam Loofer, weaving in and out of the clamorous crowds of costermongers and oyster stalls like a two-legged chess-board. Complete with a brown felt hat rounding off his wooden stave head, and a short stubble of cigar just marginally longer than the stubble on his chisel wedge face. Sam was the natural born haggler; as much at ease bargaining between stall and street, as he was between dukes and donkeys. Forever the ready source of underworld information, or of goods that had *fallen off the back of a cart*, he was often useful to Balchard as informer and supplier. Despite being in a hurry, Balchard lingered back among the crowded stalls in order to let Loofer complete his transaction with the

1

baked-potato man. As a study of human behaviour, Balchard liked to observe the moods and reactions of his contacts in their natural environment, prior to his confronting them.

While his mate up-ended his sack to tumble out a pile of potatoes beside the glowing iron stove-cart, Loofer held out a broad nicotine-stained hand to collect a pile of pennies that were dirtier than the delivered goods. ''Ere, mate, what's yer bleedin' gyme, then?' cried his Cockney mate, frowning down at the minor 'equal' share of the money that Loofer had given him. 'Ah thaht we were supposed ter be splittin' the loot dahn the middle?'

'That's right, so we 'ave; fifty, fifty. Summit wrong, then?' said Loofer.

'So 'ow come you've got more thahn my bleedin' share? We started aht with thirty five bleedin' 'tytas; we threw away three rotten bleeders and lost one under the bus wheel.'

'That's right; *them* four was *yours*,' said Loofer, with matter-of-fact surety.

'Bleedin' 'ell, mate! There's summit wrong 'ere, or my nyme is Queen Vicki!'

'Leave it out, son! What do you know about right and wrong? You've as much chance o' findin' a brain in that 'ead o' yours as you would stirrin' a pot o' Bombay mince!' Placing a consoling arm round his dim-witted mate's shoulder, Loofer proceeded to quell the plaintive pleas with a smooth flow of devious logic that was as straight as a bent nail. Pausing to remove his unlit cigar, before launching into the final speech that would finally quench his mate's protests, Loofer suddenly stopped. He forgot all else as his eyes fell on the small figure in

2

dark coat and hat, standing across the street, beside the cobbler stall, watching him. He recognised the pale face, with its cold fish-like expression sadder than a hooked cod. It was Mr B; come to spy out 'is own folk, like a fish, indeed, returnin' to its spawnin' waters. Licking his lips whilst collecting his wits, Loofer, the perpetual showman, prepared himself for a new audience, in the same way that the cardsharper shuffled the pack, or the thimble rigger reset the pea under the thimble. Signalling with a broad smile and a nod that it was safe for Balchard to come over, Loofer muttered askant at the same time to his mate: 'Look out, son, we got company. Watch what yer says an' does with this geezer. 'E's got eyes an' ears the back o' 'is knees, 'e 'as. Blink an' eye an' 'e can tell yer what colour o' shit yer last mouthful o' jellied eel laid, 'e can. So just watchit. I'll do the talkin'.'

Loofer sucked heavily on his unlit cigar and narrowed his eyes to slits as he watched the small figure approach them through the milling crowd. A right funny bloke this Mr B was, Loofer thought; a real mysterious crate o' fizz an' pop ale 'e was, right enough. After all, what bloke in 'is right mind would waste 'is time shilly-shallying around an 'ell 'ole like this, when 'e 'ad the toff job an' money to do 'imself good up town? An' if that wasn't bad enough, when 'e is 'ere, 'e goes an' blinks not as much as a bleedin' eye at the pretty painted strumpet, but, instead, goes grabbin' the ugliest female bag to see what colour o' clay she 'as stickin' under 'er bloomin' shoes! On top o' that, 'e acts like a silent partner for bloomin' Burke an' 'Are, cuttin' an' bashin' bodies an' things in the 'ospital, 'e does. An' apart from 'is music-'all magician's tricks o' tellin' yer what yer does *before* yer damn well bleedin' does it, 'e does all sorts o' other funny things, like experimentin' an' fiddlin' with bottles an' tubes an' poisons an' things, in 'is own 'ouse, no less. Blimey, I bloomin' asks yer!

Balchard stepped up to Loofer and his awry companion, greeting them with a curt nod. He looked down for a moment at the appetising warm potatoes, and then at the surrounding sea of urchins' wan faces staring back at him, their eyes sharp as bayonets with the message of belly-wrenching hunger. To buy a potato for one only would be tantamount to starting a rush that could well end in both people and potatoes being crushed underfoot in a real 'bangers and mash' rumpus. He did the easiest, cowardly, thing and ignored them all. But however much he could shut off their hungry looks, he could not shut off their cries. Those not crying out for "'Tytas", were demanding gin, not so much because they had much faith in their pleas being met, as venting a bitterness that stirred in them to ridicule the well- to-do for lamenting their woebegone poverty. Loofer took out his cigar and beamed his best smile for his next placatory piece. 'So 'ow's it goin', Mr B? Nice t' see yer again. I was just tellin' Charlie, 'ere, likes as 'ow yer can do mind readin' tricks. Go on, show 'im what I mean. Tell 'im 'ow many cock-eyed maggots 'e 'ad in 'is cheese for breakfast, then.'

Balchard found Loofer's streetwise humour contemptible, but did not stoop to showing it, knowing full well that it was his way of getting under one's skin. He also needed the man as a useful -- valuable, if he would admit to it -- informant, and contact, if not supplier of various 'goods'. His pallid cheeks twitched a second, in customary non-smiling greeting to Loofer. He looked at Loofer's companion, seeing a form that was wretchedly twisted by a mal-formed spine, and as much torn in spirit as the rags crudely adorning it. If ever depression and despair could be called a ghost, it was that which haunted the miserable countenance before him, like those around him. 'Since I cannot put a name to that which is not there to begin with, I rather fancy that your friend has not eaten at all, for some time. But perhaps he could remedy the situation by attempting to return to his former employment at the match factory. If so, I would earnestly suggest that you try the Salvation Army factory in Wick Lane, in Bow, where the new technique is now to use the safe red form of phosphorus, rather than the deadly yellow form, for the production of slow-burning fusee wind-proof matches. If you wish, I can put in a complimentary word on your behalf to the superintendent at the at the factory, through the kind office of Dr Michaels, at the Institute, who is currently researching into such detrimental effects of industry on the social order.'

The Cockney drew back in open astonishment. ''Ere, 'alf a mo'; 'ow did you know thaht, guv? Is yer from the Law, or summit? I ain't dahn nahthin' wrong. Honest.'

Balchard made no mention of his instant diagnosis of the match-maker's killer disease, known as *Phossy Jaw*, that was written on the Cockney's face, with its solvent action on his teeth. Produced by an over exposure to the deadly fumes of yellow phosphorus, it was the occupational condition that chased many a victim to the grave. Loofer released a loud guffaw at his friend's bewilderment, and nudging Balchard's arm, nodded to signal that they should leave the Cockney in his daze so that they could go off and discuss some real business. He had the merchandise that Balchard had come to collect. It was a small cloth bag containing a set of steel skeleton-keys and a tiny .22 calibre revolver. Belgian make, Balchard noted. Although a mere four and a half inches long, with a folding trigger, it was still a reassuring four and a half inches to carry in one's pocket. 'An' see 'ere,' said Loofer, pointing at the trigger, 'this ain't broken as such. It's supposed ter fol-----'

'Yes I know. *Both* of us are very clever.' There was no mistaking the irritation flaring up in Balchard's voice and eyes.

Loofer handed the goods over discreetly. He didn't question their purpose. He did, however, make a point of stressing the astronomical price over which he had had to haggle with his supplier. 'Well, anyway, I'm smarter than 'im, 'cause I says to 'im: "Mr D'Arcy," I says, "if yer wants a buyer for them goods, yer can sell 'em t' me; but not for a penny more than the price we'd agreed on, no sooner than yer can spit in a dead cat's eye," I says.' Loofer spat at the cobble-stones to signify how the deal had been successfully concluded, the spittle landing on the trouser-leg of a passing fish vendor. Balchard put the bag in his pocket. Then changing his mind, he took the pistol out and put it in his other pocket by itself. More easily reached that way.

Balchard took Loofer's point concerning the high price, and paid the requisite sum plus the agreed percentage commission. Pleased with the outcome of another safe settlement, and the money secure in his pocket, Loofer took another heavy drag on his yet unlit cigar. 'Like I says, Mr B, any deals yer ever needs doin', yer can always trust me t' do 'em for yer. There ain't nothin' t' beat a wise old fish with two left feet, I always says.'

As it so happened, Balchard did, in fact, have another such mission for Loofer in mind. He explained how he was anxious to monitor the movements of a suspected hired killer, whom he had just recently traced to Pickle Herring Street, across the river. The man, between 'jobs', had the habit of taking his young son to the stables for riding lessons, and Balchard wanted to employ a small boy to get in close. To merge in and make friends, as children do, without arousing suspicion. The boy would be his eyes and ears, inconspicuous, whilst watching the man's daily movements. He would need to keep a sharp ear and a sharp wit about him. Balchard made no mention of brutal murder and its associated treachery. He thought it better to leave that out. Sadistic killings, with all their lurid aspects, even in the domestic cases, were apt to upset people. To Balchard they were no more than commonplace statistics to be charted up in his work for Scotland Yard.

When Loofer tried to pry further into the matter, Balchard simply tapped his nose meaningfully with his finger. 'Say no more, Mr B,' returned Loofer, tapping his own nose, 'say no more. A nod's as good as a wink to a blind camel with three wooden 'umps. I know the very lad for yer. A right sparklin' little perisher 'e 'is, Mr B. Back at my place.'

From out of the blur of bleak faces blocking the entrance

to Duck' Foot Lane, Loofer plucked a most rueful specimen of human that was different from gutter filth only by a morose whimper that was an attempted smile. The hollow eye sockets were redder than usual, where the boy had been crying over the death of his mother from consumption. Loofer stood the boy before Balchard for inspection, and stood back in open acclaim of his instant prodigy. 'By 'eck, 'e's sharp, I can tell yer, Mr B.' Loofer leaned near to Balchard, and winking, partitioned off his mouth with a broad conspiratorial palm. 'Listen, 'e's so sharp 'e could 'ear a bloomin' fly fart on the roof o' the Albert 'All, 'e could. Ain't yer, boy! Ain't yer!' To confirm the point, Loofer gave a friendly tug at the boy's ear so that the boy was in danger of rising off the ground, like a human plumb-line.

As if to question the boy's hearing, Balchard, much to Loofer's curiosity, stooped to examine the boy's other ear. The boy's mouth fell open with astonishment when Balchard's 'empty' hand now extracted a 'magic' sixpenny piece from the wax-filled cavity. Balchard watched the boy's eyes light up in wonder and smiled sadly. He, too, had been in awe at his pater first performing that 'magic' on him; his pater had taught him how to do it. But then his pater had always been good at tricks, 'shifting things' and other illusions -- making things appear to be other than what they really were. Whether this had always been deliberate deceit, or a fool's optimism, was an unresolved puzzle long left alone. His brief twitch of a smile that had shared the boy's pleasure, now hardened to bitterness. 'The long lost property of the young master, I do believe,' said Balchard, trying to keep the bitterness out of his voice for the boy's sake, while holding out the coin for him. Loofer laughed and protested that the boy would not know how to spend such a sum, and that he would keep it in trust for the lad. 'The damn hell, you will!' Great anger fired in Balchard's eyes as his savage outburst ripped through his facade of gentleman's eloquence. Loofer's eyebrows arched up, but his beaming smile remained in place, the cigar stump going up slowly to the mouth. Of course, he'd known all along that Balchard was not a proper-born thoroughbred toff, in spite of 'is fine outer trimmings and fancy bridling brasses. More like an old 'orse wiv new irons nailed to 'is 'ooves, so that 'e *sounded* proper. But they both knew their respective parts in the game they played, and they both played them well, keeping to their own side of the paddock rail. After all, if that was what the stupid bugger wanted, it was no skin off his nose, Loofer thought to himself, snuffling a snort of derision behind his cigar. But he could see the stupid bugger paying a high price in the end, for staying in his so called 'winners paddock'. Oh, yes, he could see that, all right, even if the bloody fool couldn't see it 'imself.

Balchard insisted on the boy keeping the money. It was either that, or no more little deals. Loofer backed down. With no more money passing his way, he was ready to go, shifting his feet and edging away. 'Right y'are, Mr B, if there's nowt more business to be doin', I'll be 'eadin' off. Better get back to Charlie, poor beggar, an' see 'e doesn't eat all the profit before we bloomin' makes it! Blimey, I asks yer! It's been good doin' business wiv yer, Mr B. Be seein' yer.'

Checking that the bag was secure in his inside pocket, Balchard hastened off along Thames Street in search of a cab.

Prime importance required him to now seek out Detective Sergeant Dryson. A Kensington banker whose ingenious embezzlement scheme was causing much worry among private investors, was also causing acute concern at the Yard. Two such investors, suddenly bereft of their entire financial stock, had met their deaths in unusual circumstances. On the surface, these were being explained away as freak accidents occurring at the same time. The Metropolitan Police suspected it to be 'otherwise', but were so far unable to provide the evidence to sustain these suspicions. Balchard had been called in as forensic advisor. His scientific tests had since shown that the two men had, indeed, been murdered. Dryson's presence was now required for official intervention. It had been said that the banker had a mercuric temper that all too often erupted in great violence. Balchard tested the strength of his malacca cane. There was greater comfort when he felt the cold steel of the pistol in his pocket. He hailed a passing hansom. On the heels of this official duty there was a three o'clock lecture and demonstration on natal clinical surgery by Professor Bowers-Moffat at the University. Balchard tapped the cab roof with his cane and urged the cabbie to hurry. As they sped off, he peered warily out the window, shaking off a shiver. A weird feeling that had haunted his instinct all day. A feeling that he was being stalked. He hadn't seen -- couldn't see -- anyone so far. But *somewhere* out there *--eyes were watching him.*

In fact, Professor Bowers-Moffat was late, a mite more than that of Balchard. No matter. The eminent surgeon had a reputation for lightning scalpel strokes. His swift flurry of the blade made up for lost time. As it was, time lost wasn't the only thing cut. The assistant surgeon's blood ran free when the wildly slashing blade sliced his hand. Both the patient and the assistant surgeon died of 'friendly' hospital gangrene two days later. Balchard found it most opportune that the patient had died. It readily provided material that he needed for his research. It saved his having to go looking for it further afield in the city's desolate areas. The deadline for handing in his report for the current phase of his doctoral project was closing in. A *dead*line, indeed, if it was not met. His very own life and death fling. The infection festering in that putrid body could well save his project from *its* expiry.

If indication at all, luck took a dive. That day saw Balchard's young sixpenny urchin fall ill, crying for his departed mama. Before the week ended, he too would die, before he could spend his newly acquired fortune. His frail constitution having given up its struggle against that dreadful condition otherwise known as *life*.

CHAPTER 2

The evening fog pressed up against the Institute's pathology lab window, trying to join the gloom inside. The room's heavy atmosphere was cut by the doleful beat of a dripping tap. A faint tinkling came from the front bench. A solitary lamp showed a figure in shirt-sleeves and rubber apron working diligently before a glittering array of test-tubes and beakers. Standing out aloof from the glassware was a gleaming brass binocular microscope perched up on its hind legs like a giant praying mantis with a triple turret proboscis. Balchard turned to the microscope. Snapping the lens turret round into its lowest power position, he then dropped staining solution onto the slide specimen. Placing the cover on the slide, he mounted the hair specimen under the lens. Turning the milled knob gently, Balchard raised the objective lens gradually, coaxing the bubble of blurred light to burst into a vivid circle of clarity. The hair held Balchard's interest, outlined against the bright circle like a tree frozen in a lunar landscape. Swivelling the turret round to high power, he adjusted the objective lens once more. The 'moon' had now taken on a sinister darkness and the 'tree' had shot up close to touching distance. Its rugged 'bark' revealing vile secrets.

Murder, in fact, was the applicable term. The poor wretch who had fallen mortally beneath this 'tree' had done so at the deliberate felling by another. In succinct tongue, the man had been poisoned. A quick scrutiny along the hair's axis past the sebaceous gland sufficed to show that the cortex and cuticle cells were blatantly ablaze with the fiery red pigment of murder. Plainly the guilty hand was that of the estranged wife. Her rage dually vented on the husband's betrayal and the younger woman's beauty.

Balchard lifted his head away slightly from the microscope, nodding in conclusion before straightening up. Nodding his head slowly, he reflected on the plight of the female poisoners up through the centuries. How they would have stained the pages of history with the darker shade of their fair nature, had closer examination been permitted. Not until the fifteenth century was human dissection clearly sanctioned by the Pope. Before this, poisoning was the murderer's dream. Thus poison was the commonly preferred means of meting out death by the weaker sex. As sure as Cleopatra preferred the sting of the asp's tongue to that of Antony's steel blade. Prior to this papal ruling , the medical examiner had to go by the outward appearance of the body. A livid or mottled body indicated poison, though not acute poisoning. A rapid state of putrefaction was the supposed proof against this. But arsenic, alas, retards putrefaction so that considerable numbers of people must have perished by it. Diseases must have destroyed countless others with the false appearance of poisoning. But what hangman, given his pence, gnashed his teeth over a few wrong necks in the noose?

Little wonder then that arsenic's innocuous white oxide formed the murderer's favourite tool. Being both soluble and virtually tasteless, the powder could easily be mixed with food. An unsuspecting doctor could thus mistakenly diagnose the symptoms as gastroenteritis, and so prescribe the usual shilling box of Dr King's Dandelion and Quinine Liver Pills. A higher minded consultant would perhaps deem cholera as the ailment more fitting to the grace and dignity of his professional fee. To the unwary eye, then, the slow effect of arsenic was its user's trump-card, arousing no undue attention. Unlike the vegetable alkaloid atropine of belladonna which strikes suspiciously swift. Or strychnine, which arouses horror from its victim's convulsions.

Balchard broke off from his thoughts, to move to the bench's sink to wash the slide. Water cascaded off the slide, carrying the hair with it in a swirl down the sink hole. Many a previous poison had made its gurgling escape down there.

A sudden draught behind Balchard alerted him to a new presence in the room. From the deliberate cough announcing the new arrival, Balchard concluded it to be Dryson. On time for once. Officially, they worked together, but neither of them had much respect for the other. Their opinions were poles apart and their methods for tackling problems invariably clashed. They simply didn't like each other. Balchard's low opinion of Detective Sergeant Dryson was not particularly guarded. So that when he turned around, the disdain had not quite slipped from his face before it was caught by the policeman's sharp eye. Dryson's square-jawed face gave off a hardness that went well with the job. His straight-trimmed side whiskers, once all ginger, were losing ground to whitening edges. The raglan overcoat was strictly 'regulation' with its dull iron grey weave. 'As I inferred earlier, *Detective* Sergeant, this man was poisoned. Arsenic, I would venture to say. We can ascertain this for sure once the full analysis has been carried out -- if you will just bear with me a little longer.'

Dryson had to put up with Balchard, along with his cynical attitude. His superiors back at the Yard were finding the man's work, in forensic analysis, to be increasingly helpful to them. In spite of this, Dryson was instinctively wary of the man standing in front of him. He watched his every action, down to the smallest mannerisms, with a policeman's intuitive nose. There was something about the man -- something he couldn't quite put words to -- something that irked him -- *something*? 'But I thought you said arsenic was undetectable; that it looked like natural death from disease? I remember you distinctly telling me that only yesterday.'

'Your *second* observation is correct, Detective Sergeant. I did, indeed, quote the ravages of disease as often providing camouflage for the more sinister dealings of arsenic poisoning. But as to your *first* observation, *no*, I did not say that arsenic poisoning was *undetectable*.'

Dryson made to speak, but Balchard waved him to silence so that he could continue. 'Even the most circuitous paths of poisons can be traced, where the pursuer is wary of his prey.' The Detective Sergeant still didn't understand. Balchard took a long exasperated sigh before going on. 'The one disadvantage of arsenic as a poison is that it is metallic, and so remains in the body after death. If it is there to be found, it can be found. One simply requires to know how and where to look. The murderer may flee, but the murder weapon remains embedded in the victim's body.'

'Like the proverbial dagger in the back, you mean?'

'Splendid, Detective Sergeant! Now you comprehend. Though perhaps a *chemical* 'dagger' would be more appropriate.'

Dryson cocked a doubting eyebrow. 'And *you* think you know how to find this 'dagger', do you, Balchard?'

Balchard ignored the other's taunt, turning away to face the bench again. 'Observe!' He replaced the cleaned slide in its rack and then looked around to spy out the pieces of apparatus necessary for the next stage. He saw that Dryson could no more appreciate the evidence than he could see specs of soot in the fog. A solid body of proof was needed that even the most myopic policeman would blow his whistle to. This thought afforded Balchard a quick glance at Dryson. The policeman's vacant expression was convincing enough. A positive analysis was definitely needed to show that the deceased had been poisoned. Plainly nothing less would satisfy Dryson.

Balchard's eyes darted to and fro across the ill-arranged laboratory glassware and along the multiple rows of bottles and jars with their many hues of chemicals. Dryson tried to help by picking up the pieces that he thought Balchard was looking at; only to put them back again as Balchard's searching gaze shifted. He gave up with a resigned shrug.

'It beats me how you can tell one confounded piece from another. They all look much the same to me. I don't see the point of it all, really. As far as I'm concerned, good solid police work is what's needed to catch a criminal; not all this analysis nonsense.'

Balchard snatched out twice from the wall rack. He returned briskly to the front bench with a jar of copper reagent and a bottle of concentrated hydrochloric acid. From amid the glassware cluttering the bench, he drew forth a Bunsen burner. Pushing a tripod over this, he then topped the tripod with an empty beaker. Pouring out a measured volume of distilled water into the beaker, followed by an equal volume of concentrated hydrochloric acid, Balchard then held a flaming Bryant & May's Alpine Vesuvius match to the Bunsen's gaping mouth. The yellow sulphurous butterfly fluttered violently for a moment before the Bunsen burped and blew forth its white tongue to lick the beaker's bottom. Balchard tugged the Bunsen's brass collar and the mischievous flame disciplined itself into a hissing blue jet. Plucking a piggy-tail twirl of copper from the jar, he burnished it with a file and dropped it into the beaker. Taking out a gold hunter watch from beneath the rubber apron, he flipped it open to time the boiling. After fifteen minutes, the copper winked back brightly in unashamed purity. Balchard nodded in approval. The chemicals and apparatus were so far free of arsenic. Thus, any arsenic found in the analysis would have to come from the body. Balchard took up a small beaker containing the filtrate of the victim's stomach and plopped several drops of it into the boiling liquid. Noting the rapid disappearance of the dark drops in the burbling mass, he also noted the time. Sixteen minutes later, the copper still winked back defiantly. Rescuing the copper from the boiling mass with a pair of forceps, he examined its gleaming surface through a hand lens. No precipitate was apparent. Balchard frowned at the negative result, puckering his lips with forefinger and thumb. He turned off the Bunsen. Balchard's puzzled expression prompted a smirk from Dryson. Straightening up smartly, he stepped over to Balchard's side to look down at the failed test. 'Not quite what you expected, was it, Balchard? Well, I can't say that I'm at all surprised, really. All this so-called --- no, no, spare me, please!' He threw up a hand to cut off Balchard's attempt to reply. 'No more long-winded explanations for these new-fangled theories and principles of yours, Balchard. I've heard enough of them to double fill the files in our Records Office, I have. As far as I'm concerned, a crime is solved by good old -fashioned police work. It's no use shaking your head, Balchard, it had to be said. I could say a lot more, but I can see that would be a waste of time.'

Balchard's lips twitched in annoyance but he refrained from commenting. It would, indeed, be a waste of time to mount his own argument against such a tirade of doubt, he agreed inwardly. As with that other doubting Thomas, Dryson wanted his proof in the flesh. Well, with a little further endeavour, he would have his proof soon enough. Wasting no more words on the policeman, Balchard turned back to his work. Feeling confident from Balchard's silent retreat, Dryson took a different approach as he spoke to the other's back. 'Why don't you stick to what you do best --

you know, your own scientific research stuff, like you said you were doing, here in the hospital? I'm not saying as you wouldn't make a good go of it, career wise. Just leave the crime detection bit to us who do it proper.' Dryson waited for an answer, but got none. Feeling shut out by the silence now, he moved towards the door. 'Anyway, I haven't got any more time to spare. Got to go and do some *real* work. I've got responsibilities to honour, even if some of us *haven't*. See you later, Balchard.' Opening the door, Dryson stalled to turn and point randomly at Balchard and his work on the bench. 'I'll spare a minute for *that* when it lands on my desk -- when and *if* it ever gets that far. Personally, I don't see it happening.'

The laboratory door swung shut behind Balchard, but not before letting in a string of Dryson's derisive 'compliments' and chuckles fading away down the corridor. Rolling up his sleeves, Balchard scanned the surrounding glassware for his next experimental piece. The flask avoided his eyes shyly before he at last espied it and snatched it down fiercely from the corner shelf. Returning triumphantly to the bench with his precious find, he inspected it just to be sure. It had a glass stopper with a thistle funnel and a glass tap. Beneath this, another glass tube curved out of the stopper, to enter a long horizontal tube that contained calcium chloride for the purpose of drying gasses passing through it. This tube joined a finer tube toughened to withstand the Bunsen flame. Murmuring his approval, Balchard stepped sharply over to the chemical balance, a jar of zinc and a spatula in hand. The glistening spatula snaked deftly to and fro, between jar and balance pan, in a swift flurry of precision. He paused to raise the balance. Watching the needle quiver to its central equilibrium point, Balchard lowered the balance with a bump betraying his impatience. Seizing up the pan, he tipped the zinc into the flask. A pipette grew out of his hand, releasing a dribble of dilute sulphuric acid onto the zinc in the flask. Replacing the stopper with its funnel and tube arrangement, Balchard paused to watch the mixture churn up its bubbles of hydrogen gas. He then poured some of the filtrate in through the thistle funnel.

Balchard lit the Bunsen once more, placing it under the fine end of the tube. With half an hour to wait before confirmation, he decided to light a cigarette as well. Pacing the length of the room many times until his nervous energy eventually subsided, he at last plumped his lean frame down on a stool at the adjacent bench. Slouching back against the bench and folding his arms, he inhaled and exhaled his smoke in heavy thought, all the while watching the bubbling flask. With the flask quietly turning its contents over before him, he could afford to pour over his many thoughts on the general subject of poisons.

He had not yet been born into the world with all its madness when, in 1856, Dr William Palmer of Rugeley had been found guilty of murder and sentenced to death at the Central Criminal Court; the first known poisoner to have used strychnine. A mixture of wry amusement and pain crossed Balchard's grey face as he recalled next the sensational affair. It had shocked the nation some seventeen years later, in 1873, when the news of the Durham Assizes had caught all and sundry across the land aghast. The modest and somewhat naive Mrs Mary Cotton, nee Robson, had been found guilty of poisoning no less than twenty-four victims with arsenic. She had obtained her ready supply of deathly despatch from no more devious a source than the common soft soap used for killing vermin. Perhaps the stirrings of the trial had stirred something in *him* to mould his future career? He wondered on this. One thing *was* certain -- it had also been in that same year that his pater, in one of his drunken rages, had punched his mama senseless -- not long after which the household was reunited with long-forgotten peace when the man walked out of the house for the last time, to go and live with another woman. In the heat of his departure, his pater had called his mama 'a bloody *whore*'. Being only ten years old himself, he had been too naive to understand the dire implication of the word, or to fathom the reason for its scathing application to his dearest mama. Rumour since had it that his pater's continued generous beatings of female partners and his disturbances of the peace earned him periodic reprimands from equally generous magistrates.

Balchard looked around himself at his surroundings, taking in the prestigious significance of his official position in the Institute. It was all hard to believe. A giant leap of social transmogrification, from frog to prince. From a colourless backwater nonentity, to this. Only months away from the honourable title of *Dr* Balchard and currently bent under the heavy office of research assistant to Professor Felsham in the Institute's Morbid Anatomy Department. Whilst trying to squeeze in time for his own research for his doctoral thesis on post-natal genital disease and putrefaction in the 'fallen' female, under the auspices of Professor Radcliffe at the University. All this under a critical time schedule that was catching up on him. An arduous task, without question. So he had good reason to be nervous. The presentation of his work before the almighty Senatus Academicus was a nightmare on a not too far away horizon -- without even considering the many postprandial ports giving possible sway to the examiners' decision. They would have deemed it as totally improper for his dissertation to have used the word *prostitutes*, never mind his openly admitting to *associating* with women of such depravity. But from what other source could they possibly imagine he was gathering his research material? "Damned old stuffed-shirts," muttered Balchard resentfully, breaking a spent matchstick across his finger.

The muffled peal of St Paul's clock-tower bells sounded from outside, reminding Balchard of *other* church bells, *other* things, back home. His mood darkened sharply. He reflected morosely on how it had all started. How his mama had forbidden him to play with h*er,* the mill-owner's daughter. "Silly little girl" -- his mama had called her. But he had sensed his mama's uneasiness deep down inside her, in spite of her mocking dismissal of the girl. She had been most ardent on his getting his head down to study for the Belvedere Scholarship. As *Adam* Balchard, he had been her first son -- named appropriately after *that* Adam, the first son. She had intended more in her roost. But things --- *something* ---had gone amiss there. Perhaps it was only to be expected that, with *that* name, his life's voyage should first become unsettled on account of a woman, or girl, disturbing the waters. The scandal was supposed to pass away after a penitential period of morbid seclusion. In fact, his social banishment had made it easier to study for this higher goal of scholastic enlightenment. It was the beginning of his dark ascent into a higher social sphere. Away from there to here. Balchard ground his knuckles against the bench edge in grim memory of the hard fire-and-brimstone faces of teachers and aldermen glaring at him from across the table of the scholarship's award committee. But the scholarship was granted, nevertheless, albeit with reluctance. He liked to think that he had *won* the scholarship against great prejudice. There again, perhaps it was their ploy to be rid of him. To have him move on out of their area. To somewhere, anywhere, so long as it was a far distance from their puny little God-fearing community. He was made to visit her grave with flowers frequently, under the escort of his austere mama. In deliberate timing of the girl's parents not being there at the same time. *Daffodils. She* had always loved her daffodils. Just like those beautiful golden locks on her head. Now her grave was surrounded by her very own Praetorian guard of black iron daffodils. A futile protection against what had already been damnably done. When the pathologists had been satisfied in their examination of her, a satisfactory coroner's report was drawn up. It had been solemnly declared that *she*, 'a mere child, herself', had been with child. As for the cause of her death, all decisions were strained in a unanimous agreement of an absence of any action on her body, "*foreign to her person*". His mama had forcibly made him kneel before her grave and pray. As if he did not have his own anguish of remorse burning within. Funny how sin and sanctity always went together, side by side, like two eternal twins. Like the two shades of squares on the harlequin's tunic. He saw that oval harlequin mask sinking into the water -- *her* pale oval face. Those oval eyes, with their surprised fright. That oval mouth with its pleading cry, silently screaming, echoing in his head. Was it *her* screams scraping the inside of his skull? Or was it *he* who was screaming silently in his *own* head?

With the edge of his outer awareness monitoring the flask's progress, Balchard allowed his mind to come back up slowly from the past. Checking the time, he dangled the watch on its golden chain. Spinning it round and round, he drew on his cigarette for the final minutes in quiet reflection. Stubbing out his cigarette in a crucible, he leaned over to pick up a metal spatula. Striking an empty beaker with the spatula, he matched the resounding 'p-i-n-g' with a drawn-out whisper of: '*Daff-o-dils.*'

Rising from the stool, he approached the apparatus and bent down to inspect the tube just beyond the edge of the flame. No deposit had formed. Sliding the Bunsen away, he lit a wax taper from it and ignited the gas escaping from the end of the tube. It gave off a lavender tint. Splendid. Now a small piece of porcelain held to the jet grew a small patch of greyish 'skin'. Balchard added a drop of nitric acid to the deposit and warmed it near the Bunsen flame. Holding a dropper just over the stain, he delicately released a drop of silver nitrate onto it. The grey 'skin' blushed a definite brick red. *Positive.* One more test for certainty. With a fresh piece of porcelain and this time touching the stain with mercuric bromide paper, the test was once more clearly positive. The stain had turned yellow this time from the halogen reagent. Arsenic was definitely present in the body. Reaching out and pulling over a notepad and pen, Balchard hurriedly scratched up a forensic report that even the stolid Detective Sergeant Dryson could understand and act upon.

CHAPTER 3

Balchard had barely stepped out from the Institute's dark shrouded entrance, when the familiar footsteps sounded from the shadows across the street, bringing out an acid smile on his face. The same steps had preyed upon his heels the previous two evenings, from this very point, annoyingly dogging his progress all the way along High Holborn, as far as Bloomsbury Way. From there he had eluded his pursuer by a series of twists and turns before snatching a cab travelling along Oxford Street in the opposite direction from Montague Street. And yet, no sooner had he returned to his rooms in Montague Street, than the lam-post outside had grown an *extra* shadow. It had to be concluded that the man was not a casual thief or pickpocket. Not only did he know the prey's address, but no sooner than being led off course, had reappeared upon the scene with the resilience of a rubber ball bounced off a wall. In the same way that one could measure the strength of the ball's return, so also could one gauge the kindred sense of determination of the stalker. Something sinister was out there, and it made him uneasy.

A myriad of names and indexed notes flashed through

Balchard's mind in an attempt to mark and file this new entry in its proper case place. All to no avail. Even allowing for a complicated cross reference of common factors, there was no indication that this new development should be connected to any of the current cases at the Yard. That irritated him. He liked his facts and figures to fit logically into place. That bugger out there, whoever he was, was doing a good job at undermining his nerve. Damnedest luck of all, Balchard wasn't carrying his pistol. He only took it with him when he went on police work. He never carried it with him when he went to the laboratory. Tapping his pursed lips with the silver top of his cane, Balchard tried to match his wits against how his dark prowler would make his move. He nervously quickened his pace. The footsteps quickened after him.

Punctual to the minute, as Balchard had predicted, the policeman was there, at the corner of Smithfield market, sheltering in the shop doorway, beneath the Old Gold Cigarettes sign. 'Good evening, Constable,' said Balchard, handing the policeman the buff envelope addressed to Detective Sergeant Dryson.

'Evening, sir. So what's this we 'ave 'ere, then? Somethin' important is it, sir?' The rank on the envelope did nothing to dispel the constable's fear that he was going to have to move from his comfortable shelter in the doorway, in the name of duty of some form or other. Balchard's request to have the envelope , with its important chemical analysis, delivered without further ado to the Detective Sergeant, didn't help the uneasiness, either.

Biting his lip, the policeman glanced at the gentleman,

resplendent like all bloomin' toffs in his dress coat, silk hat and cane, and wondered why the bloomin' bugger couldn't deliver the bloomin' note 'imself. He also felt that his own presence seemed to be of secondary importance the moment the envelope changed hands, the gentleman's attention being elsewhere, up the street, it seemed. He looked up the street, saw nothing, and so turned back to the gentleman. A jewel thief in flight, perhaps? Balchard certainly looked the part. But, alas, there was no bag or cape for hiding the loot. The policeman's eyes wandered up to Balchard's silk hat. Spacious enough for not only a doctor's stethopoke thingummy, but also the repose of many a diamond sparkler in the past.

Balchard read the other's mind in an instant and a cold smile creased his face. Doffing his hat, he displayed the disappointingly empty interior to the policeman. 'Not one solitary diamond, as you can see, Constable. But if I could assist you in this matter, I would endeavour to give it the best of my attention. However, time being of somewhat pressing urgency ----' Balchard trailed off, affecting a hurried glance at his time-piece and looking back up the street with deliberate openness. It was his ploy to be seen talking to the policeman, to see just how bold his stalker's brass was.

The policeman could only scratch his ear. He was puzzled by the gentleman's insistence for the envelope to be delivered to the Yard, without needing to come along himself for further questioning. 'Seein' as I don't know if I should, ---' He broke off in search of words and logic. 'Seein' as p'r'aps you should come down to the station an' speak to the Detective Sergeant ---' He broke off again as a sixpence glinted in the gentleman's palm. Tugging nervously at his collar with his finger, he waited to see if the offer would increase. But it didn't.

Taking the coin, the policeman relaxed. He knew in which direction his duty lay. So he could settle once more into the comfort of his personal nook in the shuttered doorway. Balchard found it tiresome having to deal with the stupid policeman. He didn't give a toss if Dryson, or whoever, got his report, or if it got lost on the way. He'd had his satisfaction in analysing the problem for them. What they decided to do with his findings wasn't his greatest concern at this particular moment. More immediate matters of personal safety were bugging him. He assured the policeman that the envelope's contents were self-explanatory. No further mental effort was needed from the constable to enlighten his superiors at the station. 'And the name, sir?' said the constable, trying to choose the proper pocket to suit the envelope's importance. 'What name shall I say, sir?'

'That should also be reasonably explicit to the recipient, Constable,' replied Balchard, smiling inwardly at Dryson's imbecilic slowness, 'but for your sake, I think Balchard should suffice.'

'Mr Blanchard. I see, sir. Well --'

'*Bal*chard!' Balchard's anger rose up inside him. It always did when people made mistakes over his name or other personal background details. It embarrassed him so that anger came as an instant cover for it. His self esteem wavered on such instances. He had almost said: '*Doctor* Balchard', but had held back, in spite of the title having already been printed prematurely on the professional cards he carried in his pocket.

'Good night, Mr Balchard. I'll see that your message gets delivered, all right.'

Balchard walked off briskly without responding. He was noting the timing for the follower's footsteps to start up again. If they did. They did. And surprisingly soon at that. Balchard found this very significant. His episode with the policeman had also served another purpose, totally separate from that of delivering the envelope. It had served as a simple means of weighing up the follower's spirit. Normally, the ruffian intent on robbery or bodily assault would be put off at the sight of the intended victim conversing with a law officer and looking back in the direction of his would-be attacker. The ruffian's fears would be heightened by his being out of earshot and not knowing what measures of arrest were about to be sprung on him. Most ruffians would have felt their spirits quelled somewhat. With strength on the wane, the resumption of footsteps would have been delayed. The wiser stalker would have fled altogether.

But *these* footsteps still came on after him. Unhidden, undaunted, ringing out in resolute strides on the cobblestones behind him. Chasing him. Goading him, even. Balchard stopped abruptly. The footsteps stopped. He started off again. The footsteps rang out again. So was that the game? It was *his* spirit that was being measured by whoever was back there! The thought jarred Balchard's stomach.

Ignoring the passing stream of hansoms and broughams as a means of escape, Balchard let each cab hasten past in a flurry of clattering hooves and glistering wheel spokes. He was curious to test his follower's measure of stretch a little further. The opportunity he sought came to ear long before he set eye on its source. A faint syncopated jingle drifting softly over the rooftops gradually sorted itself out into the heavier metallic jangle of a piano- organ's rendering of *Champagne Charlie* and *Villikins and His Dinah*.

The dark Italian, in dark coat and dark rounded felt hat, cranked away morosely at his black piano-organ. The signora, in flamboyant striped dress of her national colours, cat- called in complete disharmony, while roasting chestnuts over a brazier: 'Castagna! Castagna! Chesta-nut! Chesta-nut!' But the Italians' joint effort was mostly wasted on deaf ears, a stronger rival enticement of Romford & Burton Ales and loud licentious revelry coming from the King Lud tavern behind them, beneath the Ludgate Circus railway viaduct.

'Buona sera, signore,' said Balchard, stepping up to the organist and tapping him on the shoulder with his cane. The Italian, somewhat surprised by the gentleman's direct approach, managed to crack a yellow ivory smile across his swarthy face. He touched the brim of his hat. 'Gooda-evening, sir.' He threw a questioning glance at his wife. The woman turned away in scorn, to tend her chestnuts, while muttering: 'Pazzo; povero pazzo.' Balchard feigned an ignorant look whilst fully comprehending the foreign mutterings of 'Idiot; poor idiot'. Offering to buy the Italian a drink, on top of some *business*, Balchard led the way into the noisy tavern. The Italian followed, pausing on the doorstep to look back at his wife, shrugging his shoulders and screwing his forefinger significantly into his temple.

'Pazzo; povero pazzo,' repeated the brooding spouse, more sure than before of her judgement. The gentleman was an idiot. How else did one classify an idler, or *poltrone*, who went around buying drinks for workmen below their own lofty social station?. The man watching all this from the depth of the shadows up the street was a little more reserved in *his* judgement of Balchard's actions.

Balchard reappeared in the doorway with the Italian. They both stood there, their backs to the street, tankards to their lips. The man in the shadows looked on intently. When a solitary cab approached slowly, the man shifted uneasily, afraid that his prey would bolt. But nothing like that happened. However, when two cabs came along together, Balchard suddenly dashed out, waving down the first one and leaping into it. The man darted out from his cover, stopping the second cab, to climb aboard and order the cabbie to follow the cab in front. Why Balchard had not used the earlier cab to foil any chance of being pursued puzzled the man for moment. But he dismissed the thought, determined not to let go of his quarry's tail. The Italian watched the two cabs rattle off down Fleet Street into the mist. Then, pushing his felt hat back, he turned and walked up to the brooding wife. 'Buona notte, signora,' he said in a clear English voice. Laying down two pence on the piano top, Balchard walked off, musing over his secret joke. His ardent stalker was now chasing a decoy to the outlying borough of Lewisham. The woman, stone-faced with astonishment, crossed herself and put the money in her apron pocket, watching the gentleman go off in her husband's hat and coat. Too numbed now to remember her pigeon English, she mouthed a limp: 'Castagna; castagna,' while the chestnuts frizzled away unattended in the pan. Balchard turned north along St Bride Street, heading for Holborn Circus, and thereafter for Montague Street. He didn't believe that his stalker would be fooled for long with the little switch-around trick. It sufficed to have him off his back for the moment. There was a second point to be observed in the trick, but the result of that would have to wait until he got back to his rooms. For the moment, though, his nerves were a little more settled.

The rancid fumes of burnt mushrooms rankled Balchard's nostrils as he entered the hallway at Montague Street. A painful reminder that this was Thursday, otherwise mushroom and cabbage day. Considering the burnt platefuls that Mrs Wallamsby, his landlady, served up as her establishment's 'homely cuisine', it was a wonder that she didn't tender her services to the Egyptian Room in the British Museum, round the corner. The ancient gods there would have appreciated her burnt offerings. Balchard winced at the odour and shook his head. He really had to make a positive effort to seek accommodation elsewhere. But pennies weighed none too heavily in the pocket and opportunities were scarce. Hopefully there would be something suitable in *The Times*. A chance for a swift, permanent departure from these lodgings. Taking up the newspaper, along with his evening delivery mail, from the hall table, he mounted the stairs silently and entered his rooms.

If the same tiny rooms had been let out to a flea circus,

those agile insect performers may well have been induced to ride piggy-back as a counter-measure to claustrophobia. Furniture and sundries may well have been eyed in horror by others as a flood-tide of chaos. But in Balchard's eye the room's contents had the ascetic discipline of a monastic cell. It secluded him from the nuisance of people outside. The very close cramped-in walls were ideal for deep concentration when he was engrossed in the logistics of his own research, or that of Professor Felsham. Most of the work in folders piled high on the shelves and furniture around him was, in fact , Felsham's. Its schedule for completion was a pressing worry on Balchard's mind. It was pushing his own research to one side, giving him a second mental burden to carry. Many things seemed to be having a crushing effect on his clear thinking of late. Some of these he could not readily identify. Balchard frowned at this last admission, with an inexplicable quiver of nausea passing through him for a moment. That moment, brief as it was, had a great effect in unsettling him further. He looked around at the massive work task surrounding him and reflected again on Dryson's remark earlier, concerning his choice of career.

A guttural sound that was neither laugh nor groan escaped from him as he remembered his distant boyhood ambitions. Long-lost memories. Rosy images swam up into his conscious mind. They had been more fanciful in their colouring than they had been realistically suitable. He shied away from the thought of his once aspiring to be a Jesuit-style theologian. His mama would not have been displeased at his taking holy orders. Not from religious fervour, but for only to get her son into a special placing, away from ordinary people. His pater wouldn't have cared. He never had. Except that he would have seen it as a 'job' where beer-money would have been lamentably scarce. If there was a 'confession' that he had to make, it was that he had been more inspired by the aura of being a bearded scholar in privileged isolation, looking down on society. With the power to affect holy wrath and chide the ungodly. Now that science, and not religion, was spearheading his personal crusade, he wondered what it *was* that he was crusading against -- *pulling away* from. He wondered, in turn, why he had posed *that* question. The thought suffered him a strange attack of nervous restlessness, so that he meandered around the room, reviewing all his scientific paraphernalia. Going along the shelves and touching the many volumes, bulging files, chemicals and scientific instruments gave him a measure of solace. A beacon in his mind, allowing him to see beyond some vague sense of incarceration. But solace from what? His pater had risen no higher than a lowly horse-shit shoveller in the stables of the Great Northern Canal Haulage Company, where the horses for towing the barges were kept. He had been thrown out of his job, to no surprise, for his continued drunkenness, and violence and finally for not turning up for work. His mama still laboured on in her secure employment as latrine cleaner in the town hall offices. But when rumours of pilfering had circulated through those municipal corridors, she had given off odd mutterings of 'another job' and worn a deathly grey expression on her face.

Shedding the Italian's hat and coat to don a brown dressing gown, Balchard sat down at the desk to tend to the mail. Sliding a Cossack silver mounted kindjal dagger from its wooden sheath, he set about slitting the envelopes open. A female voice cawed like a crow after his name from the bottom of the stairs. Arching an eyebrow at the door, he ignored the call, carrying on with his business. He had opened all the letters on the desk top when Mrs Wallamsby's knock sounded on the door. It was not too brilliant a mental feat to interpret the knock's tone as that of an offended party. Truly, the woman was hurt. If she managed to conceal her sulk, it was only because her expression matched the dark shade of her domestic tunic. However, before she could let loose her wrath, she paused to sniff around in different directions. A new smell was intruding upon all the other weird odours from Balchard's 'medical pieces', all of which her olfactory senses had now become familiar with. The source of the heavy aroma of Italian tobacco eluded her for a moment. Until her eyes settled on the coat bundled up untidily on the sofa. The woman was deriving much annoyance from the borrowed garment's scruffy appearance. This afforded Balchard a morose look of inner acid glee. Pulling her ample bosom up in solemn disdain, she turned on Balchard. 'Really, Mr Balchard; that was most inconsiderate of you to neglect to inform me that you would be coming in so late as to miss supper. You know the house rules as well as all the other members of this establishment. All those attending for supper must do so at the regular appointed hour. All those not intending to have supper in the house must let me know by early evening.' She broke off to turn on her softening tactic of emotional sniffling. 'And after me cooking all those lovely mushrooms for you, Mr Balchard. And now they've all gone off.'

Letting things 'go off' was not quite how Balchard defined the woman's pyromania with edibles. He kept a straight face, nodding in sympathy. 'Yes, I really am most sorry about any distress I may have caused you, Mrs Wallamsby. It really was quite remiss of me not to have given you fair warning. However, with my work being somewhat complicated and time-consuming, dinner rules seem to have eluded my recollection.' Mollified by Balchard's 'gentleman's words', the woman made a new offer of meatloaf and carrots. Blotting out the very idea, Balchard hastily declined. Her hackles up now, the woman surged back stubbornly with an offer of cold potato salad. Dreading a repeat sermon, Balchard lowered his resistance a little. 'Very well, then, Mrs Wallamsby, perhaps a small portion of potato salad. But only a very *small* portion.'

'And rice pudding for dessert?'

'No, really, Mrs Wallamsby. I can hardly envisage my alimentary tract engulfing such a quantity.' Politeness, of course. He refrained from saying it was the *quality* that turned his stomach.

But his manners were wearing thin. His restraint on a mounting inner rage was almost exhausted.

The woman could sense this, as he impatiently tapped out a tattoo on the back of his chair. She was nervous of the storm of agitation building up, a mere step away from her. The polite words were there, but something else, something more violent was simmering behind all that, trying to find its way to the surface. And he was struggling to hold it back. Like a boiler with faulty riveting, it would explode when the time came. He had not always been like this. He had seemed to be a decent young gentleman when he had first come to stay in her establishment. But never show your fear to an angry lion, and never turn your back on it. She stepped back, searching in her mind for an ingratiating offer to make, and so retire calmly, still in charge, as landlady of the establishment. 'If it's your insides you're worried about, I've a new bottle of Pepper's Iron Tonic downstairs in the pantry. And you being a medical man, an' all.' She shook her head at her lodger's spare frame. 'I can go downstairs and fetch it now, if you want?'

'No, please; I must insist that you do not put yourself to such inconvenience solely on my behalf. A plate of potato salad will suffice in itself, thank you.' The woman having gone, Balchard decided that an additional problem required urgent attention. That of his leaving the house permanently without offending the woman and his dear mama. His mama was acquainted with Mrs Wallamsby, and her influence had been instrumental in acquiring the rooms for him in the first place. Even mothers erred in their good intentions. He turned back to his correspondence.

There were three letters altogether. The first of these was from Dr Muir, assistant to Professor Radcliffe, at the University, on the pressing matter of "*Mr Adam Balchard providing a requisite verification of progress in his research programme, prior to entering the final phase of his doctoral dissertation*". The official date for submission of his work, stamped out in bold red, so that only a blind man could have missed it, was only ten days away. Balchard's stomach leaped. He could barely have submitted the work, given twenty days, never mind ten! 'Damn the man! Damn Felsham! Damn them all!' he cursed, crumpling the paper in his hand and casting it across the room. The second letter was from the Yard. A pink Expenses & Claims form for him to fill in, following the last forensic test he had carried out for them. Balchard's rampant temper subsided a little at the thought of some money coming his way. Not that he would get it immediately. They were always slow with that; slow to pay but fast to ask. His interest in the first two letters dissolved instantly when his attention passed to the third missive -- attached to a parcel. Intrigue flew straight at his eyes when he saw that the parcel had already been opened, re-wrapped, the cut string re-tied, with original knots remaining, and the letter, with its Scotland Yard rubber stamp mark, placed under the string and held secure with red sealing wax. No address, no postage mark on the envelope; only his name. Hand-delivered by a bobby, of course. Another conundrum that Dryson's superiors believed could only be solved by 'extra mural effort of ancillary personnel'. Dryson had either forgotten to mention this earlier at the Institute, or had been too reluctant to concede to needing his assistance. Whichever one it was, his superiors had seen fit to send it straight here.

Sweeping the other letter and two envelopes off the desk, he pulled the package over and slit it open with the silver dagger. Out of the brown paper tumbled three segments of brass tubing. The envelope contained another envelope. This contained a letter from the Bridport Constabulary, Dorset, asking for the Yard's intervention in finding a Mr Harlech's son, who had gone missing. The son had disappeared nine days ago without explanation, leaving behind these mysterious metals on the bed in his room, which had needed breaking into. Its door having been bolted on the inside. There was nobody in the room when the forceful entry was made.

Balchard examined the brass pieces. Two of the tube sections measured three inches; the third section was two inches in length. All three were of three-quarter inch diameter. The fine precision cutting was the work of an expert craftsman, but not one who placed faith in the lathe, the tooling being co-linear with the longitudinal axes. Careful examination of the interior scratches with a hand lens revealed that the pieces had been carried on a chain of large linkage. Whilst each tube bore grease deposits around the rim at one end, only the two three-inch segments were sullied around their rims by the carbon deposits of soft flames. Careful application of a delicate powder, produced a discouraging confusion of overlapping fingerprints. Balchard singled out the fragments of whorls that formed a recurrent pattern of symmetry. Using a fine pin to scratch a line perpendicular to the parallel ridges of the prints, He then counted the number of intersections of ridges along this line, between a distance of five millimetres. The number was twelve. So the print was that of a twelve, to fourteen, year old child. By similar method, all the other prints were those of adults. Two of the child's prints bore scars of cuts incised by a sharp instrument, supposedly the same instrument, at identical angles.

Those were the facts. So now for their usage as solid rational bricks of construction. Balchard sat back in his chair, twirling the dagger on its blade point on the desk as he thought. The same instrument for two incisions suggested that the incisions had been made one after the other. This bespoke of deliberation, as did the identical angles. The instrument's sharpness suggested an infrequent, delicate, usage, such as for ceremonial or religious acts. Religion pointed to candles, which would explain the grease deposits and flames marks. If candles were put in the tubes, and two of the tubes were held horizontally, the flames would stand vertical, and so mark the rims. If the third tube was held vertically, the flame would also stand vertically, and so would not mark the rim. What had been random positions of fingerprints now resolved themselves into specific positions in Balchard's mind. He now saw the tubes having been held with three sets of two fingers pointing at the apices of a tetrahedron.

The pieces now clicked together like a Chinese puzzle in Balchard's mind. He recalled reading somewhere of a sinister secret society of Hindu origin which employed this three-candle ceremony. The priest conducting the ceremony would be assisted by a young boy who held the candles, and was marked for the priesthood by cuts across his thumbs. After the ceremony, the brass tubes, removed of their candles, would be carried on a sacred chain round the priest's neck. Formerly confined to solely religious matters, the cult had since strayed, on its Western meanderings, into the devious dealings of political subversion. Assassinations being one of its finer points. He would check up on this in the Reading Room of the British Museum. Should this prove to be of no avail, then he could always consult the many smaller libraries around the city that specialised in Asian and Oriental subcultures. Balchard wrote up his notes quickly. Filing them away accordingly, he drafted a telegram for a meeting with Mr Harlech. To be posted in the morning, along with his claim form to the Yard's expenses department. With that business behind him, Balchard tried to relax. His ugly mood had faded a little, like an animal lain down, only purring quietly now. But the pain in his temple throbbed on solemnly in seeming foreboding.

Balchard finished the salad with a generous glass of Medoc to relieve his taste-buds of their anguish. He decided that he would attend the Beethoven concert in St James's Hall, advertised in *The Times* for next Monday evening. There would also be a performance of Bach's sonata in B minor and Haydn's quartet in G major, as well as Schumann's sonata in G minor. With Zerbini as conductor, Balchard reckoned that he could afford the five shilling ticket. He turned to the newspaper's Apartments & Offices section. Most of the apartments were priced beyond his meagre income. Or else were as inconveniently situated as the far- flung corners of the Empire, so to speak, in the outlying districts of the City. However, there was one at 26 Westbourne Terrace Road: ' *handsomely Furnished, for two professional gentleman, consisting of dining room and two bedrooms, with good cooking and attendance. Close to Bishop's-road Station.*' . The cooking services offered could hardly be worse than that of his present circumstances. But he could not endure sharing his living space with another. He could not allow anyone to intrude upon his privacy. Irritated, he lowered the paper with a crumpling thrust upon his lap. With his head lowered, he thought back on another newspaper article that had upset him.

When *her* death was reported in the local newspapers. *She* was no sooner mentioned, than forgotten again. Like a leaf swept over the angry weir and along the fast flowing waters, to disappear under the rushes and the overhanging bank. Just like that very weir near to where she had perished. Shame could have hung his, and his mama's heads lower, had the newspapers gone further. Beyond a mere mention of reckless youth throwing away precious God-given life by swimming in treacherous waters. The ever present hazards to human life, posed by the millwheel and its perilous weir were dwelt upon. Along with a stinging editorial on the wealthy miller's failure to provide safety measures against these dangers to his workers and the general public. This was countered by the rich merchant aldermen's plea of ever rising costs making it 'uneconomical' to provide such measures. Totally out of the question, considering the amount of expenditure already put into providing facilities for mill workers and their families.

But the miller *had* paid a price. It was his own daughter who had drowned. Balchard had also paid his price. A double price. *She* had died, and he had lived. *She* had left him, leaving him to greave and fret. He fretted that his contrition could never compensate for what had passed. His hands fell open listlessly, letting the newspaper slide to the floor, where he stared at it for a long time through sightless eyes.

His mind jolted back into the room with Mrs Wallamsby's voice seemingly coming through a loudhailer in a foreign tongue. With his brain re-orientated on his surroundings again, Balchard understood Mrs Wallamsby to have come to collect his tray. She was offering him a pot of her special brew tea. He preferred, instead, a pot of warm water for making up his nightcap. Dipping the spoon into the tin-lined packet of Epps cocoa, Balchard reflected on the evening's earlier cat-and-mouse episode. It was now time to check the result of that little ploy. Taking the cup of cocoa over to the window, he pulled the curtain aside, to look out at the lamp-post. Sure enough, there was now a *second* shadow stemming out from it. Electric sensation surged in his chest for an instant. Excitement from anticipation? Or fear? He wasn't sure. He continued to stare out openly at it until he was understood. The 'shadow' comprehended, and breaking away from the mother-stalk of the lamp-post, walked towards Number 20. Balchard timed the pace until there would be a resounding thud of the iron knocker, or a modest rap of the letter-box. It was the latter. The man, whoever he was, certainly had an interesting balance between boldness and diffidence.

Mrs Wallamsby brought the note. It stated curtly, that Balchard's presence would be e*xpected* in the British Museum, at 10a.m. tomorrow. Balchard sensed the hair's-breadth divider between polite invitation and direct imperative, in the very sparseness of words. There was nothing else *written* in the note. But Balchard read the *additional* information by detailed scrutiny of the paper through his hand lens. It was convenient that he was already going to the Museum in the morning. That way he could do two jobs at the same time. Satisfied, he put the paper and lens down on the desk, and turned back to his cocoa and *The Times.* He settled back in his chair to enjoy his cocoa and read in the quiet of the room. The only thing disturbing this was the pulsing pain in his head.

CHAPTER 4

Clearly, what had been of compelling interest to scholars for centuries had now waned in drawing power with the two men in the ancient manuscripts room of the British Museum. Neither Balchard nor the fair-haired gentleman in russet Norfolk jacket was giving any real attention to the manuscripts in the glass cases, over which they stooped, shifting and turning like dissatisfied blood-hounds. Both of them were acutely vigilant of all that was happening around them. Their senses were tuned to every creak of the floor-boards, to every voice or whisper that filtered in from the surrounding rooms of the museum. Both of them were acutely aware of *each other*. Balchard bent closer to the glass case, his nose almost touching it, all the while watching the man's angled reflection on its surface. When the reflection turned its back on him, Balchard stole a glance at the man across the room. The man's height and broad, robustly filled frame, were the first two factors which Balchard linked with his mysterious follower of the night before. The gleaming military boots, with their cocksure steel spurs, grew proudly out of the hirsute tweed breeches, and could well have been those that had strode resolutely after him last night, although they sounded differently today. Where last night's resolve had rung out stridently on cold stone from the shrouded depth of an ominous mist, this morning's caution paused and scraped on the polished floor in the decent manner of a gentleman of leisure passing his while in a public gallery. Thus did the light of day blow away the night's gossamer phantoms of the mind, like a child's nightmare dissolved with the coming of morn. All in all, the man was of the active outdoors breed. A cavalry-man most surely, from his confident rolling gait and dark weathered face and toughened hands, the latter now spread open-fingered around the corners of the display case with a firmness that threatened to splinter the seemingly fragile structure. Balchard reckoned the gentleman to be roughly his own age. But he could not envisage his sort idling away his time indoors, as like now. No, much more was afoot than met the eye.

The man moved to another case so that he was once more facing Balchard. Balchard smiled inwardly, and straightening up, went over to the same case. Standing over the glass panel, Balchard looked down at the faded yellow decomposition that was the brittle remains of the sixteenth century Goteborg Treaty. One touch of a finger, and the entire scroll would disintegrate. 'Truly a remarkable specimen of preservation,' said Balchard, his eyes remaining fixed on the scroll.

'Indeed, sir; indeed.' The tone was that of one who didn't care a damn about decaying scrolls, but only about those who stooped over them *pretending* to care.

'One would imagine,' continued Balchard, 'that it would not sustain too many prodding fingers. Like a poor party mask; finger it too fretfully, and it falls away, so revealing the face and the game is ended.' Balchard stood up straight to stare the other in the eye. The message was clear that he was more than a little peeved at being kept waiting. '*Is* the game ended?'

'Sir?' A lesser person challenged so would have shifted uneasily, or fidgeted a nervous finger, under Balchard's steely stare. But this one didn't twitch as much as a single hair of his blond moustache or eyebrows. His blue eyes twinkled with open amusement, whilst awaiting Balchard's next move, like a child dangling a frog or spider by its leg, watching its frantic wriggling, before deciding on letting it run free or dashing it underfoot. If undecided, the child often sought advice from an elder brother or companion.

Balchard pondered on the whereabouts of the 'elder' in the building. He handed the man the note from the previous evening. '*Yours*, I believe?' The man barely glanced at the paper before engulfing it in a magician's twirl of fingers and putting it away promptly in his pocket. With equal brevity, Balchard affected a frown at his golden hunter time-piece, whilst tapping impatiently on its glass panel. 'Hopefully, we are to be joined soon? Preferably before we become parched so.' Balchard cocked an eye pointedly at the ancient scroll. The man glanced round the room. A young governess, in green dress and velveteen bustle, and her three young charges, in sailor suits and boater hats, were the only other occupants of the room.

'You came *alone?*' said the man at last.

'You have not already ascertained this for yourself, then?'

Balchard smiled wickedly, tilting his head slightly to one side and tapping his upper lip with his fingers, whilst reading the man's eyes. A brief smile was allowed to touch the man's cheek. His blond eyebrow arched momentarily to emit a sparkling acknowledgement of Balchard's observational astuteness. Still spare in his words, the man moved off, pausing only to turn and beckon Balchard with a casual flick of the finger, to follow him.

The 'elder' was long in body, and dark in his apparel, just like the Rosetta Stone, along which he was casting a measuring squint; but the Stone, alas, did not possess a flowing black beard. Putting his eye to the corner of the Stone, and stretching his arms out along its edges, like a billiards player assessing his table, the 'elder' sized up Balchard for his opening shot. He looked for a signal from his man. The blond eyebrow gave a barely discernible twitch, and the 'elder' straightened his posture, coming round to Balchard's side of the Stone, patting the surface as he did so. 'To the layman, Mr Balchard, this is a mere three feet of stone; to the experts, it is a truly colossal gateway to a hitherto forbidden territory; that being, of course, the field of hieroglyphics, where our people had been quite unable, for far too long, to decipher the basic semantic key. Now, because of these inscriptions in the three tongues of hieroglyphics, demotic characters and Greek characters, our people can make considerable progress in converting former skull-cracking symbols into Queen's English. And all because, for the first time, we know what the other side is thinking, so to speak. A fundamental lesson in the strategy of communication.'

'Very interesting,' said Balchard, 'but presumably the honourable gentleman has not requested the presence of this *layman*, at the expense of valuable time, for the sole purpose of remedial recourse to a belated lesson in linguistics?' Balchard sounded vexed, and indeed felt so, at the detracting reference to the 'layman', with which he was being classed, by the bearded gentleman's presumptuous need to give this lecture. The blond gentleman smiled widely, if not rudely, in open amusement at Balchard's stilted delivery of words, with his laboured effort of affecting a 'proper' accent. He saw the complete erasure of that rough northern accent grating out at the words' edges as an elocutionist's nightmare task. Balchard's inner anger rose up sharply at the other's amusement, in his understanding its embarrassing significance. That the silken eloquence of speech should be the sole birthright of *their* class, was a constant thorn in Balchard's mind, if not his throat. His smallness in stature making him the shortest of the three of them standing there, didn't help matters any.

'I incur your pique, I see, Mr Balchard, with my circuitous choice of words. How remiss of me. Permit me to apologise most profoundly. However, such a tactful approach is all too often the only means of gaining access to new ground, where one must tread warily. The matter I am presently concerned with is a most delicate one, the nature of which is somewhat ----,' He paused, searching for the appropriate word.

'*Secret*, perhaps?' suggested Balchard. 'Or perhaps I should say *State* secret --- *Sir Basil*?'

The man's apologetic look was replaced with surprise, and this was more suddenly pushed aside by a dark anger surging to his face, his eyes ablaze with rancorous accusation, as he looked round at his subordinate. The military gentleman returned the look with his usual calm-eyed control. Shaking his head, he turned to look upon this man called Balchard with a new wonder of appraisal. Like the school prefect wanting to twist the guilty cad's ear.

'You would appear to be a bird who knows his wing, Mr Balchard. Pray, do not let us hinder your flight,' said the elderly gentleman.

Balchard took up the invitation to continue. 'Low down on your notepaper, where one normally expects signatures, there is the barely discernible imprint, many times over, of the letters *S B E*. Clearly, many documents have been endorsed by these three letters. Hence the recurrent imprint. Mere initialling, rather than signing, suggests a certain degree of rank, as does the usage of a *subordinate*,' Balchard broke off to glance round at the military gentleman, 'to follow, maintain surveillance on, and deliver messages to the particular *persona grata*, with whom contact is being sought. Rank suggests a title. A title suggests *Sir*, hence leaving two unknown factors, *B* and *E*. There is also the imprint of a three lettered word preceding the imprint of the word *Off- -*. *War Office*, perhaps, gentlemen? This would certainly conform with the military *accoutrements* befitting one such department of Her Majesty's Government.' Balchard stepped back, to pause and smile with obvious innuendo at the military gentleman, before continuing. 'A secondary source of information has revealed that a personage bearing such initials, and officiating on behalf of Her Majesty in the

War Office, would be Sir Basil Effram. I *am* speaking to Sir Basil Effram, am I not?'

'You are, indeed, Mr Balchard; bravo. I congratulate you on a most systematic mode of hunting down the fox, if ever there was one. But tell me, would this "*secondary* source of information" be a member of our Metropolitan Police Force, by any chance?'

'I would prefer not to say, sir.' Caught off guard by Sir Basil's question, Balchard felt his somewhat naked refusal to be childishly obstinate. He sought to make amends quickly. 'I am not at liberty to say, sir ---regretfully.' He was not sure, in his haste, if that sounded as cluttered an answer as the first one.

'I see. And was your contact opportune with further liberal revelations? The nature of our work, for instance? How and where we function in relation to the Ministry?'

'That whilst it was both silent and senior in service, it was yet neither of these in name, but rather, more aptly, the *Secret* Service. The degree of light shed on any specific details of operation would appear to compete with that of the snuffed candle. Nevertheless, operating as the Intelligence Branch, from Queen Anne's Gate, circa 1871; and more recently accommodated on a lesser budget in Adair House, Pall Mall, and Adelphi Terrace ----and e*lsewhere*.'

'And "*elsewhere*". Quite.' Sir Basil bit his lip with growing irritation at this gross leakage of departmental material without official inter-departmental consensus. He held no personal grievances against the culprit, not knowing who it was --- *yet* ---but he would find out soon enough. He made a mental note to send out an inter-departmental memorandum that would block the careless fool's promotion in the service for a while.

Balchard guessed as much from Sir Basil's agitated expression, but attempted no words. That matter was completely out of his power, and was entirely Dryson's worry. Presumably Dryson would not have procured such sensitive material for him without being able to cope with the consequences. A favour for services rendered. Balchard, of course, could have held back on these last points, but this was his method of convincing Sir Basil of the folly of holding back further. To goad him into revealing his hand, so to speak. Like the skilful bridge player's prompting of favourable suits from the opponent. Not that he spared much time for that card game. It being another of his points for berating the idle upper class.

Sir Basil was about to launch into his explanatory piece, when he stopped, to let a family group troop past, chattering noisily after ever important papa, on its way to the next eye- opening exhibit of the museum. When he did speak, it was to delve into the murky undercurrent of subversive politics rippling below the surface of the city's East End colony of immigrants. Separatist clubs of anarchists, Radicals, terrorists and murderers budding up among the innocent alien populace like malignant skin growths, did not appear to disturb the city's police. Far less did it disturb the Secret Service, since it could gain valuable intelligence by infiltration of the alien ranks. However, what *was* of serious concern, was the outbreaks of violence caused by *agent provocateurs* of the Czarist Secret Service. Such mounting incidents of crime, deliberately calculated to incite the anger of the police, could only result in eventual mass arrests, culminating in the deportation of large numbers of alien citizens. This would be a serious loss of information sources to the Secret Service. Proper surveillance mounted on these revolutionary groups was the only means of stemming such critical losses. This required man-power, so that the very understaffing of the Secret Service was the most immediate crisis. Sir Basil looked at his colleague. 'How many assistants is it you have at your Asian Desk, at the moment, Captain Smethers? *Three*, is it?'

'Two now, sir. One other officer and an NCO clerk on loan from Whitehall. Lieutenant Danvilles has since accepted his new commission in his father's old infantry regiment. True, he doesn't actually leave us until Tuesday, but I can't imagine him putting in much work between then and now; not 'Ginny'.'

'Precisely; two officers, one of them Captain Smethers here, and an NCO clerk. And that, Mr Balchard, is the pathetic total staff expected to cope with the entirety of the Russian Empire, Asia, China, India and Japan.'

As they passed through the rooms towards the museum's entrance, Balchard felt that the conversation's pendulum had swung as far as it could in his direction. 'Am I being officially recruited by Her Majesty's War Office for ancillary duties of a *clandestine* nature, Sir Basil?'

Sir Basil halted abruptly, so that Captain Smethers only just avoided colliding on his heels. He gripped Balchard's forearm and looked into his face with open horror at such open statement. 'I never heard such an utterance; nor shall I ever have occasion to. However forthright you may stride for your flag, no colours can ever be hoisted high on this battlefield, except at half mast, at the end of a bitter life-long campaign. You do follow me, do you not, Mr Balchard?'

'I am already actively acquainted with such a code of anonymity --- as I presume you must well *know*'

'And as yet are undaunted in your mettle by the perils of such task?'

Balchard stared back his strength of affirmative, at the same time removing Sir Basil's steely grip from his arm. Sir Basil narrowed his eyes to search into the depth of the mind before him, seeking out the littlest tremor or crack in character. Satisfied, he declared his positive finding in a slow pensive voice. 'Y-e-s. A leopard among leopards. Distinguishable from those around it only by its spots.' He looked round to Captain Smethers for concurrence. Smethers, ever smiling, changed his stance, and folding his arms, looked Balchard over from head to foot, as in rude open assessment of his fag's performance upon the playing-field. He already had the dossier on Balchard. Forwarded through Scotland Yard's new Special Branch, which had only been formed that year from the remnants of the Special Irish Branch. Where the original Irish Branch had been specifically concerned with countermanding the Fenian anti-monarchist terrorist campaign, the Special Branch was responsible for the country's security against all political subversion matters. With its commander directly answerable to the Home Secretary, and not the Commissioner of Metropolitan Police. This made them useful to Smethers, considering the political nature of his present work. His motive for recruiting Balchard was on the strength of reports that he was proving to be quite useful to the police in his role as forensic advisor, on account of his scientific and deductive skills. A good sensible fellow, in other words. And that was just what Captain Smethers needed -- a good reliable fellow who could bend to semi-official duties, without being a dumb 'yes' and 'no' laddie. A bit rough at the edges, perhaps, on account of his breeding, but that could well be to their advantage. He would blend in well with low class ruffians, if he was put out on undercover infiltration assignments. He could also be made to 'fall', for that matter, when they no longer needed him.

That, at least, was the *written* profile. Now to inspect the actual 'goods'. Smethers saw a pale nondescript face. A face that would not arouse undue attention or suspicion, or stay in memory for long. Good. The build was on the lean side. A pity, but there was a degree of boundless energy discernible in that light frame, simmering constantly for outlet. There was also a degree of nervousness playing on the face. But behind it, through the eyes, there was -----*something else?* Whatever it was, it had a fire of strength behind it. Good. That was very good. An unexpected reserve of strength behind a weak front was tantamount to the tethered goat luring in the unsuspecting tiger. Smethers recalled the file remarking on Balchard having been something of a bounder in the past. Excellent. It would serve their purposes well to have someone with a sinister side, who was not afraid to step out and wander off the straight and narrow. 'A little on the lean side, perhaps, but otherwise I should say he has the fettle for it, sir.'

Before anything else could be said on the matter, they all looked down in surprise at a tiny face peering up in bewilderment at them from their knees. Lost in a forest of grown-ups' legs, the small tearful face festooned in golden ringlet curls was biting back its fear on a toy windmill stick. *Balchard saw her golden locks, swaying like daffodils in the sun, and the millwheel turning slowly, heavy with water, turning sadly, heavy with death, turning, turning, forever turning in his mind.* Captain Smethers turned the child round, and putting a large hand to its back, propelled it gently in the direction of its squealing mama, who had appeared from behind the statue of a mythical centaur, fretting for her strayed chickling. Overjoyed to be reunited with her precious piccaninny, she rewarded it with a resounding clap across its ear, to which the child wailed out a happy deluge of tears, and to which she sobbed shakily, crushing the child to her bosom, whilst the Captain laughed aloud heartily. Balchard felt a twinge of annoyance at the Captain taking amusement from the emotional 'thunderclap' reunion. But a moment's truer thought had him conceding to envy. Envy of Smethers being ever at ease with every contingency he encountered, turning it to his advantage with the smooth aplomb that was his natural blood-line heritage.

The three men collected their thoughts from the brief distraction, re-settling their minds on the grimmer facets of everyday life. As they looked each other over without words, the silence itself was enough to say the meeting was ended.

Pulling his grey silk gloves on as he moved away, Sir Basil looked up into the air, as if pulling a distant point to mind: '*Balchard* --let me see -- could that possibly be a derivative of Blanchard? Would you perhaps know the Blanchards? -- Sussex people -- jolly nice lot; Coldstream Guards at Waterloo; only saved the Duke's bacon at Hougoumont.' Balchard felt his name come to ear as if it was someone else's, as it always did when queried after as a curiosity by toffs. He had memory of it always sounding strange and out of place among the people of his childhood, especially when barked at him by irate teachers. His negative headshake to Sir Basil's question had the gentleman's face snap shut with nothing more ado on that subject. The only reason for such a silly question being asked, Balchard reasoned, was as a reminder of who was who, and where the dividing line was drawn.

Smethers beamed a conclusive smile on Sir Basil: 'I should think *everyone* was at Waterloo, sir.' Balchard took the innuendo, if it was intended as such, to mean: 'everyone *who was anyone*' was at that now socially prestigious event of a great battle. That put *him* in his place. Balchard only just refrained from saying that but for the late intervention of Marshal Blucher's Prussian forces, Wellington's army would have been massacred outright. But there was no point in rocking the boat by upsetting the 'old boy' at this early stage.

Sir Basil held up his ivory-topped cane in parting gesture. 'Captain Smethers will be acting as liaison officer between yourself and the Department, Mr Balchard. He will contact you, as needs be, in due course. Please make a point of being available. I bid you good-day, sir.'

'Good-day, gentlemen.' As Balchard watched the two men walk away through the receding doorways, he noted Sir Basil's dark coat merging into the dark background of a bearded bronze Zeus casting down thunderbolts of Olympic fury. ' -----*distinguishable from those around it only by its dark demeanour and beard*,' Balchard murmured thoughtfully to himself. Yes, he could well imagine Sir Basil wielding powers akin to that ancient deity, with his privy labyrinth of Whitehall connections making him a sore man to cross. He could not forget how he had crossed that line once before and had only narrowly been spared being sent to prison, or at least a workhouse for young offenders. He could still feel the anger in their faces, as they questioned him over *her* death. The father, influential as industrialist and burgh magistrate, could have decided his hard fate at the flick of a finger. But to everyone's surprise, he had called for the matter to be ended there. Perhaps her dying had wounded him beyond the wish to invoke more suffering on her behalf. More likely, perhaps, he realised that further enquiries could raise matters that could well still injure her, dead as she was. With another matter to attend to, before leaving the building, Balchard turned round and headed for the Reading Room. He needed to refresh his memory and check up on some mystical aspects of Asian culture.

It was much to Balchard's surprise, when leaving the Institute, two nights later, that he was set upon and bundled violently into the brougham that had ghosted out of the fog, to stop alongside him with its door open. As the door slammed shut, and they moved off, a match flared up, to reveal the now familiar face of Captain Smethers. The face opposite them, the 'assailant', was not familiar to Balchard. Like an obedient, well-trained dog, the man sat straight-backed, staring at the space between them, watching, listening, seeing nothing, hearing nothing. The Captain watched the watching game in the other two, letting it prolong for several moments before intervening. 'Don't worry about the Corporal, here -- he only barks and bites when he's told.' At the mention of 'Corporal', Balchard concluded the man to be the aforementioned NCO in Smethers' lot's much understaffed Asian Desk. But as to the reason for, or the meaning of this unscheduled mystery journey, he was as much in the dark as the carriage's interior. Not sure if he should show anger, or a manly calm composure, at his virtual abduction, he settled for snubbing the cigar Smethers offered him. He looked to Smethers for immediate enlightenment. Reading the dithering perplexity in Balchard's expression, hidden as it was behind his overdone control of impatience, Smethers made a point of drawing out further on that control. Putting extended ceremony into crackling the cigar at his ear, and cutting it with deliberate slow precision, he then settled back to savour the taste for a few moments. Balchard found those moments tantalisingly long, as they, no doubt, were intended to be. But he recognised the pattern of play. The last time it had been a display cabinet in a museum, now it was a cigar in a carriage going to God knows where. At least they were not racing at breakneck haste to wherever it was they were heading, he noted, as the carriage rolled in leisurely pace to the gentle clip-clop sound of hooves in front of them.

Smethers held his head back to blow out a final long stream of smoke to signify the end of his sampling. Now for another 'sampling' of sorts. He turned to Balchard. He knew why the Department wanted him. But why had the man so readily consented to joining them? An academically proficient man who could go on to shine brightly in his field, wanting to engage in their work, so dark and obscure, and even dangerous? He sensed entrapment in the person sitting beside him, so still, so reticent; so near but so distant. Was it a mad craving to be singed by excitement's flame, or the need to escape from doldrums, or *something* d*eeper*? Did he see a conflict of wills in that face? As in two contesting terrible twins, with Balchard content with neither one nor the other, being at constant variance between the two? But this was real, and not some Grimm child's tale. Or was it somehow unreal in a grim adult tale? Smethers checked himself before he was drawn further into a spiral of hair-splitting logic. He had no time for such mind games, and it was not his problem. Not yet, anyway. He guessed it would appeal more to Balchard's intellect to pursue such a puzzle, ironic though it would be, like the cat chasing its own tail. He tapped Balchard's arm. 'It does good to see the new horse's form, before entering it into the big race.'

'Ah, yes -- of course, of course.' Balchard was nodding in apparent agreement, but this was an automatic stalling reaction to cover his fleeting moment of dented importance. Natural instinct made him resent having his competence questioned, but the scientist in him saw the good sense in preliminary testing. 'And does the Captain envisage this new '*steed*' having the stamina to chase those country church spires across field and meadow?'

'This is just the trotting phase. Let's wait until we reach full gallop, then we'll see' Smethers had been understandably reserved in his answer. He expected Balchard would be just as reticent. He was correct. Challenge and patriotism were the reasons Balchard gave for his joining them. And, of course, money as well, he apologetically admitted, when prompted further by Smethers. But as they talked on, Smethers noted how Balchard's words came somewhat mechanically from the mouth, while his mind seemed to follow a different train of thought entirely. Smethers considered how this could be an asset in conversing with a contact, whilst having an agile mind that could plan answers in parallel. So long as the contact did not perceive this, as he was seeing it now. In that case it could cause suspicion and mishap! He bit his cigar in serious second thoughts, but decided to let it go for the time being, anyway.

As they travelled on in a roughly circular peripheral route round the city, Smethers passed the conversation over to his NCO, Corporal Carter. The Corporal was to be Balchard's field contact, and would be responsible for conveying reports to HQ when Balchard could not report in directly himself. These instances required a coded form of communication, allowing for the contingency of material falling into enemy hands. Carter proceeded to instruct Balchard on these codes and 'dead letter boxes', to be used when personal contact in the field would be deemed to be unsafe. They stopped several times in order that Balchard could alight with Carter, to be shown the exact secret locations for concealing messages to be collected later. Balchard reckoned the points were roughly equally distanced around the city. A good strategy that made allowances for being in different parts of the city whenever urgent messages required passing on.

When at last the briefing appeared to be at an end, the carriage stopped and Smethers opened the door on his side. With neither Smethers nor Carter moving or saying anything and both of them staring expectantly at him, Balchard was puzzled for a moment. He then realised that he was being made to get out. He stepped down. Looking around he saw that he was in a desolate locality that he did not recognise, except that it seemed far out from the city centre. With the horse shifting nervously, about to move off, and the brougham door closing, Balchard cried out: 'Where are we, and how am I to get back on foot?'

Through the few remaining inches of open door space, Smethers laughed and called back: 'That's up to you, Balchie. Call it the 'canter' phase.' The door clicked shut and the carriage was away, as mysteriously as it had come, into the fog.

Arriving back in his rooms once more, Balchard had had ample time during his long trek back to turn things over in his mind. Smethers' questions, cunningly burrowing for information that lay deeper than the answers they plucked out, now reverberated in Balchard's mind, this time to a different sound. Whilst he had believed his answers to have satisfied Smethers then, he was not so sure now that they had. On top of that, he was feeling unsure over his wisdom of motivation for entering into this latest commitment;

for serious commitment it most surely was. If anything, it promised to be a very time-consuming undertaking. So *why* had he offered his services? *Why*, when time was already so critically short? For a man of ever iron-firm conviction, this uncertainty over a serious decision was unsettling. To be sure of an issue one instant, then unsure of it on another was alien to his logically organised way of thinking. It implied that he was not in full control of where he was heading. This discovery, a momentary lapse in self confidence, was alarming. Ever since studying for the scholarship had fired his imagination, he had nurtured dreams of great academic accolades. His leaving home to go to university had been more than just replacing a negative void with a positive position; it had confirmed his securing the first step on that stairway to fellowships, professorships and all sorts of professional accomplishments, along with their accompanying glories. It was this cherished goal that had enabled him to endure those long years of tutoring heckling, brainless, first year students, whilst working towards his Masters Degree; along those years he had sustained himself against the continual barrage of questions from his irate professor on the progress of his work. Now Felsham had taken over, forever crowding him, demanding to know when he would be finishing his research and publishing a paper on it. Was all this now in jeopardy?

It occurred to Balchard that he had been in dangerous waters long before Smethers had come along. The extra-mural work he did for the Yard was already taking up a lot of his time and so nailing his chance of a doctorate to the wall. So why did he allow himself to behave so recklessly, knowing all along that he was teetering on the brink of disaster? Plumping himself down heavily in the armchair, he tugged away nervously at a loose stud whilst thinking. He remembered *her* telling him to his astonishment, after his initial disbelief, that she had once swum to the bottom of the river, near the millwheel -- shaming him into accepting that she could also do something dangerous -- something which he had not done. Was *this* the devil seed in him, urging him to live on the edge of thrills and do dangerous things, break the rules, infringe on academic regulations, contravene his professor's mandates, work with disease-ridden prostitutes -- and now, venture into the dark word of espionage? Perhaps as token penance in reflection of his parents' servitude? Maybe even to meet death and so be with *her*? The pain began to throb in his head again.

CHAPTER 5

Taking up a swab from the enamelled tray with his forceps, Balchard moved in over the body. Leaning in close to take the first sample, his concentration was broken by a side glance of a tall figure in dark coat sweeping past without stopping, its authoritative strident steps ringing out on the tiled floor and walls. 'My office!' Professor Radcliffe needed no further words than these. He did not even need to stop to ascertain that his words had been heard. He *knew* that he would be heard -- that no-one would *dare* to not hear him. He k*new* that his words would be obeyed. Such was his authority, especially over squirming research assistants like Balchard -- a lowly life-form he considered to be only marginally above the bacterial insurgence, self-germinating at a phenomenal rate, in its insidious takeover of that very body. Perhaps it was because of his having to accept Pasteur's findings, whilst not being at all happy with the concept, on account of its increasing popularity across Europe, that he disliked the fool Balchard for pushing it under his nose in expectancy of a higher degree. Or was that just one reason?

The ultimatum laid down before Balchard by Professor

Radcliffe resounded with a heavier thud in his brain than that of the Professor's large paw striking his desk repeatedly to drive home the point. It occurred to Balchard, in the midst of his mental turmoil, that for a man who was in charge of everything, there was remarkably little to be seen of it upon his massive desk. But then this great ogre of a scientist did not need to be bothered with written material; he merely had to voice his will, and 'it shall be done'. Resentment stirred, somewhere deep in Balchard, and began a slow climb. It turned to anger, and started to climb faster as he took in the crushing finality of the Professor's demand, disguised as a 'last chance'. Radcliffe saw the pale face darken and the eyes steeling themselves in a puny stare of dismay turning to protest. This pleased him immensely and he smiled. Power was your making the opposition squirm, with no means of escape from your own controlled theatre of conflict. Just like those confounded bacteria in the culture dish. 'Forty eight hours?' The words came out slowly from Balchard's mouth, he was not sure how, but they did. Radcliffe simply thumped his desk again and held his chin up, to confirm this, without having to repeat the words. 'But that's ---'

'Do I hear objection!' Fury in the voice drowned out the desk's thundering. Radcliffe leaned forward, his massive eyebrows manoeuvring together in readiness for battle to put down rebellion in this insect of an upstart. Stares met stares for a lingering moment, before Balchard took a deep breath, opening and closing his fists, held down at his sides.

'In that case I'd better take up no more of your valuable time, sir. If you'll excuse me, I'll return to my work of removing samples from the body I was examining when you ---'

'No!' The desk was still in one piece, but only just, as omnipotent fury rained down on it once more. Radcliffe hunched forward on his elbows, clenching his fists together. He could see that the young man was confused and that gave him satisfaction. Rulers were never confused. Those they ruled were always confused. Radcliffe's Law. Balchard was, indeed, confused, having been told to have his work ready, and yet was now being told not to work, or had he misunderstood? Not fully understanding directives from senior staff humiliated him, and this, in turn, riled him. The Professor gave a great open sigh to demonstrate his irritation at having to lecture the naive child. Jabbing out a pedantic forefinger, he began: 'The work which you shall be presenting, *here on this desk*, shall be that which you have carried out for the completion of the penultimate phase of your research programme. I repeat: work which you have *done* --- D - O - N - E --- done, as opposed to that which you have yet to do.' Radcliffe pointed vaguely, to signify outside the room, before continuing. 'That work which you were proposing to continue with, out there, would constitute an integral part of your final phase of research, always providing that you are p*ermitted* to enter that final phase. We are not concerned with this, are we, Mr Balchard? Rather, we wish to see that which you *supposedly* have been responsible for up until now. We *shall* see this research which you are carrying out, in your scientific argument as an important furtherance of medical knowledge.' His elbows still firmly planted on the desk, Radcliffe raised his joined hands before his face, as if about to pray. To *whom*, Balchard wondered, considering that Mecca was in another direction. A mirror would have been more appropriate for the great sod appealing to his own self as deity. 'Omnipotence' spoke: 'Would it be futile to hope for the remotest of possibilities that my words have at last reached your cerebral cortex, and have been understood, Mr Balchard? As already stated -- forty eight hours from now.' Radcliffe pulled on his golden chain, to take out the bejewelled time-piece. 'That would make it at three minutes past four exactly.' He was about to reach for a pen to write it down in confirmation, then thought better of it, and left it. His spoken word would suffice. Putting the watch back in his waistcoat's fob pocket, he dismissed the pathetic little man without the courtesy of looking up. 'Close the door behind you.'

Passing through the outer office, Balchard only stopped short of exploding with anger when his passage was blocked by Dr Muir getting up from his desk. 'Everything sorted out, then, Mr Balchard?' Balchard was of no mind to see the genuine smile on the ever genial doctor's face, as he brushed past him, almost knocking his folders out of his grasp. He saw no faces of any sort -- only blind rage -- as he stormed out in mad determination to beat the forty eight hour threat coming down on him like a slow guillotine blade. No, he corrected himself -- it was now forty seven hours, fifty nine minutes and about forty three seconds. Well, no-one would be getting his neck; not just yet -- not before he had his Ph.D. Great resolve flared up inside Balchard, coming through in his glazed eyes look. He smiled at the irony. He may not yet be 'Doctor' Balchard, but that would not stop him from 'doctoring' his research report. His work, like all experimental work, was not based on established fact, but on what he, the researcher, was putting forward to be accepted as fact. Knowing the results that he wished and intended to show, he would have to enter these up falsely as having been achieved, and extrapolate backwards to enter up further false readings necessary for consolidating the final results. Since stability was not an expected feature of the diseased organ, in its state of putrefaction, all that was required was a quantity of convincing specimens to show as 'those that he had worked on'. It would still call for a colossal mountain of paperwork to be completed. But first he would have to go round the city's mortuaries and 'charity houses', to find suitable 'material'. A nun coming into the building with an injured man, stopped and turned to ask Balchard for help. But the creak of the swinging door was not much help to her, or the wounded man, as Balchard ignored them on his way out.

Luck was perhaps prepared to hear Balchard's appeal when he called in at the backdoor of the charity sickhouse just north of Spitalfields. He handed the elderly attendant documents bearing the Institute's letterheads, to show that he was a bona fide medical researcher, without actually giving his own name. But the disconnected manner in which the old man perused the papers suggested to Balchard that he was either illiterate, or suffering the normal presbyopic impairment common to that age group. According to the old man, a woman had died that very morning. 'Came in last night. Bleedin' bloomin' terrible, she was. It's what they gets in punishment for what they does, an' so they should, I says. You know.' A tap on the nose was supposed to tell Balchard what he meant, although Balchard already knew, without the secret signal. 'Bloomin' well nearly racked me back, I did, scrubbin' the floorboards afterwards. Superintendent wasn't 'appy; made me do it twice over, 'e bloomin' well did. Well, bugger 'im, I says. Bloomin' well bugger 'im.' The man's description of the woman's condition and her profuse bleeding, told Balchard that this was what he was looking for. One example, anyway. The old man normally would have bartered for a higher price than that offered by anyone asking for 'favours', like Balchard was doing. But there was something about the young man that deterred the old man from haggling further. He was initially put off by the openly hostile air of impatience hanging about the young man, along with the strong smell of liquor on his breath. But it was the sense of sinister menace lurking beneath the surface that really made the old man feel uneasy. Wasting no more time on words, he led the way through to the room reserved for the dead. The sooner the man examined the body and took his medical specimens, like he was askin', the sooner he would be off. As soon as Balchard had clicked his medical bag shut on his specimen jars, the old man could not wait to lead him to the back door again. He closed and locked the door securely, immediately upon Balchard stepping out into the dark alley.

Balchard walked for an hour, through the Spitalfields district, stepping between sleeping forms on the cold cobbles, not caring if he missed a space and stepped on a face. He stopped to stare out a rat, sitting on its haunches, sniffing his pungent human odour, enhanced as it was with alcohol.

Twitching its whiskers for a moment, it suddenly dropped down on all fours, to scurry off among the refuse, much of which was the human form. Balchard tottered round in his drunkenness to follow the furry retreat. 'Didn't like what you saw, eh? Yeah, well I wasn't too impressed with your face either. You could do with a trim of those whiskers --- great hairy bastard!' To follow up on his words, Balchard threw his empty whisky bottle after the rat, before tottering round, to continue in his original direction. His outcry had fallen on other ears, besides those of the rodent. Female voices, cooing out their indecent offers from the darkness, were shooed aside by Balchard, walking on by them, until a familiar voice came to ear, making him stop. She was generally co-operative with him in his research field studies. Apart from that, her 'personal services' were clean. He had taught her the imperative importance of this. He dissolved into the darkness with her. Having found a second source of material of reasonable avail, alive this time, he felt that he needed to release his stress. He would get back to the hard work in the morning. It would have been preferable to have collected more material, but with a little 'stretching', he believed he could scrape by. Not that the old goat Radcliffe would waste a precious moment blinking an eye at his work presentation. He would leave that to his meagre minions. Chances were perhaps greater than evens that old Muir would be one to find favourable disposition in a borderline case.

CHAPTER 6

When Balchard returned to London, from his brief visit to Dorset concerning the Harlech case, the worst pea-souper fog of that autumn was just beginning to lower its heavy mantle onto the dark outlined shoulders of the city. A faint westerly breeze was wafting the mist inwards from the mouth of the river, so that above, the blurred outline of St Paul's was choked with crumpled rags of a brooding red sunset. And yet as surely as London is apt to explode upon the wearied mind of the traveller arriving in from the quiet of the country, so it did with Balchard, as his steel-shod cab and horse clattered over London Bridge. Snatches of many tongues came to ear, inducing Balchard to lean out of the brougham, to take in his surroundings. In spite of the thickening fog, serried rows of shipping were still discernible, standing out at the river windings, hatching the mist with a ghostly gossamer webbing of rigging. These stately merchant fleets were the Empire's guard of honour, bearing golden grain from the Far East and the Far West. Barrels, bales, sacks and hides swung through the air, lightermen receiving and directing them with swinging arms. The brougham stopped in the congested river of people and vehicles, and new sounds drifted up, causing Balchard to move his head slightly in an exercise of separating and identifying each one from the other. Cranes creaked and pulleys rattled; idle sails flapped flatly and steamships pulsed as they got underway; sailors shouted hoarsely while church bells chimed from many quarters; all of this through the rhythmic 'plashy' sound of breaking waters, in private language to Balchard's ear. Somewhere in the descending gloom a river pilot commented coarsely to a pleasure party in a wherry heading for the rude enjoyment of Shadwell, while at the same time, a gentle lapping was the combined effort of stern faced Thames policemen pulling vigorously on their oars.

Stuck in the human river, up here on the bridge, Balchard thought how easily one could be stranded if one had no sense of direction from an aspired goal. Just as he could not see through the front of his carriage, he still knew where he was heading. In more ways than one, perhaps? Whereas others could see where they were going, without knowing where that was. This latter contradiction he likened to the frolicking figure of a drunk repeatedly standing up and then falling down again in his seat, in the open-top landau, halted beside him. In his happy inebriated state, the man could see what was ahead but probably without a sober appreciation of what it was he was seeing. Balchard had always known the painful past he was escaping from; but the destination he was now heading for had altered somewhat with recent developments, so that there was possible branching of his route looming up darkly. He had to choose with caution. The drunk had become aware of of Balchard staring at him abstractly, and was now leaning precariously over the side of his carriage, gesturing wildly with his bottle, offering a drink. Balchard laughed at the other's dangerous antics. 'So where do you think you're going, you brainless fool? Or does rich papa decide that for you? I don't need my pater to dictate to me where I'm going, because I'm *eshducated*. So there!' To follow his sarcasm, he gave the drunk a rude V-sign. The very sign, Balchard thought, given by ancient warriors threatening to cut off those vital two fingers of enemy archers, used in drawing their bows. And not as would be otherwise mistakenly believed by irate 'ladies of the night'. At a safe distance, in the isolation of his carriage, Balchard was reminded of Smethers' advice. The Captain stressed the need for forever having to be a self-sealed unit in the field; never trusting anyone. Never even allowing oneself to be sure of what action to take. Until that moment for action comes -- things may have changed instantly and require going off at a tangent, in a new strategy. One had to endeavour to be almost as unpredictable to oneself, as to the enemy. That was probably ' --- easier than it sounded,' murmured Balchard, finishing his train of thought aloud. He looked away from the drunk, wondering why he had said that. It was as if another person inside himself had spoken. Another side of him, perhaps? In spite of his upper-class horsy upbringing, Smethers did carry some good intelligence in his head, if one could excuse the pun.

The traffic shifted forward once more, and as the brougham jerked into motion, a coin rolled out coyly from beneath the seat, to catch Balchard's eye. He watched this 'unexpected contingency' wobble round in decreasing circles, in mild confirmation of Smethers' words. Picking the coin up, he stared out through brooding eyes at the varying combination of shapes and activities swirling around him. Ominous dark shapes loomed up like lumbering dinosaurs to give fleeting glimpses of enormous timber warehouses and crazy watermen's stairs snaking down to massive landing stages that swarmed with smudges of human parasites. Where tugs spurted their coke fumes in the faces of these unfortunates, the hazy image of the already blackened dockers was lost completely. Great forests of masts continued to stretch back along the waterfront, whilst between the buildings, dark alleys made toothless faces of ancient tenements, on whose corners the public houses tottered drunkenly from the perpendicular. Balchard observed the Empire's commerce massing itself, alive and heartily, before his very eyes, like a purring writhing beast, swelling its chest up proudly over the hum and hiss and general hubbub of hastening crowds. Dingy files of people passed into the steamships; sleepy barges lowered their masts to pass under the bridges; heavy traffic between the City and the Borough dragged over Southwark Bridge, and trains glided across the railway arches into the prodigious Cannon Street shed. Factories, mills and works, as well as barges, wherries, tugs and pennyboats all gave off smoke and steam, blurring all, while the heavy water churned from its bed, feverish in its ebb and flow, to emanate a grandeur that fired Balchard's mind. The throb of moving organisation before him was like the very arterial pulse of the turbulent stream of London life. It was also suggestive of the many activities that went on behind the wharves, outside the general scene.

Balchard's mind darkened, like the furious waters coursing between the trim array of Danish ships on his left and mysterious Greek hulls on his right, as he reflected on the Stygian undercurrent of murkier waters that gave flow to the city's festering criminal element of the populace. But from that very concept sprang his spirit, like that surging from the Leyden jar to give the otherwise mortified frog its bountiful leap of new-found vitality. For this truly was his personal stimulus, namely, the denouement of the 'insoluble' imbroglio by systematic analysis of prevailing factors trawled from this sea of life all around him. It occurred to Balchard that his dealings with the underworld, far from comfort and security of middleclass parlours, was in its own way a daring affront to society. Perhaps like the expelled schoolchild drawing his stick noisily across the school railings in a spiteful gesture against the former headmaster who had administered such punitive measures. Thus was his doing when he walked the tightrope of dabbling with right and wrong as the whim seized him -- where his genius of deductive logic allowed the fathoming of criminal darkness, perhaps akin to that of his own mind, such that he could defy crime, or commit and conceal the felony from the law if he so chose. With his fathoming of criminal minds and their motivation, he could throw light on criminal darkness or else deepen its darkness to elude lawful detection by those very methods he knew Dryson's people used, if he so chose. Like the two sides of a coin. Either one or the other, with the same ease as flipping a decisive heads or tails. A game that he could enjoy. Looking down at the coin as he turned it over slowly in his fingers, he was not sure if this was a serious temptation, or a passing thought. Like that of the faithful bank manager appreciating how easy it would be for him to rob his masters' vault, since he holds the vital numbers in his mind. Letting the philosophical exercise pass, he grunted and throwing the coin up, caught it, to look at it. 'Heads. Would that be heads for: go ahead, or 'heads' for: off with his head?' He wondered. Taking hold of the cloth tag on the door, he lowered the window. Extending his arm out as far as he could, he flicked the coin over the side of the bridge. The thought of it hitting the water, even out of sight, to sink down deep into oblivion was enough to turn his expression grey. *Just as she had done*, he thought morosely, *just as she had done*. Closing the window, he sat back, forgetting the outside view. 'No daffodils down there,' he muttered dejectedly.

He said this as he remembered how *she* had remarked how every little drop of water in the river was joined to the next one, and so on, to join every drop in every ocean in the world. A tiny, tiny, drop could go all round the world without going on rough land, and encountering trouble with rough people. It is only when we become too big, and hope for dreams that are too big, that we find trouble. Was she cautioning him on his academic aspirations and social ladder- climbing? He had told her that in the aquatic state, there would be no daffodils. She had replied in her tauntingly kittenish manner, that *daffodils were everywhere -- they were simply a state of mind -- a state of being happy -- to be seen if you were happy, or wanted to be happy*. Well, he could only see the lead coloured water of the Thames pulsing away, and he was not happy. 'No daffodils down there,' he said morosely once more.

Balchard alighted from the brougham at Scotland Yard. Detective Sergeant Dryson was in not much of a lighter mood than Balchard, when they met in his office. With the Commissioner, Sir Charles Warren, being fastidious over legalities, it seemed that their hard work, in collecting scientific evidence to incriminate the Kensington banker murderer, was encountering legal problems. With Balchard being away out of town, Dryson had been unable to vent his irritation on him, over this setback. He tried to do so now. It didn't help any, that Balchard was defensive, on a stand-off point. 'Such a predicament, regrettable as it may be, can hardly pertain to me, Detective Sergeant. *My* concern, my *understood* and *officially agreed* concern, as stated in written contract, is restricted to the purely scientific. All else beyond this, alas, must waylay the brain of some other unfortunate, I fear.'

Dryson took the cold remark with withering patience. He was familiar with Balchard's interest dropping like a brick, after the last slide was examined under the microscope. He saw it as a shirking of duty. Like the deserter fleeing the frontline engagement. But he was not fool enough to expect Balchard to see it that way. The man was a purist, if not a bit loony, with first loyalty to his scientific work, before all else. Any shortcomings occurring outside of that dedication were not likely to weigh heavily on his conscience. 'It always comes down to *that*, with you, doesn't it, Balchard?'

'I beg your pardon?'

'*Scientific*! Everything has got to be scientific, with you. With all this scientific lot they're bringing in, I honestly think that I'd be better off handing in my warrant card, and letting those clockwork toy automatons take over the work.'

Balchard rubbed his chin slowly, his eyes looking afar. 'It is foreseeable, that in some future society, with a more advanced ----'

'*Joke*, Balchard! For God's sake, it was a *joke*!' Clearly Balchard had not been theorizing along humorous lines. Furthermore, he felt insulted that his professional opinions should ever be associated with anything remotely resembling humour. Dryson saw that he was making little headway with the other. He virtually snatched the buff envelope from Balchard's hand. 'Is this the report, then? On Harlech?'

'The *initial* report. Yes. I chance to say that a return visit to the locality is imperative, in order to assimilate matters in relevant perspective.'

Dryson cast a sharp glance at the other. 'So you think you need to have another look around -- get a better picture of things -- right?' He held up the report sheet in one hand, giving it repeated backhanded slaps with the other. 'And you think that what's on this flimsy piece of paper is enough to persuade my superiors to hand out more expense money for you to go down there again? Do you?'

Balchard shrugged his shoulders. Dryson saw a strange thing called the beginning of a smile nick the corners of Balchard's mouth for a fraction of a second. He suspected that its significance would be the reverse of what one would normally expect of it, when it appeared on *that* cold countenance. He threw the sheet into the wire tray on his desk. 'Right. Leave it with me; I'll see what I can do.' Dryson stepped over to the hat stand, to take down a new-style head piece of soft gold-coloured felt -- a homburg. With his planting the hat firmly on his head, it was not too brilliant a deduction for Balchard, that the Detective Sergeant was of a mind that they should both exit the office. They were both spared annoyance from further heated discussion, by the fact that they both had other pressing matters to attend to.

Having been allowed to proceed into the final term of his research programme, Balchard had experienced a definite release from pressure -- from *that* pressure, at least. However, with War Office assignments on the increase, along with those of the Yard, he had once more become lapsed with his medical studies. His hours of attendance in the hospital laboratories and tutoring and lecture sessions had fallen to the barest minimum allowed, to the critical notice of senior staff. Thus, he was incurring the disapproval of the Pathology Department's head, Professor Jeremiah Aloysius Smelfors, M.D., F.R.C.P. The venerable professor was apt to be mild in his reproof of the hospital's juniors. Satisfied with his three and sixty years, and the decades therein that had put his name to a noble lineage of medical volumes in the Department's library, to the keen interest of no-one but adventurous spiders, he could well afford to be lenient. His eyes shone brightly. But Balchard was not deceived. For whilst the merry sparkling in the Professor's eyes may have misled the lesser layman, it was, in Balchard's diagnosis, the peripheral haze of onsetting cataract. Professor Smelfors noted the silent, peering examination, and nodded sagely at the young man's successful recognition of the ocular ailment. 'And yet there was a time, Mr Balchard, when their visual acuity was perfect --simply perfect. But like as one when one looks down the unfocused microscope, the decision to rack the instrument up or down must be adroitly concluded lest there be too little illumination, or lest, indeed, the specimen slide be damaged. Perhaps like one standing in the closing doorway of the illuminated room; one is compelled to step forward or backward, to be either *included within* or *excluded without.* '

The Professor peered closely at the Napoleon barrel clock on his desk, and then inclined his head back, beaming a broad smile, as a means of measuring the young man's reaction to his words. But as far as the elderly gentleman's failing vision was permitting, it would take a sculptor to chisel out some form of expression on that granite-like face of the young Balchard. The statements occasioned by general rumour of the staff were true, it seemed. This young man Balchard was a social iceberg. Brilliant in his clinical precision, with a singularly zealous approach to chemical analysis, undoubtedly. But with a definite lack of the requisite social graces that made for better working relations with fellow staff members. The foreseeable result of this could well be the detrimental lowering of work output and general standards in the Department. With only his retirement to look forward to, after the New Year, the Professor had no desire to leave a disorderly house behind him, as memorial to his lifelong work. He would have it no other way. This would have to be rectified. A glass of claret was poured and proffered across the desk to Balchard.

Balchard accepted. And so it was, with little more words, that Balchard was paroled on the basis of improving his hospital attendances, as well as his liaison with colleagues in the department, and so come a little closer to the fold. As an initial step, he was *invited* to dinner. Whilst having no undue craving for socialising, Balchard nevertheless did crave for the laboratory facilities permitting his scientific experiments. He therefore made the enormous effort at inner self constraint and bowed, albeit most slightly, to the behest.

Simpson's, in the Strand, was quiet for that hour of the evening. Waiters in black jackets and immaculate white aprons flitted like penguins from table to table in a diligent effort to lesson the doleful atmosphere -- or so it seemed to a bored Balchard. But for the cracking of lobster shells at the next table, Balchard was in introspective detachment from his immediate surroundings. He could almost hear the moth snoring on the chandelier across the room. His interest had long departed from the meal, after the initial delight of the exquisite salmon plate, so that had the grouse been served still in its full feathered regalia, his palate would not have been unduly troubled.

Dr Pilkington-Greeves found it only too obvious that Balchard had not much to contribute by way of ordinary social conversation. Rather, he was mostly inclined to watching, listening, or was 'elsewhere', only joining in occasionally. When he did speak, it virtually brought a stop to all else around the table, on account of his 'railroading' out stiff long scientific pieces. And old Smelfors had especially asked that they make an effort to bring the young man in out of the cold, so to speak. Oh, well, he thought, if he had to get the 'train' started, then how better, than with a scientific topic. God help their indigestion. He interrupted Balchard's thoughts. 'If I'm to understand you correctly, Balchard, you would have us believe that the eye has some sort of retaining power long after the body has ceased to function; when it's dead, in fact? ' Pilkington-Greeves looked more of a soldier, with his rigid, upright bearing and steadfast jaw, than he looked senior physician at the Institute. If this was coincidence, it was only because his family had always been either of the Army or the Church, or both, for nigh on two centuries. Since his present generation had already contributed fair stock to each of these noble vocations, it had only remained for him to take up the third noble profession as his personal metier. His family were also longstanding landowners and so had the further tradition of giving a fair hearing to the serf, if only to clear the lungs for a long day's toil over the soil. He was plainly interested in Balchard's answer.

'I am suggesting,' said Balchard, 'that the final image impinging on the retinal pigment epithelial layer, at the moment of the individual's death, is left there, somewhat like a black -board that is not cleared of its last chalk markings. Considering Hering's research on the continual chemical regeneration process facilitating colour changes in the retinal cells, by bleaching in accordance with the light wavelength, it is surely reasonable to surmise that if this process is arrested at the moment of death, then the changes in the retina will also be arrested, so leaving that final image. Like the final solitary picture in the closing gallery, if you wish; just waiting for closer inspection by the curious mind.'

' "*Curious*" is the word. That is utterly ludicrous!' This jeering exclamation came from Guy Du Mont, seated between Balchard and Pilkington-Greeves. Virtually all gold in hair, complexion and probably blood as well, Du Mont was of the rich Norman aristocracy that had flooded over the land in that tidal wave of eight hundred years past. His family motto was simply to crush underfoot all that lay before. And that included Balchard. As consultant in obstetrics at the hospital, and sometime lecturer at the University, he had a strong distaste for seedy researchers infiltrating and demeaning the medical profession.

'Hold on a moment, though, Guy. There may just well be some sense in it.' Pilkington- Gtreeves lowered a forkful of gateau *fromage* for a moment's thought. 'I've read Hering's papers on the effect of metabolic changes as regards stimulation by spectrum wavelengths in the visual pathway, and there does appear to be some ground for credence. It certainly corresponds with the Helmholtz-Young theory, I'll grant you.' He took another mouthful from the fork, before looking up expectantly at Balchard. 'Go on, Adam. Assuming this final image *is* suspended indefinitely on the retina, how do we isolate it, and to what purpose, exactly?'

Balchard noted Pilkington-Greeves' gentlemanly effort in addressing him, *for the first time ever*, by his Christian name. At the same time, he felt a touch patronised, as in the case of the teacher being extra kind to the disabled child -- the special attention having the reverse effect of alienating the 'freak' child even further from the normal children. It was not too difficult to guess the extent of Professor Smelfors' part in all this. Only *he* would have been capable of such benign intentions to bring him into their precious flock. He pursed his lips for a few seconds, his eyes directed downwards, as he tidied the crumbs specking the brilliant white tablecloth. 'Like all systems in their embryonic phase, the words are the next easiest stage, following the initial seed of concept, after which the ground can all too often be barren for long periods of dormancy before germination occurs. True, we have no instruments at present capable of such delicate precision, but should our scientists provide us with the means for such at a later date, the rewards could be manifold.'

'For instance?' The very terseness of Du Mont's question was a measure of the loaded backhander for what he suspected would be the answer.

'For instance, in the field of criminal investigation, the part played by forensic analysis could well --'

'Just as I suspected ---"*criminal investigation*"!' Du Mont's rude interruption of Balchard's words was accompanied by his rocking his chair backwards and forwards, and finally slapping the table edge loudly with his fingers. 'One could hardly fail to guess that it would descend to that lewd subject. Nothing, but nothing whatsoever, to do with true medicine. Indeed, one could well say that we've come round in a circle, back to square one. It's rather a cart before the horse situation, with the whim preceding the need, is it not, Balchard? Personally, the whole thing strikes me as positively immoral.' Du Mont quietened for a moment, sure of a crushing victory, to adjust his cuff-links. 'Besides, what possible good could it serve, even in your so called "*forensic*" techniques? If the wretched victim falls to his death on the floor and sees, as his last thing, the heel of a boot, what good is that, I ask you, Balchard?' He held his head back in bold challenge, with a haughty sneer on his face that was another belated sword swipe at the feudal Saxon vassal.

Balchard pondered over his 'assailant' through ice-cold eyes, recognising the over-surety as that with which the carelessly arrogant hunter stormed blindly through the undergrowth, only to step on his own pre-laid spring-trap. 'To the unknowing fool --nothing; but to he who has an insight for that *beyond*? --' He left the statement suspended for emphasis, giving Du Mont a heavy slow nodding of reproval, before continuing. 'Alas, poor Achilles, whom one recalls as being waylaid by a mere "*heel*". Such tragedy, alas.' Balchard tut-tutted in mockery, again nodding his head solemnly, whilst thrumming out an equally solemn drum- roll on the table.

The air was tense with stares for several seconds, before Pilkington-Greeves intervened. '*Touche*! That about evens it up for that round. What do you say to that, Stolling?' They all turned to the fourth member of the party. But the young Dr Stolling was of no weighty opinion, being there solely for the food. He couldn't otherwise afford it on his meagre salary as a surgeon's assistant at the hospital. Du Mont, in disgust, beckoned the waiter to replenish the empty port decanter, and heads went down once more to continue the meal. By the time the plates had been cleared and coffee was served, the topics had changed multi-fold, with Balchard's interest waning rapidly with them, so that he once more found his nervous restlessness mounting within. His head was beginning to hurt, and it was not the wine.

Outside the restaurant entrance, Balchard declined the invitation from the others to drink elsewhere, as the doorman made a timely intervention with a note which urgently demanded his presence at a locality far across the city. In the sheltered solitude of the cab speeding off towards Trafalgar Square, Balchard crushed the note and cast it out the window. It had been written by himself earlier as a pre-arranged means of taking his leave of the others, without his seeming to be uncivil, *or suspicious*. Once out of the Strand, and safely out of sight of the others, Balchard ordered the cabbie to change direction and hasten for a new address in the sinister shadows of Drury Lane. Stopping at this address to make a sinister purchase, Balchard redirected the cab to return him to Montague Street. Standing in the shadows, counting and pocketing Balchard's money, Sam Loofer touched his hat brim at the cab speeding away: 'An' a bleedin' good night t' yer, *Mr B.*'

Securely secluded in the privacy of his rooms, Balchard loaded the steel syringe and feverishly sought the venous channel in his arm. Pressing the plunger in, he watched the cocaine solution pass from the one hollow shell to the other 'hollow shell'. Withdrawing the needle, he closed his eyes in relief for a moment, dropping the despicable devil's tool onto the floor. Then he sank down onto the bed to fall into a deep sleep.

CHAPTER 7

With the shadows growing longer and the evenings moving in on the closing days of that September, the heavily overcast weather did nothing to alleviate Balchard's brooding agitation. Waiting between developments from Scotland Yard and the War Office, he was gripped by a mind-grinding impatience. It was in his nature to see every action he performed as an experiment, like those in the laboratory, with readings to be taken on its completion. So he was always anxious to take 'readings'. With Dryson being none too receptive to his enquiries when he called in at the Yard, and Smethers being nowhere to be found, matters were not made any easier for Balchard's anxiety. For this reason he had thus on one occasion rushed out on a moonlight sortie to Camberwell, to measure the wheel diameters of a blind knife-grinder's barrow. The result had yielded nothing more dramatic than the anticipated confirmation of what his forensic tests in the laboratory had indicated, but the effort had provided temporary relief for Balchard's nerves. It was another relief for him when Corporal Carter unexpectedly turned up at Montague Street, to 'collect' him and take him on a reconnaissance exercise. 'Scrapin',' Carter called it.

'Scraping?' As he put the question, Balchard's mind already held a dark picture of them inflicting facial injuries.

'As in scrapin' the ground, to see what's disturbed underfoot, sir.'

'I see.' The faint tone of disappointment did not escape the Corporal's notice. He had been instructed by the Captain to watch the funny bloke's every move carefully. Like polishing boots, buttons and buckles for parade --- leave nothing out.

'May one ask after the grounds of your certainty that I was to be found here, and not perchance, elsewhere, at work?'

'*We knew*, sir.'

Being accustomed to examining other people's efforts through a microscope, Balchard found it strange that *he* should be put under the microscope by someone else. He was not sure if he was annoyed more by this, than by his being led by the nose by a mere NCO. But he was sure of one thing. He was warming to the stirring undercurrent of devious intrigue. Contenting himself to be led on by the Corporal, Balchard followed him into the night. The places they visited struck Balchard as being *different* from those that he frequented in his research. Dark doors, with forbidding airs, opened only to coded knocks, or after long scrutiny --- from where, Balchard could not see --- but could somehow hear and *feel*, a little uneasily. Doors were opened back by wardens from Hades, giving access to dark dens of even darker iniquitous dealings. No society gentleman's 'endeavouring of French lessons' from harlots would be hosted here. Balchard let Carter do the talking. He had to, as he had no idea what the man would be talking about, or what it was they were doing specifically.

But the concept of a guinea pig being monitored in its cage by Smethers did occur to him. He could feel himself in that cage. While doing so, he watched and listened, around in all directions, familiarising himself with what was supposedly an expansion on his theatre of activities. An occasional face he recognised, seen elsewhere, in his field work about the city's poor sectors. The other faces did not register, being as rough and uninteresting as the surrounding walls. They seemed to be prisoners more of their own inner wretchedness, than of those grim walls pressing in on them.

Piercing words brought Balchard's attention back to his side. '---bloody *giant* wiv yer, then?' Carter did not suppress his grin quick enough to escape Balchard's eye, with its injured look. Humour faded when rage replaced injury. The ruffian speaking to Carter rose from his chair and motioned them to follow him into a black recess of a backroom that Balchard had not noticed in the gloom. They were spared the amenity of a candle. 'Told yer not t' come after me 'gain. 'Ow d' yer know I was 'ere? ' A blade scraped stone beside them in the man's expression of anger. 'Told yer t' leave me 'lone!' Knife-blade fury lessened to quieter scratching on the stone, as Carter calmed the man down. Balchard could imagine the Corporal having a campaign ribbon in skulduggery. He could barely hear the other two speak, as they stood tete-a-tete, the knife hovering between them. They shifted apart. 'Right. So what's it t' be this time? What's yer askin' for, eh?' The man leaned forward. 'An' 'ow much yer *givin*?'

Balchard suddenly realised the man was addressing *him*. He looked round to see what Carter had to say. Carter was not there. Balchard spun round, looking everywhere that he could in the unrelenting darkness, but could not see what he wanted to see. Carter had gone completely. So *that* was their game. He had been deliberately dropped in at the deep end, in trial measure of how he would cope, with his 'back to the wall', in an 'unexpected contingency'. Good one on you, Smethers! It was not outside Balchard's logic to reason that if this was only a trial run, then there would be little lost or gained if he made a wrong move or a right move. He thus reverted to his normal role of medical researcher, putting his usual line of enquiries, concerning 'females in distress', and illnesses in general, to the man. The man thought the questions were 'bloomin' barmy', and only wanted to know how much was going to be put in his palm. For once, a rare instance, Balchard could appreciate the curses cast at him through sprays of saliva. The questions *were* stupidly inappropriate, put to a mind which at that moment saw only money at the point of a blade. But they were Balchard's lever for prising himself out of a tight corner. Balchard concluded that his false promise of money for information had been successful when the knife stopped hovering, to bury its point firmly in the top of the wooden table. Both parties satisfied, one returned to its drinking, the other re-emerging out into the night, to rediscover the phenomenon of fresh air. On his way back to Montague Street, Balchard turned the 'practise run' over in his mind. It came as none too great a surprise that he had derived a degree of pleasure from it, in spite of the tension and danger. Or was it *because* of the tension and danger?

Entering his rooms once more, and pleased with his

earlier performance, Balchard's confidence was jarred by a problematic thought. It suddenly occurred to him that if his War Office assignments entailed his associating with ruffian anarchists intent on bringing down society, especially the hierarchy, then his image as a highly educated professional gentleman could well prove to be somewhat incongruous. Reaching between two piles of folders of Felsham's work, he plucked out one of his half-painted lead soldiers. He wondered how the little hussar would look with a complete change of uniform. As it seemed his own 'colours' would need to be changed. Sinking down into the leather armchair, he held the soldier up close, to peer at it pensively. Otherwise, apart from these brief nocturnal interludes, a streak of lightning was welcome in his sullen rooms.

Sam Loofer provided these 'thunder-flashes' with his bright suit, now blue and white check, when he called in on his occasional 'deliveries'. 'Not a friend of yours, I 'ope, Mr B?' Loofer remarked, cocking his head at the pair of eyes staring out dolefully at him from a jar of formalin standing on the workbench in the corner. The sight of these gave Loofer the urge to grab the coins quicker than Balchard was dropping them into his palm, and so be off. In his haste to get out, he almost forgot the other matter. Turning round in the doorway, he took out an envelope and gave it to Balchard. ' 'Er downstairs, the dragon, asked me t' give yer this. It came in through the letter-box just after I came in.' It was a ticket for the concert that evening at St James's Hall.

The 'cats' were squalling in the pit, as the orchestra prepared for its opening rendition of Mozart's *Eine kleine Nachtmusik*, when Balchard entered his box. The soft andante of the second movement was not particularly to his fancy, if not to say spoiled in his anticipation. It was the piece frequently savaged by the fellow lodger along the landing from Balchard, to the point of stretching his nerves, like the violin strings themselves. He was thus looking forward to the performance, if only for an improvement on this. This was not his sole object of anticipation. The seats beside him were empty, resolutely so to demand strict privacy of the box. Balchard scanned the auditorium, just as 'it' scanned all. A whole sibilant sea of conversation echoed back, as if by two giant sea shells held to the ears. Here before him, in the fleeting glances exchanged between fluttering fans and sweeping binoculars, was all that of which the 'cultivated' Londoner never tired. From the highest wit, to the lowest impertinence of gossip and scandal. The seats remained vacant beside Balchard even when the hall's gas lights dimmed. Mozart's vigorous strains had given way to the lyrical lilt of Schubert, when the darkness behind Balchard split into a bright slit and a tall figure ghosted in. It sat to the rear of Balchard, partly shrouded by the box's partition and curtain.

'Good evening, Captain Smethers,' greeted Balchard, his eyes still to the front.

'Good evening, Balchard. You'll please forgive my late arrival,' returned Captain Smethers, a little disappointed that his surreptitious entrance upon the scene had not had its intended effect on Balchard.

Balchard turned to make a glancing inspection of the other, before returning his apparent attention on the concert. 'I see that the snow has fallen in Surrey. I trust that, but for the delay of a wheel repair, your journey was otherwise comfortable, Captain?'

'How the deuce ---!' Smethers was utterly astonished at Balchard's accurate deductions, but broke off to hide this. He continued, a little more slowly, a little more cautiously, trying to sound un-perplexed in a casual manner that would have fooled all but the sharpest mind. 'Yes, as a matter of fact, I've just come up from Guildford. Right nuisance about the wheel. A little spot of dinner. Nothing important. Purely a personal engagement.'

'For which you nevertheless deemed it necessary to carry a *loaded revolver*? A '*Bulldog*', or the new *Schofield-Smith & Wesson*, perhaps?'

'Schofield, point three two calibre, actually.' Smethers controlled the surprise in his voice this time, although he was again caught off guard. 'You'll just have to tell me this time, how you do it, Balchie.'

Pleased with the accolade of open acclaim, Balchard allowed a warmer expression to melt a little of his cold reserve. 'In the same way that the blind man's absence of one sense sharpens the other; so then, with the dimming of light, do we have an accentuated smell of gun oil. It would appear that you ascribe some considerable attention to your particular piece. Also, bulges by objects *semi* concealed beneath the vestments are apt to convey those certain characteristics wherein lie their very identification. A subject which I am considering researching, with a mind to writing a monograph.' 'You make it all sound very simple,' said Smethers, chuckling at the ease of explanation.

'Simplicity, alas, is the keystone to that bridge crossed by the many --- so readily paced, yet not so readily *placed*.' The sombre tone denoted Balchard's return to his former aloofness. He was annoyed at the belittlement of mystique in his methods. Captain Smethers attempted to discuss the contact, the very reason for their being here, but Balchard was insistent on hearing the soprano complete her beautiful ballads. Smethers could only find interest in the beautiful silken swell of her ample bosom. With the concert ended, the doors opened on cue, and 'culture' oozed out, a distending bubble of people bobbing and babbling, its volume increasing with the mounting pressure within. Balchard and Captain Smethers just managed to burst forth from it before the people spilled out onto the road behind them. Waiting for them, in the dark shrouded shadows of an alley down the street, was a four- wheeler. Inside, moulded into a dark corner, was a dark figure in astrakhan coat and brilliant red fez with its own blue cobra of a tassel dangling down the side.

'Inspector Fieseen Bijali, of the Cairo Police,' said Smethers to Balchard, not bothering with introduction formalities, as they climbed into the carriage. The light shafting in from the street lamps, as the carriage moved off, did little to brighten the man's swarthy features. Had he been matched with a racing camel, he would have undoubtedly won the race by a long nose. When he chose to smile from time to time, half the gold of the ancient Pharaohs shone forth from his mouth, in a tight grip round the ivory cigarette holder. Reading into the sharp crevices cutting the man's gnarled face, Balchard saw the devious chasms that pitted the face of the Law, like the labyrinth of back alleys running through that ancient North African capital. The Inspector leaned near to Balchard to speak in a low secretive tone. There were strong rumours of an anarchy plot that could well ruffle the plumage, if not endanger the lives, of Her Majesty's Parliamentary Members. Fieseen Bijali was anxious to track down and arrest the infidels responsible. It would have been perhaps nearer the truth, Balchard inferred, to say that the Inspector was anxious to uncover the route sometimes used by the villains for gold smuggling between the Middle East and England. Balchard made to scribble the details impromptu down on his cuff, but the Inspector put a hand sharply to his wrist to stop him. He would prefer that nothing be committed by the written word. He leaned closer to whisper, so that his teeth were scathingly close to Balchard's ear. Balchard reflected on how the Pharaohs had a fetish for crocodiles. The carriage stopped and Balchard alighted onto the pavement, outside his front door in Montague Street.

Balchard's work, assisting Professor Felsham in his research into the disintegration of the VIIth cervical supra-scapular nerve's myelin sheath in sclerotic paralysis, along with his work on the osmotic exchange at the nerve's terminal synapses, kept his head down over the laboratory bench for the next two weeks. This entailed not only the practical side of setting up and 'running' experimental processes, but also the further time-consuming mountain of paperwork to be attended to afterwards. All this in maddening detraction from his own important research. Laden with all this responsibility, there was the subdued feeling in Balchard that he was the one who would be liable if experiments proved unsuccessful. Felsham's theories, Felsham's tests. But if anything went wrong, it would be *Balchard's* fault. Just like a strip of litmus turning red. Felsham's Law. With Felsham constantly standing so close, either at his side, making a dual incision, or peering over his shoulder, his diamond sharp eyes searching for error, Balchard's concentration was disturbed. Felsham's constant improving of Balchard's already perfect incisions greatly riled Balchard.

His nerves were put on edge, an insidious undercurrent of paranoia creeping in. Into the second weekend, two levels of thought were running parallel through Balchard's mind. Upper thoughts were the systematic processing of scientific proceedings through their progressive stages -- monitoring, calibrating, assessing. At a deeper level, nervous signals were picked up, upsetting him. False readings which should not be there, flew up at him. Sniping criticisms cut in on him, with prying questions over his own research, which he did not wish to share with anyone, least of all Felsham. He was keeping that close to his chest. As he worked on in this twilight of thoughts, his peripheral vision seemingly darkened, giving a tunnelled view that made dangerous objects stand out before all else for his attention. *Bottles of strong acid gave invitation to be seized up and thrown in a face, burning out eyes. Steel scalpels, surgical saws, glinted their urge to be swiped at something other than an inert cadaver -- at Felsham's jugular vein! 'Go on, slit the bastard's throat!'* The voice, with its goading enticement, startled Balchard, jolting him. But when he looked round, the only person there was Felsham, quietly preoccupied in the precision task of pulling aside a section of myelin sheath from a motor neurone axon. Balchard fought to keep these delusional temptations at bay, struggling all the while to understand them. During this time, his syringe had remained locked up in its case back in his rooms. But the pain throbbed in his head.

Only when his intense concentration ended, with the completion of the preliminary setting for Felsham's experiments, did his nerves begin to prickle outwardly. A smashed retort only just escaped Felsham's notice by the swift requisitioning of a new one from the Supplies Department, by Dr Michaels, Balchard's nearest thing to a 'friend'. Suffice it to say that Dr Michaels limped upon a modified shoepiece that carefully concealed a clubbed foot, and was never known to put acrimony in anyone's direction, not even Balchard's. Furthermore, when George, the hospital's porter, handed a telegram to Balchard a day late, having absent- mindedly left it pinned up on the staff notice board, it did nothing to soothe Balchard's rapidly soaring temper.

Balchard almost burst a blood vessel in a frantic dash along the station platform to leap aboard the 4.15pm train for the part journey to Dorset. The South Western Steam Locomotive Company, if not the most comfortable of services, was one of the most reliable services as regards time-table efficiency. At least his lung-stretching effort for departure would be compensated by a reduced stretching of impatience to arrive. And yet a fear of being too late gnawed like a rodent in his brain. Putting his head back against the velvet head-rest, Balchard closed his eyes to concentrate on the bizarre dream that Mr Harlech had recounted to him at their earlier meeting. With the rhythmic reverberation of steel and steam beneath him simulating the trance-like voice in which Harlech had related his dream, Balchard was able to see the setting vividly. Improvising with imagination, where logical conjecture saw fit, he could see it all now, in his mind.

He could see the insect darting away as the portentous shadow fell across the boulder. Blinking up at the blazing sun, the faceless man sat down on the polished rock, grateful for a rest. He breathed out freely through the mouth, bending his head backwards. A rill of sweat followed the bald head curve to run down the face. The insect tried to land on his scorching bald head. He swiped at it, a second too late. It had already gone, sensing that three was a crowd. As far as the man was concerned, he still had the tranquillity of the glade to himself, as he basked back idly on the rock. He closed his eyes for a short while and then opened them. He was not alone.

The new figure, despite its wrapping of heavy woollen scarf and thick leather gloves, still shivered from the cold, <u>unlike the man on the rock</u>.

There was no alarm as the shotgun materialised in the gloved hands. The man on the rock was no longer interested in the figure menacing him, and followed the flight of a raven, just as the double-barrelled blast lifted him puppet-wise off the rock in a half somersault, his arms flailing out lifelessly. Stepping up to the faceless corpse, the killer carefully avoided the pool of blood flowing freely from the semi-decapitated body.

One brown limb, now speckled with a new pigment, curled

beneath the body in a position that only the dead could enjoy. The other arm reached backwards, fingers turned up in a mocking farewell bid. A pink gap in the head was nauseating, as the brain mass spilled out like jelly over the jagged bone onto the grass, which was now adorned by a bright red congealment of oxidising blood. Only the primitive ritual sign was missing from the grotesque sacrificial setting.

The killer gave a grunt of satisfaction and turned to go. He stiffened at the sound of breaking twigs coming from the undergrowth on the far side of the glade. The figure looked around furtively, then strode swiftly over to, and disappeared among the fir trees. Out of the trees on the far side came two open-shirted men. The plumper one panted and sweated after the other, who had now sat down on the rock, beside the corpse. Fatty joined his friend on the rock. They both had their feet in the blood, _but this did not seem to bother them_ as they basked contentedly beneath the scorching sun.

The man watching from the trees was very puzzled and _very cold, shivering all the while_, as he looked on.

A chirping of shrill voices turned attentions to the stream, where two small figures came along, jumping like frogs from stone to stone. Their yelps coincided with the ricochets and splashes made by stones thrown with great exuberance into the water. Abreast of the two men, the two young adventurers decided to come ashore. _The white frost crackled under their feet_. Yet, with only 'several square inches' of trousers, and their shirts tied like ropes round their waists, _the boys sweated in the heat_.

The taller boy stooped to pick up a stick and raced up the slope, followed by his tiny tot companion. There was a near collision as *the two of them, full of giggles, careered round the two men on the rock. Their head down sprint brought them up to the dead man where they halted abruptly.*

They exchanged glances and then the tall one, with squeaks of delight, prodded the body with his stick. He tried stirring the blood. Just like tomato soup, only more oozy with that grey stuff. It was smashin' fun! The smaller lad, with both hands on his head, blew out a continuous rasp as he side-stepped playfully in a circle round the top of the bloody corpse.

Having seen their fill of dead bodies, they let out great whoops of glee, and jumping and twisting in the air, they scarpered off up the path. Their tumultuous retreat was traced by a bas-relief of bloody foot marks. The boys vanished over the ridge and a tranquil silence returned to the clearing.

Some time elapsed before the two men reluctantly gave up their lazy rest in the sun, to proceed in the same direction as the two boys. The two heads gradually dropped below the ridge, and the heavily clad figure re-emerged slowly from the trees, very much mystified.

It looked around cautiously and then made off along the path to the right, pulling in its leather collar and exhaling twin jets of condensed breath through the nostrils, like a thick- skinned dragon. The sun had vanished from the tiny glade, along with the hallucination that had brought it. Only the cold body remained.

Balchard opened his eyes as the dream faded away and he became aware once more of the train thundering onwards towards its destination. Putting that dream aside, he turned to look into another one, beside him, in the window. Poor illumination made his face, and those of the compartment's other occupants, stand out in pale reflection against the dark background, like spectral characters in some opera macabre. A trick of light through a defect in the glass rendered Balchard a distorted visage, like a grotesque phantom ball mask. Or was that his imagination? Would it be purely his imagination if the 'stage curtains' opened behind them and *she* was to step out to take her bow? He waited longingly for a long second, but no prima-donna came out to light up the 'stage' -- only a flaring match. He turned away from the window, to look at the man in the far corner applying the flame to his pipe. The man, in turn, watched him over the pipe's glowing bowl. Naked embarrassment seized Balchard as he imagined everyone staring at him, having read his mind, with its foolish yearning, He shunned them. Taking out a cigar and cutting it, he put it to his mouth, his mind tensed in readiness for deep concentration on the Harlech enigma, with all its bizarre anomalies.

CHAPTER 8

Stepping down lightly from the roadway, Balchard began to climb the slope, his form bent forward to match the gradient. The view from inside the glade opening was really quite enchanting. A little dent in a hillside transformed to a picture card by lighting from above. With moonlight splashed up one side and a bold impasto soaking the other side, the ragged trees were projected right out of the Dickens-style Christmas card scene. The snowy carpet was perfect so that no printer's artist was necessary for that sparkling effect, where there were stars and a stream readily provided. His mind took momentary flight back to a night of similar celestial glow. *The moonlight was gracing her naked body with silver skin, plucking her lithe form, leaping like a wood nymph, from the darkened foliage of Grangehill Woods. Straight but for the small bumps of her breasts and buttocks, her diving form pierced the river with barely a sigh for a splash. He had followed on awkwardly, hindered more by his own nakedness, than by stiffness of parts, save but one. After that escapade, on returning home, his mama had been too worried over his catching pneumonia, to have any thoughts of his being guilty of doing anything untoward.*

Balchard crossed over to *the rock*. The 'yule-log' was there. He smiled down grimly at its 'Christmas spirit' shrouded there beneath the snow. He grimaced slightly as the stench came to him. With the snow covering it, there was the semblance of a tree open at one end. But the odour was too strong to be stifled by the frost. "Face to face with the faceless man," said Balchard solemnly, looking down at the body. He turned at the sound of squelching footsteps. A dim fatigued figure approached, brandishing a club. It also carried a policeman's regulation bull's-eye lamp.

The old village constable looked up, panting, and handed the club to Balchard. His exhaustion after the climb was almost too much as he tried to speak. 'Found this down by the bridge, sir. Beside the body. I thought you was comin' to inspect it, sir; you bein' from the City, an' all?'

'The *body*? Am I to understand that there is yet *another* one, Constable?' Balchard's initial surprise and annoyance gave way to an eye-glinting satisfaction at the thought of a problem increasing its folds of complexity.

'*Another* one, sir?' Just then the constable caught the smell and looked at the 'log' with widening eyes. He pointed at it slowly. 'You mean to say that *thing* ---?

'Precisely, Constable. Some wretched fellow most drastically removed of his brain. But perhaps we could now see the *other* body?'

Of all the stones and debris washed up under the bridge, the body was the largest piece. All wrapped up in saffron robes and bangles. 'About one 'undred and sixty pounds, I'd reckon,' said Tom Meadows, Harlech's gamekeeper, assessing the weight of 'game', and prodding it with his shotgun where the water sluiced over the sandalled feet. Mr Harlech remained morosely tight-lipped, looking to Balchard for a lead in this terrifying nightmare that was most surely taxing his sanity.

'A further fifteen pounds would perhaps be more precise,' said Balchard, kneeling down over the body, and pulling the policeman's lamp closer to aid his examination. Leaning in close, he inspected the head and neck for several long seconds during which the others waited in tantalising silence.

'Well?' said the constable at last, unable to keep his patience any longer.

'A severe blow delivered sharply to the base of the skull, undoubtedly.'

'I could 'ave told yer that ages ago,' said Meadows mockingly.

'An' we 'ave the club what's did it, an' all,' chortled the constable, in automatic collusion with his fellow rustic.

'*However*,' continued Balchard, with a stabbing look at the gamekeeper, 'eventual death was caused by the application of a firm pressure to the front of the throat, resulting in constriction of the tracheal passage. Asphyxiation -- *suffocation* -- from strangulation, is the end product. As far as the bruises on the throat indicate, it would appear to have been a firm object, broad and heavy, with metal attachments.' He looked round at the gamekeeper's shotgun, as an example of what he meant, but said nothing. A catching of the man's ferret- sharp eyes was sufficient message. 'A pathologist's post-mortem examination will no doubt reveal the abrasive damage to the respective cartilages, thus confirming my conclusion.' Balchard looked at the others. His summing up had a finality that made them shift uneasily on their feet.

Meadows turned and spat into the stream, beside the corpse. 'A foreigner, 'e was; a bleedin' 'eathen. We shan't be buryin' 'im in the same soil that's 'eld my folk for 'undreds o' years. Not the likes o' 'im that don't 'ave no religion, will we, Mr 'Arlech?' But Harlech was too caught up in bewilderment with the situation to do anything but stare at the corpse, clasping and unclasping his hands in pent-up emotion.

'Contrary to your statement, sir,' said Balchard pointedly to Meadows, 'I would venture to say that the deceased was *very* religious; a devout follower of the Hindu philosophy, in fact, to the extreme degree of embracing fanatical mortification. The 'club', apart from bearing no indication of its being used as such, is actually his flute. A most serious piece of the sacred ceremonial ritual.'

'You knew 'im, then, did you, sir?' said the constable, looking at Balchard with new fired suspicion.

'In a manner of mind, Constable, in a manner of mind,' replied Balchard abstractedly, visualising first, the dream, and then the mystical effect of Indian fakirs' flutes on snakes. Sonic vibrations that induced the venomous reptiles to many acts of a seemingly entranced nature. And what of the human mind? How many temples of incense could it be led through in swirling dance before breaking out in final torment? Balchard pondered deeply.

Seeing that he could get no more out of Balchard, who was steeped in thought, the constable turned to the gamekeeper.

'There's another one on the 'ill, Tom. Un'erneath the snow, so's likes it's not surprisin' that we didn't notice it before.'

'Oh my God!' Harlech blurted out, almost choking over the words in his anxiety. 'Who is it?'

'It looked like it be Dan, Mr 'Arlech. For all that I could see of 'im, that is, for seein' as 'ow 'alf 'is 'ead is gone, an' all,' said the constable. It *was*, in fact, Dan Chuddley, Mr Harlech's chief farm labourer. Thus, Harlech's son, Mathew, was still missing. Now with the heavy suspicion of a double felony of murder hanging over his head, as far as the local constabulary was concerned. The gentleman down from the City, Mr Balchard, was not fully concurrent with this frame of mind, it seemed, much to the annoyance of the *local constabulary*.

Flora Chuddley was normally of a strong, robust constitution. This was natural, as she had been born and had lived all her life on a farm. She had learned to work, eat and fight, like a man. This was not so now. The last few hours had changed her manner completely. Outwardly, she was still the same slovenly figure of a farm worker's spouse. Her back, however, had sagged into a humbler position as she emitted wailing sobs. So unlike her usual verbal profanities. The body shaking all the while. She sniffled and choked out her grief, pushing large rough knuckles into the red-rimmed eyes. At least her little lad was being looked after by the Pratts.

That was how the whole horrible thing had started. The little boy had wakened her early in the morning. Sunday, it was. Dan had not been with her, but that was nothing to fret about, after all these years. His erratic whims for village bitches were commonplace now. But there was this unusual pleasant feeling that she had felt. It was the screams of her otherwise tough young son that had alarmed her. Groping her way , swearing, into the musky bedroom, she had sat down on the putrid smelling bed. What was wrong with 'im? What was 'e yellin' for? Could 'e not speak? No answer. The boy had simply bubbled out his tears as an impatient mother sat beside him. Annoyed, she had struck him a fierce blow to the side of the head, with the result that the boy now moaned as well as wept. She had finally silenced him by seizing the narrow shoulders and shaking him wildly, the head rolling back and forth but not quite coming off.

Strengthened by the fear of more punishment, the boy had sputtered out his trouble in blurting stages. A horrible dream of his father lying faceless, while his friend, Davy Pratt, had poked the body with a stick and played with the blood. He had just looked on, and laughed at his dead father. The tale had earned him a rapid delivery of more vicious blows to the head, the hollow sound of its bumping on the wall competing with his yells. What rubbish! He would get a proper whoppin' when 'is dad got back. The fire of fear was lit later by the news from her neighbour, Mrs Pratt. Davy, along with the husband and brother-in-law, had had dreams similar to that of her own boy! Mrs Chuddley was not superstitious, but these circumstances had been too much, a great feeling of hysterically inspired fear engulfing her inside. Besides, her Dan was still absent and she could not even remember his being present the day before. That was the other chilling fact. Nobody could remember yesterday's happenings. Only that it had been extremely warm *on an extremely cold day*!

The final heart-wrenching message had come when the policeman had entered and told her enough to send her into hysterics. Flora Chuddley was now resigned to misery, while Mrs Pratt tended to her and the little boy. He was wisely removed to the relative peace of the Pratts' dwellings next door. It was late in the evening when little Davy Pratt ran into the house to say that a stranger was approaching.

Balchard walked down the muddy farm road, avoiding the puddles as best he could. He noted the small buildings clustered together with no sense of line or order, and badly needing the company of one another in the eerie wilderness. Thrown together like a fortuitous hand of dice. A door opened up a few inches and then opened fully, throwing out a shaft of yellow light, broken by a silhouette. A smaller silhouette appeared and squirmed round the legs of the larger one. The man muttered and pushed young Davy Pratt away from himself, back into the house. He faced Balchard again, his finger trying to assist his brain with a finger thrust up the nose. 'Are yer from the police?'

'In an ancillary capacity, yes. But I should like to express my condolences with Mrs Chuddley,' said Balchard.

'Oh aye? Wha's'at mean, then?' The finger wiped its pickings on the door jamb and burrowed up for more.

Balchard immediately identified the specimen of *homo sapiens* standing before him as the possible inspiration for *The Origin of Species*, as postulated by the controversial Mr Darwin. He persevered. 'It was I who found Mr Chuddley. Supposedly that makes me somewhat responsible for the present situation, in a manner of speaking. Is Mrs Chuddley available?' The man gave no reply, and Balchard sensed that he was wasting his time here. He should have gone next door. Apparently there was something going on there. But the man stepped down, with a hostile muttering, to bar Balchard's way to the next house.

'Bloody well get lost, Mister! We don't want yer 'ere. Clear off, do yer 'ear?' Balchard whisked up the shilling piece in front of the crude face. A not too remarkable transition occurred. The man's aggressive grimace softened. He snatched the money and tramped in through the doorway, gruffly announcing the visitor. Balchard had seen stables that were less squalid and had brighter oil lamps than this dingy abode. Better slating, too, judging by the green stains on the rafters. The cobwebs were dry, but the atmosphere they tried to catch was unpleasantly dank. Rotten fruit had its reek reinforced by the refuse piled up in the corner, beside the ingle.

Pulling a knife and loaf over and cutting himself a generous slice, the fat man called out a second time to someone. Balchard looked at the primitive plank shelf nailed to the dirty wall. On it, two faded daguerreotype camera obscura plates tried hard to preserve some human dignity above all the mess. Balchard inspected them. Why was he sweating? It did not show openly on his face, but he was conscious of the moisture, with a strange guilty association, around his eyes and around his neck and elsewhere about his body. The unpleasant feeling engulfing him carried a shameful mental throwback to similar childhood surroundings of such squalor. Dim grey memories swam to the surface, embarrassing him. There was a vague recollection of an 'Uncle Morton'. It had been a single visit by him and his mama to this drab rundown ramshackle dwelling that could have seen better days as a hog's swill- house. It had been his mama's and his secret. Pater had not accompanied them. There was never any mention of it between them, nor letter or word from 'Uncle Morton', thereafter. But something else was making him feel uneasy. Something from deep down, trying to scrape its way through to the conscious surface, but not quite making it. He let it go. The strength of relief that he experienced from letting this go puzzled him. That, in turn, made him feel uneasy. More precisely, *nausea*?

A faint reflection flickered over the plate surfaces, making him turn around. Balchard gave a slight bow of the head to acknowledge the gauche woman standing in the doorway of the adjoining room. He repeated his reason for being there, at the same time trying to meet the woman's cross-eyed leer, but finishing up watching her hands. Cleaning her hands on her apron, Mrs Pratt walked over to the table to heave the bread and knife out of the fat man's grasp. She buried the knife in the loaf's hard black top. The brother-in-law shrugged his shoulders and massacred the bread he had kept with his molars. Having put one pest in its place, the woman now turned to stare, with unequal eye concentration, at Balchard for a moment. She jerked her head sharply, to indicate the inner room. In the depth of the candle- lit room there was a mourning heap, crying quietly on the bed. The situation was a delicate one. Balchard paused over his choice of words, considering how best to explain his involvement without appearing to be hypocritical. His thoughts were suspended abruptly as as a man came barging in the front door in full fury.

'Little Davy says there's a man in ---' began the man, before stopping short. Pratt took the message from his brother's darting eyes and followed their indication. He saw the 'snooper' in the inner doorway. Pratt looked at the others again. 'What's 'e after, then? What did yer bleedin' well let 'im in for, eh?' said Pratt to the others. He knocked the chair aside and walked right up to Balchard, to stare him in the face. 'What yer be lookin' for, *Mister*? Come sniffin' aroun' for somethin' for nothin', 'ave yer? Well, I'll bleedin' well give yer somethin' t' sniff with yer big beak 'ooter!'

The woman's squeal from the bedroom came just as the fat brother grabbed Pratt. ' 'Ang off!' cried Pratt. 'What yer be blabbin' 'bout?' Pratt's anger subsided as his brother's whispered words got through. Money? Oh, well, that was different; why didn't 'e say so? Pratt wiped away what remained of his hostile spirit. 'We've 'ad that much bother from these other interferin' folk, likes. Strangers like yerself, they was.'

'Only they was proper foreign, they was,' added the brother for confirmation. 'With monkeys an' all t' 'ang 'bout the place.'

The issue was becoming too intriguing for Balchard to be vexed by the insolence. 'What exactly did they want, these "*interfering folk*"?' Balchard asked.

'Dunno, really. Couldn't understan' it, we couldn't. Lots o' silly talk 'bout minds outside the body an' all that sort o' 'og-wash. Said my body was a shell, they did.' Pratt laughed and nudged his brother. 'I asks yer, can yer see me 'avin' a shell for

113

a body like some bleedin' great crab, eh? Proper mad, they is. I reckon it's the foreign food they be eatin'. All rice an' dry weeds an' no pork, like we be 'avin'.'

'Aye,' agreed the brother, 'an' they played lots o' funny sounds on them flute things an' kept wavin' them tin pots with the coloured smoke on the end o' their chains.'

It did not strike Balchard as ill-mannered to shake his head in open disgust at the inane mentality confronting him. Comprehending the two men was a task, considering their accents and vernacular twists. Much patience was required to extract the more valuable points. Apparently a colourful, if not weird, group of dark skinned Asians had visited the farm on several occasions over the last week or ten days. Their music and chanting had filled the crude farmworkers' heads with strange words and sensations no less intoxicating than the heady fumes from the ceremonial incense burners swung on their dazzling chains. E*verything* was dazzling and sparkling when the 'darkies' came.

'And these strange speeches that they made? Perhaps you can tell me what they were about, or what you *think* they were about?' Balchard put the words across tentatively in the faint hope of striking a spark in what he sensed was an otherwise discouraging void of mental darkness.

'Nobody ever remembers anythin' 'bout 'em, 'cept that they 'appened an' we 'eard 'em,' said Pratt.

' 'Cept that they make you feel good an' relaxed, like,' offered the brother.

'Were these people here on *Saturday?*' persisted Balchard. The three Pratts exchanged nervous glances. She did not like the trend of the topic and so joined the other woman in the bedroom, leaving the men to paw out their greedy ends. To meddle with the unknown was to tempt Providence.

'Funny thing is, nobody remembers anything 'bout Sat'rday. Like we missed out a day. Nothin' 'cept it were awful warm. An' that's daft 'cause it be *snowin'* Sat'rday,' said the brother, dazed by the 'memory'. His enthusiasm overcame him. 'It must 'ave been a dream. We wouln't 'ave let Dan lie there like that. It's *got* to be a dream.'

Balchard's mind kindled with a mounting fascination as he listened on.

'It were like this, Mister. Me an' my brother an' little Davy an' Dan's little lad, we all dreamt that we saw Dan the way the police found 'im,' said Pratt, in a sudden anxious burst that suggested an inner frenzy of belated soul cleansing. 'Everything were same, 'cept there were now't snow. All that blood runnin' like a little stream past our feet, down t' other stream. It were 'orrible nightmare.'

There was no more to be said. Nothing that anyone wanted to say. But the silence in the room was heavy with a common pondering over the realms of metaphysical phenomena. *Incubus extraordinaire?* Yes, indeed, a nightmare, but for the part of it that had chosen to crystallise into a horrible truth, so as to be discovered and bring them all together like this. And how could a common thought share itself out over a multiple of minds? Mass hypnosis, perhaps? Balchard had certainly seen the adept illusionist perform his amusing 'magic' before the deceiving limelights of the music-hall. But only on individuals, and never to a strength of inducement that could nullify the natural alienation of death by outright slaughter. The concept of such a possibility with its far-reaching applications in the militarist's theatre of war was truly terrifying. Even in this modern age of great learning, the mystical powers of the Indian subcontinent could sometimes drown the Western scholar's vast wealth of knowledge in the ocean of a mahatma's far-seeing eye.

Scientific, solid and sensible --- that was how Scotland Yard expected forensic evidence to be presented to them. That was how they wanted Balchard to deliver it to them, all tied up and neat. Something they could use in court. Sympathy was therefore thin on the ground, with his current findings delving into dream-orientated killings. Dryson was having a field day, using this lull in official support as a lance to pierce Balchard's scientific armour. '*Dreams?*' Dryson slapped his desk top with glee, his voice loud, so as to be carried beyond the open door of his office. He had an audience of colleagues to reach and entertain in the larger outer office. He didn't see it as mocking and humiliating Balchard. Rather, it came as a definite policeman's duty to cleanse the Force of Balchard's kind, with their interfering 'ancillary work'. This weird little man who had attached himself to the Department, like some nasty fungal growth. All crime work was police work, to be seen to by real policemen. Bringing in outsiders to do their work was an audacity. To hell with the Commissioner's 'modern scientifically balanced outlook on policing in the metropolitan area'! Dryson found it easier to fault Balchard on this basis, than to admit to having this almost stomach-turning

116

dislike for the man that could only be classified as uncanny. Totally unfounded, as yet, but still there, deep-rooted inside him and making him uneasy in his biased judgement. 'I know some old 'beaks' have a tendency to doze off under their great wigs, and who can blame them, considering the boring dross these *learned councils* can all too often pour out? But a Crown prosecution case based on *empty intangible dreams*? That's carrying it a bit too far, wouldn't you say, Balchard?'

'Concluding a road to be *going too far*, without actually travelling along it, may well carry more hazard of error than to merely to follow that *straight* road's *bends.*'

'I'm sure that means something clever, Balchard, but we need something *practical* for this one. Something solid and substantial, to pin somebody down with a double murder charge. Until you come up with something like that, you're out there on your own. That's how I see it. And I'm not alone in that. I believe, from what one hears, that the Superintendent, himself, wasn't exactly over the moon either, with your *theoretical postulations*, as you would put it.' The Detective Sergeant was contriving to force Balchard out on a limb. But try as he did, he began to see that this was a futile tactic. Balchard was *always* out on a limb. The cold message of defiant indifference emanating from Balchard, as he stood there across the room, said just that. Even if Dryson's disparaging spiel was having an effect on the man internally, nothing as such registered on the frozen grey face. In readiness for an onslaught of scientific gibberish to come back at him in retaliation, Dryson put up his own barrier of indifference by sifting through the papers on his desk.

None of the cringing excuses that Dryson hoped to hear came to ear. Balchard made no pathetic spectacle of pleading his case; no stance was taken to expound his ridiculous scientific principles. If one was free of faults, there was no need to plead for mitigation on their behalf. He simply made to leave the office. This disarmed Dryson, not knowing quite where he was on this one. But he knew --- he could *sense* --- that something was eroding that wretched man's calm control inside that head. He could swear his pension on it. But he could also lose his pension if something horrible happened; if he was there when it happened, without preventing it. That cold thought was one to bother him for a long time.

Balchard turned in the doorway, a strange smile announcing a departing repartee. 'You would maintain that evidence comprising part dreams is worthless on account of their being an 'empty intangible nothingness?'

'*Y-e-s. So*?' Slow caution was in Dryson's voice, unsure as he was of what was coming next. His head tilted back, the chin tipped up at an unusually high angle, ready for attack. Despite the defensive posture, he was still nervous of that attack, not knowing how it would come.

'Should we seek out darkness, Detective Sergeant, or merely the absence of light? For that it truly is. One is *nothing* beside the other. Yet shroud all manner of felony, it most surely does, that very same *empty intangible nothingness*. Goodnight, Detective Sergeant.'

Balchard's cold encounter with Dryson earlier had not done anything to help his worsening mood. Having hidden his feelings from Dryson, his silent burden of restrained anger was doubled by that weight cast upon his shoulders by Professor Felsham. It was not enough that he was buried under an ever increasing mountain of work. Felsham's continual barrage of overriding remarks, while peering over his shoulder as he worked, grated his nerves. Many things were grating Balchard's nerves, of late. Each arduous task struck Balchard to be as taxing as that proverbial mountain of toil --- once it was ascended, a new mountain of problems was visible from its summit; and from that, another. It seemed never ending. At this escalating rate, Balchard saw a horrid forestalling of his own important research. Only through the consideration of Dr Muir had he scraped through that time. It would be unrealistically calling on angels to expect clemency from that quarter a second time. Disaster was looming up as a sure bet. He cringed at the thought. That would please this bastard. He glanced at Felsham. He really felt that Felsham would relish his falling on his face, disgracing himself. The Professor's blood-stained apron had gone. Its soiled image replaced by the resplendence of evening dress cloak and silk hat, and polished wood cane in place of steel scalpel. As if reading Balchard's thought, the domineering smile came out, with the usual reproach behind it. 'I gather that you'll not be in tomorrow morning. That you'll be over at the University. Is that correct, Balchard?'

'Yes.'

'Very well. But do see and not take all day. Try and get away when you can. You're needed here. We have a lot of work to get through, as well you know.' Balchard knew that, all right, but thought that the 'we' should be changed to 'me', where the onus was on his back. 'And for God's sake, Balchard, see and not make a pig's mess of it over there with Radcliffe, like everything else you do.'

The storm raging in Balchard's mind over Felsham's unjust remark was lessened later, through a distracting remark by Dr Stolling passing by. Balchard recognised the name of the charity patient taken in by Stolling as one of his own 'research cases' that he had seen only recently. In the Bluegate Fields district, if he remembered correctly. Putting Felsham's work aside, he went along to the ward to inspect the woman's situation. From what he could remember of the case, her deterioration was inevitable. He was only surprised that she was still alive, and had made it to here. His surprise was even greater when he saw the patient. Under delirium from morphine, the woman did not see Balchard as a face that was any different from that sea of faces normally seen through gin-crazed eyes. But Balchard's experienced eyes immediately appreciated the difference in the patient. Her condition had improved. Although still weak, the outlook was hopefully positive. There was good chance that she would fully recover. Balchard was normally unmoved by the rigours of disease and the deaths it imposed on the wretched that he was dealing with. Not only his professional discipline, but his frozen personality made him immune to such feelings. But in this instance, he could not escape a strong wave of annoyance invading his inside. A moment's examination of these feelings told him that it was not on account of his prognosis having been proven to be wrong. It was the fact that she was not going to die that was angering him. This wholly unprofessional attitude made him rummage in his mind for explanation. The scouring pain deep inside him increased as he searched.

Was it because this woman here was spared, while *she* had perished, that long lifetime ago? That this woman lay before him, reprieved in her extended lease of life, while *she* had gone away from him into death, caused a burning grievance. But not just an answer to this eluded his brain. His work was sliding away; his control was shifting, ready to desert him; even his mama was slipping away. The most recent of her monthly visits had not enjoyed her usual maternal fuss and concern. Rather, the atmosphere had carried a conspicuous numbness in conversation that had put distance between them. He had not been able to fathom a reason for that then. Nor was he able to think of one now. But why was he mindful of *that*, right at this moment? A bolt out of the sky totally irrelevant to his scientific work, here in the Institute? For the second time within twenty four hours, he felt a puzzling great relief in surrendering his effort to answer a strangely unsettling *emotional* question. That in itself, seemed irrational, in its eluding of insight. Like that butterfly escaping the naturalist's net. Only dogged persistence would see the trapping of those ephemeral wings; and a strength of will to do that had to prevail.

CHAPTER 9

'If the honourable gentleman would care to step down and examine the subject and verify the findings for us ---- *in his own good time?*' The words cut into Balchard's mind like a surgeon's scalpel. The fact that they had been uttered along with a polite cough and a heavy accentuation of the last words perhaps accounted for their success, second time around, in gaining Balchard's attention. Balchard came out of his inner concentration to look at Professor Radcliffe staring in his direction from the platform of the University's steep-tiered lecture theatre of Materia Medica. The Professor's extended hand. His polite expression of dwindling patience told Balchard that *he* was the 'honourable gentleman', being seated alone on the bottom tier, nearest to the platform. Rising from his seat, Balchard stepped down from the heavily scarred bench, to approach the platform. Creaking boards beneath his feat echoed the faint squeaks of amusement drifting round the theatre, to emphasise his humble passage across the floor. Like a lowly insect crawling across the floor of a forest of academic 'oaks'.

Balchard stooped over the subject to peer at it closely.

Administered with the sleep of death from vapours of chloroform, the subject now had a long steel needle inserted into its cranial cavity, behind the eyeball, via the optic foramen, for the purpose of introducing oxygen to the brain by subcutaneous injection. Running out from the trunk end of the needle, a bright red rubber tube snaked back to the reservoir of oxygen, where a small bellows syringe was worked by the brown-coated theatre attendant, to deliver the gas to the brain.

'And if we examine the relevant aforementioned vessels, pray, what do we find?' The Professor's guiding finger led Balchard to where the abdomen had been opened by an incision in the linea alba, the intestine drawn to one side, and the peritoneum membrane covering the iliac artery skilfully divided. The sheath had been opened up to reveal the common iliac veins lying behind the artery. Balchard leaned in closer to inspect these, along with those of the upper vascular system. Truly, as had been forecast, the iliac vein and the inferior vena cava were charged surprisingly with a brilliant red or arterial-like blood. This in reverse of their normal role of carrying dark deoxygenated blood. In direct reciprocation, the blood in the heart, on both sides and in the lungs, was dark, unlike the usual bright oxygenated form.

'Quite remarkable,' muttered Balchard, tapping his chin with his fingers as he straightened up slowly.

'Indeed, as the honourable gentleman says, gentlemen, "quite remarkable". A positive, if somewhat concise confirmation, but a confirmation nevertheless of our earlier predictions.' The Professor's address to the audience was cheerfully informal once more, pleased as he was with the result of his experiment, and so ready to overlook the moments of awkwardness that had threatened the lecture several moments before. 'Yet another *eye opening* indication of how the functioning system may have its physiological pathways re-routed, so to speak, by the appropriate application of external stimuli. But if we may now proceed to the next phase, gentlemen.' He beckoned the attendant to remove the body on its trolley, and then looked at Balchard. 'Thank you for your *invaluable* assistance, Balchard.'

But Balchard's mind was preoccupied once more with that which had held his attention earlier. He thought the findings were 'remarkable', indeed. But in pertinence to an issue that was much more sinister. Namely, that of 'applying external stimuli' to the mind so that it lowered its moral guard to perform actions that it would normally refrain from with great abhorrence. Normal hypnosis would not facilitate this effect.

Muffled laughs filtering out once more around the theatre brought Balchard's attention back to his immediate surroundings. A fleeting glance around him gave a flashing glimpse of blond, among the sea of black and silver beards, that was the clean cut Guy Du Mont. Radcliffe's surgical assistant sought to politely dismiss the unheeding Balchard with a repeated thanks. 'Thank you, Doctor Balchard.'

'*Mister*,' said Balchard, turning to nod curtly to the Professor, with more malice in his gesture, than there was courtesy.

'Ah, a fellow surgeon. Thank you, *Mister* Balchard.' Balchard returned to his seat, accompanied by more laughter caused mainly by Du Mont.

'Some 'systems' more readily than others, it would appear, *without* requiring the preliminary *"external stimuli"*,' remarked Du Mont in wicked jest, in private audience to those within earshot, as he referred to Balchard's trance-like 'absence'. Professor Radcliffe waited, along with those who had not shared the private joke up at the back of the theatre, for the laughter to subside, before proceeding. While they waited, they watched the attendant set up a 'magic lantern' and screen. In addition, an adult human brain was taken, dripping from its jar of formalin, dried, and placed on a marble cutting block on the table, beside the Professor. As the lecture continued, with a stress on the cerebral hemisphere's influence on personality and personal reflexive behaviour patterns, Balchard thought along his own parallel lines. Just as temporary damage to certain areas of the hemispheres could inflict temporary blindness, so also could simple 'sleep' be induced by depriving other areas of oxygen. In the very way that the stage magician's dangerous trick of inducing instant hypnosis was to deliver a heavy slap to the subject's carotid sinus, so momentarily cutting off that artery's supply of oxygen from the aorta to the head.

Balchard watched the glint of the Professor's scalpel in its precise transecting of the corpus callosum, that enormous strap of millions of nerve cells which lay beneath the cerebrum and was responsible for holding the two cerebral hemispheres together in eternal bondage. The cut completely severed the link between the two hemispheres, and this, according to Gustav Fechner's contemporary school of thought, in his newly conceived science of psychophysics, was tantamount to splitting the brain into two separate minds. The Jekyll and Hyde syndrome, perhaps? Balchard's mind bristled with excitement at the possibilities. It also made him feel insecure at the thought of another side, a darker side, to things. The very concept, with its underlying implication, was so striking that his normal logical control deserted him in a moment's scary questioning. Could their brief spell of unbridled joy in the meadows, under the sun and the stars, have been marred by clouds? Had he been unhappy with *her*? How could he ever have been anything but happy with *her*? *The yelps ringing out in his mind were those of her lunging and grasping at him through the branches, as she taunted him; goading words, making him angry, in her daring him to jump fully clothed with her, into the river. Angry? Was this how it had been, before she had plunged into that water that she loved -- all those layers of underskirt and drawers clinging to her lashing limbs, snagged in viciously snatching, grabbing branches -- fighting a merciless fury of undercurrent, all to no avail -- that water that so jealously loved her as to take her all to itself, in its eternal embrace?* His unsure mind clawed back through misted veils of distant memory for something satisfactory, but nothing of that ilk came through --- *or did not wish to come through.*

A droning background voice brought Balchard's mind back into the lecture theatre. He remembered how as far back as 1840, the mesmeric trance had been used as an ancillary aid to medicine. Elliotson in London and Esdale in Calcutta having performed painless surgery, including leg amputation on their patients. However, since the blind could also be hypnotised, it followed that the magician's theatrical sensation of visual fixation points such as spectacular flashing lights and spinning discs were, alas, totally unnecessary. The only thing necessary, in fact, was the voice. In other words, sound. Hence in *this* case, *flutes*, aided by the soporific effect of some fiendish narcotic disguised as incense.

As the Professor's pointer stick moved over the screen, tracing out Wernicke's speech region in the temporal lobe of the cerebrum, Balchard noted how the shadowed characters of the diagram stood out upon the stick against the flat background. This made another point stand out in Balchard's mind. In the 'dream' shared by Harlech and the others, everyone had experienced a feeling of great heat. Everyone, that is, *except* one solitary individual who had felt the need for heavy winter clothing. Likewise, everyone, including two mere children, had shown not the least attack of nausea or conscience at the open bloodshed and death of a near-one, whilst this same odd individual had found it necessary to seek confinement in the undergrowth. It had thus to be inferred that this person, the very perpetrator of death, was not acting under the influence of the drugs and hypnosis that had given the others their 'dream', but was an intruder within that 'dream'. This was the uninvited bogey that had turned innocuous fantasy into a live, killing reality.

The floorboards creaked out in agony again, this time in an upward direction, as the lone figure at the bottom bench suddenly stood up, to turn and bound up the narrow wooden stairway between the towering tiers, taking the deep steps two at a time. 'Good Lord!' exclaimed Professor Radcliffe, at the astonishing sight of Balchard fleeing up and out the exit at the top. 'He surely isn't going to be sick, is he? One really ought to be able to stomach unpleasantries at this stage in one's studies. If one is the least squeamish, then one ought not to enter the medical profession at all.'

'Quite,' said Guy Du Mont succinctly, amidst a general murmur of agreement from those around him.

But Balchard's hasty departure from Professor Radcliffe's prestigious symposium lecture and demonstration had nothing whatsoever to do with an unsettled stomach. Rather, his premature exit was for the purpose of hurrying to the telegram office in Euston Square, and thereafter to the Upper Thames Street warehouse office of the East India Shipping Company, in the duty of tracking down a murderer. Having executed these important measure, Balchard had then gone round the corner to enter an approved gridiron chop-house. He then found that he had insufficient pence to procure himself even a mouthful of victual. This was hardly surprising since he was having to reach deeper and deeper into his pockets to pay the cabbies and other *extras* involved in his cases. He thus resigned himself to entering the greasy dark timbered cavern of an oyster-shop next door. At least as a gentleman he would get his oysters on a wooden platter, unlike the rough around him who noisily sucked the steaming molluscs up off their thumbs. This was in preference to his walking all the way back to Montague Street just to face another gruelling portion of Mrs Wallamsby's culinary torture. It was too much to recall what frightful dish that day of the week would bring forth, and so he shut the matter firmly out of his mind. As he did so, it struck him as a most puny point to be bothered with, in comparison with those burning his mind earlier. Trivial, yes --- and *yet*? And yet such trivialities were irking him frequently of late. It further struck him that he was experiencing alternating, if irregular, periods of light and morbid temperament. Like a swinging pendulum, or a train passing in and out of tunnels. A medical point to be noted.

When Balchard finally did return to his rooms in Bloomsbury, his mental turmoil was such that he was unable to recall if he had eaten or not. The most interesting item among his mail was a note from Captain Smethers pertaining to Inspector Fiseen Bijali. Following the note's *request* from the Captain, Balchard later that evening found himself mingling with the crowd of destitutes lolling round the Church of England Temperance Society tea stall on the Victoria Embankment. United with his impoverished brethren in his disguise of tattered coat and forlorn expression, Balchard joined them further in their misery by thrusting his hands in among those held out around the urn's stove pipe and over the glowing brazier below. No matter which eyes he looked into, the only brightness there was the spotted reflection of globular lamp-lights curving round in the night like a pearl necklace hanging over the Embankment's heavy balustrade. Balchard noted the tin tray of scattered ginger cake crumbs and the tea cloths drying on the silver urn, along with the cake wrappings in the bucket beneath the stall, concluding that business was rife. With the workers' cheap tram and train fares having ceased some hours ago, those who thirsted, but could not afford a threepenny pint of ale or even a twopenny dram of gin, were apt to find the stall a good stopping-off point. On cue to this thought, another crowd of 'parched pilgrims' surged over to the stall from the road's river of passing vehicles. But much to Balchard's disappointment no-one from this new lot proved to be his contact. People came and people went. The bucket emptied and started to fill again, so that Balchard's patience began to wane.

Suddenly, the cup of tea which he clenched in a frozen fist was half spilled over his front as a filthy beggar lurched drunkenly into him. The words rasping out through the beard scraping Balchard's face like a wire horse-brush were as unclear as the alcoholic blast warranted them. 'Beware the blue knife, near the rope.' The cryptic utterance alerted Balchard instantly and he glanced around, primed for imminent danger. Seeing none and not fully comprehending the message, he looked again at the man. Whilst the man's breath may have felled a regiment of dancing bears, his eyes were as sober as a judge's, so that Balchard followed them as they signalled. Following their direction, Balchard looked at the orange double-decker knife-board omnibus that was moving away from the kerb under the heavy steamed snorts and stamping of the sweating horse team. His eyebrows twitched and enigma exploded into clear understanding as his eyes fell upon the large boardings proclaiming: OAKEY'S **KNIFE** POLISH and RECKITT'S **BLUE**, on the upper deck, at the rear of the omnibus. '*Between*, rather than "beware", I fancy,' muttered Balchard to himself, over what he had misheard. For sure enough, *between* the two large lettered boardings there was another smaller advertisement hailing: **PEAR'S SOAP**, above which sat a character with a profile that caught Balchard's attention.

Removed of his exotic Egyptian headgear, the man looked different from his earlier appearance, but the prominent 'camel's nose' was enough to set Balchard running after the vehicle. The 'vacuum' Balchard left behind him was filled by a mad bustle of those fighting for the abandoned half cup of tea.

CHAPTER 10

If Fiseen Bijali was acutely aware that his country was being wrenched to and fro like a dog's bone between the Anglo-French alliance and the Russian Czarist Empire, using Turkey as its puppet, he made no show of it. Rather, he behaved, as far as Balchard could probe beneath the leathery skin, just as any enforcement officer of the Law would behave in the course of pursuing his duty to track down and apprehend the criminal instigator. Whatever personal ulterior motives existed could be temporarily put aside, where the common cause carried them like a breeze winging two birds of different plumage to the same shore. But whilst considering this, Balchard bore in mind the plight of national affairs that possibly flickered like a quiet furnace behind the Inspector's placidly diplomatic expression.

With Egypt's recent 90 million pound bankruptcy in '76 leading to the deposition of its Khedive Ismail and the succession of his son, the Khedive Tewfik, there was great concern over political unrest. A growing hatred for Turkish overlords and European intruders was causing a new nationalist movement to rear its ugly head in Cairo, under the leadership of Colonel Arabi Pasha, much to Prime Minister Gladstone's consternation. With these new usurper vibrations threatening to topple Khedive Tewfik at any moment, needless to say that Gladstone's Question Time in the House had been one of few ready answers and very many headaches. With this new Egyptian problem once more in their lap, the headaches would be those of the Marquis of Salisbury, now Prime Minister, replacing Gladstone.

Such was the political instability, poised like a potential avalanche, ready for shifting with minimum effort to achieve maximum catastrophe, that there was much delight for revolutionary activists and anarchists alike. Any violent act of political dissent, however small, that could lead to the deportation of Egyptian nationals and so weaken Anglo-Egyptian relations, would be playing into Russia's hands. To avoid such a disaster, it was necessary to have more information on the situation. So it was that Balchard had to seek out and fraternise with the *agent provocateur*. To do this he would have to infiltrate the criminal underworld in low profile and once established, listen to the 'grape-vine'. The Inspector could partly provide the lead through some dubious exiles from his native soil.

Rough clothes were a simple measure against outsiders' throats being cut by the shadowy inhabitants of a dark backstreet world that was so different from the civilised world of the city's brighter thoroughfares. As a further precaution, Balchard had a small knife strapped to his wrist, inside his ragged sleeve. He would have preferred the comfort of his revolver in his pocket, but such an item, in the event of its usage, could prove to be too conspicuous, and so lessen his chance of approaching the right people without arousing undue suspicion.

Hailing a hansom whilst still in the awkward descent of the open rear staircase of the moving omnibus, they alighted briefly in Fleet Street, to mount their new transport and head eastwards for Smithfield. In a mere few minutes, the safe illuminated London was gone behind them, taken over by a dark unsure land of twisting alleys that swarmed with grey rivers of squalling poverty. The cab slowed down, seemingly blocked by noise alone, where vision was poor, trundling jerkily over the hard cobblestones, between black shapeless houses, where only the corners showed light at the open doors of crude gin palaces. The sinister forms that skulked in the night were kith and kin to those openly crowding the cat-meat barrows and bird cage stalls of Newport Street, Seven Dials, in the daytime. The very cousins of those innocents up from the country to reap their golden harvests in the gold-paved capital.

Fieseen Bijali's devious contact was no different from the rest of the featureless figures filing up to the refuge hall doors except that he had only one eye, where a Turkish bayonet had stopped short. The Turk responsible for this memento had fallen with a third 'eye' in his forehead. Mehemet Kahamir, ex-soldier come banker, come 'diplomatic courier', come murderer, stepped forward to wave the cab to a halt. Balchard dismissed the cab and they proceeded on foot, facing the same dangers confronting those brave missionaries first entering the realms of darkest Africa. Balchard tested the blade at his wrist for its readiness to slide from its sheath. Not understanding a word of the foreign dialogue ensuing at his side, Balchard made it clear by repeated hand signs that he patiently waited for his two companions to converse in English. The three eyes stared back at Balchard for a moment, as if caught out in a foul act of conspiracy. Then, by shear *coincidence*, there was very little verbal exchange in English after that.

Looking at the charity worker outside the hall in Whitechapel offering reading lessons, Fieseen Bijali remarked to Balchard: 'I am sometimes wondering if it is not altogether a grave error to be educating the criminal element. Do we not then put before the criminal the opportunity to assess and steal the dearer article --- to outwit us, in fact, with an improved mind nearly equal to that of our own?'

'If his mind is made equal to our own, do we not then have the opportunity in turn to understand and so predict and counter his action with a stratagem of our own? Is this not the very basis of the militarist's intelligence strategy -- to see, hear and *know* the enemy -- as, indeed, we are supposedly *now* endeavouring? No, Inspector, I foresee no bottomless pit of horror in bringing light upon the enemy. When we do finally fully understand the criminal mind, perhaps only then shall we be able to commence curing our cities of their rank afflictions of crime and 'darkness'.' Balchard looked away, irritated more by the Inspector's inept theory, than by the 'darkness' around him.

The Inspector studied Balchard and saw a man in love with his work. 'You are most surely a man who follows his craft with earnest sincerity, Mr Balchard. To do so to such a degree must undoubtedly require a close study of the subject. Just like the doctor researching with his diseased specimens and patients, in fact.' Fieseen Bijali paused to inhale on his ivory cigarette holder and blow the smoke out at the criminal vermin scuttling past them in the night. 'But in so doing, there is surely the danger of some of the contagion -- how do you say -- rubbing off on your shoulders?'

'In that instance one could perhaps be consoled by the knowledge that part of the burden has been removed from *some other unfortunate's* shoulders,' replied a faintly cynical Balchard, while watching the starving mother carry the stolen carpet on her shoulders, along with a dying babe at her dried up breast, the older child walking behind, choking with asthma. *His mama had not been well that day of the funeral. But she had spared herself visiting the town for medicine and food, despite her discomfort, for fear of encountering venomous tongues. Stale bread had therefore comprised their Lenten repast that solemn day. The dry taste in their mouths had been no fault of the bread. The church bell had lulled out its miserable departure message across the fields where daffodils should have swung their bright cheerful bell heads to and fro -- like the golden curls on her head had done --and she had loved her daffodils, tauntingly so, such that she would force him to adorn his head with them, as she did, when she would later ask after his 'golden curls', bringing curious glances from those around. But there were very few flowers that day -- only a desolate muddy expanse seemingly bereft of benevolent natural growth, and cruelly punished by pelting rain. A sad torrent of countless teardrops from the heavens. The dark heavily overcast sky seemingly crushing everything and everyone with their personal inner grief into the earth. What few daffodils there may have been were flattened into the ground. To be later resurrected in staunch cold iron.*

For the best part of the night Mehemet Kahamir led them on a fruitless tour of the densely packed haunts of poverty and crime. They searched hideous tenements stacked far and wide in such locations as Bluegate Fields in Shadwell, where 'lived' hundreds who had never had the chance of escaping to the comfort of 'education'; victims of drink and sufferers of every kind of horror and crime to which destitution had driven them. The only divider of the forlorn crowds was that while some cooked and ate, others looked on and starved. With the penniless poor sharing dwellings with the most rascally company in the City, Balchard wondered how to differentiate the two. How did one curb corruption when thieves shared the same bench with the paper flower maker girl -- when hussies of Whitechapel Road sat before the kitchen fires with the yet virtuous orphan girl?

As the night hours grew smaller, nowhere was there to be found any substantial snippets of information of the kind sought by Balchard and his companions. When Fieseen Bijal and Mehemet Kahamir decided to suspend their effort temporarily and take their leave of the area, Balchard pressed on. To get to know his terrain it was essential, he felt, that he enmeshed himself in the surrounding 'undergrowth' however prickly the thorns. To find the real raw diamonds of earth, one had to dirty one's hands in the muddy soil. Balchard's fascination with his surroundings was highlighted when, in the fuggy corner of a common lodging house in Shoreditch, he was confronted by an oriental seaman enshrouded in a 'sea of dreams'. A much wrinkled old whore smiled sleepily in the opium fumes as she stirred the black mixture over the flame of a tiny brass burner. The seaman sucked the poison up through his long wooden pipe, his eyes glowing like coals. Taking in the fumes, Balchard felt himself stilled and drawn into the scene, the pimples bristling up on the back of his neck. Realising that his morbid interest was straying from the more important issue at hand, Balchard snapped himself out of his gaze and after a thorough check of the smoke-filled den, removed himself to the clearer night air. But with fatigue touching his brain and a cold invisible drizzle spiking the night air, Balchard's immediate thought was for to secure himself some proper shelter and rest.

Rather than return to the privileged comfort of his region of the city, Balchard decided to remain and merge with his kind. He chose to join a file of vagrants entering the refuge where a lump of hard bread and a de-lousing bath were standard regulation. Even with the comparative security of the Bible reader voicing his stentorian peace over the somnolent forms huddled like mummies under their thin sheets, Balchard could not allow himself to close his eyes completely. Not when all those other eyes were staring, drilling holes in his brain. Hundreds of them, trying to pluck out the very thoughts in his mind. But he was wisened to their game, when they came at him without bodies. Balchard shook his sweating head, alerted now to the symptom. Under cover of the rough horse-hair blanket, he stealthily took out the small phial and the steel syringe. As the fluid entered the one limb, the other limbs relaxed, and so throughout his body. Making a final sweeping inspection of the slumbering forms around him, he settled back into a comfortable position for a short rest. He also checked the knife on his wrist once more.

Having hurried out of a rough night, to come here to the Institute, Balchard's haggard mind was having to climb up out of its stupor to meet what would be an equally rough day. With Felsham's work out of the way for the moment, there was the much needed opportunity for him to proceed with his own work. Optimistic as he was, the bogey of unease still perched on his shoulder, awaiting further interruption. Approaching the laboratory fume cupboard to retrieve his retort, he saw the shadow fall across its front, a second after his dreaded prediction. He turned around. It was one of the students. Forever under his feet and constituting an unholy nuisance in themselves. He could not recall the name with certainty; Collins, perhaps. 'What do *you* want, Collins?' Balchard's surly mood sought no refuge in sophisticated words for a mere underling of a student.

'It's *Coles*. Professor Felsham wants to see you; "*immediately*", he said.' The student did not have much respect for Balchard in return, and showed it with his blatantly wide grin openly mocking the other's sour expression. Moreover, he was savouring the fun of seeing Balchard's belittlement in being hauled up brusquely by his superior.

'You can tell him to go to hell. He can wait.'

But Felsham could not wait, as was his usual trait of high office. He came striding into the laboratory. 'Ah, Balchard, there you are. I'm not at all happy with your last report. I cannot honestly say that I am in agreement with the layout of your findings. I have to say that the logic of your overall conclusions is not at all explicit. Not in the least. I'm having to carry out the entire examination once more, myself. You will assist me.'

Balchard's annoyance was not successfully hidden by his turning his back, to put down his retort. The extra loud crash of the fume cupboard's front being closed down with force betrayed his anger. He turned around again. 'I would have thought that my report contained a sufficient degree of clarity to render it wholly satisfactory. The conclusions to be derived thereof are self evident as to be -- *explicit*.' He refrained from saying that they could be read by an idiot.

Fumes of indignation uncoiled, like shifting reptiles, in the Professor's mind, as he stared at the impudent worm that was Balchard, standing there insulting him with his defiance. Coles, rooted there between them, was agape with inner delight at witnessing the conflict. He relished the sight of Balchard being crushed. 'Am I to take it that you are questioning my authority, as well as my greater experience and expertise, Balchard? Because if you are, let me remind you that I am your superior and head of the research department in which you are privileged to work --- perhaps further to that, a serious reminder would be that the question of your remaining on staff, here in this hospital, is essentially provisional, depending on your work performance. A further reminder, to be taken wisely as a caution, is that incidents of gross insubordination will not greatly enhance your chances of submitting a work performance that is acceptable to the Board. I, myself, am Deputy Chairman of that Board. Am I making myself clear, Balchard?'

'Quite clear, sir. Only, I was simply saying that ---'

'Then I shall expect you in readiness upstairs in fifteen minutes.'

'Yes, sir.' Balchard watched the whirlwind of power, Felsham with Coles on his tail, blast its way out through the doorway. Thereafter he released his own power by dashing the retort down into the deep bench sink so that it shattered. Turning on the tap, he cursed at the contents of the broken vessel seeping out through the crack, to follow the water down the drain. Down the drain! All wasted, down the drain! Damn Felsham! Damn Smethers and his damned bloody 'unexpected contingencies'! It soothed Balchard's bile only a little to know that his resources were not on immediate call by either the Yard or the War Office. Not yet, anyway. He almost smashed another retort when George, the janitor, came in to say that a man was waiting out at the entrance with a message. A one-eyed man.

CHAPTER 11

Whilst some cat-napped in the precarious peace of Shoreditch hovels, others across the City treaded lightly lest they should wake the fathers of their heritage staring down from paintings on the wall. Captain Smethers entered the large room without knocking, closing behind him the heavy oaken door which bore the brass plate deeply engraved with: **WAR OFFICE: MILITARY INTELLIGENCE**, with a lesser cardboard square pinned below the plate stating in red ink: **EURO/ASIA.** The heavy riding boots being padded underfoot by the thick carpet, the only sound in the room was the earnest scratching of a pen on paper. Sir Basil Effram darted his hand assiduously over the parchment in a typical emergency redrafting of a treaty that was required to please both his political and military superiors. Only just returned from the House, where a raging debate was still in session, Sir Basil was now, as always, under close scrutiny from his masters, endeavouring to preserve the country's security by the surest measures that his office and the means at its disposal could devise, official or *otherwise*. Unofficial, as a word, did not exist in the corridors where he walked, and so was unutterable as it was inconceivable; otherwise Her Majesty would have derived some considerable displeasure.

Captain Smethers approached Sir Basil's desk, opening his folder to take out a sheaf of papers and place it down on the desk top that was already flooded with paperwork. Sir Basil paused in his diligence to look up, leaning back to make way for the fresh onslaught of work. He put a forefinger and thumb to his eyes to relieve their ache. Stooping over the desk to point out where the specific clauses were to be initialled, Smethers then helped himself to the iron handled rubber stamp, banging each document in turn, as it passed from Sir Basil's hand. He sifted out one sheet from the others, lifting it up for closer inspection. 'I'm really not too happy about this one, sir. I'd much rather that we had more time to collect more information on it. Can't Sir John delay his trip to Germany for a few days until we have a clearer mind on it?'

Sir Basil reached out to take the document, peering at it through his pince-nez reading lenses. 'Ah, yes, our old thorn-in-the-foot annexure to the Berlin Treaty that makes the Treaty's stipulations stretch like elastic. Yes, I agree, the possible ceding of the small Thessaly territory to Greece would appear to be a knife-edge balance, on the wrong side of which the Prime Minister would not be too anxious to topple. With the miracles of landslide by-elections and our establishing protectorates over Southern Nigeria and Bechuanaland, as well as the Burmese War just fresh in our wake, I don't foresee the Prime Minister being too overjoyed with more *surprises* --- especially with these confounded Boers doing their best to stir up a wretched colonial war, as it seems. No, leave it with me and I'll see to it personally in the morning. Speaking of the morning ---' Sir Basil reached across the desk for his open hunter watch, the steel of which had ripped heads apart indiscriminately as a Russian cannon-ball at the Balaclava battle of the Crimean war. The deep scar on the back of his hand gave vivid testimony to where the very same metal had spared his body but scraped his soul with the pain that he had stood while the dearest of comrades had fallen. 'Good gracious! Is that the time already!'

Putting his watch down, Sir Basil removed his reading lenses and sat back in his chair, pausing for afterthought. 'Suffice it to say that we can be thankful that the Treaty does facilitate our sending a fleet through the Straits into the Black Sea whenever we wish. Added to that, we are able to post our military consuls in Armenia, where they can supervise the fortifying of the northern frontiers of Turkey-in-Asia.'

'Quite, sir.' Captain Smethers picked up the other papers and returned them to his folder.

Sir Basil turned to look, with not a little dismay, at the wooden block on his desk that held a refulgent array of six brass-headed speaking tubes, clipped by their necks to the block, like captive serpents. Hesitating for a moment, he reached out and then stopped just short of the tubes, dithering over the choice. 'I'm damned if I can come to terms with these new -fangled contrivances! Which one is which, for instance?'

Captain Smethers leaned over to unclip one of the brass heads and gave it to Sir Basil. 'I believe it's this one, sir, for the night-watchman's lodge.'

'Thank you.' Sir Basil flipped back the combined whistle/cover cap on its hinge and blew into the shining mouthpiece. 'How on earth did you know that I wanted the night-watchman? You reminded me of that fellow Balchard, for a moment.' Sir Basil heard the tube squeak back with its insect's voice, and for a moment was unsure if he should hold the tube to his ear, mouth or eye.

Captain Smethers suppressed a broad grin, not wishing to tell Sir Basil where else he could try putting the rude-looking open tube-end. 'No one else in the building, sir.'

'Of course; how forgetful of me.' Sir Basil spoke into the tube, with an awkward deference for it, ordering a fresh pot of tea. The brass cap closed easily enough on the tube end, but it was not so easy replacing it in its original holder. Captain Smethers leaned forward once again to snap the bright metal neck back into its clip.

'Incidentally, how *is* our Mr Balchard progressing?' said Sir Basil, looking at the 'snake', glad that it had resettled with the others, but not quite sure if it would jump up again and bite.

'Coming along quite splendidly, I'd say, for this phase of the operation, from what I've read of the report, that is.'

'And the operation itself? What state of advancement have we reached there?'

'I'd say we've gained a fair footage of ground, considering the short time that we've had the plan in action in the field. It's too early to expect Balchard to make any positive contact with the other side just yet without it looking too obvious. At least we have him in where he can keep an ear to the ground.' Smethers paused for thought, pursing his lips. 'Y-e-s, I'd say that the fellow should manage to fit in squarely with our plans.'

Sir Basil's bushy eyebrows crouched closer together and he inclined his head back, stroking his long beard, his expression darkening as he examined the Captain. 'You sound uncertain -- almost as if you were fighting to convince yourself of your soundness in judgement. Are there grounds for uncertainty? If so, it's better that we know of them now and so plan our way round them, rather than flounder over them in the field.'

Captain Smethers twisted the corner of his buff folder for a moment and then looked up into the room's high corner, as if it would help to pin-point a difficult subject. 'It's just that he's a most peculiar fellow.'

' *"Peculiar"* ? In what way?' Sir Basil's inside tensed, throwing up a jagged spike barrier, in the manner of the old *cheval-de-frise* defence against oncoming Russian cavalry, in readiness for a unfavourable report.

'Difficult to say, really. Like a good nag that you instinctively know is good, but have never seen run fully in form so that you don't know exactly what to measure it by. By all accounts he's certainly a lone operator ---brilliant, in fact, as regards observational and deductive reflexes. Indeed, I'm not quite sure how he does it, but he appears to be continually ahead of your own thoughts to the point of astonishment. But apart from that, I would almost say that he's a very solitary and embittered individual. I say *almost*, because although in normal circumstances the lonely recluse would most surely be classified as such, h*e*, by virtue of some magical zeal for his work, does seem to hold back from falling into that pit of a character mould. I suppose one could say that he's the direct reversal of that old adage that no man is an island. Indeed, he's like a ruddy ivory tower on its own ---a great ruddy citadel on wheels.'

'Whence he sallies forth in moonlight pale, to seek his inmost Holy Grail,' added Sir Basil poetically, in a moment of personal recollection. And what of it, if a gentleman in chivalrous vein quests after his own destiny? A lingering look at the cannon-ball time-piece brought the reminder that the year of that campaign was also near to the beginning of young Balchard's 'campaign'. Just some nine years before he was born. He shook himself out of his reverie. 'I seem to recall that our early ancestors found the wheeled tower to be most useful as a war machine for scaling and surmounting the enemy ramparts.'

'Yes, well, whatever it is, the old boy has certainly got his guard up about something. He can be a trifle too snappish with his answers, for my liking. But otherwise, all right, I suppose. Come to think of it, he doesn't seem to hold too high an opinion for women. Maybe that's it --- some stubborn filly, withholding her consent for 'favours', or whatever.'

Sir Basil relaxed and lowered his inner defence. 'Oh, well, in that case we have nothing to fear. From the solitary operator point of view, he makes ideal field agent material. Remember, it doesn't pay to become too personally involved with your rank and file. You're *not* becoming involved, *are* you?' That solemn note of misgiving had crept back into Sir Basil's last words.

'I shouldn't think so, sir.' But Smethers *was* thinking, quite seriously, over the possibility of trouble looming ahead. In his overall assessment of Balchard, there were naturally patches of personal obscurity that were left to one side. So long as they had the main part of him to do their job, these blank spaces could be left out. It was none of their business, so long as they did not interfere with the serious work of the Department. But these blank patches kept floating back to Smethers' mind for re-examination. Whether or not Balchard realised it, his muttering small talk was occasionally letting out odd messages noticeable only because of Smethers' acute observation. If it was not suicidal or self-destructive strains that Smethers saw in the man, what was it? Whereas other men reached out eagerly for success, this odd character Balchard, whoever he was, *whatever* he was, seemed to be juggling with his professional career, ready to throw it away almost, as if he hated it. Smethers saw something ticking away in that strange mind. Something they had missed out in his personal background file. Something that appeared to seek out danger with the same mad compulsion that sent other brains screaming after alcohol or opium. Was it a trait for self-punishment for some old skeleton in the cupboard, that was crucifying the inner Balchard? Maybe that skeleton was taking on flesh to haunt him? Old boy Balchie did seem to be determined to bang his head on the wall about something. Smethers did not care what it was, so long as it did not upset his plans for the Department. Balchard could do whatever he wanted to do. Go jump from the Tower, if it made him happy. So long as it was after he had carried out his assignments for the War Office. Concerned as he was over this issue, Smethers made no mention of it to Sir Basil.

'Good. Then all is well.' A twinkle came into Sir Basil's eyes as his inner trepidation left him, like Elsinore's foreboding battlement spectre departing, haunting Hamlet no more. 'I venture to suggest, Captain, that you are perhaps a trifle annoyed because your latest recruit doesn't jump to your command as you would have your subaltern do.'

'Annoyed? *Me*, sir? Hardly. Debatable, I'd say.'

'Ah, *debate*; trust not debate, when it chance holds back a dark dagger of fate.'

'Shakespeare?'

'No, Captain -- *me*.'

'Jolly clever, sir. So you also think that there is another side to Balchard -- a side that doesn't quite see daylight?'

A chiding arched eyebrow came with Sir Basil's response. 'You're not the only one holding back on information, Captain.'

'Sorry, sir; just thought you had enough on your plate, as it is. I'm glad that's settled.'

'Splendid. So we have naught to fret for the present.' Sir Basil hunched forward, taking up his pen once more, ready to launch another attack on the redraft. He looked up suddenly. 'That *is* all, isn't it, Captain? We have nothing further to concern ourselves with unduly in that aspect, have we?'

'Not that I can think of, sir.'

'Good.' The word was final and Sir Basil set about his paperwork again. After several strokes of his pen, he paused, to spare a second to look at the infernal ensemble of shining brass 'serpents'. A moment's thought allowed him to change his choice, for a more reliable messenger. 'Oh, and, Captain.'

'Sir?' Smethers turned and waited, his hand on the door-knob.

'Before you get on with writing up your report, perhaps you could be so good as to tell that man downstairs to hurry up with that tea.'

'I'll see to it at once, sir.'

Balchard strode swiftly into his front room, making a bee-line for the leather arm-chair. The door-slamming, which he normally would have avoided doing, did not bother him. At this moment he had eyes and ears only for the precious chair. A near intruder in his own room's dormant privacy, by virtue of his whirlwind entrance, he collapsed down into the leather chair. His eyes, normally set deep in their hollows, were even more deepened and haggard, their scleral whites reddened, by three nights without proper sleep. And for all this, he was still none the wiser as regards contacts.

Removing his unfinished laboratory report and thesis on linear absorption analysis of chromosome fluids from the chair arm and putting it down on the floor, he put a leg up over the side of the chair. That way he could lie back and read his mail which he had snatched up off the hall table on the way in. The letters fluttered open, the pages stalling in his fingers according to their degree of importance, before flying up into the air in varying arcs of disinterest, like a conjuror's doves. None of the letters commanded the urgency to demand his attention at that immediate moment. He could safely see to resolving their individual problems later in the day. He looked round through bleary swimming eyes at the abandoned thesis. Part of his dissertation for his doctorate, it was already four days late and should have been on Professor Radcliffe's desk on Friday last. Without making drastic cuts in his experiments, Balchard could not see himself finishing the report before the coming week-end. This was especially so with those other serious issues clamouring for his precious time and energy.

Suddenly remembering the problem he was having in extrapolating the graph's inconsistent figures, he made to pick up the report. But it was out of reach, so he relented in his effort. Lying back again he relied on his memory, which was beginning to dim, as fatigue gradually took over. Perhaps he could consult Dr Michaels at the hospital later in the afternoon. No, on second thoughts, Dr Michaels would not be in until Thursday, having gone off to Manchester, in the course of his research into industrial diseases. Further to this setback, Balchard foresaw his having to make another trip south from the City in the next few days, in connection with the Harlech case, so delaying his seeing Dr Michaels. So that was it, then. The report would have to wait until next week before it was finished. Damn!

It occurred to Balchard that he spent a considerable amount of his time waiting. He wondered drowsily how much of his life was spent in fruitless waiting. At the same time his brain screamed for sleep, his chin sagging down in a slow curve towards his chest. Was he waiting for the wrong things, or was he confusing his vocations? If only one could filter off all of life's waiting periods and so be left with only the long awaited essentials. Just like removing the space between the lattice structure of the natural crystal, or that between the molecule's atomic structure. Was it the clever Italian physicist, Avogadro, who not so long ago said that all the atoms of the Universe, removed of their inner space, could be contained in the mere volume of a thimble? Balchard's fuddled mind attempted the concept, but the proper proportions eluded him. Wait, wait, wait. Ironically, the tingling sensation in his arm that was brought on by his waiting would also have to wait. He was too tired to fetch the syringe from its clandestine repose in the bedroom. Likewise, Mrs Wallamsby would have to postpone her complaints of his door-slamming in the early hours of the morning. His ears were closed to her irate jabberings and knockings, as the blanket of fatigue descended heavily over him. A different image came into the rapidly slipping mind, tormenting him. H*er* beautiful young face came up at him and then twisted, to fall away, further and further away, never to return, as he waited, as he had *long* waited, before sleep finally clapped his brain tight to its dark abysmal bosom.

A most wretched specimen of a human it was that Balchard brought into the Institute from Spitalfields. But not without the bitterest of effort. With the Board of Governors thoroughly opposed to the artificial termination of embryonic life, Balchard's initial hope of bringing in his patient for an abortion was nil. Not only the clergy on the Board held this disapproval. Everyone else who mattered was absolute in the resolve not to allow the Institute's facilities be used for such immoral purposes. Balchard had thus performed the operation elsewhere, in the seediest of surroundings.

Such surroundings were congenial to the mother. Any discomfort that she voiced was on account of the 'business' that she was missing out on. 'Make it a quick 'un, Doc,' her pungent breath had rasped in his face. Her health being poorly, Balchard had noted her life fading fearfully. He had all but carried her to the Institute. There he could monitor her with medical accuracy, as her health spiralled down. As regards legal proof, there was no blemish on his gaining admission for the woman; she was an unfortunate whom he had 'encountered' in the course of his field research, and was in urgent need of medical care. Though words were spared, minds were brittle, heavy with the loaded implications behind Balchard's actions. His very act of bringing in a *fille de joie.* It was another knot in the tightrope he was already walking with his research time factor crisis. No less, he supposed, than the danger involved in his handling of these bodies where raging infection was rampant --- one cut on his hands, and he was in mortal danger, if not a certainty for death, himself. But strong in spirit, the woman surely was, in spite of her borderline health. She had brutishly insisted on her paying him, instead of accepting his usual payment for her services to medical research. After he had performed the foetal extraction, he had taken her money promptly. Rather than collect it another night, as she had suggested, for payment of another sort, for fear that she should expire in the interim. He hoped that she would live on a little while yet; just long enough for him to take some more decent experimental readings. Why, oh why couldn't these women live like decent women, instead of dying like the sluts they were? It would make things a lot easier for his research, instead of all the trouble it was giving him.

With his mind still laden with this curse of a 'female problem', Balchard was no less embroiled to hear the prattle of unfamiliar female voices, when entering the hallway at Montague Street. Filtering out Mrs Wallamsby's high pitched sound, he puzzled on the other two. His greater surprise, on seeing the face in the guest room, was in realising that he had not recognised his mama's voice. Of the third woman, he had no immediate recollection. But he did recognise the situation, after a moment's intake of the scene, much to his dismay. The youngest of the three, in fact, roughly *his* age, coupled with her plainness and her nervous awaiting of his mama's introductions, the message was clear. His forced smile hid a budding anger at his mama's fresh attempt at match-making. A careless sigh betrayed his feelings. His orderly mind mathematically saw four persons in a room. Three women and himself. Each to a corner. Him in his corner -- trapped -- mentally suffocated. An odd, indeed, silly thought, he told himself, wondering how it had managed to find its way into his otherwise scientifically disciplined mind. Perhaps the bloody nature of the work he had just left behind him in the Institute was the reason for his feeling nakedly guilty in front of these ladies. That and the records of it which he now carried in his medical bag, making him hold it self-consciously slightly to the rear of his leg. The very bag his mama had bought him on his graduation. Was that why she was looking at it? Was he imagining their stares boring into his back, up in his room, when he self-consciously put his bag underneath his desk chair. It was joined by a pile of folders containing that sort of 'medical material', to make room for his guests on the vacated chairs. .

Teaspoons tinkled and cups clicked politely on saucers, courtesy of Mrs Wallamsby providing tea in Balchard's room. But conversation broke the silence little more than this. His mama said very little, but her attitude toward him was different. Had it not changed a long time ago? Or had he chosen to ignore it, refusing to see it as such? Wishing there was a lifeline there, giving refuge from his madness? Something in her quiet caring manner had turned hard. Like sculptor's clay settled, no more able to change face. The transition phase of her fondness for him was difficult to see, looking back, in precise instances. But it had transpired nevertheless. As they spoke, she would glance briefly at him, as if catching a stranger's eye, and then look away abstractly around the room. Almost as if some secret between them was awakening afresh, but could not be born openly.

'Did she suffer great pain in her death? How could anyone possibly leave someone to die like that -- to die alone? It's un-Christian. How could you?' The words came at Balchard like a sharp bayonet, slicing into his vault of sacrosanct thoughts. The woman's question, if it was not an accusation, cut a disturbing cleft in Balchard's memory of a horrendous scene that was his private excruciating hell. But how could this woman possibly know anything of *that* day? She was not of that locale, if he remembered correctly. He could barely remember her name from his mama's brief introductions several minutes ago. Not that he had held any intention of retaining her name in memory beyond those few moments of confused annoyance. The very idea of anyone ferreting out details of *that* day touched him like a personal desecration. His anger soared. 'Does your Institute not have a chaplain to keep company with the dying, so that they can meet their Maker in strength, Mr Balchard?' That the woman had been referring to other deaths, and not *that* one, stalled Blachard's anger, but did not quell it entirely. A second before this realisation reached his brain, his anger cracked the delicate china cup in his hand. Only one pair of eyes looked down, startled, at the china fragments and tea soiling the carpet.

Balchard held his mama in a long cold stare. His mama returned the look, but with sadness, not anger, in her eyes. Balchard's expression was one of rebuke for his mama's bringing this woman to intrude upon him, with an ulterior motive for matrimony -- that and her unpleasant questions. But at the back of his mind, he knew that this was a front for his putting the same question to himself. Just what *had* he been doing, that it had resulted in *her* dying like that? When Balchard's mama and her companion took their leave later, it was like an emotional re-enactment of that time long ago when he suffered the silent chastisement of his mama's pained face. It would have been unmanly, and totally out of the question for him to have mentioned that he had a headache. It throbbed on and on. Like something in his brain *trying to get out.*

CHAPTER 12

When Balchard eventually raised his portcullis to the world outside his door, just after breakfast, it was to permit Detective Sergeant Dryson to enter. The policeman was wryly amused as he came in. A hard smile cracked out on his face giving the semblance of soft yolk oozing from a cracked egg, as it did when he visited Balchard's part laboratory, part museum rooms. This was how Balchard saw the policeman, except that, perhaps, the egg was not as hard-boiled as Dryson. For all that the 'observant' servant of the Law took in with his sweeping gaze, he attached no significance to Balchard hurriedly rolling down his dressing-gown sleeve over his elbow. The syringe had gone in only moments before, behind the bedroom door, just prior to Dryson's authoritative rap on the front door. Nevertheless, Balchard's twinge of guilt caused him to rummage through his files in false preoccupation for several moments. Then standing back against the fireplace and thrusting his fists down hard into his dressing-gown pockets, he steeled himself against his own conscience and the imagined scrutiny of the Detective Sergeant.

Dryson's grin widened in curiosity as he gingerly picked

up the shrunken head of a Polynesian pygmy by its hair, from beneath a bell-jar on the chemistry bench. 'A most intriguing study of miniaturisation by chemical reagent, wouldn't you say so, Detective Sergeant? Eyes, bones, even the *brain*, all *reduced* in perfect proportion. You'll notice, of course, the interesting variation in nostril widths compared with the African cousin of the Ogooue River region.'

'Sure, Balchard, sure.' Whether or not Dryson had understood Balchard's jibe was not made clear as he replaced the skull and continued to scan over the chemicals and objects on the bench, tweaking his nose with forefinger and thumb in wry humour. He turned round at last, to take a long depreciatory up and down look at Balchard standing there in his loose -fitting domestic apparel. 'Well, I must say it's good to see that *some* of us have been enjoying the soft comforts of home, while others have been up and about at a more proper hour, pounding the pavements for the best part of the morning, no less.'

'Really?' Balchard did not give way to the taunt, but avoided staring Dryson straight in the eyes. 'But I'm sure that the good Detective Sergeant hasn't come all the way here, braving the ghastly road repairs of High Holborn, in the precious time of Scotland Yard's Criminal *Investigation* Department, simply to discuss the variation in matinee habits of the metropolitan denizen.'

Dryson smiled at the genteel banter, and then frowned as he pondered over Balchard's deduction of the route. He looked about himself for clues, as he had seen Balchard do in previous instances. His eyes finally fell upon the dark messy substance encrusting the edges of his brown boots. Balchard saw enlightenment spread across the face like in a child that comes to understand the complexities of its new toy for the first time. 'Oh, I get it now --- Holborn. Very smart, Balchard, I'm sure.' The frown returned to his face. 'Here, but wait a tic --- how do you know it was Holborn and not Theobold's Road, further up? They're doing repairs along there as well, you know.'

Balchard closed his eyes and raised his eyebrows in a moment of quiet exasperation. 'If you really wish me to elucidate on such simplicities, Detective Sergeant, perhaps I should summon Mrs Wallamsby and have her prepare us a small luncheon that we can partake of, while going through the procedure, step by step.'

'All right, Balchard, that'll do now. I *had* come to tell you that you were right in finding the arsenic in that body, just proving that we were right all along, just like you said.'

'Of course, Detective Sergeant. Do forgive my manners.' Balchard winced inwardly at Dryson's wording, so that it was *we* who 'were right all along'. It was either that, or a complete omission of the fact that anyone outside the Force's manpower had helped solve its cases. The article marked in red pencil, on page three of the *Times* lying on the breakfast tray, bore testimony of this. It heralded the brilliant work of Scotland Yard in tracking down and apprehending the lady murderess of the Clerkenwell art gallery proprietor; without a solitary mention of any other name that could threaten to encroach on the Yard's exclusive efficiency. It was just possible that the printer had run out of ink. But otherwise, Balchard derived his satisfaction from meeting and defeating the challenges that a case placed before him. Just like the singularly intimate bond between the mountaineer and his personal 'Matterhorn'.

'Mind you, Balchard,' continued Dryson, in afterthought, 'you were lucky to find the poison before it passed out from the body, like in that difficult case we had last month. Our own doctor at the Yard couldn't find anything of a positively incriminating nature in the body. Not a thing to warrant criminal charges, until we uncovered that vital witness.'

Balchard turned away, shaking his head in faint annoyance, to kneel down and shift the coal in the grate. 'And tell me, Detective Sergeant, *who* was it, who led you to uncover that '*vital witness*'?'

Dryson's instinctive dislike of the man turned to anger, burning in silence as he stared into his back.

'Furthermore, Detective, I beg to point out that *that* case was entirely different in that the poison was of an organic nature.'

'I always thought a poison was a poison, in my book. Perhaps you could expand on that.'

'Simply, Detective Sergeant, that since the poison in the former case was organic in nature, it follows that it was more easily 'passed out' , as you would say, by the body's fluid system. However, in the latter case of the unfortunate late Mr Pardy, the administered substance, arsenic, was not only detectable because of its metallic character, but also by virtue of its entering all parts of the body, including such remote regions as the hair and finger-nails, to the extent of being very much evident after death.'

'Do you mean to say that if we'd dug the body up after a month of Sundays, for instance, we could still have found the poison? Is that what you're saying , Balchard?'

'If not in the body's decomposing tissues, then in the soil itself, no less, Detective Sergeant. A sample of this soil compared with a sample of the surrounding soil would give a fair indication of the quantity of arsenic originating from the corpse. Indeed, Detective Sergeant, if you would fret over the time factor, it is a noteworthy point that the toxin itself can serve as a fairly reliable 'clock' for measuring the time of the foul deed; by way of its presence in the hair filament, which has a regular growth of approximately point four four millimetres per day. Thus, in Mr Pardy's case, for a five point three *centimetres* length of filament impregnated with the poison all the way up from the root, the period of poisoning is roughly one hundred and twenty days. Four months of carefully administering the poison in specifically small dosages that would arouse no suspicious ill-effects. So much so that the doctor attending the victim never suspected that his more rapid deterioration, pallor, loss of flesh and appetite, and vomiting were due to anything but natural causes. Now, had a more e*xpert opinion* been called for, and a hair or nail clipping sample taken, the dastardly crime would have been brought to light at once.'

'Yes, well, that's all very interesting, your fancy figures and all, Balchard, but I still say that we would have got her in the end, with or without your fancy barber shop hair-chopping antics.'

'Of course, Detective Sergeant; how remiss of me to

overlook a certainty like that.' Balchard crossed over to the side table to pour out a glass of water from a small carafe. Opening a tin of Dinneford's Magnesia, he took out a spoonful of the salts, pausing with it over the glass. Looking to the Detective Sergeant, he proffered the heaped spoonful of magnesium sulphate and sodium bicarbonate salts. He did not imagine that Dryson would accept, guessing that he would have preferred something more strong in 'spirit', but it aroused a sinister amusement in him deep down, to tease him, nevertheless.

Dryson gave a negative shake of the head. He considered *his* constitution to be a cut above those who had to resort to the silly remedies prescribed for weak-kneed gentlemen or kiddies. Or perhaps it was all this talk of poisonous powders. 'To those that need it, I always say. But you go right ahead, Balchard. Don't mind me.' He hoped that Balchard's stomach was giving him hell.

Balchard stirred the salts into the water, watching the violent effervescence of bubbles protesting their fizzy discontent, before raising the glass in mock salutation. 'To your health, Detective Sergeant.' Pouring the sparkling waters back slowly, Balchard watched Dryson over the rim of the glass. 'If not in the stomach, then possibly elsewhere there is *some other issue* unsettling the Detective Sergeant --- in the *mind*, perhaps?'

'As it so happens, there *is* another matter I want to pick a bone over.'

'Not that I would have suspected that for a moment!. But pray, do continue, Detective Sergeant.'

'You'll push my patience just too far, Balchard. But like

I was saying, here was I just enjoying my annual four days autumn leave, until I come in this morning to hear from the desk sergeant that you've been having a mind to instruct my men to go chasing Indians. Ruddy Indians in the middle of London ---I ask you! Sounds like Buffalo Bill's Wild West Show!'

'I'm sure the Detective Sergeant deliberately jumps the continents in his geographical error.'

'You know damn well what I'm referring to, Balchard --- so perhaps we could be having it straight from the horse's mouth?'

'Taking that somewhat enthusiastic metaphor as an intended compliment, yes, I do believe that I can provide you with an explanation, Detective Sergeant. But in the more appropriate environment of that relating to the matter in hand --- especially one where there is a lesser abundance of *ears*. 'Balchard accentuated the last word with a lingering look at the front door which gave directly onto the landing. Stepping into the inter-room doorway leading to the bedroom, Balchard removed his dressing gown to replace it with his waterproofed sovereign tweed overcoat from the coat-hanger on the bedroom side of the door. Taking up his tweed cap and stout malacca cane, Balchard ushered Dryson to the door. 'If you can spare your precious time for a brisk perambulation to a certain shipping office in Upper Thames Street, Detective Sergeant, I rather fancy that you will find the topic of conversation much to your interest. Failing that, then perhaps at least the air will serve to invigorate your lungs. After you, Detective Sergeant.'

Mrs Wallamsby was immediately there by 'shear coincidence', doing her dusting, as the door opened, like Balchard had implied. Balchard smiled his artificial greeting. 'Splendid breakfast, Mrs Wallamsby. Absolutely splendid breakfast. But perhaps a teeny bit less heat on the toast and a teeny bit more heat on the teapot next time.' A gross understatement as the tea had been cold like the Newgate condemned's last sweat before the gallows. The toast had been sufficiently hard and black to warrant it as a museum's proud piece from the City's horrific conflagration in 1666.

As they made their way to the vicinity of the East India Shipping Company, and thereafter to Scotland Yard, Balchard laid out his plans -- *suggested* plans -- to foil the flight of a killer, as well as clipping the wings of a larger flock of dangerous 'birds'. Alas, the more Balchard unfurled the intricate folds, the more Dryson shook his head in disbelief. Balchard was familiar with the sceptical reaction, hiding his inner vexation behind a gentleman's wager that time would prove him to be the shrewder of the two. It was later, when Balchard was leaving the Yard by himself, that he first noticed the *Walrus Man*.

The title registered itself aptly in Balchard's mind immediately at the sight of the heavy black moustache drooping down in semblance of that other great species of mammal. Further to this likeness with the sea-lion, the man was powerfully built, with an openness of manner and facial expression that dispelled the sinister, yet failed to completely eliminate that uncanny air of intrigue that accompanies the inexplicit. That the man was of the outdoor type, without lording extensive estates of stables and carriages, was easily inferred from his general air and the rough norfolk knickerbocker suit and cap. The large tricycle beside him said the rest. Not immediately averting Balchard's returned look, as the stalker is apt to do, the man eventually shifted his attention to the object by his side, on the tricycle seat. The box, heavy from the way that the man handled it, was what really held Balchard's attention. Innocuous in its brown paper wrapping and red twine, there was that one aspect of it that made Balchard's spine tingle. For there, in the middle of the front surface, just perceptible through camouflaging flaps of paper, betrayed by glinting sunlight, protruded the ominous brass barrel. As the man stooped to adjust his instrument, Balchard darted swiftly into the shelter of the crowd of people streaming along the pavement. Looking back from his cover of the thronging mass, Balchard watched the man peering in dismay in his direction, like the hunter who has just lost his quarry. Balchard felt instinctively that this was only his first encounter with the *Walrus Man*.

A second instance of being watched alerted Balchard's overwrought nerves, only streets away, when he paused to browse at a pavement bookstall. His sudden turn and a sweeping glance at surrounding faces did not reveal what he had thought he had seen. For a fleeting moment he had thought he had seen his pater. But he was not there now. His imagination playing up on him? What would his pater have been doing hovering around a bookstall? He had never had a high regard for books or his son's learning from them. The only books he understood were those kept by the turf accountants at racetracks. Or had he come to see the 'zookeeper'? The origin of that term came back to Balchard with a sharp pang. He remembered that *she* also had once teased him over his books, calling him a 'zookeeper'. He had not understood until she had explained that books, with their white pages and black lines of words, were like striped zebras --- 'zeebers', she had called them --- so he was a 'zookeeper'.

' 'Ere, mister! It'll cost yer a tanner, if yer tears that book! Show me yer bloomin' money, then!' Balchard's attention was suddenly drawn to the stall owner pointing at him. Following the direction of the pointing finger, down to his own hands, Balchard saw the man's cause for consternation, at the near-tearing grip of his hands on the book. Casting the book down, Balchard gripped the book-barrow's side, with a mind to tip it over in fury. He restrained himself at the sight of a policeman approaching to investigate the commotion. Striding off, Balchard took his own private 'commotion' with him, in his head. The thought of his pater and *her* sharing the same philistine attitude towards books seemed to upset him with a strange feeling of disillusionment. The first crack in the mirror? Nausea began to come on.

Back at the Institute, Balchard sought refuge from his troubled memories in the solitude of his work. Adding the concentrated sulphuric acid to the platinum wire, he held it over the Bunsen. Seeing the gradual green colouration, he added the sulphated hydrogen to obtain the dark precipitate. Satisfied he stood back. Watching the soft yellow and blue flickering flames intermingle, *he saw her golden locks play with her ribbons, in the sunlight. He saw the silken strips dancing in the air, as she did, taking them out, one by one, to cast away into the air, before starting on her clothes. These came off slowly at first, as she teased him with her prancing body -- before quickly taking them all off completely, to run wild, through the meadow's gorse and bracken, which carried its own emancipating fragrance.* Looking round, Balchard concluded that the chlorine fumes coming from a retort along the bench were influencing his mental visions. Angry, he knocked the retort aside, only to be further angered in watching it fall off the bench, to shatter on the floor, its liquid contents swelling out in a bright green pool around his feet. Staring down at the spillage for what seemed long moments of subsiding anger, he was suddenly aware that he was being watched from the doorway. Raising his head with measured slowness to conceal his embarrassment at being caught out, he looked around.

It was Dr Stolling, standing in the doorway, holding a tray of phials containing fluids for his analysis. 'Another lot for you to get on with, Balchard, old boy. I say, you have made a bit of a mess of it there, haven't you?' He smiled with open amusement while Balchard's anger resurged inwardly. In Balchard's mind, the spilled fluid had already been thrown in Stolling's face, glass fragments and all, burning the flesh, and gouging the smiling bastard's eyes out.

Balchard stepped away from the bench briskly, trampling on the broken glass with deliberate nonchalance, to disarm Stolling's urbane mockery, and all but wrenched the tray from Stolling's grasp. 'So let's *get* on with it, *shall* we, *old boy!*' Returning to the bench, he planted the tray down with no lack of noise and rattle from jumping phials, and busied himself in his new work, completely ignoring Stolling's prolonged staring into his back. Stolling's further taunting remarks brought no response from Balchard, other than the occasional loud clink of a beaker. Stolling remained there for a few moments more, leaning against the door jamb, arms folded, shaking his head slowly in wonderment at that before him. How in God's name, they managed to let that wretched fool in was something beyond his understanding. There wasn't even mention of a decent school. Instead, some puny northern backwater school -- penny exercise books, no doubt, and then some provincial place daring to call itself a university. He sighed in resignation of what he couldn't fathom. With a curt: 'Oh, well, can't dally around all day,' he straightened up briskly and went off.

'And may you rot in hell, as well, *old boy*,' was Balchard's measured reply *sotto voce*.

The publican was quite adamant in his statement. 'Not seen 'im round 'ere for ages, mate; not likely to, either, seein' as 'ow ' got chased by coppers for knifin' a bloke in Seven Dials, two nights ago, I 'ears. Be keepin' 'is 'ead down, 'e will, if 'e knows 'is business. Talkin o' business, what yer 'avin', then?' A heavy hand thump down on the bar was the signal for beer money to be slammed down beside it. That would be when Balchard and Kahamir would leave. Similar words, or a shake of the head, were the continuing empty responses, if not rebuffs, that kept the two of them moving on in their determined search through dangerous neighbourhoods. The two men walked in a silent solidarity of seemingly God-forsaken pasts, Balchard with his sullen grimace, and Kahamir with his one-eyed leer. Ruffian and killer that Kahamir was, Balchard felt a weird affinity with him -- perhaps it was because of the missing eye. A handsome man, but for that flaw, Kahamir's image had been dented, just like Balchard felt his own dignity scraped and fallen short.

Casual enquiries, made through Kahamir's acquaintances, took them everywhere and nowhere. Whenever a scent was picked up, it only led to where a useful contact had been. Balchard began to wonder if their enquiries were the only ones circling round. Was there a concentric circle of enquiries going on around them, *about them*? A name that sounded like it could be what they were after came through. Vlarda. By that time, Balchard was very tired, and as much enquired after as he was enquirer. With guarded questions passing in both directions, a discreet distance was being kept between the two sources. Balchard and the supposed Vlarda kept to the periphery of each other's notice, making no show of direct interest in the other. To each of them, the other was 'somewhere around' or 'near at hand'. But Balchard felt the disadvantage of not knowing which one, if he was here, was Vlarda; he could be any one of these bastards around him. He would have to wait until this 'Vlarda' put in an appearance.

Kahamir took himself a woman and left. With a drunken stagger and a boisterous refrain, to meet his adopted ruffian guise of Irish rebel, Balchard left shortly after. He headed for the nearest mission hall, to bed down for the night. As he lay down on the coarse straw bag bedding, he noticed the blood on his cuff, and puzzled, found his knuckle bleeding; the result of his stumbling against a wall, or something. Alcohol was not without its effect on his senses. Like the bruised knuckle, he was taking his chances and just scraping by. He thought of the subtle remarks that had come at him, cutting through raucous laughter, to hone the suspicions of Vlarda's cronies all around him. But as the room spun wildly around him, a remaining speck of sobriety told him that he had perhaps only just escaped suspicion and a knife across his throat for the night. What would it be like tomorrow? The fear and thrill of it all had him muttering himself quietly to sleep.

But what sleep that Balchard managed to catch that night was greatly unsettled. A river of nightmares swam through his mind. Through the darkness came the putrid odour of bodies rank with sweat and excrement, reminding him of the endless story of human desolation and wreckage all around him. Dozing fitfully, he jerked awake between ragged patches of disturbing dreams, trying to orientate himself to his surrounding, and so escape from the scenes that had alarmed him. Distorted dream visions, ungoverned by daytime's sanity, ran amok through his mind, playing havoc with his emotions. Convoluted mood changes took him from a morose past, to a precarious present that harboured a great fear of the future. Overriding all these melancholy wraiths spiriting through his mind came the scary questions. What would happen if Vlarda's lot tumbled to his ploy? Could he be connected to Smethers? Had he overlooked any thing in his cover story -- even a tiny point, that could be the difference between life and death? Did he let *her* drown? Did they quarrel that much, that night? Did he *push her*? Sleep at last claimed his mind solidly, so that he rested inwardly undisturbed, until the warden announced it was time for morning prayers.

CHAPTER 13

London, October, 1887

With the calendar turning over a new month page, so also did the City turn over from its slumber of the two preceding 'summer' months. For as surely as the badger needs to hibernate during the unsociable months of winter, so also did that select section of society need to live covertly behind closed doors and shuttered windows of 'empty' houses; this was preferable to the admittance that many of the 'country residences' were non-affordable and hence non-existent beyond that of polite fabrication. A 'coming out' mood was thus prevailing, where aspiring socialites welcomed the new season of evenings highlighted by the ball and soiree. At least Balchard certainly found Oxford Street's atmosphere livened so by people stepping out briskly with wide swinging sticks and parasols, hastening along like new sprays of butterflies bursting forth from their pupae. Perhaps this theme of sticks played on Balchard's mind as he swung his in similar spirit along the way. He finally turned purposely into the reputable gentlemen's stick-dealers that proclaimed its noble repute in bold gold lettering across three storeys of the shop's tall facade. Inside, with the magical tingle of a doorbell, the cheerful light of the street was lost to the dark austerity of umbrellas, riding crops, sticks and other woods in sufficient quantity of a miniature Sherwood Forest.

Balchard took up an Irish blackthorn from its stand, testing it for weight and matching its firmness of girth with his own stick. Whilst fussing about with the stick, and shifting round the stand to poke and prod at other models, he kept a wary eye separate from the myriad of sporting woods for his real quarry. The man was just entering the premises now, striding up to the counter, with a mind to having the loose ferrule on his cane repaired. Like Balchard had foreseen from earlier evidence. Just at the right moment, Balchard stepped back, 'testing a stick', into the path of the other man. Limbs and sticks collided with resounding cracks that sent woods and oaths flying with equal vigour. 'Bloody cad!' blurted the man in instant fury, glaring at Balchard with bulging grey eyes. Balchard's apology was a silent bowing of the head, whilst holding the man in the vice-like grip of his steely return stare. Stooping down, Balchard retrieved the sticks, holding one of them out to the gentleman. The man held out an expectant hand with iron-stiff brusqueness, in the manner of the bullying squire accustomed to deference from servile staff. It was not even necessary for him to look at what was being placed in his hand since his orders were always obeyed.

But Balchard's unyielding stare set the man's facial muscles twitching on one side. 'I say, sir,' the man said at last, unable to sustain the 'hold' in eyes alone, 'have we met?'

In answer, Balchard slowly nodded his head up and down in inner conclusion, weighing up the characteristics before him with those that had been deduced from earlier insight. 'One may have seen the other *from afar*. That is possible, is it not, perhaps?' Venomous humour sparkled in Balchard's eyes for a second as he sought to unnerve the other with a half truth. For truly the half truth, so close to home, was the more deadly dagger that that struck down, not from the enemy afar, but from within the safe cloak of one's own mind.

Ill at ease with the enigmatic statement, the man smacked his cane in his gloved hand. 'It couldn't have been at my club. We're jolly careful of those we choose to select for membership. Good day to you, sir!' With a sour grimace of open distaste, he turned and strode away with a non too discreet muttering of: 'Bloody damn cad!' which said little for his club's rules on politeness. Only when he spared a moment to inspect his stick, between hectic bangings on the counter and angry cries for service, did the man let out a different-toned shriek denoting new-found horror. He turned and rushed back to Balchard. 'Are you a thief, sir, as well as an absolute bounder? You have my cane there, sir! Kindly return it at once, or take a good thrashing!' With that loud-voiced imperative he cast down Balchard's stick like a leper's staff.

Balchard voiced a meek apology for his 'error', and handed back the stick that he had 'accidentally' taken. Watching the other storm off again, Balchard nodded sagely once more at the receding back, emitting a faint smile like the wizard divining an imminent black cloud of retribution gathering over the head of the condemned. Collecting his stick up off the floor, and touching his hat in mock courtesy, he turned and made for the door. The glove which he had put in his coat pocket was carefully wrapped round a small cardboard lid that contained a soft wax mould. That mould now had clear imprints of the grooves and scratches on the ferrule of the gentleman's stick. Those same prints were but one step in a series of steps that would lead a cunning embezzler to a lengthy *sojourn* in Newgate Prison.

Immediately outside the shop, the crouching form of Sam Loofer straightened up from its snooping position behind the door's glass panel, as Balchard opened the door. 'Givin' you a spot o' bother, was 'e, Mr B? Should 'ave given us the whistle, you should've. We would 'ave put the 'ammer on 'im. Flattened 'im proper like a jelly-fish, we would've. Ain't that right, Charlie, son?' He turned, with this remark, to the twisted figure of his Cockney mate beside him.

Ever mournful, the Cockney's face seemed to darken in deeper dismay at this new suggestion of violence. 'Thaht don't seem ter be a good idea, Sam. We always seems ter be lahndin' in trouble with efferyfing you says. I mean, look aht thaht job we did on Sahterday behind the dairy. I near lost me blinkin' 'ooter.' He rubbed his nose in painful memory. 'Ahn' all 'cause you tells me ter jahmp through the bleedin' window.'

'Sure I told yer t' jump through the window, son, but you're supposed ter bleedin' well *open* the window first! Stupid git!' Loofer tucked his thumbs under his armpits and shook his head in mock wonder as he looked down in sad judgement at the forlorn expression of his mate. 'I honestly don't know what your old woman was sittin' on when she 'atched you into this world. Must 'ave dropped you on your 'ead, she must've, I swears. Pushed your brains right up into your feet. That squeakin' noise what we 'ears from your boots when you walks is your brains squealin' out for 'elp. An' God 'elp 'em, I says, 'cause no-one else will. That is 'cept you, of course, Mr B, beggin' your pardon.'

Admonishments over, Loofer turned back to Balchard. 'Anyway, Mr B, 'e'll be the bloke that you'll be wantin' us ter follow, right?' Loofer jerked his head in the direction of the shop to clarify his meaning.

'The very same. And *please*, if I can insist, see to it that you tread lightly. Your methods can prove to be somewhat *rumbustious*, shall we say, as past records have shown. Balchard looked at the Cockney, in reference to the 'dairy job'.

'Sure, Mr B, sure. You can always trust us,' replied Loofer, tapping his nose with a broad finger. At the same time he held out a broad palm. 'There again, there's always the cabbie fares.'

Balchard looked down at the hand, heavily calloused with its network of scars that mapped the City's illicit activities. He tapped it lightly with the silver knob of his stick.

'There should be ample recompense at the end of the day, after your errand is completed. In the meantime, the non-too paltry sum that I allotted you this morning should suffice, I think.'

Seeing that he would get no further with that plea, Loofer pursed his lips and then blew out. 'Right y'are. Just one other thing. What 'appens if 'e sniffs us out an' turns on us? Does we scarper sharpish, or does we stand an' give 'im the old boot in the goolies?' Balchard was about to elaborate on the details of action for such a contingency, when he suddenly broke off and turned away from Loofer, to hurry off up the street. A tingling doorbell behind Loofer, followed by a frame-jarring door-slam, told him that the prey had emerged from the shop, so causing Balchard to make himself scarce, like he had done. Signalling Charlie with a wink, Loofer turned round casually and they sauntered after the man. From across the street, Balchard saw Loofer's flamboyant black and white chequered figure hail and clamber up into the black obscurity and comfort of a hansom cab. The less fortunate Charlie was left to struggle up onto the wobbling frame of a rusting penny-farthing bicycle. Balchard saw wisdom in the division of labour since. If the cab was halted in a traffic jam, at least the bicycle could still make progress ferreting in and out around the larger vehicles. But no doubt the ill-fated Cockney wouldn't see it that way.

The Union Jack hanging from beneath the three faced clock jutting out over the gun dealers caught Balchard's attention and he checked the time with that on his own gold hunter. He had fifteen minutes to keep his rendezvous with Dryson. If the policeman had heeded the time, he would have already moved his men into the specified Dockland locations. *He had not possessed a watch of his own that day. Yet he had still managed to time it so as to get across the field to the church, to see her coming out at the end of the Easter Morning Service. The sun had also waited on her patiently, to embellish her with its golden rays, as she emerged from the doorway --- along with her father. All pretty in festive bonnet, adorned with bows and ribbons, it was the first time that he sensed a restriction in her frivolous spirit. The 'grown up' dress and the bonnet holding her golden locks down in check, gave her an unfamiliar formality. Standing there, on the arm of her beloved papa, she was resolutely the daughter of the town's important landowner and industrialist, chatting among her own people. He had not dared step out from the cover of the lesser crowd, to show his association by smiling to her, or catching her eye. Not with her father guarding her preciously in all his austerity. There was great envy at the sight of those parental hands, hard, yet gently, lovingly possessing the child; the way he yearned to possess her. But was it the fear of the father that gave him trepidation? Or was it the fear that she would not have acknowledged him -- him from his working class? Was she as much trapped by her own people, as he was by his? Or did she really feel that way inside herself about him?* Coming out of his reverie, Balchard increased his pace and hurried across the road.

'Hey, you! Gerrout the bleedin' road! What's yer bleedin' name, then -- Dr Death?' The brewer's dray-wagon, with its angry driver, rumbled on past, narrowly missing running over Balchard.

CHAPTER 14

'Late as usual, are we, Balchard?' An acid-smiling Detective Sergeant Dryson stepped out from the depth of the alley, like a shadow detaching itself from the warehouse wall.

Balchard did not bother to consult his watch to contend the taunt. 'I rather fancy that precision in timing depends much on what we find inside, Detective Sergeant. Your men are in position and have been issued with detailed instructions, I take it?'

'Down to the last hobnail boot, Balchard. And anyone who doesn't follow his lot is in for a right earful from me, I can tell you.'

'So I see,' said Balchard, looking over Dryson's shoulder, towards the corner of the building. For sure enough he saw the two white plumes of condensed breath issuing out in heavy snorts from around the corner of the alley. This, along with a soft jingling of harness and a restless shifting of steel-shod hooves, told him that a black police wagon sat waiting in readiness in the alley. 'In that case, Detective Sergeant, shall we proceed?'

At that, Dryson lifted up his polished steel whistle and

then, after second thoughts and a reproving look from Balchard, held it down, concealed in his hand, by his side. The enormous gaping black mouth of the building's entrance beckoned Balchard and Dryson as they walked slowly towards it, the cobble-stones echoing their steps and glistening from the gossamer drizzle just starting. Inside, the atmosphere seemed even damper. It was certainly much cooler. To some, it was also eerier. Dryson shivered in the dank darkness. The darkness around them was almost as sticky as pitch. It was more than a mere spectral cancellation of colours. It was like a thick tangible substance present all around them wherever they looked. They could virtually feel themselves stepping through the dark wallowing medium, their limbs totally immersed in it in front of them. With nothing for the eyes to focus on, the mind was apt to swim, and several times Balchard felt the searching fingers tip on his arm as his companion searched out to navigate himself over unsure footing.

'Bloody hell! What kind of deranged beggars want to live in a damned hell hole like this, where the eyes are no good? They've got to be foreigners. Must be something to do with their skin being darker than ours, so it fits in better with the darkness. That was a joke, Balchard, before you give me one of your philosophical spiels. I can just about tolerate this damn darkness more than I can your raving on.'

The manner in which Dryson's speech had broken down into idle banter not befitting an officer of the Yard, was enough to make Balchard smile. Apparently his companion did not perform to full form in this dark enclosed environment.

Dryson, in fact, was thinking that anyone who could derive pleasure and be in his element, as Balchard obviously was, in this unearthly blackness, had to be sick. To Balchard's ear, the weird noises around them signified the shifting of frightened pigeons and bats and scurrying vermin. As well as other forms that gave him an exciting exercise in identifying the unseen from the acoustics of movement. But with the unsure mind, these sounds played havoc with the spine-jangling imagination. Each flap of a wing sent a fresh army of goose pimples marching up the back of Dryson's neck. The Detective Sergeant fumbled and clanked about with something metallic until at last, with the help of a mouthful of profanities, he managed to light up the bull's-eye lantern. He held it out at arm's length. 'Christ!' he muttered, in outright surprise, at the colossal shapes towering over them out of the blackness. Like a long lost legion of Titan insects advancing on them, the monster fifty foot vats, once part of the City's malt industry, now stood there empty and abandoned, on their massive legged wooden stages. 'For a moment there I thought they were bloody beetles. They would have made good pets for the mother-in-law. There again, maybe not; *they* would've been frightened at the sight of *her*.' Dryson moved his lamp around, at arm's length, as a diversion from his silly talk.

'Yes, with the imagination at its ripest, the 'legs' do give a limited semblance to the order of *Coleoptera*, or perhaps the *Blatta orientalis*. Beetle, or common cockroach, Detective Sergeant. Clearly a mistake, of course, and, alas, so easily trodden underfoot.'

'There's no need to be funny, Balchard. We all makes

181

mistakes.' Dryson's normal aplomb for ignoring Balchard's sarcasm was clearly at a low ebb because of his being out of his depth in unfamiliar territory.

'Funny? Dear me, no, Detective Sergeant. Whatever gave you such a thought, I wonder?'

As the light reached out, it caught the retinae of 'millions' of eyes staring out from the nothingness between the vats, so that Dryson felt the hair on his neck rise up like the best of kites in Hyde Park. 'Go on, gerrout of it!' shouted Dryson, kicking and punching the empty air to no avail, the 'millions' of luminous dots remaining stock-still. He drew back the lantern and stopped just short of throwing it when, with a tight knot of nerves in his stomach, he thought of the consequences of having no light in his hand. Balchard queried the action, with raised eyebrows. Dryson adjusted his hat in nervous defiance. 'Yeah, well.'

The violent shift of light had apparently had some effect, with 'millions' of tiny feet retreating in a furry soft-padded flurry, as the two heavier pairs of feet advanced. Watching the light spread round the curved surface of the vats, Balchard thought of the convoluted cerebral surface of the human brain. How shedding the light of knowledge on it meant the advancement of man towards his ultimate civilisation, pushing his savage side, with all its primitive instincts, further back into the decreasing unlit and unexplored horrific dark corners of the great cavern that was his mind. 'What the ---! Did you see that, Balchard?' blurted out a much excited Dryson. 'Over there, between the ---'

'Yes, Detective Sergeant, I was aware.' Balchard had

indeed caught a moment's fleeting side glance of an orange blur between the vats. But when he looked straight in that direction there was nothing but the unyielding gloom relinquishing none of its secrets. It happened again, seven times, in seven different directions, and each time the eyes looked directly, there was nothing to hold them but space. 'No, not hallucination, Detective Sergeant, but more so a time for positive communication.' At that, Balchard removed from his coat pocket what Dreyson mistook for a long sausage with a lump on its end. He put the 'sausage' to his lips so that it began to emit a series of hauntingly willowy notes made all the more eerie by their falling on the heavy silence around them. While Balchard's fingers danced on the pipe, Dryson's pulse danced in time to it, his eyes darting here, there and everywhere, half expecting the Indian fakir's rope or something, anything, to appear and so satisfy his leaping imagination.

Suddenly he started. Balchard's notes were now not the only ones climbing up into the darkness. There were now two other flutes entwining their mystical notes with his. Dryson also swore that he could hear what sounded like a large muffled heart beating, beating, beating, on and on and on back there, somewhere. Moving his head to and fro for a moment, in rhythm with the soft hypnotic beat, he looked round about himself. His eyes widened in amazement. Where there had previously only been blank space, there were now standing on the dim periphery of light, eight dark-skinned, bald-headed figures clad in saffron robes and festoons of bangles and beads. Two of them accompanied Balchard on flutes, while another one tapped out a solemn beat on a small drum under his arm. A half-sized replica of the figures strutted into the circle's centre, in semblance of a stiff-legged doll with no knee joints, swaying in trance-like motion to the music. The three brass pieces danced on the chain around his neck. 'God, he's only a nip of a lad!' muttered Dryson.

A large lump of fur jumped up out of nowhere onto an orange-clad shoulder, the monkey twisting its head and clapping its tiny paws in praise of the policeman's brilliant deduction. Dryson lifted his whistle, but Balchard caught sight of this and turned to him, whilst still playing, shaking his head violently to caution the other's restraint. On and on Balchard played his serpentine notes, closing the gap between the minds, in ever increasing nearness of unison with the Hindus. Dryson's impatience mounted. All right, that was it. He had had enough of this tomfoolery. Dryson blew his whistle and stepped forward, tapping Balchard's arm. 'All right, leave it to me. I'll take over from here.'

Whatever mystical spell of communication Balchard had begun to set up with the Asian minds was now broken by Dryson's horse-footed intervention. The ritualistic peace of the Indians gave way to an ear-splitting babble of voices that was all the more mind bending because of the unintelligible foreign tongue. Dryson's whistle shrieked out again and large inky blobs with buttons down their chests loomed up to apprehend the assassins. Knives flashed from beneath the orange robes, and three of the men seemed to rip at their vestments, pulling off their necklaces and casting them down. 'Here, don't start taking your clothes off,' cried Dryson, now fully recovered in his official capacity as servant of the Law. 'That's against the Law, and I must hereby inform you that as an official representative of Her Majesty's Metropolitan Police Force, I am vested with the power to ---' But before Dryson could finish his phonograph-like recital, one of the men snapped together two slats of wood suspended on a leather thong round his neck. The 'necklaces' on the ground suddenly came alive, slithering about in ominous zig-zag motions, much too near to many feet. The dutiful zest to arrest evaporated instantly and the policemen vanished as quickly as they had appeared. Dryson wasn't the last to jump back in panic from the deadly snakes.

Balchard also leaped back, but as he did so, part of his stick sprang away from just below the ferrule, so that he was now holding a glinting sword. Slashing fiercely at the wriggling snakes he managed to strike home only once with his blade, but succeeded only in driving the other vile creatures away underneath the vats. That still left eight blades to contend with. Whilst his was the longer steel, their fanatical minds would urge them on relentlessly, undeterred by death. Much as Balchard hated irrational superstition, it was but the one extreme measure open to him. For one incredible moment amidst the commotion, Dryson thought that Balchard had succumbed to a weak bladder in a fit of fright and was having a pee, the water cascading down his front. Balchard poured the water carefully from the large hip flask onto his left palm which held a bundle of silver coins. Moving his hands closer into the light of Dryson's lantern so that it caught the glint of the coins, Balchard dropped the coins one at a time in a steady stream of water until there were eight coins lying on the ground. Dryson thought that Balchard had taken leave of his senses. At this crucial moment when action, and not silly clowning, was needed. Dryson also noticed at the same time that the vociferous snarls of the enemy had given way to weaker moaning sounds. Balchard now held a small mirror to the coins, and then picking them up again, threw one at each of the men, uttering the soft incantation: 'Ahyhani, ahyhani, mogaba,' over and over again to each individual.

The transformation was astonishing. The circle that had been steel-pointedly aggressive melted back in one wave of fear, mumbling feeble-voiced prayers. Balchard stepped forward uttering the words again, this time very loud. The prayer mumbling halted and the expressions froze into blankness, the knives falling to the ground in a single unified clatter. Like clockwork dolls that had started up together, they had now all run down their spring windings to an absolute standstill. 'Well, I never!' said Dryson, amazed and pushing back his hat to scratch his head. The silence was virtually overpowering, making the pounding in his chest and temples sound like drums of the Grenadier Guards. While his men handcuffed and marched their charges out, Dryson caught the boy by the ear to deliver two kicks to his rear, before letting him run off to join the main throng. Watching the strange figures being bundled into the police wagon until the lock clicked securely behind the last of them, Dryson turned to Balchard. 'So what was *that* all about, then, Balchard? Why did they crumple up like paper bags, like that? Is there something you're keeping from me, then? Something *you* know and I *don't*?'

'The dividing line between awareness and nearness, Detective Sergeant, is a matter of personal perspective. How much does one see and know, and how much does one not know and hence not see?'

'Yes, well, go on, I'm listening.'

'I rather fear that this is neither the time nor the place to enter into an elaborate treatise on Asian cults. Moreover, to linger here after such happenings is possibly to tempt the anger of the gods. None more so than that of Mkuyani, of the million and one temperaments, and so bring his eternal wrath down on us wretched mortals in a never ending hail of stone javelins.'

Dryson looked back at the blackness of the warehouse entrance for a moment and then at Balchard. 'Here, you're havin' me on, aren't you, Balchard? You surely don't believe in all that nonsense, *do you*?'

'As before, Inspector, the state of one's being *on* or *off* is dependent, surely, on the degree to which one ascribes belief in that particular doctrine.'

'Yes, well, what do *you* believe in, Balchard, if I may ask?'

'Oh, you may *ask*, Detective Sergeant, you may well indeed *ask*.'

As they climbed into their carriage, Balchard turned to look at the still dissatisfied Dryson. 'Let us say that one allocates the very minimum of personal energy to dabbling in the realms of the supernatural.'

'You don't mean that you don't believe in God.'

Balchard held his stick to his lips in a call for the other's discretionary silence. Dryson reached out to take Balchard's stick. 'That's quite a nasty piece you have here,' he said, pulling the blade out several inches. 'Not the sort of thing I would have imagined you carrying about with you; you being---' Dryson stalled from saying: a quiet little man --- little pale-faced shit, would have been more fitting, '--- being a man of science, and not force.'

'*Force* is surely the basis of science, Detective Sergeant. How else would things move, plants grow, blood flow, chemical reactions occur, without one force succumbing to a greater one? Indeed, where would your drunken street brawler be without the alcohol molecule superseding the oxygen molecule's affinity for the blood's haemoglobin molecule, in the brain, to produce inebriation?'

'I'm not sure if there were two words side by side in that lot that I understood, but I'll take your word for it. Although we certainly could do without the damned drunks.' Dryson handed Balchard back his stick, musing aloud slowly. 'Just like magic, it was -- like magic.'

Balchard frowned, not comprehending Dryson's line of thought. '*Magic?*'

'Back there -- the way their fanatical aggression just suddenly dropped -- the way they changed like that into docile dummies. You saw how they were -- like loose-limbed wooden puppets; maybe zombies would be a better description. Seemed to have no more thought left in them. Only mechanical movements. Tell me how they did that, Balchard; you seemed to have something to do with it. Can you give me a great scientific answer for *that?*'

But Balchard's mind was no longer dwelling on this

topic. It had flown out instantly to another such 'magical transformation'. *She had first stolen up silently upon him that sunny day; too sunny a day for him to be 'dutifully attending his scholarship studies', when he had been trilling the spokes of the millwheel with a long stick. She had crept up, to entwine herself mischievously, like an elf, round a wooden pole behind him, watching him all the while. For a long while after they had acknowledged and accepted each other's presence. The trilling on wood sound, and that of her plopping stones in the water and other soft sounds of nature from the two banks had been all the conversation they needed. Her face spotted with impish freckles, a mere schoolgirl she had still been then. It was later -- a full year later -- that the magical chrysalis-like transformation occurred, as if by some garden fairy's touch of a wand. A mere child had totally vanished, blossomed out in shape to comely womanhood, with urchin's spots replaced by a honey-glazed pale skin. What had been a child's expressions of naughtiness or boredom, were now beautifully sparkling blue eyes of absolute entrapment. And the golden 'daffodil' curls. After that, there were still times when words were not needed, but by then it was not the enchantment of turning millwheels that held them in silent rapture, but that of each other.*

Balchard shifted in his seat, uneasy, thrumming the window pane with nervous fingers. It was not without some satisfaction, that Dryson noted Balchard's agitated state. 'Something's wrong? What is it? Did we miss one of them?' Dryson made to open the window, to order the driver to stop. Balchard shook his head, waving Dryson's misunderstanding aside. Dryson settled back in his seat again, puzzled. But some deep instinct in him perked up its wolf's ears, telling him that the uneasiness twitching in Balchard's eyes had nothing to do with the prisoners they had just apprehended. It had to be something totally remote from this business that was digging him. He watched the wavering emotions passing across Balchard's face, like cloud shadows rippling in undulating waves over a grave convoluted landscape. It mattered little that whatever it was that was bothering Balchard did not concern him directly. He still wanted to needle the bastard. He was enjoying seeing Balchard in this rattled state, instead of his usual smug attitude that hid him behind his barrages of clever scientific answers. If this was a crack in his armour, if he could find out what it was, he could insert his own wedge, and with a little careful manoeuvring, begin to get rid of him. 'So if it's nothing to do with them --- *what*, then? Let's have it, for heaven's sake.'

Balchard simply continued to stare abstractly into space.

'Well? Don't bloody well waste my time, Balchard; official police time, at that. Out with it!'

Bristling with anger at Dryson's persistent probing of his thoughts, Balchard lurched for the door. 'I'll walk!' With these words, he leaped from the still moving carriage, into an outburst of hollering from angry drivers. Good, thought Dryson, pulling the door shut on what was a most satisfactory conclusion of action. He had him out of the carriage. Next move would be to get him out of the Force. Just like scraping the turd off one's boot.

Darting between and around dangerously close oncoming vehicles was that much easier, Balchard thought, than evading the many questions that were inundating him like poison darts. He had managed to put Dryson's little inquisition behind him. Now had to face Felsham and his confounded clinical schedules. He searched in his muddled mind. Today was Wednesday --- no, Thursday. That meant that he was required to put in an appearance and assist at a demonstration tutorial with those contemptible medical students. His snort held less steam, but more irritation, than that of the horses pulling the heavy wagons past him.

Back at the Institute, his peace of mind was no less disturbed when he was confronted by a dark unshaven face. ' 'Ullo, 'aven't I seen yer afore, somewhere?' The dull eyes, slit down narrowly with suspicion, searched Balchard's face with devilish intensity. 'Yeah, course, I remembers now; 'twere th'other night. So whats yer doin' 'ere, then?' Fright seized Balchard only a split second after he recognised the man. He was one of Vlarda's rough lot, that he had encountered the other night with Kahamir. Balchard's brain froze in total blockage for what seemed eternal seconds. During this numbness, he heard a faraway voice -- his own voice -- faltering between admitting and denying that the man had seen him. His mind had been too confused to register the question, and yet he was answering it. The other night, Balchard had affected a guise of a rough unkempt Irishman speaking in uncouth Irish vernacular, with a brogue accent. Now he was dressed as a professional gentleman, speaking polite Queen's English. A contradiction truly loaded with questions for the suspicious mind.

As Balchard floundered for words to escape suspicion, he was only too aware of the man's probing stare. He recalled how the other night, a knife had come out from beneath the man's jacket. To be placed on the table near to his hand, in readiness, as he asked his questions. 'Tavern? Which tavern? I know of no such tavern, nor would I wish to visit one of such. You are mistaken, sir. If you will excuse me.' Balchard spoke in what he hoped sounded briskly professional, fraught as he was with nerves. He made to step away smartly and be about his duties, along the corridor.

But the man reached out to catch him by the arm. ' 'Ere, not so fast. I knows a face, when I sees a face.' The man was taller and heavier, and no doubt more experienced than Balchard. Balchard had no intention of fighting him. Not here, in the Institute. Balchard realised that as the man grabbed him, he would have to do likewise in return. To play the man's initiative as psychological momentum against him. With his official position as shield, Balchard gripped the man's arm firmly, to march him semi-military style down the corridor. 'This way. sir. The Admissions Office is this way. A brief consultation there will most surely provide remedy for all present misunderstandings.' Balchard, in fact, was heading for the porter's office, where, with a little help, he could have the man thrown out. Caught off guard, he was rummaging among his muddled thoughts to recall Smethers' instructions for dealing with such a 'contingency'. He also wondered what procedure the Captain would employ, in rendering the man as a 'non-nuisance factor', as he had euphemistically put it. Just as they were passing the Surgical Theatre, its doors opened, to release its crowded complement of doctors and surgeons. To the forefront, outshining all others with his resplendent frock coat and diamond-pinned cravat, was visiting surgeon, Professor Bowers-Moffatt. Pilkington-Greeves stood close at his shoulder. 'Ah, yes, the volunteer patient! Good man. Good man.' The Professor's attempt at kindly words failed to hide his impatience at getting down to hacking open another body. 'Bring him in; bring him in. Come along, we can't have the patient dying *off* the operating table. Heavens, that would never do!' A nervous titter of laughter rippled through the students somewhere in the background. Bowers-Moffatt's such remarks for cheering the students never ever carried any thought for the patient's comfort.

'All right, Balchard, we'll take over now. Thank you,' said Pilkington-Greeves, in his usual soft controlled voice, bringing a calm seriousness to the air.

Balchard's realisation that the man was here for a free operation, in return for voluntary demonstration purposes, gave him part relief. But not complete relief. The man may not have followed him, as he had first feared. But he *had* recognised him Or 'rumbled' him, as the good Captain would have put it. In whatever tongue, it was a worrying factor. He struggled with his many inner images, trying to filter them out into different levels -- rotting whores -- decapitated bodies -- murderers -- anarchists -- sunny meadows -- moonlit millwheels -- that frantic drowning face, losing life rapidly -- the black funeral sky. Balchard now headed for the Pathology Department.

Pulling on his rubber apron slowly, in preparation for his

demonstration tutorial with the students, his mind was not all there, where it should have been, in the laboratory. Moving among instruments and chemicals in slothful preoccupation, Balchard's air of detachment didn't go unnoticed. Whilst Professor Felsham didn't much like, nor care for Balchard, neither did he like having his work and staff ridiculed by students. He saw the danger of Balchard's behaviour bringing such disfavour on this clinical session. 'Look lively, Balchard. For goodness sake, look lively in front of the students,' he said in a none too discreet aside. Balchard wanted to comply. But he somehow felt unable to escape an inexplicable fuzziness that was akin to inebriation without the alcohol. Working with the mechanical stiffness of an automaton, he succeeded in raising murmurs of amusement among the students. Not least of these was from troublemaker Coles. Beakers clattered down with unnecessary noise, and jar lids missed their jar necks, to fall and roll in silly circles on the benches. The murmurs rose in audience approval. This was great entertainment. Quiet remarks became jocular catcalls. Coles led these. Felsham became concerned, so cautioning Balchard. The warnings from Felsham made Balchard more anxious, more clumsy.

Unnecessary noise with the glassware developed into unnecessary spillages. 'For God's sake, control yourself, Balchard!' Anger had now replaced mild anxiety in Felsham's words. Simple spillages became dangerous ones. A broken thermometer's blobs of mercury rolling on the bench had Coles stepping in promptly to throw sulphur on the silver fluid, to counteract the poisonous metallic fumes rising from it. 'Well done, Mr Coles,' said Felsham. He glanced sharply at Balchard. 'Perhaps I have myself the wrong assistant.' The derisive remarks all around Balchard united to make a buzzing beehive of anger in his already confused mind. Tranferring itself to his limbs, awkward wavering hand movements became sharp movements of focused fury. Snatching up a bottle to finalise a test, he was frozen in mid action by Felsham's alarmed cry. 'Stop! For God's sake, what do think you're doing! That's concentrated acid! Do you want to blind us all, splashing it about there like fool's champagne!' He moved over to reach out for Balchard's bottle of acid. 'Here, give it to me. I'll finish this. You get over there and filter the pigment solution.' He sighed, giving a piercing look at Balchard. He saw his assistant as an embittered student, masquerading in gentleman's attire, who nurtured a mysterious resentment deep down. Like an experiment that was not properly monitored, that could get out of hand and cause problems. 'God only knows, we should all be out of danger, with you tucked away safely out of the way, over in the corner.'

Mild laughter ringing out around Balchard impinged on his ears with an exaggerated volume that pounded in his brain. He didn't catch Coles' words, although Felsham curtly cautioned him for it. 'That'll do, Coles.' But it was enough to detonate his inner fury, blowing self-restraint to the heavens. Whirling round from the bench, he rushed at Coles, to grab him. Taken by surprise, Coles jerked back on his high stool, shifting his feet off its leg-bar. The unbalanced sway, caught in the impact of Balchard's rush, knocked him over, stool and all, onto the floor. The great explosion of laughter defused the bomb that could have been. But two minds were highly charged. Balchard took insults like wounds that remained open indefinitely.

Felsham was enraged. His serious tutorial clinic, and his precious time given to teaching students, had been turned into a calamitous circus show. He readily blamed Balchard, with his incredibly outrageous performance, for the session's disastrous failure. Balchard was humiliated by Felsham angrily dismissing him from the laboratory, along with a threat of possible temporary suspension from clinical duties. This, pending a hearing before the Committee. Word of the fiasco, with all its comedy, travelled quickly through the hospital. It eventually reached Professor Smelfors' ears, so that Balchard was summoned to his office.

On his way upstairs and along the corridor to Smelfors' office, Balchard became aware of an overwhelming lassitude spreading through his body like mild fire. Realising it to be a purely mental syndrome, he also appreciated the mood swing. He had been all right earlier, when he was with Dryson. He had been in control. Now he was in *its* control. He was barely aware of his feet touching the carpet as he walked along, *glided* along, smoothly. Counting the vertical seams in the wood panelling as he moved along, he became increasingly alarmed as each one passed. The very same way he had dreaded the passing of each iron school railing, when he was reporting for punishment. Driving his hands deep and hard into his pockets, he felt something metallic. His key; or was it his toy soldier? On those occasions he had always relied on his little soldier for strength, thumbing its head in his pocket. A good soldier knows only one way to go -- *has* only one way to go --*forward*. Who had said that? Balchard thumbed his key fiercely, causing pain in his finger.

From what he had heard of the incident in the pathology tutorial session, Professor Smelfors had been somewhat displeased. It was not that a student had been attacked. Students mattered little. It was that a member of his staff had behaved irresponsibly by losing control. Smelfors expected his staff to behave like gentlemen. Gentlemen never lost control. Smethers expected his staff to practise self-restraint by being gentlemen -- *always*.

'Grossly unjust, is how I see it. A minor misdemeanour warranting such a reprimand?' The voice, thinly plaintive and far away, was his own, Balchard realised. He was speaking to Professor Smelfors standing over there, somewhere. Everything seemed distant and dissociated. Not only the room swam around him, with all its paintings and marble busts, but also the thoughts in his head. He was not sure if he was appealing for fairness against something that had occurred just now, or a long time ago. Far, far, away. Smelfors followed the young man's lost look, as it wandered round the room, apparently seeking, apparently speaking, to someone who was not here. His old eyes searched the room, along with Balchard's, trying to help, trying to find something of significance. But he could find nothing. The young man was not well. Fatigue was the most likely cause.

'You do not look well, Mr Balchard. Perhaps you have been working too hard. Professor Felsham tells me that you have been working most irregular hours lately. I would suggest a good rest as the best remedy. This is Thursday; I seriously suggest that you take the rest of the week off, and come back on Monday. The rest will do you no end of good. We can talk about this again when you come back. I'll call you back in sometime next week.' Balchard made to protest, wanting to make his plea now, and clear the matter up, rather than await a delayed sentence. *As it had been before.* But Smelfors officially shooed him out of the office. He could see that Balchard really was not well. Perhaps he could get the Committee to see a way to accepting a plea of mitigating circumstances for the young man.

On entering at Montague Street, and climbing the stairs, Balchard paused on the landing. He wondered why Mrs Wallamsby was not coming out to investigate the heavy drumming that he was hearing. It was the pounding in his head, with its intense pain. Not bothering to turn up the gaslight as he went into his rooms, he made straight for the bedroom. Impaired by darkness, both outside and inside his brain, he fumbled around wildly in the drawer. Anguish released itself in a short cry as desperate fingers located the cold steel. Lying back on his bed, Balchard let the syringe deliver its river of relief. But as he slept, that part of the brain which never sleeps kept on knocking, knocking, knocking --- wanting its own release from its dark deep-down vault.

CHAPTER 15

BRIDPORT **BROILERS**. The gaudy title flaunted itself across a glaring red board. Much to Balchard's distaste, clashing as it did with the green fields that humped and rolled around in their wild freedom. But for this commercial announcement, Harlech's farm building was no different in outward appearance from any other of its kind. 'Truly what the mind doesn't know, the eye doesn't see,' mused Balchard aloud as he stepped up to the building's front. Facades could be wholly misleading. Two enormous doors running on iron rails awaited Balchard's strength. The effort was not needed. Just as he was reaching for it, the right door roared open and the bloody knife missed his face. The sticky liquid ran down the handle, into Pratt's fingers, to end in the sodden cuff of his corduroy jacket. The green material was spotted all over with blood, as was his face.

A red spray of blood fell short of them, and their surprised attentions on each other turned to the interior. The picture was vastly different from that suggested on the outside. Heat and noise hit Balchard full blast in blunt reassurance of the change. Nature had hitherto predominated with its pastoral quietude and unseen horrors. Now man had moved in with all his brazen contrivances necessary for wholesale slaughter. The sight that impressed Balchard was where it should have been, in the centre of the stone floor, bolted down firmly. Basically a tank-like structure, with a monorail running along one side to turn into its front end, the large machine vibrated to an internal rumbling. Rectangular frames suspended from the monorail moved along with a stealth that was eerie. For others, it was inevitable doom. The chicken at the front still flapped limply on its frame even as it was being drawn up the chute to its infernal end. It disappeared in the steaming gap, leaving its blood to drip down onto the tiny mountain of congealed gore rising in the channel beneath the monster tank's belly. 'All but for the want of a few paltry poultry, eh, Mr Pratt?' said Balchard with a searching look at Pratt. But Pratt was not sure if he understood, or wanted to understand, any innuendo from the city meddler. He continued with his work of slitting chicken throats.

Balchard turned back to the blood bath. Half a dozen empty frames swung by, separating two birds at the back from imminent doom. The first bird drew near to the chute and Pratt the executioner stood ready over the inverted form. Eyes blinked and wings quivered in panic. A stroke across the side of its head and life gushed out. Before the second hen could make a nuisance of fear, Pratt reached out and slashed its carotid. The languid bird now exploded into a maelstrom of fury, the body jerking violently in all directions, sending out a scarlet jet of blood that arched out across the room, to refresh the dried stains on the walls. The dying bird wrenched upwards, straining the frame's chain, as it struck out and pecked Pratt in the face. Balchard watched the bird fight gallantly to its end and thought of the previous day's episode where equally zealous spirits and slashing blades had also featured prominently. But for his hasty reading up on the doctrines of that fanatical rebel sect, his could have been an equally hapless fate. That he had called upon the sect's chosen idol of death, Mkuyani, and threatened to steal their souls by washing away the silver moonlight spirits that were guardians of the assassins, as represented by the silver coins, and imprisoning the spirits in the mirror, had been his vital stratagem of survival. But such explanations delivered over a pot of tea in the orderly atmosphere of the police station had struck the duty sergeant as a little far-fetched.

Balchard watched another swirling bundle of birds joining the death line. This was systemised death and the individual's plight did not count. Only the end product was of importance. How true that was, thought Balchard. Considering not only the two recent human deaths, but also the fanatical dedication of those other anarchists that he was currently tracking down with Captain Smethers. He had a mind to speak to Pratt, but the noise was deafening and the fellow was pouncing again, more claws mixing the man's blood with that of the fowls. Drainage was being blocked below the machine and so Pratt mashed the crimson jelly of congealed blood with his foot, watching it rush away along the stone furrow. It was now all logically clear to Balchard. How the bloodstains on the shoes that Sunday had not caused a fuss. The 'dream' being a reflection of what went on here six days a week. Ample blood, the 'stream' under the machine, grotesque head wounds and everything else that a stolid mind could be expected to transform from reality into fantasy and vice versa. The stream of blood on the floor matched that up in the glade, whilst savaged chickens there were not too distantly reminiscent of the semi headless Dan Chudley. Without solid evidence, it was apt to look like the Hand of Providence meting out chastisement for sins long forgotten. Hence the penitential reproof on the faces, some more than others. Upon this last thought, Balchard looked up and around, but that certain person had not yet put in an appearance. He could wait.

Pratt's brother shouted from the back to attract attention. His work at the plucking machine was getting on top of him, with dead fowls continually swinging out of the boilers back end. Here they were unclamped from the moving frames and deposited on the table beside the plucker that removed the feathers with a revolving steel drum studded with rubber protuberances. The man held a bird to the tremulous steel mouth, the devilish contraption shuddering with a force that spared neither bird nor man, gobbling up the feathers and spitting back the fluff, to plaster his face and goggles. He leaned in too far and Gatling-gunfire seemingly broke out as the plucker pulled savagely at the bird's leg. Balchard noted the table was overloaded with slumped bodies, as well as the other plucking machine sitting motionless with rubber apron and goggles lying idly over the metal cover. The deceased Chuddley's working apparel, of course.

The Pratt woman caught Balchard's enquiring look, but turned her eyes down again, to continue gutting the fowls.

She did her job with a clinical expertise that could have been an improvement on some of those professing as surgeons at the Institute. Crossing flesh with steel, a deft stroke removed the head and neck from the body. Two more snippings at the knees and it was one stage short of being a fine spit piece. She slashed the rectum, her hand going in to withdraw again with the entrails. Balchard cut the silence with pretentious interest. 'Mrs Chuddley? Is she about?'

The blade sheared through the cartilage viciously. She threw the feet away and pointed with the hen's head. 'Back in there, 'avin' rest. Poor little lass. Known 'er all me life, I 'as. Knew 'e was nowt good, but never dreamed owt like this would 'appen, God forgive us. It's been too much for 'er. Why can't yer not be leavin' us 'lone, sir?' She was genuinely upset and Balchard wondered how to answer in a way that she could understand. He watched her make a special point of gutting and clipping a select number of birds, separate from the rest, that would hang fully limbed from the monger's hook in the shop window.

'*Special* customers?' asked Balchard, once again in feigned innocence, to conceal his ulterior motive.

'The local squire likes 'em this way, sir,' replied the woman gruffly, without looking up from her work. But when she did look up, she saw that the gentleman was not giving up that easily. 'An' there's Mr Tokely as well. 'E always 'as some like this way for special business fren's o' 'is, 'e does.'

'Ah, yes, *Mr Tokely*. He's the dealer who buys your stock for the town market, is he not?'

'That be right, sir.'

'Aye, an' what 'bout Tokely? What's 'e been askin' yer, woman?' asked Pratt, coming over to the table to hone his knife on the stone.

Balchard turned to Pratt. The knife looked sharp enough. 'The question concerned the subject of favours, and whether or not your Mr Tokely enjoyed any *special* deals.'

'What yer be talkin' 'bout, mister? *Special* deals? An' what business o' yours be it 'o 'as special deals round 'ere, eh, mister? Bloody nowt!'

'That would rather depend on what the *special* deal *is*, I fancy.'

Pratt was becoming more prickly by the moment, and the amusement creeping into Balchard's face didn't help the man keep his calm. 'What yer be sayin', then?'

'Perhaps the trouble, the *real* trouble, is in what one is *not* saying.'

The man was truly getting worried. 'So wha's'at supposed ter mean, then?'

'Only that the local constabulary is likely to deem the withholding of evidence vital to a murder investigation as indicating that one is party to that felony.'

The woman let out a low groan of distress and held a handful of chicken hearts to her chest. Pratt paused with derision at the woman's emotional release. He glared hotly at Balchard. 'Is you sayin' it be me 'o killed Dan?'

Balchard's steely stare, with raised eyebrows, said enough to goad the man.

'You dirty bastard!'

The woman shook her head and squealed at the rising

voice, and Pratt repulsed by dashing the hone down in front of her. It was a clean crack right through the stone. They all looked down at it, and then Pratt, clenching his fists, got back to work. Casting Balchard a fiery look, he put the knife between his teeth to tuck in his sleeves and get on with his job of killing. Hackles flashed and stout claws thrashed as Pratt grabbed out to seize holds on the doomed. Scratched and annoyed, he looked round at Balchard. 'You still 'ere? 'Appen as some folk 'as nowt brain ter take 'int.'

'How very true,' taunted Balchard, in a further effort to loosen a frightened tongue. To push his own 'hint' in further, he took up a dead chicken, and applying a 'noose' of forefinger and thumb round its neck, swung it to and fro to the sombre whistling of Chopin's *Funeral March*. In a moment's distraction elsewhere, he thought of *her* taunts, and their effect on him. Had they *pushed him* too far? Had *he*, in turn ---? A shiver touched him with its chilling finger for a second.

Pratt spun round, his eyes blazing with rage. He was not sure how much he could say or not say, now that it had all come this far, but by 'eck, he was sure that he felt like shutting the meddler Balchard up. The knife handle felt good and solid in his hand. Aye, by 'eck, he would show the meddlin' town bastard how to cut a neck or two. Balchard saw the hostile look and made ready to seize up a wooden crate.

Light cut off in the doorway, and they turned to see that it was Mr Harlech looking in. Pratt's blade dropped its aggressive angle and tensions dropped, so that it was back to work again. Harlech was instinctively aware of the heated seconds that he had just entered upon, and stood inside at the corner, like a schoolmaster returning to his pupils, trying to assess the degree of mischief that had been afoot. He nodded in nervous distant acknowledgement, and Balchard nodded back, wondering what the man was really thinking. Balchard was about to speak to Harlech, when he paused, his attention caught by the face of a new arrival going into an outhouse across the way. He excused himself and went out, stepping briskly across the yard. He passed carefully through the first section of the outhouse that was alive with hundreds of little yellow balls of fluff cuddling and chirping under the heat of the oil stoves and their neighbours' bodies. Avoiding the young chicks as best he could, Balchard opened the door to the building's inner section. The noise blared out, as the fowls ran riot in all directions away from him, away from fatal selection. Balchard quietly watched the man.

An apparent expert in his trade, the man was feeling bird after bird for solidness, and if it was near to the mark, lifting it up to test it for weight. Two were already 'sentenced', struggling as they hung by their legs in the man's steel grip. Balchard opened his mouth to speak, when he felt the sudden piercing sensation in his throat and nostrils. Pungent ammonia fumes. One of the natural by-products of decomposition of bird droppings on the litter. He should have known better. It was much easier breathing through the handkerchief. The pickled air did not seem to affect the other as he went about his task. 'It does not trouble you, I see,' said Balchard, by way of introductory remark to catch the other's attention.

The man looked round, to smile at Balchard's personal

bother. 'Yes, it does nip a fair bit when you're not used to it.'

'Presumably this is your trade, then, sir?'

The man straightened up and turned to face Balchard. 'That's right. Tokely's the name. Albert Tokely. General dealer and supplier in the poultry trade. And *you*, sir?'

'Balchard'

'You're thinking of going into this line of business, maybe?'

'My preference is more so for the *larger* prize bird.'

'Yes, I do some turkeys meself, but that's more usually for Christmas. Still, not long to go now. Maybe I'll have to keep a look-out for you. Rivals, eh?'

Balchard could but only smile at the play of words in their irony. 'Perhaps, sir, perhaps; and possibly *sooner* than one anticipates,' he returned quietly, nodding his head and thrumming his chin with his fingers.

Tokely turned away to continue with his selecting, and Balchard looked around the dim interior for a sign of his own particular bird. A 'fowl' stood up, grinning cheekily and picking its nose. Young Davy Pratt was a chip off the parental block. Dirty and untidy like his father, but with a child's privilege of sprightly mischief. Balchard, who had given the boy instructions earlier, along with an initial payment of two pence, now signalled secretly to the lad by nodding his head at Tokely's back. Buck teeth shot out in a broadside smirk around a mash of masticated bread crust, but otherwise the boy stayed put stubbornly. So that was the young scamp's game. Balchard took out a sixpenny piece and tossed it up and down in his palm, the boy's heart rising and falling with it. The boy's jaw dropped as Balchard put the coin away. He nodded zealously as the coin reappeared. Money changed hands. Increasing the shine on his newly gained wealth with a rub on the elbow, the boy leapt up and away into Tokely's corner. Saltant like a grasshopper, making a mockery of the soft peat bed that retarded Balchard's steps.

Balchard nodded. The boy nodded back cheekily, balancing his coin on his knuckles at arm's length, while tugging at Tokely's coat. Annoyed by the boy's action, Tokely swung his clucking 'club' at him, causing the lad to dodge the swipe in hasty retreat, to continue skipping out of range in defiance. Birds fluttered up in Tokely's face, stalling him before he attacked again. Crashing backwards over a seed hopper, the boy forfeited his precious coin, he and it taking different orbits in the air.

Uproar was tremendous, the loss catastrophic, as pandemonium seized the house, the birds taking to the air, and the boy taking to the ground, in common panic. For fowls, there was life to be lost, while for boys, it was a sixpenny piece. All around, squawking bundles leaped up and over one another in a minor cyclone of terror. Loud painful cries came from the figure searching on the ground with one hand whilst sheltering from the stinging blows with the other. Tokely scythed through the defence to fetch more yelps from the boy until there was a wink of silver on the peat bed. Balchard flipped the coin with his foot and it rolled up to nestle with a smile at the boy's knees. Snatching it up, the boy was recharged with pertness, reeling over outside the assault to spring up towards the door. Beating the slaps by only an ear's length, he made his retreat through the door, behind a yammer of words so foul that even the fowls were embarrassed. The birds settled like sand after a storm. Tokely looked at Balchard, shrugging his shoulders.

'At least you still have your catch, I see,' said Balchard. 'A fine pair.'

'Yes, they are, aren't they. Would you like me to help you pick one out? It takes some practise to be able to judge by eye.'

'I have already made *my catch*, but perhaps you would care to come over to the main building and *confirm* my judgement?' said Balchard.

'A pleasure.'

Sealing off the din and the acrid air behind them, they crossed over to the main building. Back inside, there was a long stony moment where it seemed that no-one was sure what was afoot, so that eyes darted about exchanging glances like pointed daggers. Balchard took the initiative, stepping over to Pratt and significantly prodding a nude chicken in the belly. 'Well? Shall it be Queen's Evidence, or shall it be the noose for your neck, sir?'

Not quite yet alerted to the situation, Tokely looked at Balchard with a new eye-narrowing caution, and then at Pratt. The look between Pratt and Tokely suggested something more than a mere business deal. Their entanglement something more twisted and odious than chicken entrails. Tokely looked around, smiling an enquiring face of innocence at everyone.

But Pratt could bear the tension no longer. ' 'E says I can be 'anged for what you did,' Pratt blurted out suddenly to Tokely, whilst pointing at Balchard. 'Is that right? Can I be 'anged for what you did? 'Tweren't *me* that's did owt. That ain't fair. I ain't not is 'angin' for you or any other ---'

'Shut up! Fool!' Tokely's innocent expression was gone, replaced by a hardened grimace that betrayed the trapped's fear of the tightening snare. Harlech, an apprehensive background face of few words, looked to Balchard for a rendering of sanity to the scene.

Balchard stepped forward to take hold of Tokely's sleeve, so removing a slender fibre of bright saffron material from around the button on the cuff. He held it up to Tokely's astonished face. 'I should imagine that we are all of us able to infer the identity of the original owner of this piece of material, and how it comes to be *here* on your person. That very same owner who was murdered here of late! *Murdered*, I say, by *you*, sir!' With this, Balchard seized the startled Tokely by his lapels.

Tokely pulled himself free. '*Murdered? Me? How?*' The man's brain was too perplexed to cope beyond the stunted monosyllabic utterances, his innocence drowning in the rushing whirlpool of events.

Pratt had suffered enough of the sordid dealings with Tokely, the heated frenzy of the moment taking hold of him. Grabbing up his knife from the table, he brandished it menacingly before Tokely's face. '*You* did it, you cheatin' bastard! *You* killed Dan!' This was too much for Tokely. With no alternative left open to him, he turned tail and bolted out the door. Pratt ran out in hot pursuit. In the calmer wake of the heated departure, Balchard began explaining the situation to the bewildered Harlech. It was, primarily, that Pratt and

Tokely had been pilfering off the farm's stock in a sideline deal of their own.

'You mean they were stealing my chickens?'

'An operation which I can imagine to be none too difficult, considering the multitude of the stock that I have just seen.'

'And Chuddley?'

'His, alas, was the misfortune to discover the illicit transactions of the other two, and subsequently threaten to expose them; that is, unless he was given a generous share of the takings. A *most* generous share, one can surmise, which left the other two founder member *shareholders* somewhat in dismay.'

'But that's blackmail.'

'The very same.'

'And so they killed him.'

'*Tokely* killed him. Pratt was not party to such fiendish action. Tokely merely took advantage of the artificial opportunity where everyone else was temporarily in a mentally suspended state. Induced so by a combination of drugs and hypnosis. Unfortunately for the Indians, who were testing their Western observers' addled minds, one of them was incidental witness to the murder and so had to be disposed of himself.'

'Ah, yes, the Indians,' sighed Harlech, finding that subject a painful one. He tried to delay it a moment longer.

'And *all this* on account of my chickens?'

'To kill for so little truly calls for so little courage in the stomach of the stranger.'

'Supposedly one should summon the police to arrest Tokely before he gets away.'

'Have no fear. The miserable scallywag will find his exit from the farm to be a keen point of 'debate' with the local constabulary, that already awaits him at the gate; upon my instructions, of course. From thereon, his expedience of fate could well hang on the slender thread of some arcane judge choosing between a final glass of port, before resuming court, and another portion of luncheon.'

'Slender, indeed. A considerable stroke of luck that you found that thread on his sleeve. Or even that it was still there after all this time.'

'Indeed, sir, indeed.' Balchard smiled inwardly. He had secretly torn the piece off one of the other Indian's robe, in the police station the day before, with the intention to use it, as he just had, to trigger off the nervous confession. His investigations had revealed that today was the day on which Tokely made his weekly call on the farm. The boy had done the rest, planting the fibres on the man's coat in the outhouse. There was the considered possibility that the coat which Tokely wore today would not be the one that he had worn on the day of the murder. But Balchard had gambled on his general observation that frightened minds tended to bolt ahead of their logic. Thus not having the composure to argue out discrepancies. He had won his wager. But it was now time for the final issue. Balchard looked round at the woman and then tapped Harlech on the forearm. A signal that they should remove themselves to a more remote point for the sake of discretion.

Outside, he caught Harlech's arm again, this time to plant three pieces of brass tubing down in his palm. 'You were aware of the significance of these most intriguing objects from the very first instance, were you not?' said Balchard, with a clear tone of reproach coming out in his words. 'Of course, the door was closed from the *outside* by your hypnotised son, through the agency of a mere trifling of loops and special release knots on a string passing between door and jamb. The melodramatically mysterious manner of departure being merely to convey a cold message through shocked awakening. Of dark memories associated with these sacred ceremonial pieces. And, of course, you knew exactly what these brass pieces meant. I am correct, am I not, sir?'

Harlech nodded solemnly.

'And yet you still chose to not inform the police of the true circumstances behind your son's disappearance?'

The man's pained silence was sufficient indication for Balchard to continue. 'But of course. There was danger of the police uncovering matters of a somewhat *ungentlemanly*, if not horrific, nature. Thus your plight was not *what?* but *where?* Your anxiety was not in finding out what had become of your son, Mathew, but in locating his exact whereabouts. It helped, that I am not of the official police force.' Balchard sounded piqued on this last point.

'No, no, it was not like that, I assure you, Mr Balchard,' Harlech lied limply.

'No matter,' said Balchard, holding up his hand, 'you did well in your eventual realisation that Scotland Yard, with its *forensic resources*, was your only hope of recovering your son.' Balchard's sardonic humour did nothing to encourage Harlech from his silence. Further prising was necessary. 'And this--- *indiscretion*? It chanced to happen a long time ago? A young *woman*, perhaps?'

Harlech kneaded his cheeks nervously with his knuckles, looking up into the sky as the tears welled up in the corners of his aging grey eyes. He was able to speak at last, despite the choking lump in his throat. 'She was only a young flower of a girl --- fresh as a spring lily. She was of the fourth Sudras something or other Hindu caste. Came down from a village in the Satmala mountain district to work as a servant, as did many of her kind, in the Officers' Residence, at Regimental Headquarters.' Harlech paused for a deep breath, before the worst still to come. 'I didn't mean to --- none of us did. It must have been the drink. Too damn much to drink.'

Balchard dropped his gentleman's air, to try a blunt question for a personal poke at the man's sensitivity. 'She wasn't asking for it, then?'

'Asking for it? Sorry, I don't ---'

'*Enticing* the men -- you know -- offering *favours*?' Balchard saw that his innuendo had got through, to upset the man. He did not give a damn about the man's feelings, or the moral issue; he simply wanted to make the landowner squirm. Like that other landowner had once looked down on him and made him squirm. But the insinuation carried by the question would have implicated *her* also, Balchard realised, too late. He wondered why he had asked the question. That thought puzzled and upset him.

'Alas, no.' Harlech rubbed his hand over his eyes in the

torment of his recollections. 'Afterwards -- the others --- on the mess table --- they used the Regiment's mace for --- on top of the Regiment's *silver*, too.'

'Ah, yes, alas, the *silver* -- that *it* should be desecrated so,' said Balchard quietly, in unnoticed sarcasm.

'She was still alive --- but only just. It was the shock, you see.'

'I would believe so,' replied Balchard gravely. 'One can well envisage such. Do continue.'

'Anyway, she lived and was returned prudently to her village so that the incident died away and was forgotten. But after about ten months, the others --- there were nine of us that night --- the others began to fall like flies in a series of most unusual accidents. I was the only remaining one. So I obtained a transfer for duties back over here, in England. Now, after all these years, it's happening all over again.'

'Your son for their daughter. The endless arm of retribution reaching out across the sea of time and generations to seek out your seed and cast it out barren, alike unto theirs.'

'They would have turned him into a zombie. A killing machine. Until he no longer served their need. At which time their degree of revenge would have been deemed completed. I've witnessed it with my very own eyes. Like the many weird things over there, in India, that have to be seen to be believed.'

'Quite.' Balchard felt not a little uneasy at the thought of how he and Dryson had found the son virtually drugged to the eyeballs when they had returned to the warehouse for a second, more thorough, search.

'But thanks to your timely intervention, Mr Balchard,

Mathew is now receiving medical attention of the best possible counsel. A most reputable physician, I am told?'

'I am able to give assurance that Dr Pilkington-Greeves is most proficient in *his* profession.' Balchard's words were cutting. There was much want for similar assurance in h*is* profession of forensic analyst. He made little effort to conceal his disgruntlement as he turned to take his leave. The empty fields round about him offered little else of interest. Balchard was eager to get away. With a last glance around him, something sounding like '---dils,' escaped in low morose murmur from his lips.

Harlech didn't catch the word clearly. 'Chill? Yes, it is getting cooler.'

But Balchard didn't respond. The country atmosphere, and all it entailed from distant memory, gave him a shuddery motive to leave it behind and hasten back to the City.

Balchard's movements carried a nervous caution as he shifted about his bench, in the quiet of the laboratory. He was awaiting news from 'above'. Professor Smelfors had called him in on the Wednesday after his return, for a brief review of his situation. Exactly what his working situation was, had not been clearly specified, except that it was under consideration. Under the Institute's statutory regulations, he should not have been performing any laboratory duties, pending a decision on his status. Professor Smelfors, however, had turned a blind eye to this ruling, upon its being mentioned by Balchard. Thus Balchard should have been busy examining slides of sliced sections of Felsham's specially dyed myelin sheath. Instead, he was bent over his microscope seeing nothing, through eyes that looked elsewhere in his mind. A tinkling of of glassware distracted him from his distraction. It was Coles, supposedly clearing away equipment, rather than deliberately trying to annoy him. Balchard had taken it as an affront that Coles should have come into the laboratory at the same time as him, considering their last confrontation, but had said nothing.

Without looking up from his microscope, Balchard spoke in a quiet controlled tone that fought hard to conceal its irritation. 'I think that will be sufficient, thank you.' The words apparently had fallen on deaf ears, the tinkling continuing. Again, without looking up from the microscope, Balchard spoke, the anger in his voice slipping out this time. 'You still here?'

'Won't be a minute; just this ---'

'Why don't you just leave it, and go!' Balchard's pain in holding down his anger was now openly evident. He looked up from the microscope, in Coles' direction, without directly meeting the other's mocking eyes. 'All you're required to do is empty the contents down the sink, wash the glassware, and place that on the draining racks. That, I see, you've successfully done. So, fine. You can go now.' He lowered his head to the microscope again, in his dismissal of the mere student.

Coles was very much enjoying the frothing anger he was stirring up in Balchard. He knew full well that Balchard's neck was hovering over the chopping block, such that he could not afford to strike back at any impudence put to him, as he had done the week before. 'Sure; give me one more minute with the chemical balance. I overlooked the ---'

'Leave it!' Balchard's fury was no longer concealed.

With the knowledge that Balchard's fate was currently being decided by the Committee upstairs, Coles was feeling bold. He sidled mischievously halfway down the room, towards Balchard, drying his hands on a cloth. 'I hear the gods on Mount Olympus upstairs already have your lot burning in the crucible. If you ask me ---'

'I'm not!' Balchard pulled his rage back from the brink, pleased, indeed amazed, that his clenching fist had refrained from smashing the microscope, along with Felsham's precious slides. Taking a deep breath, he spoke in as controlled a voice as he could manage. 'Just ---,' he gulped back a mouthful of furious words, before continuing, '-- leave it with me. I'll sort out what's left. You can go now.' The words now hissed out softly, slowly, with a menacing sound that was totally unintentional.

Not sure if there was direct threat there, from the odious little toad, Coles froze his hand -drying movements for a moment. Smiling in brazen defiance, he resumed drying his hands for several long seconds, before casting the cloth down on the bench. Turning around, he walked out, whistling with a deliberate discord that pointedly heralded doom.

Professor Smelfors was not happy with the general mood of the Committee. It was felt that Balchard had challenged, however indirectly, the authority of his immediate superior, Professor Felsham, and that of the Institute, by his very act of disorderly behaviour. He should be reprimanded. Murmurings round the table concurred in majority with this view. These condemnations strayed with uncomfortable alluding into the delicately unmentionable area of Balchard's 'rumoured' use of *personnae non gratae* as medical subjects for his research. No one round the table actually stated that he was using prostitutes for his experiments, or admitted that he was doing so; no one said that research in this area could be done without using that kind of 'material'. But it was agreed that he must stop doing what it was that had not been openly stated that he was doing. It would not have done to have admitted to such procedures being carried out under their very noses, in the Institute, no matter how valuable they were to medical advancement. To have done so would have meant sharing the blemish. This was Professor Smelfors' worrying concern, namely, to have his fine record spoiled just before his retirement. Dr Du Mont ventured into another attack, over rumours of Balchard being similarly examined before his university disciplinary body, over allegations of academic misconduct.

'Totally unfounded,' cut in Professor Smelfors hastily, wishing to put all such unpleasant matters to the side.

'Perhaps we should enquire further, Mr Chairman,' said Du Mont, hanging onto his subject like a leech.

'Absolutely out of the question. It is not on this agenda, so does not concern us. Valuable as our time is, we cannot afford to waste it on totally irrelevant issues. Are we agreed, gentlemen? Nevertheless, your remark is duly noted, Dr Du Mont.' Smelfors did not like Du Mont's persistence, in what had seemed to him to be a purely personal attack. Nodding heads round the table were in favour of Professor Smelfors' statement of bypassing irrelevant issues. After all, luncheon was approaching, and no-one was of a mind to be late for that. Smelfors believed Balchard to have admirable qualities as a scientist, which he felt, in spite of personal faults, could well facilitate his making a valuable contribution to medical research, and science in general. He also believed that the root of Balchard's present misconduct could be found to be simple fatigue from overwork. Another complimentary proof of the young man's professional dedication. He believed that it would be ungentlemanly to deny the young man the right of special consideration on account of mitigating circumstances.

Professor Felsham, not saying much, but thinking deeper than Smelfors, was seeing Balchard from a different perspective. A social nonentity, of poor parental background, Balchard was forever antagonising his superiors' authority on some matter or another of unfair treatment. Not content with obtaining his scholarship and access to university, to free him from the squalor of his class, he still complained of personal injustices. The nature of these, Balchard never ventured to say. But the bitterness emanated from him, most surely, to be felt by everyone he worked with. Balchard's seemingly lifelong crusade to exalt his social status had given him such a supreme assurance of his own genius, that it was next to impossible to accord him the merits that he anticipated. Rewards came in their own good time, with everything accorded in its own rightful scale, without the rushing impetus of Balchard's impatience. That was how Felsham saw it. Balchard may well have possessed a fine intellect and brilliant scientific acumen, but he lacked the professional grace of accepting his due. But Felsham also appreciated the colossal amount of his own research work that Balchard was carrying on his shoulders for him. He may not have liked the horrible little man, but without him, who else was there in the Institute who could do the work for him? No-one. Balchard, with his devilish brain, was the only one of subordinate rank in the department, who was remotely capable of seeing his important work through to its completion. Felsham ceded his vote to Smelfors' motion.

Balchard was greatly relieved at his reprimand going no further than nominal admonishment. But he felt a little thwarted on the imperative forbidding his using prostitutes for his research. He would have to tread more carefully there, than before. The good news was that Vlarda's man, who had come in for the free operation last week, had just died in the ward, some twenty minutes ago. Complications had arisen, it seemed. Brought on by an unforeseen pulmonary embolism, with its blockage of arterial blood to the lung, resulting in heart failure. Good, that got rid of that bastard. One point less to worry about. Balchard, lightened in mood, was about to do the rare thing and whistle, when he suddenly remembered Coles' impudent whistling earlier. The dark anger returned to his face, and he made his noise, instead, by pushing the corridor door open with a violent bang.

CHAPTER 16

Luncheon, and bridge thereafter, at Pilkington-Greeves' club in Pall Mall, was a minor accolade in itself, if one was not already a member of that sanctum sanctorum. Such an invitation, when it came rarely to junior staff at the Institute, was apt to inspire hopes of the penultimate step of a fellowship in the hospital, followed by nomination for club membership. To Balchard it was another exercise in touching his forelock. Or perhaps fetlock would have been more appropriate, considering the lowly station that non members were assumed to accrue from, with the same mysterious spontaneity as fungal growth on the compost heap. As he entered the hallowed lobby, the heat touched Balchard with an evenness that made him appreciate the rude jostling from the wind that he had just escaped from. Supposedly higher beings lay back in armchairs, like indoor plants preserved behind glass. Only the soft snores and twitching cheeks testified to an inner thriving. It was a life-style that Balchard had almost forgot existed, whilst others had no inkling of its existence at all. Others took it for granted and used the birthright assurance for taking an afternoon nap, between strenuous bouts of nodding the head and making the right sort of grunt, in deals that served to increase the wealth of ancestral family estates.

Time was no threat to the tired and conservative, as it ticked away sleepily from somewhere. Balchard located the pendulum clock and saw that it was twenty one minutes slow. There would be a revolution now, with the hour about to strike. Several seconds late, the whirring commenced, the sonorous chimes shaking the mausoleum and stirring weary bodies to life so that they shifted over onto the non-aching elbow. Balchard saw the establishment as an exclusive bastion of the nation's rulers, its vastness of proportion, along with the Odyssean wanderings of far flung rooms, reflecting the dominant and nomadic nature of society's privileged male. With such extravagance in baroque marble and oak, with sufficient timber to fend off a second Spanish Armada, it was a great pity that dining guests were afforded such meagre portions of victuals on their seemingly over-large Worcester plates. Indeed, Balchard concluded, were the venison to be sliced any thinner, it would serve admirably as book-markers. The wine, however, was commendable.

Pausing for another sip at his Hennessy cognac, Pilkington-Greeves raked in the last cards of that rubber, before totting up the points. 'Really, Adam,' he said in mock horror, 'this won't do. We're lagging behind terribly. You're really going to have to pull your weight in the next lot, otherwise these two ruffians will have me over a barrel for paying for dinner.' He laughed with the other two 'faceless' members, their stony smiles etched in facsimile of the gargoyles staring out from larger stones throughout the city. Theirs was a trust to respect, solid and silent, like the legions of fluted Corinthian columns of veined marble standing on guard all around throughout the premises.

'I think, perhaps, you need another drink,' said Pilkington-Greeves, looking at Balchard's empty glass. He beckoned a white-gloved servant to replenish the glass, in spite of Balchard declining the offer. Inhaling heavily on his thick cigar, Pilkington-Greeves examined his new cards. He looked over them, across at Balchard. 'This doesn't seem to be your game, Adam. But then one rather gathers that you win your tricks from much further afield. I must confess that I find all that gallivanting around a little too much for my stamina. Enough is enough, I say, for one lifetime. One needs an extra life and a half to endure anything beyond all that bash and swipe we take on the fields at Eton.'

'To each his own,' said Balchard quietly, his eyes held down on his cards.

'Quite,' returned Pilkington-Greeves, inhaling slowly on the cigar, whilst studying his enigmatic partner across the table. A decent Establishment man, settled comfortably in his married life and most notably in his profession, Pilkington-Greeves was not averse to giving a helping hand to another decent fellow; but he was not keen to push a lame horse, lest he should increase the burden on that afflicted leg. Admittedly, he was really pleased with the unusual case that Balchard had brought in, with its most peculiar background of circumstances. However, it also occurred to him that Balchard was *personally* disturbed, beyond the interest of purely scientific study, by the acuteness of the patient's condition of narcotic poisoning. 'That was a most interesting case you brought to my attention the other day. When was it, again? Anyway, you know the one. The young Harlech fellow. A critical borderline balance, alas. Where was it that you found him, again?'

'His father hails from the southern counties; landowner, I believe,' replied Balchard, with covert succinctness. He knew that Pilkington-Greeves was referring to the more recent location at the Docks. But the very mentioning of such a squalid vicinity could well have inflicted acute cardiac arrest on the other two gentlemen at the table. Anxious not to betray his full degree of feelings on the next subject, Balchard put it forward cautiously. 'Upon mention of that case, perhaps you would care to comment on the prognosis.' Pilkington-Greeves' forecast on the patient's chance of recovery was a pessimistic one. As the details ensued, Balchard felt as if it was he, himself, who was being discussed, and that the other three were seeing him seated there, bereft of his clothes. Balchard's dejected spirit affected his playing such that the game ended with he and Pilkington-Greeves losing by a miserable trailing of points. Taking his leave of the austere establishment, Balchard was confronted by a bearded 'stranger'. It was Sir Basil Effram in close tete-a-tete discussion with an Eastern gentleman. Both Balchard and Sir Basil were too absorbed in their separate problems for one to show recognition of the other. At least that was the excuse that they both attributed to the mutual non-acknowledgement.

Thus it was for many days after. Balchard's morose spirits

dogged his steps like a black spectre, weighing him down like divers' boots. He was a mere shadow of himself, his work deteriorating badly. The troubled mind gave very little account of itself to those round about it, and then, only like a snarling dog disturbed as it ate. Like the canine afflicted with rabies shunning water, Balchard shunned human company. Even Felsham saw the sense in keeping verbal communication to a minimum, letting Balchard get on with his work in silent seclusion. One important sound caused by Balchard was the agonised scream of a fleeing thief crushed in his flight between two heavily laden barges. Balchard heard no further, perhaps cared little, of whether or not the unfortunate wretch's body was recovered from the river. He was too sunken in his own murky waters. It was whilst in deep introspection, in the midst of throaty traders' calls, in Smithfield Market, where he was once again accumulating forensic evidence for Scotland Yard, that Balchard felt a heavy hand fall upon his shoulder.

Dryson's stern face, with its sudden appearance, did little to lighten Balchard's downcast mood. 'You'll not have heard the latest on that head-case, Harlech, that we brought in, Balchard. He tried to kill himself twice today, no less! First he tries to escape from the hospital and nearly gets run over by a municipal water wagon. Still not satisfied, he next tries to hang himself with hospital sheets. Get that! Talk about being ungrateful! What's the whole place coming to, that's what I'd like to know? Can you answer me *that*, Balchard?' Balchard could not. But he was not blind to the game Dryson was playing. He could see that all the while that Dryson looked him over, his serious expression belied an inner smile of triumph of sorts. For that surely was how the policeman was seeing him; he was comparing him with the disturbed Harlech, and finding a near match. An individual of mental instability, a person of miscast character, a social leper? Any of these, perhaps. And was Dryson really that far wrong? *That* question troubled Balchard.

It was not long thereafter that the young Stolling came across a similarly tormented Balchard in the pathology laboratory. He was astonished. There before his eyes was Balchard, unaware that he was being observed, battering the back of his hand upon the bench with an iron tripod, so that blood welled up out of the wound. It was his new-found experimental way of using physical pain to distract him from his inner craving for the evil drug. He jerked, none too discreetly, at the sight of Stolling watching him.

'*Good Lord*, Balchard, what *are* you doing there?'

'A comparative study of the effect of force on living and dead cutaneous tissue,' lied Balchard sarcastically, and not too concerned with manners, now that he had been caught in the act.

'That's stretching it a bit far, don't you think? Here, let me see it.' Stolling took the bloody hand and held it to the light, in spite of Balchard's effort to pull it away. He tut-tutted with professional aplomb over the patient. 'We'd better get this seen to, before infection sets in. Especially in a place like this.' He glanced round fearfully at the forest of test-tubes with their hideous contents, glad that he worked mainly in the wards, where he dealt with normal 'good, clean' illnesses. 'Hold on a second, and I'll get some tincture and bandages.

You don't want the Old Man to see you like this, do you, old boy?'

'It's all right, Dr Stolling, I'll tend to it. You can run along,' said a voice from the doorway, behind them. It was Dr Michaels. Like Stolling, he had come to investigate the cause of the beating sounds. Unlike Stolling, he had held a dreading suspicion that it would be something as unorthodox as this, having seen recurrent signs of it over the last few weeks. Stolling was not familiar with the daily routine of the laboratory. So everything had seemed in order, among the clutter of apparatus on the benches, as far as his inexpert eye could be expected to tell. But for Michaels, working intermittently as he did in the laboratory, there was saddening significance of little points that stood out like cardinal sins against the precision of a properly run laboratory. Such little items as too many spots of spilt chemicals; too many spent matches around the Bunsen; the Bunsen sitting flamingly too close to inflammable substances; more than the usual quota of broken test-tubes; the waste of wooden spatulae, crumpled up in seemingly invisible wrath, and all the other telling signs of a mind losing its control. There was also Balchard, *himself.*

Michaels waited for Dr Stolling to disappear out the door, before turning to look into Balchard's haggard face. Torment certainly lurked there, not too far from the surface. Being a trusted colleague at such times as this could prove to be most difficult when, after all considerations, one should have acted otherwise for the ultimate good of the patient. It was as unfortunate as it was unavoidable that his own industrial survey research was frequently taking him away from the hospital and out of the city, to Manchester and other northern localities. Otherwise, he may have seen the critical signs sooner, and been of more help here, where it was needed. Did Adam not realise that he needed help? Or did he shiver at the thought of help from another? He made a long sigh at Balchard's wounded hand. 'Stolling is right, you know -- open cuts like this are not good policy in a place with high risk of infection like this. But then you hardly need me to tell *you that*.' He gave Balchard a reproachful look. Fetching tincture of iodine and bandages from the cupboard, Michaels applied them to Balchard's hand in silence. The brilliant whiteness and orderly neatness of the binding strips made everything else stand out all the more in bizarre disorder. Michaels looked round about at the mess, blowing out in playful exasperation and trying, without success, to understand it all. 'I think that you'd be better running off along home, Adam. It's all right, I'll tidy up here.'

'Incidentally,' Michaels called out as Balchard opened the door to go, 'I looked at your figures for *'differential capillary absorption of organic solvent mixtures'* --if that's what you're calling them. A bit long-winded. I'd call it chromatography, myself, but that's up to you -- it's *your* experiment. Anyway, they're not quite satisfactory, in my opinion, I'm afraid. There's not enough there to constitute solid scientific argument for what I think you're trying to prove. I can see what you're getting at, but I'd strongly suggest that you carry out the analysis afresh -- perhaps from a different approach. Provided you get a good night's rest, I don't see you having any difficulty in repeating the experiment tomorrow. *Right?*'

'Right,' murmured Balchard, with a special effort to push down his inner repugnance at this humiliating reprieve. The door closed quietly behind Balchard. But his footsteps beyond it rang out with a pounding resolve that worried Dr Michaels. What way was that resolve heading, he wondered, and for how long? Balchard had a great need to release his inner volcanic build up of fury, but he felt that he could not do this in Dr Michaels' presence. The singular sound of Dr Michaels' club-foot clumping behind the closed door was that unique control valve. This caused Balchard considerable anguish. He had to get out of this building before he exploded.

As Balchard trudged wearily back to his rooms in Montague Street, the monotonous downpour of rain did nothing to elevate his morbid spirit. Even once in the shelter of his rooms, he could not escape from the dullness of the grey deluge outside. Unable to apply his mental resources to any gainful task of the work strewn forlornly about the room, urgently needing to be done, he stood at the window, staring out solemnly. His mind was solidly united with the rain, united with its unfailing determination to bombard all that lay before it with its cruel coldness. Showing no mercy; no mercy to anything, or anyone. Rivulets ran down the panes, twisting all the while, changing their routes, changing their destiny. The street, as he looked down into it, seemed to answer his curiosity with a silver spectral glow, reflected off the wet stone. No one was about, everyone swept indoors, off the street, by hostile sheets slanting down from the sky. Correction, a dark form skulked about the railings two doors down, across the road. The prowling figure looked up, to meet Balchard's eyes. They were as of two minds alike, in their furtive stealth. The cat disappeared back down the basement stairs. Depression had glowered down on the city all day long, earlier with a choking blanket of fog, and now with icy rain granting no quarter. Street-lamp flames flickered feebly through the watery mesh, in futile effort to lessen the drabness. That other great deluge of biblical times may have sufficed in purging mankind's wrong-doings, but this great splash-down would not be enough for that -- not in this city, anyway. Balchard felt drained of energy. He turned round, and with weighty strides surprisingly noisy for his size, crossed over to the fireplace.

He sat in silence, staring into the gaunt recess with its cold ashes, their energy also exhausted. They were grey now, but had started out black. And in reverse? From light to dark? Was it as simple as that? As simple as black and white? And if so, what was causing the changing, not only in one direction, but in its to-and-fro oscillation in his brain? The fog may have gone from the streets outside, but in his mind it persisted still, swirling around and around at his rational attempts to claw at it for clearance and explanation. As he pondered over this, the haunting strains of a violin coming from across the landing came to ear. Following the lamenting notes, his mind reached out, winding down the darkest alleys of the city with their happenings, and the darker recesses of his mind. As the privileged gentry might partake of 'slumming' these lowly regions of the city, so did Balchard travel through the twisted passages of his ever increasingly sick mind.

CHAPTER 17

It was well into the dark hours of one wet and blustery evening in October that the Reverend Nathaniel Blintook came to call on the professional service of A Balchard, forensic analyst. Despite the wind's fierce rattling of the window, and a spirited rendering of Wagner's *Die Walkure* on the violin from across the landing, Balchard still caught the note of urgency in the small, but sharp, door-knock. He noted a concealing of the knock's importance, by its softness. That was a disavowal of the person in uncertainty. In its being placed in diffident secrecy on a low part of the door. *How much of that was applicable to his very own self, he wondered*? Balchard waited for a tall nervous person to enter. Indeed, the man was very tall and thin, like a lamp-standard, in fact. He was also 'light' on top, by virtue of a receding hairline, so that with long flowing sideburns he had an image that was reminiscent of the Bard, Shakespeare.

'Blintook?' said Balchard, as they sat down by the roaring fire. 'That has a Dutch root, I suspect. Do I surmise correctly?'

'My great grand papa came originally from Apeldoorn, in Holland, to this country in 1827. His was a family of many generations of cheese curers. Splendid people, really splendid people.'

'I'm sure,' said Balchard impatiently, waiting for the man to settle down from his bubbling banter of uneasiness. Such snippets of trivial information were hardly the real reason for the Reverend's pressing presence. The man did not appear to be of a generally nervous constitution, but only so for this occasion. Perhaps the man's nervous state was contagious, for it was testing Balchard's patience, just short of his violently ejecting the stupid clergyman through his front door. Balchard looked away, fidgeting deliberately with a pair of callipers, in order to allay the clergyman's difficulty in finding his opening line to the real issue. Blintook noticed the other's apparent nervous fidgeting, so that for a moment he was having second thoughts on the wisdom of his coming here, to seek this gentleman's help. But he put this down to illusion, on the part of his own nerves. After all, the good people at Scotland Yard had redirected him here. To the person they said could render him a service that they themselves could not provide. He didn't notice the wild aggression lurking about Balchard's haggard eye-hollows, or the hostility spiking in the eyes themselves.

Clasping his lengthy thin shins just below the large knee nodules, Blintook leaned forward, like an oversized grasshopper. 'You really must think it silly of me to impose myself upon you by crossing your threshold on a night like this, Mr Balchard.'

'Not at all, Reverend. One learns to see the reasons for stepping abroad on nights such as this as being most crucial in their timing. Besides, if everyone who crossed that threshold was decreed silly on sole account of that act, then it would surely follow that *I, myself*, would be the most silly.'

'Oh, no, Mr Balchard, I didn't mean to imply that ---'

They both laughed at the deliberate joke, one with more acid than the other, giving Balchard the opportunity to observe the other's release of nervous tension by the lightness of topic. But in spite of this informality, the Reverend Blintook still fidgeted with his hat, turning it round and round by its brim. Balchard saw before him a sporting man of sorts, from the very way that the clothes, especially the bright coloured muffler, hung about the long-boned frame, to the large rounded fists and the bent nose. It was worth another stab at starting the conversation. 'I would have chanced to be a pugilist Blue, myself, save that nature, alas, decreed a critical shortness of limb. And *yourself*, Reverend?'

'How interesting. It just so happens that I give instructions on that art to some of my younger parishioners. I'm a rowing man, myself; Trinity, '78. Did a spot of rowing until I broke my nose. Got hit by an over-excited oar. Left quite a mark, wouldn't you say? Now I give lessons in the noble art to the little scamps in my modest little parish. It gives them, and me, something to do. I'm going to die.'

Balchard's eyebrows twitched at the bluntness of the last remark. He stopped spinning the callipers. 'I see,' he said impassively, a smile nicking the corner of his mouth, at the Reverend's comically nervous manner of uttering the vital words only at the last moment, against a background camouflage of trivial chatter. What the alienist doctor would perhaps classify as 'defensive inhibition', from the futile attempt to delay a morbid truth. *And what was he, himself, hiding from? That thought had him looking into his own mind's mirror, to see whatever dark image cowered back there from scrutiny.* Averting *that* truth, by promptly dismissing the effort, Balchard returned his attention to Blintook. 'You put it most succinctly.' Shifting back slightly, he leaned his head to one side, to take in the 'new angle' of the man before him. 'Presumably, Reverend, this forecast of your imminent demise, with which you are so acutely concerned, is one of an unnatural character, and not that of the 'final calling', of which you, yourself in your vocational capacity would otherwise warn us in your Sunday Lesson, from your pulpit?'

The man shifted with unease. 'It's difficult to explain, really.'

'I am forever your faithful listener.' Balchard's lies matched the tightness of his clenched fingers, as he fought down the anger of his impatience over a long wait. Just how long did he have to endure this pathetic churchman's equally pathetic spiritual nonsense? As a fanciful distraction of thought, he reckoned that the two points of the callipers could have pinioned the clergyman's eyes neatly through the pupils.

A small rill of sweat ran down Blintook's temple. He wrestled with his inner self for a moment, finally winning, to wrench out that which troubled him. 'I've had an apparition.'

'Perhaps we could be a little more *bountiful* with details, Reverend.' But the Reverend had not lost his hesitance completely, so prompting Balchard to get up and cross over to the cupboard from which he took out a colourful tin commemoratively stamped with royal heads. 'A kindly muffin or two, with a glass of sherry, should serve to warm the innards, and give one substance.' He knelt down, impaling the muffins on a four-pronged fork, holding them to the orange flames leaping up the chimney. Rising at last, Balchard put the muffins on the table and poured out the sherry. 'Butter, or honey, Reverend?'

'Oh, yes please, thank you.' The man was clearly too preoccupied to give definite choice.

'And now, Reverend, if you could find it in yourself to continue.'

'Of course.' Blintook took a sip of sherry, and after that, a long deep breath. 'The parish of St Ogdburg's, where I am pastor, is an ancient one reaching down through the centuries, the church's stones being worn smooth before some of this city's newer pieces were even hewn from the quarry. As one can well imagine, superstitious tales can arise and grow in great abundance over such a long span, passing by lip from generation to generation of the illiterate, so that there can be some difficulty in stamping out such silly pagan nonsense.' The man, much abstracted, clasped his knees tightly in nervous plight. 'God knows, I try earnestly to redirect them from their misguided paths. I really do try.'

'Possibly one has to reassure one's *own* self against straying from the righteous path?'

But the Reverend was now unheeding to all else but his own mind as he went on. 'It has been said that upon certain sinful acts of desecration in our flock, the Lord's wrath is such that it manifests in His sending down an angel to take away a member of the flock, not necessarily the sinner, as a measure of retribution. Sometimes it is more than one person. But first they are warned by a foresight of their departure. Some say that it is the Devil, and not God, who sends out the Angel of Death.' The man's distant look came back to Balchard, the eyes losing their glazed appearance that had held them, as the words had held the mind.

'And you, Reverend? You, yourself, of course, find no substance in these *silly* superstitions?'

'Of course not. That is to say ---' The man faltered. 'At least I didn't until two days ago.'

Balchard leaned forward, his elbows on his knees, to catch the final vital points, only to be disappointed as the man stopped yet again. Further prompting was needed to stir him from his far away state. 'We have so far not come upon the part of the tale so pertaining to your own personal involvement, Reverend.'

The words seemed to have their effect in recovering Blintook's lost attention. 'It was two nights ago that I saw my very own self in my own study.' The eyes left Balchard, focusing again on that distant inner image, the head nodding in self conviction. 'Yes, I *did* see myself, as surely as I see you now.'

'And there was no-one else there as witness to this most remarkable --- *apparition*?'

'No-one, Mr Balchard. I was entering my study, whereupon I had a vision of myself, first facing and greeting me, then turning to depart, and bidding me farewell thereafter in the distance.'

'Ah, one moment, if I may.

'Yes?'

'You say, *in the distance*, and yet your *vision* was there before you in the study. How did you infer that it was distant? Was there a tree or something beside it to signify that it *was* so? A *burning bush*, perhaps?' Balchard could not resist the humorous note, deriving some pleasure at seeing the disappointment flicker across Blintook's face at the thought of not being believed.

'It was *smaller*, finally receding into the distance to gradually disappear.'

'I see.' Balchard sat back again, a light of serious concern coming into his eyes. 'Please do continue.'

'As if matters weren't difficult enough, there has since been the disappearance of my verger to contend with. Gone completely without a trace. And yet the peculiar thing is ---'

'Yes?'

'He left his boots behind!'

'In your study, that same evening?'

'Yes.'

'Is there any other means of entering or leaving that study, other than by the door by which you entered?'

'None, except the windows, and these were securely locked from the inside.'

'You will forgive my putting the necessary question to you, Reverend, but is there the remotest possibility that you were *slightly* inebriated ---that first glass of communion wine extending into a second one ---*et cetera*?'

'As a man of God, Mr Balchard, I implore you to believe me when I say that I was of sound mind that evening.'

'Of *that* point, you have convinced me, Reverend.' Balchard tapped his fingers on his lips. 'And there are no items missing, along with your verger? No diamond-studded crucifixes, or chalices, for instance?'

'Good gracious, Mr Balchard! You're not suggesting that my own trusted verger ---'

'One must be systematically thorough to the minutest detail in such investigative matters.'

'Of course, Mr Balchard. I see your point. You are quite correct. But Mr Goodfellow, my verger, has not gone off with the church's silver. That is the truth.'

'Do we ever really *know* the *truth*, Reverend?'

'Surely, Mr Balchard, the truth is ---' Blintook stopped, to lapse back into his vacant-faced inner conflict.

'And so we have it,' said Balchard, with a finality that declared the consultation to be virtually ended, slapping his hands down on the chair's arm-rests in readiness of rising. He paused on the final point pricking his mind. 'So why are we here, Reverend?'

'Sir?'

'Your problems seem to be of the *spiritual*, and yet you consult the auspices of the s*ecular* for aid. I am only a scientist of this world. Should you not, therefore, be seeking help among your own people? If there is trepidation in approaching your bishop, is there not a more immediate brother of the cloth from whom you can draw confidence?'

Having shared his problem with another person, if only for the moment, seemed to have restored Blintook's sporting strength of character, the cheer returning to his face. He smiled compassionately at Balchard's ignorance of the circumstances. 'You do not know the predicament of loneliness of my ministry, Mr Balchard. Be it spiritual or secular, either way, I fear that my final act would be one of departure from my parish, if I were to toll my troubles aloud like a requiem bell to fellow churchmen. How can a shepherd be allowed, by fellow shepherds, to guide his flock from wanderings if he, himself, is seen to be astray?' With a coy grin, he symbolically hanged himself with a tightening tug at the muffler round his neck, and then joined his hands in mime of angelic departure.

Balchard surprised himself by warming to the man for the openness of his naive sincerity. It was a quality he had not foreseen in the cleric on his arrival. But for the intriguing oddity of the Reverend's tale, Balchard would have found only impatience and contempt for him as a dithering priest whose spiritual 'cloth' would have seen better purpose adorning a scarecrow. Balchard was drawn into closeness with the Reverend, in that he was also out on a limb from his fellow holy brethren. Somewhat like himself and his lot, back at the Institute. There was possibly a hitherto unseen tightrope connection between the high-wire balancing of isolated pastors and that of solitary forensic analysts. 'Never fear, Reverend. We shall tread lightly, that only the lithest of spirits thereof shall know of our passing in the night.'

Pulling on his coat and hat, Balchard held out an arm towards the door to signify that he and Blintook should be on their way. 'Let us seek the sanctuary of your church, Reverend.'

Blintook was a little surprised. 'I really hadn't intended

that you should trouble yourself on my account by going out at this late hour on a night like this.' He looked round at the rattling window that held back the rage of the black night outside. Sure enough, with the wind howling like a demented banshee, and the dimmed gas jets on the landing flickering in the draught, as in the Gothic novel, there was much to discourage the faint-hearted from venturing abroad that night.

'To see the beast firstly at its most demonic, is to see it thereafter at its most meek,' said Balchard, locking his door behind them. *Must he, therefore, face this totally alien feeling of madness in the fullness of its suffocating grip, before he was permitted to comprehend its meaning and reason? And would that deep-down troll inside his skull be removed of its claws when brought out from its 'mountain', into the daylight of his full understanding?* Revulsion suddenly stirred Balchard's inside. The unsettling message of how little he understood, or was in control, screeched like swirling harpies in his head. With the sickness welling up inside him, Balchard swung round to make, what seemed to Blintook, to be a frenzied attack on the keyhole with his key. Puzzled, Blintook watched Balchard rush back into his unlit rooms. The mutterings coming out from the black void were inaudible, but by their vented energy, some were most likely blasphemous, Blintook reckoned. As Balchard injected the cocaine into his arm, he feared that it would not be enough to ward off another oncoming attack of a black mood. It was as if he was possessed by a chilling fear of going in and out of black tunnels. It was of no reassurance to know that he would come out of the 'tunnel' into the daylight again -- that his dark mood eventually passed away. The horror of the experience in the black mood blocked out all else. Whenever sick moods had taken him over as a child, he had always found secure refuge in his mama. The alternative would have been his having to face up to his pater's belt lashings. His pater would have it that he faced up to things, rather than hide. So why was he reverting back to that distant thought? Now there was no maternal comfort to fall back on, and the alternative was something more fearful than leather and buckle. But *what* was it?

While he waited on Balchard, Blintook's attention was caught by a noise downstairs. He stared down into the hall. A hunched figure bumped and hobbled up the stairs, like a deformed Harlequin in chequered tunic. Sam Loofer swung his heavy sack from his back, planting it with a heavy thud on the landing, at Balchard's door. He took the smaller bags out of the larger bag, putting them, one by one, onto the floor. A ghostly apparition of Balchard, ashen-faced, materialised in the black opening. The silent reappearance of Balchard in the doorway seemed to have disturbed Blintook's nerves, as if it reminded him of some other unsettling 'appearance'.

Loofer broke the sombre spell. 'There y'are, Mr B, a little bit of England in each one, just like yer asks me.' Taking off his hat, he had to scratch his head in wonder. 'But I can't for the likes o' me reckon what yer wants it for, I can't. Still, that'll cost yer a tanner. Yer'll be wantin' these in your rooms, then, right? 'Ere, lemme do it for yer.'

Balchard swore in annoyance at having this interruption to his immediate plans. He directed Loofer to put the soil samples on the floor, beside his desk. There was no room on the desk itself, with all the folders already piled upon it. Loofer's haste caused some spillage of the earth onto Mrs Wallamsby's precious carpet. Scraping the earth with his toe, Balchard only succeeded in making a greater mess on the carpet. He swore louder, paying Loofer his due. Loofer touched his hat, looking at the Reverend Blintook and then at Balchard in turn, a mischievous gleam touching his eye. 'So what's this, then, Padre, someone gone an' pinched your bell? Don't you worry, Mr B 'ere'll put yer right, 'ave no fear.' He followed them down the stairs to catch Blintook's arm. ' 'Ere, Vicar, how d'yer like a nice brass 'andle for yer chapel doors?' He took a brass handle, with some fragments of wood still screwed to it, out of his pocket. 'Nice one ennit. Worth five bob easy, but it's yours for a shillin'. Go on, take it. That's a bargain, that is.'

'I don't know that I quite need a handle at the moment, thank you,' said Blintook shyly, put off by the broadside onslaught of Sam Loofer salesmanship.

'Course yer needs it. 'Ow can a good minister like yerself, Vicar, not need a good brass 'andle like this? All right, Vicar, just ter shows yer I ain't mean, yer can 'ave it for thruppence, an' that's a bargain, no kiddin', short o' 'avin' me parrot's wooden leg thrown in wiv it. I ain't mean, y'know. 'Ell, I knows a geezer --Charlie is 'is name -- 'e's so mean, I swears that 'e's got rubber pockets for stealin' soup from the Sally Anne kitchens!'

'Sally Anne?' Blintook was confused.

'I rather fancy that our Mr Loofer refers to a cousin of

your cloth, the newly aspired Salvation Army,' said Balchard, guiding Blintook away from the loquacious Loofer, so that they could proceed on their mission.

Loofer was not one to be put off without a good haggle, stepping in front of Blintook, and polishing the brass with a spit and a rub on the cuff. 'See that shine there, that's as good as a wink from God's right eye, that is.'

'Oh, I don't really think it is wise for us to mock the Almighty,' said Blintook, upset enough already with his own stretching of Divine tolerance.

'Perhaps *another time, another place*,' said Balchard, intervening to give Loofer a menacing look of dismissal. His words carried an icy menace that was matched by the malice in his eyes cutting through like broken glass. Blintook noted the change in Balchard's mood, contrasting sharply with his earlier bonhomme. Feeling a somewhat leadened atmosphere descended upon them now, Blintook was nervous at the thought of him possibly being responsible for it. He was anxious to know what had caused the hardness that had come over Balchard. He searched his mind to see what he could have said to upset Balchard like this. Putting the question to Balchard, he received only the muted response of a testy shake of the head. This, in place of muzzled anger held behind a tightly closed mouth.

Blintook also noted what seemed to be a drainage of strength in Balchard. A faint sleepiness seemed to have come over him, especially on his sullen grey face. It was just possible that he had inadvertently upset Balchard by making him go out on a night like this. He saw how it could possibly cause even more rancour if he suggested cancelling their trip, after their having set out at this late hour. He considered it to be the better policy to pursue his suspicions on the issue no further for the moment. Perhaps he could return to the subject when they got to St Ogdburg's. That, and possibly whatever other personal problems Balchard was burdened with. He certainly did appear to be carrying his share of those. They could discuss all that in the settled peace of the rectory. This thought brought a touch of uneasiness to Blintook.

'Right y'are, Mr B. G'night, Reverend. An' like I says, Mr B there'll take care o' yer, good an' proper, 'e will.' Wishing that Balchard could perhaps break his neck on his way to wherever it was they were going, Loofer watched them go off into the screaming night.

CHAPTER 18

The flame from Balchard's Lucifer match fought fiercely with the wind to light the end of his cigar, and for a few seconds succeeded only in throwing his and Blintook's shadows about the brougham's interior, as the carriage headed off at a trot, out of the city centre. Blintook leaned out of his window so that the night's invisible turbulence seized up his muffler, to throw it back in a cautionary gesture. He moved back a little, pulling in the muffler. 'It's a terribly rough night,' he said with a tone that suggested a foreboding of something more than the elements. But the wind had already snatched his words away too quickly for them to be heard by Balchard. Blintook repeated his remark and Balchard muttered something about fresh air, between long nervous draws on his cigar. 'That would appear to be about the only thing that hasn't been fouled by some means or other, in the community,' said Blintook, watching the city crack up, with side streets opening back onto slum rookeries. There was a vague nod from Balchard, that did not really confirm if he had agreed or not.

Blintook settled back into his corner, snuggling more deeply into his seat, and clapping his arms despite the air being too chilling for this action to dispel his shiverings. He smiled for a second when he saw Balchard pulling his own collar in tighter. But the smile was dispelled and replaced by a frown, when he noticed the sweat running down Balchard's brow. Balchard was experiencing a chilling shudder running through his inside, and that had nothing to do with the cold night air around them. The two faces were continually slapped by the street lights, on and off, as they looked out at the shifting buildings steadily losing their grip on the carriage. The crumbling continued until at last the city disintegrated into a random scattering of houses. The horse seemingly took advantage of this to step up its pace, giving free movement all round as the carriage cast off its shackle and headed for the country. Wheels turned faster, so that the town decreased to a roadside colony that held on as long as it could, before being snatched away with contemptuous snuffle, as they broke clear of it, into the open countryside. Mischievous country air attached itself in a siffling joyride to the new night traveller, the current streaming round the carriage to freeze their faces, ruffling the driver's hair, but not affecting his tobacco-chewing concentration.

With nothing more outside to hold his attention, Blintook fixed his gaze on the red glow from his companion's cigar. Balchard, steeped in thought, focused his mind on the distant star that peeped out from behind the ragged clouds racing across the silvered sky in great rips of Wagnerian fury, to the screaming horn and violin crescendos in his head. Conversation was limp, the topics being of no relevance to the current concern, and so dying off soon after their utterance.

This was so for the entire journey but for one instance when, as if the star had dimmed in lustre, Balchard suddenly pulled his cigar out to turn to Blintook. 'Your verger, he is small?'

'Yes, as a matter of fact, he is. Is it important?'

But Balchard gave no answer, only looking back again at the bright point beckoning from the other side of the universe. The very remoteness of that pin-prick star was serving as a point of refuge on which to hang his attention, in faraway distraction from that tormented part of the universe inside his own head. Blintook's announcement that they would soon be there had Balchard casting his cigar out the window, so that the red cinder flew backwards, to disappear where the road had also folded up magically. As the way twisted and straightened ahead, earth shifted aside and lights sprang up, approaching quickly to give rise to a tiny hamlet preceding the village. With the spread of cottages increasing, a twinkling effect arose from the spotted lights competing with black bulks moving across their paths. Trees were there and gone in moonlit flashes, the great growths masquerading behind ghoulish nocturnal habits giving easy panic to the faint-hearted. Something that was too large to be nurtured by soil was moving up out of the distance, but it was hard to see what it was with the road twisting around at violent angles. The road straightened out and the village was there, ahead of them, almost within reach. A final devilish contortion of branches leapt up round a crooked trunk and then dropped away to leave the way open for them.

The biting slipstream became a soft breeze as the brougham slowed its pace to enter the village quietly. Rough grimy stone took over from wrinkled bark in protecting indrawn life, as they passed along the narrow street. Lights from the windows all around had a warming effect, after the cold journey across open country. A dozing communal spirit emanated from the cottages, multiplying itself where the street opened out into a tiny square. Over and beyond this space, ultimate grimness tapered off into the Divine infinity.

Balchard leaned out to look up.

The black mass stood imperiously over them in its timeless watch. An awesome ferocity of flying buttresses and narrow stone piping ascending to a terminal profusion of barbed pinnacles and Gothic arches wrestling with the sky. The towering steeple needed no lighting, unlike the lesser cottages around it, being as structurally and dogmatically firm in darkness as it was in daylight. The overbearing presence was sufficient testimonial of its Godly formation.

A lonesome peal reaffirmed the holy allegiance. 'Simon, my bell ringer,' said Blintook to Balchard, who did not seem to think that this piece of information was of any vital importance.

The lonely tolls drifted across the cobble-stoned square as the brougham crossed it, while dark figures entered from the shadows beyond it. Dark piety trickled past in white collars and stiff clothes as ill-fitting as the erect backs. The service almost over, souls were safe for another week, so that dark gold-tipped prayer books could be replaced with beer that was also dark and tipped with gold. This was how Balchard's mind, with its disbelieving scorn, interpreted the scene. But the village was most particular about its visitors, so that as the carriage passed through them, curious eyes stared up at it to see who the stranger was seated with their pastor. Privacy was strictly guarded here, and anything upsetting its indolent pulse was apt to be met with some degree of hostility, verbal or otherwise. The people ebbed away, while the true flock within the church rent the air with a final burst of its evensong chorus. But the noise no more did pull the walls asunder than the bell had done, lolling out its unchanging message through the centuries, from somewhere amidst the cold mountain of reverence.

Balchard's eyes searched the broad stone face for an opening. They turned off sharply, into a lane, to be swallowed up through the opening beneath a lychgate in a lichen-velveted wall, the driver's haste almost slicing off the carriage's side lantern. Circling round to the rear of the huge building, the carriage stopped with a jolt outside the comparatively tiny rectory that huddled close to suckle from the mother. The reason for so large a basilica in so remote an area escaped Balchard just a little more than he was able to envisage the original temple of pagan worship that had stood before it, near to the site. After introducing his aging housekeeper, Blintook insisted that, following their bone-chilling journey, the next immediate course of action, before embarking upon matters of a more serious nature, would be to partake of some body-warming beverage. The old lady soon afterward brought them two earthenware mugs steaming with brandy toddies. As she leaned down to give Balchard his mug, an innate mothering instinct saw persecution and pain torn across the young man's face. 'You look unwell, sir.'

'I'm all right.' Balchard was openly irritated by the woman's close attention.

'It's no wonder you don't feel well, sir. It's terrible weather for anyone to go travelling about in. I don't for the likes o' me, know why anyone would have a mind to, I don't.' She looked round in soft reproach at the Reverend, then turned her mother-clucking attention back to Balchard. 'Now just you see and make yourself more comfortable over there, in the armchair, while I go fetch you a woollen blanket to keep you warm. No use drinking that warm toddy if you can't keep the warmth inside you. After that, I can make up your bed in the guest room.'

'Why don't you mind your own business! Go and do --- whatever it is that you do, and leave me alone, in peace!'

'Sorry, sir.' The old lady was very much offended by Balchard's harsh outburst. 'If you'll excuse me, I have to prepare the oven for tomorrow's bread. Goodnight, sir.'

Blintook was taken aback by Balchard's rude words, perplexed between apologising to his housekeeper for Balchard's rudeness, or apologising to Balchard for his housekeeper inadvertently upsetting him with her offer to help. He did neither. Instead, he sat and said nothing. Balchard leaned forward, elbows on his knees, his head drooping down to partly obscure his view of the austere surroundings, that were dragging his feelings down. He gulped the warm liquid, burning his mouth, hugging his hands round the mug, using the heat to ward off his shiverings. All the while *she* was screaming away silently in his mind, competing for his attention, against the pain pounding his brain.

Sitting there in the quiet stillness of the bleak parlour, now seemingly more bleak after the brightness of the city, Blintook felt the earlier uncertainties of his situation return. He began to have misgivings over his wisdom in hiring, as Balchard, himself, had put it, a 'scientist of this world'. This lapse of his faith in a person seated just across the room from him made him feel guilty. He felt that he should not be judging Balchard like this, considering that the man seemed so heavily laden with his own inner conflict of personal problems.

'And the other such incidents?' asked Balchard, as Blintook led him along the long narrow passage to the study.

'As far as superstitious tongues will ply the simple mind, I gather that there have been three such incidents. The first occurring round about the time of a discovery of the live practice of witchcraft in the parish, in the sixteenth century; the second one thereafter was about the time of a hideous slaying of a young milkmaid. About seventeen sixty, I believe.'

'And the third? You did say 'three', did you not?'

'Ah, yes.' Blintook's attack of the taciturn had him hesitating with a hand on the study door-handle. 'The third, it would seem, was a fellow predecessor and occupant of this very house. The Reverend Alkinsop, who, as far as old wives' tales go, was supposed to have had such a vision prior to his disappearance a week or so thereafter.'

'Never to be seen again?'

'Never to be seen again.' There was a resigned heaviness in the Reverend's reply.

'When?'

'About seventy years ago.'

'And in *his* case?'

Blintook looked blank at this question.

'And the act of desecration that bade the Almighty take His toll?' prompted Balchard. 'Some say rape, but this, as ever, has never been confirmed,' said Blintook quietly, his voice falling with his awkwardness on the subject.

'Confirmed, not in writing, but by the frivolous cackling of old hen-hag grannies,' said Balchard, amassing his material aloud, with such an emphasis on the latter case to give no small measure of discomfort to Blintook. Once again Blintook was silent and blank. 'And altogether, there are no officially written records?' said Balchard.

'If there ever have been, they have long since been removed, leaving my superiors from the synod most reluctant to discourse on such.'

'A not altogether uncommon reaction, one learns,' remarked Balchard as an aside, referring to Blintook's own attacks of temporary paralysis of the tongue. 'And now the study, if we may, Reverend.'

'Of course. Allow me.' Blintook entered first, stepping aside inside the doorway to let Balchard pass. Balchard stood still for a second or two, looking around, to take in his fill of the atmosphere. The room was of a long rectangular shape, greyish in its nondescript simplicity, with nothing remarkable or out of place to the unsuspecting eye. At one end of the room there were lattice leaded windows with staunch stone pillars in their centres. Each window appeared to be securely bolted. With only a writing bureau, bookcase, two plain wooden chairs and a small side table for furniture, the room passed as spartan. Disciplined like a monk's cell, devoid of the temptations of brighter materialistic luxury, there was much inspiration for philosophical insight. Failing that, there was peace to write the Sunday sermon.

Removing a small hand lens from his pocket, Balchard carried out a systematic examination of the floor, the walls and the furniture. Then, with an adroit swiftness that suggested that he had kept this action to the last, but not least, he whipped out a handkerchief to cover the small table, and with the Reverend's permission, mounted it, to examine the top of the bookcase. Blintook winced in fearful anticipation of the frail piece collapsing under Balchards' weight. Balchard found the dust layer to be undisturbed, so concluding that the bookcase top held no importance in the issue. He was a little disappointed since this had been where he had expected to find his trump card of a vital clue. The fact that the boots had been left behind suggested a hurried departure. That was simple. But at the same time there was the question of what it was that had caused, not so much the abandonment of the boots, but their having to be *removed* from the feet, in the first place. In mental association with his recent 'Indian' venture, Balchard had first thought of the Eastern custom of removing footwear prior to entering a holy place. Whilst not for a holy reason, one did, nevertheless, in this country remove footwear of a filthy nature before going indoors. But the boots were already in here, so one could infer that they had been removed so as not to scratch or mark something that one intended standing upon in the room. Hence Balchard's earlier question to the Reverend of whether or not the verger was small. Just as Balchard could reach the top of the bookcase only by standing on the table, so would a small verger have needed to stand on the table.

Balchard next set about inspecting the ancient volumes of Holy Scripture in the bookcase. Blintook, whose spirits were waning, especially at the useless feeling of standing idle, excused himself so as to be about his other pastoral duties in the vestry. He went off to compliment the deacon on his evensong service, leaving Balchard to his peace. Balchard went through the books carefully, one by one, finding nothing of value to the investigation, so that his hopes, like those of Blintook, began to fade. Suddenly his inside leapt.

For there, in the Book of Deuteronomy, he espied the last page being slightly out of place, with a differing shade of bleached colouring at its edges, as if it had been taken out. It *had* been removed sometime before, it seemed, and being loose, came away easily in Balchard's hand. Where the last page should have been bound to the spine, there was just perceptible a long slit that was the opening to a secret compartment between the spine and the hard outer cover of the book. With soaring spirits, Balchard prised the ancient parchment out, almost tearing the fragile sheet in his excitement. As far as time had allowed, the faded ink and widespread cracking of the brittle material made the document barely legible. One further difficulty was that the words and symbols were of a language that Balchard was none too familiar with. He sat down slowly at the bureau to study the faded sheet. Confronted by a confusing mixture of Old English of King Alfred's ninth century and a later Middle

English, along with weird Teutonic runes and illuminations the likes of which he found fascinating, as well as perplexing, Balchard rose continually to consult the more orthodox texts in the bookcase.

And yet as Balchard read on, there was the impression that the difficulty in comprehending the final message arose from the deliberate cunning of the original scribe. A simple message was being put to confusion by coded *inference*. The key to understanding lay, not with the reader's knowledge of the *code*, but with the knowledge of the *subject referred to* by the code. Balchard read on.

Some time ago, supposedly a long time ago, something terrible had happened, to endanger this very church. Something so horrific that a bishop had been despatched by urgent order of the Crown to hasten through the dark night, that he might seek out, to rout and ultimately destroy, the vile force of blackness threatening the church.

Balchard paused for a moment, reflecting on how he and Blintook had likewise hastened through the night. He returned his attention to the parchment. As the night wore on and Balchard persevered with the deciphering, he began to feel his flesh creep and his hair prickle up on his scalp.

A shattering clang made him look up in fright, at the sight of *her* father stepping in through the wall, ringing *her* funeral bell. A steady, calming voice and a clearing mind allowed him enough sense to realise that he had fallen asleep. He had been dreaming. Having slumped down over the bureau, he had knocked a silver bowl onto the floor. That had been the 'bell'. The 'father' figure approaching him was

Blintook, come to investigate the noise. Blintook's loaded curiosity turned to dismay at the sight of the expression on Balchard's face. Balchard truly appeared to be experiencing some considerable degree of fright, beads of sweat running down the forehead, into the eyebrows arched over the eyes with their dilated pupils. All the time he stared down in alarm at the document in front of him. 'Is everything all *right*?' Blintook's statement was hollow-voiced, seeing as he did, that something was dreadfully *wrong*. Fear was infectious, spreading to Blintook and gripping him inside, as Balchard failed to answer immediately, or even to hear at all.

At Blintook's stepping over to the bureau, Balchard jerked out of his stupor and rose up from his chair, making an effort to conceal his state of alarm. He waved a hand to dismiss the other's acute concern. 'It is nought that cannot lie well till the morn.' But these words had little effect in quelling Blintook's inner anxiety, seeing as he did, the fear in Balchard's eyes. He could see that Balchard was holding back on something, but despite both of them knowing this, both were fearful of mentioning it.

'Is there something that I can do to help?' asked Blintook, his eyes darting round the room in a frenzy of despair to find something to support his words and so banish his feeling of inadequacy.

'To say a prayer, perhaps, or light a candle, or anoint me with holy oil, Reverend?' Balchard's acid words cut deeply. He condescended for a moment, but his grim effort to force a smile fooled no-one, his difficulty in bringing out placatory words being overshadowed by the inner-dwelling horror.

'Thank you, Reverend, but the guest room that you have so kindly put at my disposal would seem to be the best answer. We have both contributed a colossus of will-power this one single night.'

'Of course. That is probably the best remedy, as you say. It is just along the passage, and second on the right beyond the stairs. I will show you, if you will just follow me. I bid you goodnight, then, Mr Balchard. Sleep well, and God be with you,' said Blintook stonily, in limp acceptance of the most damned befalling them. In his mind he cringed from what he had glimpsed for a second prior to Balchard snatching it up quickly to put it in his pocket in a furtive crumpling between trembling hands. It had been a piece of paper that Balchard had been scribbling and sketching on, while studying an old parchment that he had apparently found. Depicted on that paper, in shaky-handed sketchings of the most diabolical features conceivable, were demon figures all cavorting round the Prince of Darkness, Himself --- *Satan*.

CHAPTER 19

As Balchard lay back on the ottoman in the guest room, trying to marshal his thoughts, he was continually interrupted in his concentration, so that he raised his head from time to time to look around him. His earlier ruse of requesting adjournment for the night for the sake of rest, in order to conceal his inner anxiety from Blintook, was having little effect in allaying his uneasiness. A thick claustrophobic sense of evil pervaded from all around, like dense smoke emanating from a flameless fire, choking the mind but not the body. Voices gurgled and cackled in hellish mirth, not from beyond the walls, but from the very walls, *themselves*; the walls pulsed and bent inwards menacingly, as if alive, under the green satanic power glowing in the corners of the room. Balchard rose to peer closer, at which the supernatural effects died away. Pulling on his coat, he went along the passage, to let himself out by the small side door.

His weight sunk into the gravel, slowing his walk along the side of the building. The crunching beneath his feet emphasized the stillness of the night, from which all other life forms were curfewed this side of the darkness. He rounded the corner into the obscure entrance way, to be confronted by a legion of stalwart shapes clad in silver armour of moonlight splashed down their slender boles. There was a seeming rush from these, bent in readiness for combat with the nocturnal intruder, where the wind had pushed them over from time immemorial. Ignoring the martial threat of the trees, Balchard entered the wood. His mind swam fuzzily all the while, as he threaded his way with a drunken gait through the trees. His mind and body seemed to be functioning independently, the legs carrying him hither and thither with an apparent will of their own, leaving him only the choice of which trunk to try best not to bump into. Stunted growths appeared to come more and more across his stumbling path until he was able to realise that the stumps were too regular in shape to be tree trunks. He had strayed into a small burial ground. The crude stones jutted up at odd angles, like the decaying fangs of some giant beast lying dormant in the earth. The obvious extrusion of these graves, with their eternally damned souls, outside the sanctified soil of the church graveyard, was significantly sinister.

In a small clearing further amidst the trees, a silvered grass mound swelled up in a classical roll to meet the waxing moon in its silver ascent. Where countless victims had solemnly awaited the rise of the high priest's dagger to signal their mounting the summit of the natural sacrificial altar, there now stood only one. Balchard stood at the foot of the mound, feeling within himself the tremors of association between that before him and the unhallowed ground of those buried behind him. A leathery bat flapped its way past overhead, to disappear into the church belfry that was steeped in its own leafy-leadened torpor behind the lacework of branches. Balchard looked around for signs of other midnight prowlers, but the goblins and harpies did not hearken to his summons. Only the trees closed in with ominous shuffle. And yet, out there, somewhere, there was *something*.

He entered further into the wood. Much to his own surprise, he found himself turning round to check if he was being followed. And he was surprised. For the silver mound had now turned to flaming gold beneath the moon that was now a blazing sun! Startled eyes blinked at the incredible vision and a confused head turned to locate the weird wailings that sounded out all around from the trees and from nothing. When he next turned to see the mound, it had vanished completely, so that his mind now spun in total disorientation. Odd shapes and colours danced before his eyes, while an evil smell swamped his nostrils, causing suffocation. Striving forward frantically for breathing space, he was struck savagely by the trees stepping in his way. Sinking to the base of a trunk, he paused for breath, his heart pounding, until the slothful rumble of *that behind him*, *pursuing him*, caused him to rise hurriedly and hasten on. When he finally broke free from the wood's strangling hold, the mind was momentarily cleared by the bone-slicing wind. He looked around for direction, but saw that he had been forsaken. The moon had deserted him by taking refuge from the macabre behind shifting cloud.

Macabre it was, for he could not as yet give full credence or explanation to what he was seeing and experiencing, save that it was most fearsome. Strange inexplicable phenomena with no logical sustenance of theory. As much as he had been sceptical, he was now seeing and virtually believing. But what was it that was being believed? Both weird and mysterious, the 'grounds' were unfamiliar, like that under his feet. With only shades of darkness to differentiate between the sky, the ground and the wood, he groped his way onwards awkwardly, stumbling over uneven turf, so that progress was slow. The alien sensation came over him like cold sleep, only that he was awake with open eyes. He stopped and turned slowly to face, with mounting apprehension, the black face of the wood from which he had escaped. Standing there in a cold-sweated trance, he waited for *it* to emerge.

When *it* did emerge, his inside jolted with fright. For there, coming towards him in unnatural spectre of glow and slowness, the feet not touching the ground, was his *own self*!

Balchard trembled for a moment, then, snapping out of the shock, his mind fired with panic, he shifted the blocks of stone that were his feet, to turn and flee with the fullest power that his wretched mortal limbs could command. He ran on under a heavying body, his strength draining out until he was carried on by shear momentum alone. He tripped and fell once, twice, only to rise and run on doggedly. The falls became more frequent and enduring, so that he felt the jerks with increasing pain, and needed greater effort to rise again each time. His initial power gone, he sank forward onto his hands and knees. Hanging his head down, he breathed heavily and with difficulty against the stifling wind blowing in his face. One glance to the rear, at the ghostly doppelganger approaching, was enough. He heaved himself up and bounded forward under a pounding chest, his only surety being the pain in his side and the increasing nearness of that *thing* behind him.

Lurching forever onwards and onwards, he suddenly twisted violently, toppling over the top of a hill, his heart in his mouth as he plummeted through space for an eternal few seconds. His hand reached out touching something then nothing again. The sloping hill suddenly arrested his feet, the impact jerking his body forward like a matchstick, his arm buckling under him, against the hill face. He landed brutally on his front with only slightly more pain than shock, continuing to roll until something smashed into his side and then his face. A momentary footing was gained and then lost as the body slithered down the steep slope to what seemed inevitable destruction. His racing mind dropped its resignation abruptly as sharp hairy claws rushed up out of nowhere into his face. The thorns ripped past the face and through the clothing, slowing the body's downward passage. He reached out desperately for something, anything, and found a holding on a bush. But the branch bent over to slip through his grip like a rope, the thorns slicing the flesh. Another grip, another slashing, and then he felt the solid stalk in his hand. The stem did not yield and he clung on grimly with his bleeding hand, the world and its meaning ceasing to whirl through his brain as he hung there exhausted, grateful for his narrow escape. Limbs ached dully and the pulse throbbed sharply through the surface wounds.

Releasing a hand gingerly from the slender shaft, he stretched out as far as he could reach, searching about. His hopes sank as he felt no pathway, footing, or even any more bushes to grasp onto. He dug his hand into the cruel wall of earth and stone to support himself. It was a harsh hold, the distorted fingertips bearing the weight to the point of virtually tearing the nails out. Panic flooded his brain. He was slipping again and it was too awkward a distance to regain his double hold on the bush. With no clear concept of his actions, he followed the fate of his sliding body and scrambled like a crab, sideways, across the hill face. The frenzied motion carried him a fair footage, but not enough, it seemed. Vertical displacement was greater, so that he was accelerating towards an imminent free fall. Blunt fear and emergency adrenalin gave him that vital boost to haul himself unbelievably onto a ridge. Hands, feet, knees and elbows all bustled together in an overwrought commotion as he slithered down through the dark to no certain end, hugging the hill's surface like an oversized breast. Spirits rose as the hill face swelled out to a more gentle slope, so that he progressed more easily. Mastery was just his, when the hill resumed its hostility to drop down suddenly in an almost vertical gradient. The change was drastically unexpected, causing the legs to kick in empty space, levering the torso outwards, so that he overbalanced. Falling over sideways, he cascaded downwards, bumping and bouncing off the rugged surface, the hill sweeping outwards near its foot, to catch him and send his body rolling over freely like a spindle.

His body came to a gradual rest, lying face downwards, his electrifying moments still flashing through his mind. His nightmare descent over, it was a wonder that he was still alive, in one piece. The breeze was soothing, and he rolled over on his back to breathe in the air in long draughts, as it wafted over his recently aged face. As he sat up painfully, stars dashed about everywhere, most of them in his head. A rough inspection by prodding fingers revealed no bones to be broken, despite the general feeling that he had just passed through a mincing machine. With a surprising reserve of energy, he pulled himself to his feet, only to lurch brokenly over the pain in his ankle. The shoulder also throbbed out an illusionary displacement of several feet. Life had been too rapid and urgently at stake for him to have noticed these things in the whirring moments of his fierce fall.

And yet, as he had learned from his experiments at the hospital, pain could well serve as a worthy distraction agent, clearing the mind of the unwholesome; so, when he looked up at the hill's summit, there was no sign of his bizarre Angel of Death. But his peace of mind would not last forever, so the situation was still critical. Swaying round on the sore ankle, he limped off hurriedly in the direction of where he judged the village to lie, from a light he had glimpsed momentarily in his fall. With a subdued cry and a great wince, he stepped up his tottering pace.

The Reverend Blintook continued to stare at the empty place prepared for Balchard at the breakfast table. His heightening concern was marked by the heavy ticking of the mantelpiece clock, as he glanced at it from time to time, between nervous snaps at his toast. When his patience ran out and diffident knockings on his guest's bedroom door received no answer, he was forced to make an embarrassed entrance into the room. He was immediately shocked. The general disorder of furniture and sundries was like that left in the wake of some ravaging beast of the night. Thoroughly alarmed, the Reverend conducted a hasty search of the rest of the house, lest his wanton guest should have mistaken the lie of the rooms and somehow become lost. This proving to be fruitless, he carried out a frantic search of the church grounds and the church itself, all to no avail. Going through to the church's tiny side chapel, Blintook flopped down on his knees at the altar rail, before the glowing red repository lamp. He bowed his head in earnest soul-proffering covenant with the Almighty. 'Help us, Lord God, Eternal Father, especially those of us who, at this moment, may be most dearly in need.'

CHAPTER 20

When Balchard prised his eyelids apart, the first thing that came into focus was the shining steel cylinder of the syringe lying against his face on the desk. It seemed gigantic in its closeness, its needle stabbing out dangerously near to his unguarded cornea. He continued to stare at it while he lay inert, scraping his brain, like a ladle in an empty pot, in an effort to recall the happenings of the night before. A trickle of vague scenes filtered through slowly at first, then, as the floodgate burst, a great torrent of sharp images rushed forth to pierce the mind. They had been hallucinations, of course. With his body crying out for the fiendish cocaine, the mind had resorted to producing its own devils to the extent that all around reality was distorted into its own grotesque world. Also, with the supernatural element placed before him by the Reverend Blintook, it was perhaps only to be expected that his mind should run amok with ghosts and ghouls like drunken roisterers on a typical Saturday night in Piccadilly Circus.

It was rather unfortunate that Blintook had caught him in this state of agitated craving and almost out of control. But how exactly had Blintook interpreted that man shaking before him? Balchard paused to consider which of the two alternatives was the more detrimental to his professional image. Had Blintook seen a man shaking because he was afraid of silly ghosts, and therefore incapable of rational separation from such nonsense; or had he recognised the shakings as the debasement of intelligent man's dignity over the beast, by a puny, yet wretchedly commanding, few drops of narcotic? Either way, Balchard felt that he had lost, with a black stain in character, before the Reverend's eyes. He reached out for the syringe and threw it violently at the wall, feeling only then the full effect of the pain racking his muscles and limbs, especially at the joints. This was little wonder, considering the jarring that his poor frame had endured. An additional pang of remorse stabbed his chest when he saw that he had broken the syringe's needle. Such was the frailty of his penitential plight --- to concede to wrong and banish it for one moment, only to crave out for it the moment thereafter.

He leaned forward on his aching body to rest on his elbows and put his face in his hands, only to stop and look at the dried blood on his throbbing palms. There were also blood stains on his coat. He felt the burning sensation in his cheek and so recalled afresh that particular incident of rushing thorns. The cutting pain had, indeed, served to clear the mind of its twisted state, but only for a brief period. Otherwise, there had been the urgent need to return to the City to procure another injection of the bestial fluid. His folly had been to venture so far afield on an overnight case without including the cocaine in his travel bag. Vague recollections of the irate cries of the village carter, outraged at being wakened by thunderous door-bangings in the middle of the night, came back to Balchard with a small degree of acid humour. The man had not been too keen at first to take a fare up to the city at that time of night. But a handful of coins had duly subdued him, that little bit more than the blood stains had inhibited him. Balchard could not recall in accurate detail what had happened after that. But he could well imagine that his state of arrival back here in his rooms had been much in keeping with that of all the rabble of a maharajah's elephant entourage. That, needless to say, would have been much to the consternation of dear Mrs Wallamsby. This afforded him a further measure of his sadistic satisfaction.

Now that the mind was clear, Blintook's problem was solved, the pieces fitting together like a jig-saw puzzle to show that the issue was not spiritual in essence, at least not in its immediacy, but one of mechanical cunning. Balchard looked around and stretched over for paper to draft up a telegram to the Reverend Blintook. Yet again his limbs screamed out for mercy. Considering that he could well do with a bath to soothe his aches, it suddenly occurred to Balchard that, out of all his fresh recollections, he had not yet determined what day of the week it was. When it did come to him, he swore and clenched an angry fist, for it was not the day on which Mrs Wallamsby had allotted him the privilege of having a bath. Still, a swift cab to Northumberland Avenue would see him well to a rewarding Turkish bath. The Turkish issue brought to mind his appointment with Captain Smethers, and his brow furrowed into an extra crease. But one thing at a time. Continuing with the telegram, he explained to Blintook how he would return to the scene with its complete solution in due course, in the meantime having to first attend elsewhere to other matters of a more pressing nature.

Finishing the message, he rose and crossed over to a drawer to look for some clean handkerchiefs to use as makeshift bandages, after washing his hands in the basin, with a mind to obtaining proper bandages later at the hospital. Searching through the drawer's contents, his hand came upon a small cardboard box that hugged the secrecy of its being hidden away beneath everything else. His hand froze upon the touch. Forgetting everything else for the moment, he took out the box slowly and went back with it to sit down at the desk. He stared down at it solemnly for a moment before opening it. The first photograph was of his dearest mama. The other one was of *her*; young and pretty, with her teasing smile that had once fanned a flame in his chest as he had never known before, disarming him like a centurion removed of his shield. Strange, that the feeling now partly shamed him; that he had been at a loss in knowing how to reciprocate the feeling in her. What was perhaps stranger was that he should be having these thoughts now? Why? Why was he thinking this now? Had they not, after all, been together body and soul? Lest it had all at best been a charade. *Her* charade. That a man should have the geometrical precision to circumscribe himself within his own circle, but not be able to recognise its beginning or ending, and so be trapped within it; such was the despair of being without the savoire-faire of communicating such delicate emotions to the female. The very word love, made Balchard shiver from memory. He struggled to discipline himself in maintaining a rationality that elevated him above such foolish sentiments.

She still looked as lovely as she had then. But she had laughed, and that had pained him greatly. Perhaps she had not meant to hurt him so. But could he be sure now, under a calmer cloud, that she had not, in her fairest heart, meant it so. Nevertheless, he had felt it so. His control snapped. The brutal bitterness of that time flared up again inside him, and he was seized by an impulse to crush the photograph in his hand, only just stopping short of doing so. If he had not been seated, he would probably have swayed, from the light-headed sensation he was experiencing. A situation not unlike that induced by the notorious nitrous oxide, or laughing gas, in that it promoted laughter, without reducing the seriousness of the mind. Balchard was disturbed by this strange mode of thought. Almost as if it were outside himself. As if it were of another mind. *That* disturbed him above all else.

Mrs Wallamsby's sharp raps on the door had the box closed and re-hidden in the drawer before the second barrage of blows rained down on his privacy. Staggering to his feet, he snatched up a retort from a shelf to make himself look busy, before letting the woman in. The woman was truly upset by Mr Balchard. Unless his behaviour saw an immediate improvement, he would have no alternative but to leave the establishment. Whilst not wishing to upset her friend, his mama, standards were standards. And those of this establishment were being lowered by his actions. Thus, it would be better for everyone concerned if he started looking for alternative accommodation, so as to be out by Christmas.

Apart from the questionable nature of what he called his 'work' already littering the room, one could only wonder what it was that had him gadding about at such ungodly hours, much to the disturbance of the other guests, especially the female guests. And if it was not enough to debase her rooms and furniture with all those smells of chemicals, there was that mess of earth on her carpet inside his door last night. That would cost him extra this week.

It was only the sight of blood on Balchard's hands and face and coat that caused her to pause in her verbal onslaught, just managing to stifle a gasp. Wondering if she would next have to further humble the good name of her house by calling in the police, she left, slamming the door behind her to the further agony of the much fatigued hinges. But it was the woman's nerves that had suffered more strain than the hinges. Frightened of upsetting the strange Mr Balchard, and bringing out his latent fury, she had summoned all her strength to put up a brave front, to say her piece. A genuine complaint, gathered from her other guests, it had been her excuse for having him leave the establishment. Relieved as she was at the safety of Balchard's door being closed behind her, she was touched by an afterthought that stirred up regret. Or was it fear? Should she have demanded that he leave sooner -- a week, perhaps? Between now and Christmas was a long time for anything to happen. She dearly hoped that Mr Balchard would not take it the wrong way and do something unpleasant. In spite of her acquaintance with his mother, there was something very frightening deep down about that man. She almost tripped in her nervous steps down the staircase.

Stepping down into the safety of the hall, Mrs Wallamsby paused to turn and look up in reflection at the landing. She had felt quite -- yes -- alarmed -- she admitted to herself, at the sight of Mr Balchard standing there arrogantly, holding that glass bulb thing, almost as if he wished to crush it in his hand. The other hand, opening and closing, seemed to be seeking something in the empty air to strike. An overall aura of subdued violence had seemed to surround him. Without doubt, a strange man. This was the common opinion among the other lodgers, on Mr Balchard. His communication with them was zero. No-one in the house knew him, and he had plainly never wished to know them. Worst was that he had become somehow unstable of late. Whilst he had always worked fitfully, like a restless dog, keeping irregular hours with his 'doctors' work at the hospital, at least his mood had remained reasonably consistent, as it should with a gentleman. But now his temper flared and fell like that dog now gone snarling mad. Mrs Wallamsby saw his behaviour as that of someone labouring under unbearable stress. The pressure that was crushing down on him seemed mercilessly unending. His irascible manner never seemed to leave him. If she did not see him fretting, she would hear him so, as she passed outside his room. His angry pacing and curses from within. His spasmodic outbursts of anger, accompanied by the sound of paper being ripped and heavy books being cast down on the floor. On Tuesday, there had been the tinkle of broken glass; but she had found no trace of that when she later went in to dust his rooms. Perhaps oddest of all, was his growing tendency of talking to himself. Strain an ear as she would, listening at his door, on the pretence of dusting, she could not make sense of his words. It was all terribly upsetting. Perhaps she should write to Mrs Balchard?

But otherwise, Balchard could not have been more delighted by Mrs Wallamsby's ultimatum. *He* would be glad to be rid of *her*. As far as he was concerned, she was the past, as good as dead and buried. That concept had an eerie ring to it, Balchard thought, considering how it could be equally applicable to another in the past. It was as if the thought had forcibly come up on its own accord, not his, to remind him of something. That *he* was not in control. That something else *was* -- commanding its own programme of thought, and countermanding his, was something he didn't wish to concede as happening. Or to be remotely possible. He folded *The Times* at the page advertising furnished apartments to let. But before studying it in detail, he made a quick perusal of a rough work schedule lying on top of a pile of folders, where it had long lain abandoned. Contrary to his earlier intention of going out, he was now deciding to remain in his room, to do some work. More truthfully, to put a thorn in the ear of that meddling bastard of a landlady downstairs. 'And any other meddling bastards who can't mind their own business!' The words came out in an angry shout that shook the room, to frighten the walls, and any other ears that may have been hiding behind the nervous silence of the house.

Balchard worked for the best part of the afternoon in a diligent silence. Where there was the occasional explosion of his temper, with his fist striking a surface, and jars of chemicals jumping and clinking, the stairs also creaked, as Mrs

Wallamsby, feather duster in hand, listened in apprehension. Balchard's floorboards also groaned out beneath his agitated pacing of a wild animal. When Balchard's room did settle down to an eventual silence, it was as if the very beast it was had taken to slumber. It was then that Mrs Wallamsby took heart to once more knock on *that* door. On her pretence of bringing fresh towels, she inspected the effect of the noise. Things were as before. Untidy and scientifically unintelligible to her layperson's eyes. Then she saw the vase. Its handle missing. The neck also missing several pieces! The broken fragments lay on the floor, hastily pushed, with furtive guilt, beneath the table. Her prize blue Minton! The vase had been a present from a former lodger. A most grateful patron of her establishment, now in gainful employment of secretarial duties at Lambeth Palace.

Balchard caught the vexation in her critical eye. 'It was an accident -- couldn't be helped,' he lied, snappishly. He saw that she did not believe him, and this pleased his sadistic mood. 'Don't fret, woman, for goodness sake! I'll pay you what's due. Since I'm already owing to you, for your silly carpet at the end of the week, tote them both up and let me have the reckoning. Never entertain the thought for a moment that I shan't honour the payment. I'm a medical man, as you well know. You'll get your damned money, have no fear!' He turned his back on her, to busy himself with his work. 'Unless there's something else you wish to discuss --- don't let me keep you from your *precious* housework,' he said, without looking round. His belittling of the other's work had its sting.

Gathering up the broken cup pieces in her apron, Mrs Wallamsby straightened up and paused to look at him. Even looking at just his back was intimidating enough. All the courage she had plucked up to ask him to leave earlier than she had already specified, was suddenly drained out of her. There was no knowing how he would react. If he would whirl round in fury, at her going back on her word. If he could break her best china, he could well ------. She left, quiet as a mouse. Subdued into carrying in her apron the breakage that, in its shameful circumstance, was blemishing the peaceful harmony of her respectable establishment. She had no wish to upset that peace by having a scene with Mr Balchard. Mrs Wallamsby pushed to the back of her mind the fact that a mere scene with Balchard was not what she really feared from him.

With enough work done for the time being, Balchard made to leave, the coat over his arm, to be taken to the laundry. Pausing by the table, he picked up the small bottle beside the microscope to note that the level of the haematoxylin acid was low. It was invaluable for staining his slide specimens, so that he would have to requisition further supplies from the hospital stores. Casting an eye over everything else to check for further needs, he caught sight of a haggard 'devil mask' in the mirror, looking back out at him. Leaning in closer to the mirror, he winced at the dilated pupils and the red spider's web of blood vessels crowding the lower halves of the scleral 'whites' that were dull grey, in his tired eyes. The tongue, with its sickly yellow precipitate, was no less discouraging. It was conclusive that he, Adam Balchard, Esquire, was gravely in need of medical attention. He made a point, there and then, to consult Dr Michaels on the matter in the near future. Going out the door, Balchard changed his mind, deciding that he would *mention* the matter to Dr Michaels only after he had dealt completely with Blintook's situation, and made out his report to the Yard. Or perhaps even a little later.

Before turning to greet Balchard, Captain Smethers, in full military ceremonial dress, took the salute from the resplendent detachment of Scots Greys trotting along Birdcage Walk towards Storeys Gate, where afternoon crowds thronged into St James's Park to make most of an extended weekend. When he did turn to look at Balchard, it was not without a little mirth that he grinned at the other. Despite Balchard having since repaired from makeshift handkerchiefs to proper bandages on his hands, the change did not seem to have its intended effect in deflecting the Captain's humour. Grinning openly, Smethers took up one of Balchard's 'mummified' hands and turned it over, looking at the ugly purple patch of iodine on the palm. He saw the same message on the other palm and on the left cheek. 'You look as if you've just crawled out from under a pyramid. Did they shoot the elephant that did that to you? On second thoughts, they don't have elephants in Egypt, do they? Must be fair, I suppose.'

Balchard pulled his hands away, putting them in his pockets and looking into the distance across the park to save face. 'Upon your mention of *Egypt*, Captain, you have presumably read my report on the issue pertaining to our mutual acquaintance, Fieseen Bijali?'

'Yes, I have, as a matter of fact. The Inspector confirmed it only yesterday that his man -- what's his name? -- Kahamir -- has been clucking his tongue in cahoots with the 'other side'. So the time is just about right for you to jump over, into their lap. It's just the opening we've been looking for, so you'll have to make sure that you walk through it carefully, without kicking anyone's shins, laddie.' They turned to move off in a slow saunter of synchronised steps in the direction of the Palace. Smethers took the opportunity to to have another critical look at Balchard. 'But I say, you do look positively awful. What in God's name have you been doing with yourself? A good party, was it?'

In spite of the reference to God being nearer to the truth than the Captain suspected, Balchard did not much like being sized up and hung like a butcher's prize ham. He tried to sound his most piqued at the other's remark. 'Pain can well serve as a chastising agent and sharpener of the senses and reflexes.'

'Maybe, but aren't you letting things get a little bit out of hand, old boy? We don't want to overdo it and spoil things just when you're poised for your big jump over to the 'other side', do we?'

Balchard cast a razor-sharp glance at Smethers, and then looked beyond him. His eyes scoured the tasselled bonnets and 'boaters' competing for place with rainbow-ribboned sticks and penny windmills around the maypoles and stalls bordering the footpath along the way. Camouflaged amongst all the chari-vari of children frolicking with their parents and nannies, was the source of interest that Balchard sought.

Balchard watched the man in the distance, *who in turn was watching him.*

A stab in the arm from Smethers' forefinger interrupted the silent vigil. 'The trouble with you, old boy, is that you haven't yet learned to draw the dividing line between work and leisure. You've got to leave the ruddy horse behind in the stable some time, you know. Can't ruddy take it with you everywhere -- especially not in the old *boudoir*, what?' He paused to smile and finger his blond moustache at its ends. 'You know the old saying that 'all work and no play makes --- -' Smethers broke off to look behind at the 'clip-clop' sound of an approaching carriage. He touched Balchards' arm to stop him as well. Putting a white-gloved hand to the hilt of his sabre, Captain Smethers saluted with precise military sharpness. The hirsute face of Edward, Prince of Wales, floated past as he beamed back from amidst the customary bevy of 'easy ladies', not the least noticeable of which was the beautiful Mrs Lillie Langtry. She, however, had no time for the silly toy soldier and his ghost-faced companion standing to the side, looking away from them, behind her twirling pink parasol.

Following the passage of 'Bertie' with shrewd eyes, Balchard nodded solemnly at Smethers' last remark. 'Perhaps there is some truth in what you say, Captain Smethers. Supposedly one can now look *up* to licentious philandering as an *accepted* social grace of the E*stablishment*.' Balchard emphasised his words with burning anger directed at Felsham's lot, and their prohibitive rulings on his research 'subjects'. Smethers made a face as he took Balchard's general meaning, following

279

the progress of the royal carriage past Wellington Barracks, where more white gloves shot up in salute, and one nervous cavalry mount dropped its shit beside an even more nervous trooper. When Balchard and Smethers passed the Barracks themselves, there was only a solitary Coldstream Guards bandsman crossing the road with his drum, to return the Captain's salute. The nervous trooper was still waltzing with his nervous back-stepping horse, and it was still dropping shit. They stopped at the corner of the Walk and James Street, Smethers looking at his fob watch and then significantly across at the Palace. 'Got to push it, old boy. Can't keep the Old Girl waiting. Tea in the Garden, and all that. Invitation, of course. Sorry you can't come.'

'Of course.'

Smethers suddenly became serious, looking fretfully at Balchard's pockets, where his hands had been 'invalided' out of sight. 'I say, old boy, do you think that you can handle dynamite with those ruddy things? Can't have you dropping it around you like that ruddy nag over there, blowing up the wrong people, least of all yourself, can we?'

Balchard removed his hands from his pockets to flex his fingers and demonstrate there versatility, but not mentioning the considerable pain it was causing him to do so.

'Right, fair enough. The next question is, do you *know* anything about dynamite? I mean apart from the fact that it was invented by some Swedish fellow called Noble?'

'Nob*el*, I believe, is the name, Captain.'

'Yes, well, whatever. Well -- *do* you?'

'*Only* that the main constituent substance is nitro-glycerine, which, strictly speaking, is a misnomer as it contains the N O three, or nitrate group, similar to that in metallic nitrates. It should, in fact, be called glyceryl trinitrate. This is absorbed by the suitably porous material, kieselguhr, which is composed of marine organisms, or diatoms, to be more specific, to give us the explosive, dynamite. It may contain up to seventy five per cent 'nitro-glycerine', with the addition of sodium nitrate, potassium nitrate or ammonium nitrate with sulphur. Although not unduly sensitive to shock, it does appear to have a destructive force of about eight times that of gunpowder. *Apart from that*, and the *reasonable* probability that my knowledge of the substance would far surpass that of Scotland Yard's incompetent herd, who do not seem to have coped too well with such matters in the past --- *yes*, I think that I have a *fair* smattering of the subject, Captain, if I may be permitted to say so, myself."

Smethers looked unconvinced for a moment. 'Yes, well, that's as may be, but I would still like you to attend several days training in the field with the ruddy stuff.' He held up a hand to stop the other's protest. 'No, hear me out. I can imagine how you feel if you are as good with it as you say, but I don't make the rules. It's merely my responsibility to ensure that they are carried out to the last letter as they are dictated down to me. This is a new statute from the Old Man, by way of the War Office, which stipulates that anyone we take on to serve in a specialised field should be given some basic training in that specialised subject. In this case, a minimum of three days attendance on one of the Army's Ordnance ranges. Do I make myself clear?'

'Quite clear, Captain.'

'And do you accept the terms?'

'I accept.'

'Good. That's about all there is to it, then, for the moment. I'll send you word of where and when to attend. Probably not later than Wednesday.'

Smethers stood balanced on the kerb's edge, ready to dash across to his Royal Appointment, when another thought struck him and he turned round again to Balchard. 'I tell you what, Balchie, old boy; my cousin, Archibald -- he's a biffer, is Archie -- his old lady, Lady Caroline, is giving a party next weekend. Why don't you come along? Carlton House Terrace; Lady Caroline Ethelwaite-Coombes; you can't miss the place.' Smethers paused to perfect his moustache yet again. 'Lots of nice ladies, I shouldn't wonder. Knowing Archie, he'll have half of Haymarket's *sweet canaries* along, if only to have his old mama choke on the cholic.' Although Captain Smethers did not really see the enigmatic Balchard as one of his social station, he did imagine that having him at the soiree as a social curiosity and outlandish topic of discussion, would be to win the honour of the evening.

But no wool fell over Balchard's eyes. 'I think not, Captain; but we shall see for sure 'pon the night in question. Providing, also, that time is permitting, away from the Army's *stipulated* field exercises. We shall see.'

Watching Captain Smethers hurry over to the Palace, Balchard turned away, pausing before going off along James Street, to look back up along the Walk. Sure enough, there, still following him, his ever watchful eyes still trained on him, whilst pretending to linger for a 'penny buy' at the sherbet vendor's stall, was the *Walrus Man*.

The rain had been off for several hours, but it had still left its mark, a very wet mark, of shiny puddles for Balchard to dodge round, cursing, on his way to the Institute. Misty haloes hung around the gas lamps, reflected in what looked like large pools of mercury, to Balchard's scientific eyes, in the slanting light. His preoccupation in avoiding puddles was pulled away by a shrill female scream. A young child, breaking away from her governess, had strayed into the path of a fast-moving omnibus. Near death rumbled past, with only inches clearance, throwing up a great spray of black puddle water to drench the frightened child. Onlookers were seized with relief at the child's narrow escape.

But Balchard was momentarily transfixed by the transformation before him. That of dignity being swiftly and cruelly replaced by shame and embarrassment. The happy frolicking child was now a motionless trunk-form emitting pitiful sobs. Soaked clothes, now seemingly darkened in their disgrace, clung to the child's body in cold harsh mummification. *Just like she had been when they had taken her body out of the river, watery green reed tendrils still jealously trailing after her, and lain her on the bank. From bright butterfly to dull pupa. Metamorphosis in reverse.* Reverse? Going back? He was not unaware of his acute tendency of looking back. Going back to what? To the peace of nothingness prior to life, whence we came, perhaps? A death-wish, perhaps?

Curious glances followed Balchard along the hospital

corridor, clinging to him in his own mounting curiosity. Passing an open doorway, the word 'police', along with his own name, caught his ear. With his nervous impatience bristling, his mind raced over the avenues of possibility covering his many diverse activities. Had that confounded landlady complained to the police? Had one of his whores tried a bobby's patience too far, and blabbed on him and his work? He had barely donned his rubber apron, when the laboratory door flew open, almost striking him. A head came round it in sly slowness to reveal the impishly searching face of Stolling. 'Ah, there you are, Balchard. Everyone's after you today, apparently. Even the police are looking for you. So what have you been up to, old boy? Spot of bother? You haven't stolen the Crown Jewels, by any chance?' Stolling's playfully wicked words did not go far in hiding his hope that it *was* trouble of some sort for Balchard. In his young mind, a bit of hot gossip was to be relished in this deadbeat place. Balchard tied his apron strings with deliberate slowness to conceal the racing speed of his mind, checking and back checking. He felt that his best security was to remain silent, so as to prise more out of the bubbling Stolling.

'Two other chappies were also looking for you, it seems. I didn't like the look of those two -- seen better faces on the wrong end of a twelve bore blast. One had only one eye. Proper ruffians, I'd say. Didn't leave any names, not that you'd expect that sort to be dropping names freely.' Balchard concluded it to be Kahamir; and it had to be Carter with him. Kahamir would not have brought any of Vlarda's contacts here. And if Dryson could afford to send a bobby, instead of coming

284

himself, it could not be too urgent. In that case it could wait. They could *all* wait.

'Burke and Hare does not strike me as too inappropriate a title for the two,' said a new voice that made Balchard's anger soar, the very instant he recognised it. Stolling shifted aside to let Guy Du Mont come in from behind him.

'Indeed,' said Balchard, giving the other two no more of his attention than was needed for his succinct response. He had no intention of revealing to them what was not theirs to know. He also needed the precious seconds to think, moving things about the bench without point, to cover his mental block.

'No, in *mis*deed, Balchard --- in *mis*deed! Where on earth do you dig them up, for God's sake!'

'The good doctor errs, for grave-robbing ghoul I most categorically am not. Our infamous two gentlemen were purveyors of the already departed. My work is with the living, I need not remind you!' Balchard stamped a flask down on the bench to push home his point.

'No, you need not, because I find it all most questionable --- *abominable*, in fact!' Du Mont also had a mercuric temperament, like Balchard, especially when confronting him, and had now cast jest aside. 'But for Old Man Smelfors' near tears pleading, I would have had the Committee see it my way. The proper way, and had them throw you and your despicable work out into the gutter, where you belong. Their decision for reprieve was nothing short of pathetic. *Pathetic!*' Balchard could see Du Mont's eyes ablaze with something that went far beyond mere discord on a committee's majority ruling. There was personal hatred there. On that, at least, they were mutually agreed. Du Mont paused for a moment, to look at Stolling for support. He got a meek nod. That was the usual best that Stolling ever contributed to a debate when it became heated. 'I find your particular concept and *practise* of experimental medicine to be an absolute defilement of this establishment and of medicine as a whole. I personally believe that respectable medicine should be left as it is, and jolly well always should be.'

Du Mont's very much 'personal' declaration came as no surprise to Balchard. He could well appreciate Du Mont being satisfied in his safe social equilibrium; in everything that he held precious. His family background, his professional status, his club, all his 'gentleman's acquisitions'. Secure in these traditional rights, nothing, not even an earthquake would see him moved.

No such earthquake shook the room, but both Du Mont and Balchard looked in surprise when Stolling spoke. 'But how are we to progress?' Both faces, not removed of the surprise, stared on at Stolling, awaiting further wondrous revelation. 'Medicine --- how is it to progress, if we do not allow for an experimental margin?'

With Du Mont distracted by Stolling's unexpected interruption, Balchard found initiative to extend on the theme. 'For how else has medicine advanced from its Dark Ages infancy of wizard's magic spell and herbal potions, to its present day status as the science of life? And if such people die from their ailments in our failing efforts, would they not have done so otherwise, had our attempts not been made?

Or perhaps you would have it suffice that the nurse is simply reminded to fold the bed sheets properly?' Balchard's sardonic smile dissolved that on the other's face. Du Mont's dark anger deepened as he considered these points, searching for words. But as Balchard's eyes bored into him, he knew and enjoyed the thought that Du Mont's argument was stalled, not so much by the lever of logic, as by the betrayal of a junior colleague, Stolling, whose loyalty he had automatically believed he commanded.

Stolling continued. 'But there again, could *you* kill anyone -- a loved one, even accidentally, and be immune from grief on the basis that that person was going to die anyway -- that we all die eventually? *Could* you?' It was a general question put to both of them. He turned to Balchard. 'If you think you could, would you be lying to that person in memory, or to yourself?' It was still being posed as a general hypothetical question, but Balchard took it very personally. Challenged by these words, he experienced tremendous confusion of feeling in his chest, being neither sure of what he was *really* asking himself, nor of how it should be answered. His mental turmoil was suffocating. A sinking despair gripped his inside.

Balchard's downward spiralling mood was halted abruptly by the typical 'air-rushing' effect of Professor Felsham's crashing entrance through the swing doors. 'Right, Balchard, presumably we are ready to get some work done?' Standing there rubbing his hands enthusiastically, Felsham looked around, surveying his work layout. Second to his scientific interest, and only on the edge of his attention, were Du Mont and Stolling. He turned to them. 'Gentlemen?' But the fire had gone out of Du Mont's attack. For the moment. So that he and Stolling excused themselves and took their leave. As Balchard worked in silence alongside Felsham, with nothing but the cadaver to hold them in common thought, he was taken by a curious question. Was it pure coincidence, or was he somehow psychologically drawn to all the women in his life having two common factors? Namely, that they were, firstly, faulted in the eyes of society, and secondly, that they were beckoned soon by death. *She* had qualified for both of these. And then he remembered his mama. Since she as yet did not qualify for the second 'requisite', what then, of the first?

'Right now, just hold them back .' Felsham waited for Balchard to fold back the thoracic flaps. Turning aside to get cutters, he turned back and deftly snipped the cartilages joining ribs to breastbone. Felsham next cut the small joints connecting the sternum to the clavicles. With only three remaining vessels to sever, he paused for a second. Pressing on, he cut through the aorta, then the superior vena cava and finally the inferior vena cava. Lifting the heart out of the thoracic chamber, he held it there, waiting for Balchard to hold out the bowl. '*Bowl*, Balchard, *bowl!*' His words landed on deaf ears.

Felsham looked round. Balchard, eyes closed and his face twisted in pain, was slowly rubbing his head with the blunt handle end of his scalpel. Felsham's anger was instant. 'Dammit, man, you'll do yourself, if not someone else, an injury, flapping that thing about! If you're not fit to do your work, then you shouldn't be here. If you're going to fall asleep over your work like this, then you're a great waste of everyone's time, not least of all mine. I knew it was a mistake to let Smelfors have his way.' Balchard looked round, surprised, if not just remembering Felham's presence, before apology fought its way into his expression. But Felsham was having no more of it. Half assistance was *no* assistance, and that was an encumbrance he could not afford on his tight schedule. 'Go home. Go home and get some rest. Before you really become ill.' He waved Balchard's mumblings for remission aside. 'No, no, we'll hear no more of this. Now go on, get out of my sight!' A possible solution came to Felsham's mind. He called out after the departing Balchard. 'Before you go, find the porter, George, and have him locate that Coles boy. He's in the building somewhere; I saw him. Have George send him to me. God willing, perhaps *he* can provide me with some assistance, if others can't.'

CHAPTER 21

The Reverend Blintook's black cassock flapped in the soft breeze, emphasising the tight gird of the rough leather belt pulled in at the waist. A reminder of the meagre stipend that was his pastoral penance to survive on. Muddy boots and a long-shafted spade suggested that he also did a lot of his own messing around, otherwise called 'gardening'. 'Breezy, but not without its mildness,' he called out, by way of greeting to Balchard, who was approaching up the drive -way. Balchard looked around him to acknowledge the statement. He had already noticed the daylight's metamorphosis effect on the trees and church, so removing their macabre black mantles and chasing away all goblins and ghouls on a sojourn elsewhere. Blintook let his spade fall to the ground so as to pull off his earth-caked woollen mittens. Balchard had since also laid his hands bare, the bandages proving to be too conspicuous, especially to the sore point of inviting disdainful comment from Guy Du Mont. But the haggard look of fatigue and latent illness was still there, so that it did not escape Blintook's notice. He also noted the purple palms, with their liberal application of ointment in a hindsight of after -treatment.

'I was very relieved to receive your telegram, Mr Balchard although I must confess to not fully comprehending its meaning. Is everything all right, as you would have me believe?' There was grave concern in Blintook's voice for the man standing before him, who seemed to have undergone some terrible personal ordeal since last they met. 'You did say that the problem had been solved, did you not?'

'I did, indeed, Reverend, and the very solution we shall see in due course. But to do so we must first return to the scene of your 'vision'.'

Blintook was not quite sure what to anticipate, and strode with swift steps that clumped aloud from somewhere beneath the swirling cassock. He turned round sharply in the middle of his study, expecting Balchard to be there on his heels, like a performing dog, ready to perform before the circus audience. But Balchard had fallen behind to linger in the narrow passage that joined the study with the parlour. Looking up and down the passage, he all but closed the door to the parlour, so cutting down the light.

'Don't you think that you could see better with the door open, to let in more light?' Blintook's sincere effort to be of some help did not fully conceal the fact that he was absolutely baffled by the other's action.

Balchard smiled at Blintook's misunderstanding of the mechanics of the situation. 'One can well appreciate a man of your calling seeking the *light*, Reverend, but this is a situation where we, in fact, benefit from the darkness.' Blintook was not sure if he liked the sound of that last part, and fidgeted in uncertainty with his belt. 'Indeed, it is a pity,' continued

Balchard, 'that here in the daytime we have insufficient shadow to play upon the mind and senses, like it does at night. It happened, after all, at night, did it not?'

'Yes, like I said before, I saw it there. Right there.' Blintook pointed with positive assurance at that part of the study facing them straight on and so just visible from where they stood in the passage.

'Ah, yes,' said Balchard thoughtfully, leaning on the parlour door's edge, tapping it with his fingers, 'you *saw* it there. Truly, what the mind sees in presupposition, the eye can only witness in humble obedience. Somewhat like Galileo renouncing his heretical beliefs, to concede to *seeing* the Earth as the centre of the solar system, with the sun and all else revolving around it, *as Church decrees*.' Although the last remark was of a low muttering, Blintook still heard it, but chose to ignore the sarcasm as such. 'Very well, enough of that for the moment,' said Balchard, walking into the light of the study. He looked at the walls for a moment, before opening the bookcase to take out the *Book of Deuteronomy*. From it he removed the parchment that had given him so much concern on his last visit. 'Do you happen to play chess, Reverend?'

'I haven't played for many a year. Not since my student days.' Blintook laughed for a second, shrugging his shoulders, to look around him. 'There isn't really much scope or opportunity to indulge oneself such; not with all the parochial duties that need seeing to. Besides, I can't imagine that many of my parishioners would play such a game.'

"Your verger most certainly did."

'Really?' Blintook could not see the importance for such a trivial point to intrude, so that the puzzle registered on his face.

The look did not escape Balchard's notice. ' "Oh ye of little faith", indeed. Be most assured, Reverend, that everything --- every little point --- is of paramount importance in so intricate a situation as this.' His eyes gleamed with the surety that sounded in his words, so lifting his air of melancholy, and giving heart to Blintook. He opened out the parchment on the bureau, flattening it out with his hand, while peering down at it in close scrutiny. 'In much the same manner that an absent-minded banker may need to write down the combination number of his safe, so also do we here witness another 'banker' with pressing need to record such a 'number'.' Balchard leaned nearer to the parchment to consult some of the more faded inscriptions. 'To the unprepared eye it is a gruesome account in sepulchral undertones of all that is evil in the dark happenings of the night. It tells of the bishop commanded by the Crown to travel through the night in haste to save this church.' Balchard paused to pose the loaded rhetorical question. 'So?' He paused further, to look up at Blintook and around the room and at the whole aspect of their surroundings in general. 'So it is a recording of the supernatural, or religious, in a book of the religious, in a house of the religious, and as such is inconspicuous; much to the design of the 'banker', who does not wish to have his secret 'number' attract the attention of the wrong party.'

Balchard now tapped the parchment heavily with his knuckles, to ram home his final point. 'But to the 'banker', who has the inner knowledge and the ulterior motive for its usage, it tells of a *bishop*, a Crown, or *king*, a church, or *castle*, and a dark night, or *black knight*! Perhaps n*ow* you begin to follow my reasoning?' Balchard looked at Blintook, at the same time lifting the parchment up and dropping it down again onto the bureau, so demonstrating that it was an ordinary object obeying the law of gravity, unlike some warlock's piece that should have flown off by its own power of flame and fury.

Blintook's expression was as empty as ever, but he managed to move his lips like a dozing goldfish. 'Sort of.'

' "Sort of ".' Balchard repeated Blintook's words with a faint sigh of impatience. 'An improvement, nevertheless. Suffice it for the moment.' He came away from the bureau, to stand in the middle if the floor and look around the room. 'But as yet we have no chessboard. Or *have* we?' His eyes darted randomly round the room, in a moment's fun at misleading Blintook's following eyes. 'If one recalls the verger's need to *elevate* himself on the table.' Balchard's voice took on a more serious note like a tutor closing the Euclidean triangle for the pupil. 'For *what purpose*, one asks?' He looked at Blintook and then pointedly at the two opposite walls, waiting for the other's eyes to rest on that which they had been led to see. 'Lo and behold, the chessboard -- or rather, the two opposite *halves* of the chessboard!'

Sure enough, two wooden panels, both positioned at about nine feet up the walls, one above the study door, and the other on the opposite wall, ran the full length of the room. About eight inches deep, each panel was divided into four horizontal sections, each of which was divided along its length into eight alternating rectangles of faintly differing shades. Projecting out from the centre of each rectangle was an iron peg ending in a nodule. As Balchard had said, to the unprepared eye, the panels bore no strong resemblance to the conventional layout of the chessboard. Four pieces, now presumably king, castle, bishop and knight, sat above each half-board, further up on a timber beam running the length of the room. About ten inches in height, and of heavy wrought iron, the pieces easily weighed several pounds each. The two sets of four differed in colour only by a slight shade. Fashioned in the ancient craft-man's mode of gnarled expressions portending the anguish of the damned, the pieces could only have been seen by a knowing eye as something beyond the traditional religious theme. Symmetrically spaced along the beam in the customary manner of ornaments, they looked like something that came with the rest of the house's fittings. As such, they were not only as old as the house, but also as 'immovable' as the house, and so left undisturbed, by the unsuspecting.

'The moment, I would venture, for *quod erat demonstrandum*,' said Balchard excitedly, stepping up onto the table to handle the pieces. As he has expected, each piece had a short tubular projection on its back to accommodate it on a peg. The tedious need to rise and descend four times to procure and place the pieces on their appropriate pegs demonstrated a further safeguard against accidental discovery of the secret. This was doubled when one considered the other wall's set. Following the development of disguised chess movements from the 'tale' on the parchment, Balchard climbed up and down on the table at various positions along the two walls, placing the pieces in their strategic positions on the board. He had but one chessman left to place. Climbing up onto the table for the last time, Balchard held the final piece in his hand whilst looking across at those on the opposite board, and then those on his own board. 'A most ingenious amalgam of cunning and mechanics. For not only is discovery averted in the event of the pieces being put at random on the *wrong* pegs, but further, when seven pegs are placed on the *correct* pegs, still there is yet nothing for the eye to imbibe in wonder. But when the *eighth* piece is placed in its position --- *voila*!' At that, Balchard put the puzzle's ultimate unit of clarification, the bishop, onto the peg and waited confidently. For a moment there was nothing but silence and the beauty of purring excitement; then, to Blintook's amazement and Balchard's satisfaction of completing a solution, the bookcase facing the study door swung inwards silently, to reveal a hidden passage.

Silence continued for another few seconds before Balchard climbed down from the table to approach and peer into the dark clandestine opening. There was insufficient light for either of them to see beyond several feet along the secret passage. But the chilling damp air was sinister enough message that this innermost compartment was different from all the other warm inner compartments of the house's ancient structure. Blintook looked round at Balchard. 'This is incredible, Mr Balchard. But what does it all mean?' Balchard moved the new-found 'door' to an angle of roughly forty five degrees with the study wall, and then walking out of the study in the direction of the parlour, beckoned Blintook to follow him. Turning round Balchard pointed. Blintook, by following the line indicated, could now see not only right into the study, but beyond it into the secret passage, the length of which was reflected in the specifically angled 'door' as a patch of blackness 'straight ahead' of them.

'Perhaps now you begin to see almost, but not exactly, as you saw that particular evening, Reverend?'

Blintook's mind turned hot and cold with relief and confusion as he thought over that before him. 'Are you saying that what I saw was in *there*? That *something*, some *creature*, came out of there that evening?'

'What you saw that evening was, indeed, inside that passage. For all the years that you have entered this study in the dark, you have grown accustomed to all reflected movements, however obscure, being those of your own self reflected in that panel. Thus, when the panel was moved in, so reflecting the movement *inside* the passage as being 'straight ahead', your brain automatically registered it as your *own* movement. That the figure was moving in the opposite direction, with a motion out of synchronisation with your own movements, gives substance to the supernatural effect that you experienced. Without doubt, the addition of some background illumination by oil lamp, or torch flame, or even moonlight, would serve to enhance the spiritual quality of the vision. Do you recall the type of illumination that made the figure visible that evening?'

'I can't really remember. This is all so bewildering. But you said moonlight. Do you mean to say that this passage leads from my private study to the outside?'

'Most surely. For what other reason would we have such a convenient means of refuge and escape? There is more than a morsel of truth reflected in the parchment's record, however cleverly disguised. In former times of political and religious unrest, with the countryside swarming with Roundheads and Royalists eager to run each other through with cold steel, it was passages such as these, and not the Church, if you will forgive me, Reverend, that gave 'sanctuary' to the fugitive.'

'You speak of *then*; but what of *now*? I feel a fuller explanation, however sickening, is necessary to connect the two.' Blintook gestured vaguely at the dark opening, in anguish of all its dastardly implications. 'And where is my verger?'

'Alas, we move from the safely remote strifes of the past, to a present day counterpart of fatal curiosity. In this case, *murder.*'

'Oh, dear God!' Blintook clapped his hand to his mouth in shock.

Balchard lit the oil lamp and they went with it into the passage. Moving along slowly between the damp stone walls, they stopped suddenly at Balchard's warning of steps falling away immediately at their feet. Whilst making no mention of it aloud, Balchard now considered his earlier theory of illumination by moonlight to be unfeasible because of this changing of levels in the passage. It was unlikely that even the most brilliant lunar glare could be the sole provider of light in the passage. It must have been a combination of some hand-held light, along with a diffuse filtering in of light from the study or parlour, that had given the 'holy vision'. The stone-slab walls gave way to a mixture of small stones, earth and wooden struts that formed a crude tunnel that led eventually to another flight of stone steps. This time the steps climbed upwards. With the lamp held aloft, it was plain from the shape of the stone rectangle above them, that they were standing inside a grave. A shiver ran through Balchard. He put on a brave act, more to chase away his own fears, than to impress others.' "Alas, poor Yorick", the stairs to the stage and the final act, I presume.' Balchard handed the lamp to Blintook so that he could apply his strength to the stone above them. After several efforts, the heavy lid finally rumbled aside with a loud grate and an internal hollow groan that reminded Blintook of grinding teeth, while Balchard thought of the surgeon's bone-saw back at the Institute.

Stepping up and out into the blinding daylight, they looked around them to see that they were standing on the very edge of the graveyard, facing outwards towards the wood. An excellent position for the tunnel's exit, whence fugitives of the past, Cromwellian or Cavalier, could make their swift transference to the cover of the wood. Just beyond the trees, out of sight within the wood, lay the ancient, or perhaps not so ancient, sacrificial mound, Balchard recalled. He pointed to the trees. 'Your unfortunate verger lies buried over yonder, not far from the mound. I ascertained this fact this morning, before coming here.' He did not say that standing over that grave had unnerved him. Bodies in the laboratory were a totally different issue altogether; he could cope with them as scientific 'material'.

But a body buried out here, in the open greenness of the

country, stirred up haunting memories. Just looking at the wood made an uneasy feeling come over Balchard. *She had absolutely loved the wood, with its trees and bushes and overall emerald mischievousness, if not mysticism. She had once said that she would have liked to have been a witch, living wild among her friends, the trees. It had been her teasing ploy to climb up into the branches, deliberately entangling her ribbons and petticoats, so enticing him to climb up to rescue her.* But these trees glaring back at Balchard did not have that friendly air that *she* gave to everything with *her* presence. These had a menacing whisper, a howl, that whirled round his ears in the wind. His tumble down that hillside had winded him not only bodily, but had seemingly caused a landslide shift in his mind. That, and other things. He felt different, but how so, he was as yet unable to specify exactly. A nausea and faintness came over him for a second, so that he swayed unsteadily.

Blintook reached out to grab Balchard's arm. 'Are you all right? You look a bit pale.'

Balchard instantly jerked away from the helping hand. 'Leave it! I'm all right!' But the voice was angry, not thankful.

Blintook was otherwise greatly upset, turning and looking round and round aimlessly in pained question. 'But who would do this? And *why*? Can you tell me *why*, Mr Balchard?'

'I fear that your verger stumbled upon and witnessed that which he ought not to have seen. For that he was silenced -- for ever -- in order that no other forbidden eyes would see.'

Blintook shook his head. 'I don't understand.'

It was Balchard's turn to shake his head 'Is it possible, Reverend, that you surround yourself so well with your good flock, that you do not see the dangers that threaten the outermost sheep of that flock? Forgive me, but I must say that whilst the 'good' may pay homage to your God by day, do they not also pledge their allegiance to a pagan deity by night?'

'You mean *witchcraft*? A *coven*?' Blintook buried his face in his hands in great dismay.

'Precisely, Reverend. It is most probable that your late verger, in his preoccupied act of spying, did not realise that he, himself, had been spied upon. He was then followed back to the church house, where, with barely enough time to return the chessmen to their original positions, he was then abducted. The release mechanism on the inside of the door supports this theory. It was the very last part of that abduction that gave you your apparition. The door was either closed from behind by an accomplice, or perhaps the draught rushing through the tunnel from the outside caused the door to close.'

'This is terrible. Truly terrible. And all within my very own church. My very own parishioners. I see and meet these people every day. I *know* these people.'

'Does one ever *really know* another, Reverend? *There* we have the crux.'

'I suppose I must now strengthen myself to the horrible task of summoning our village constable to arrest these wrong-doers -- sinners from my flock for whom I must bear responsibility.'

Balchard looked round sharply at this remark. 'A serious word of caution there, Reverend. I would strongly advise against enlisting your local constabulary for this task.'

'You don't mean to say that *he's* one of them, as well? Our very own constable -- assistant church warden -- a member of a witchcraft coven? This is all really too much.'

'Whilst I have not stated anything definite as such, Reverend, one learns that it is fairly difficult in situations such as this, to differentiate between those who kneel by day, and those who cavort by night.'

"So what am I to do, Mr Balchard?"

'The time factor is clearly of no crucial importance, since the evil act has already been committed, and the perpetrators, themselves, dwell here. I would thus suggest that you leave the matter in my hands, that I may put it to an acquaintance of mine at Scotland Yard. He will see to it that the necessary measures are carried out in strict accordance with the Law.'

'And I, in my humble part, must surely pray for forgiveness. Most wholeheartedly, I must.'

They did not return to the church house by the tunnel, Blintook deeming it to be vile under the circumstances of what he had just learned. When Balchard was ready to set out on his return journey to the City, Blintook had one further question to ask. 'But why did poor Mr Beggs -- my verger -- not come to see me if he knew about the secret passage, instead of fooling around in the dark by himself, as you say he did?'

Balchard was hesitant in giving the final, saddening, truth. 'Regretfully, it is likely that he linked the secrecy of the passage with a romanticized vision of great hidden treasures, and wished to keep such wealth to himself.'

'Oh, dear God. That means that he went forth to meet his Maker with theft as his last intended act!'

'Could it be possible that his 'passage through the tunnel' was more revealing than ours, Reverend? Perhaps what he saw in its startling finality was sufficient to incite his inner contrition?'

'I really do hope so. I pray to God that it *was* so.' As a last resort at making amends for his failings as a pastor, Blintook looked keenly at Balchard. 'And you, yourself, Mr Balchard? You are at peace? You were not without your own distress, the other evening. Can I possibly be of some help in easing any personal burden?'

This last minute personal probe caught Balchard off guard and he looked away at the crows in the trees as cover from his embarrassment. 'A little matter of fatigue from overwork, Reverend. The human brain partly deprived of its normal supply of oxygen is apt to induce the senses with some traumatic effects. Fortunately this is only temporary.' While he could have lied with ease to anyone else, Balchard felt his words come out his mouth like awkward bricks, before this sincere man of God.

'Of course, Mr Balchard, of course.' But Blintook was no longer so easily deceived, having been wisened by a lifetime over the last few days, and especially by this morning's stark revelations. But he held his distance. All things considered, good against evil, with souls gained and lost, it was thus with a mixture of sadness and gladness, that Blintook watched Balchard depart down the long drive-way, on his own personal 'long journey'. 'God be with you, Mr Balchard.'

'Of course, Reverend.'

When Blintook had prayed to the Lord for Balchard's

safety several nights before, it had been in earnest covenant of his own safety being offered in return. Now that the Lord had bequeathed Mr Balchard's sparing, what of his *own* sparing?

Early evening saw Balchard slicing up sections of placenta, and preparing them on slides for microscope inspection. Professor Radcliffe stood by, waiting in silence, to make the inspection. But for the sound of his fine blade, Balchard was finding the silence between them to be heavier than usual. He sensed that something was bugging the old bastard. He would get it off his chest soon enough, as he always did. As Radcliffe looked down his microscope, examining the specimens, Balchard noted the distinct absence of critical mutterings that the Professor was apt to make, on passing from slide to slide. The sharp click of the slides being put down on the bench too briskly was an indication that what was troubling Radcliffe could not be seen down his 1600 high power lens system. He swung round, holding out a specimen to Balchard. 'What in heavens is this supposed to be, Balchard? It needs to be done again. They'll *all* have to be done again! A complete waste of my time, if not yours. Perhaps you don't value your time here, as others do, and wish only to fool around?' Radcliffe pushed the slides, with one sweeping hand, across the bench to Balchard. 'Get rid of these, and set up a fresh set. Quickly; don't stand around gawking.'

'I'm sorry, but I don't understand what's ---'

'The sections are horrendously thick -- like tree-trunks. And you have overdone the staining agent; it's so heavy as to be indistinguishable from everything, the maternal lakes and blood vessels especially. Do it again.'

'Sorry, sir, but I would have thought that the foetal villi, the prime point of focus, are very much discernible and easily distinguishable from -----'

'Do it again, and don't argue with me!'

'Sorry, sir.'

'Your work is undoubtedly deteriorating rapidly, Balchard. Is there a *reason* for this? A reason that I should know about? If there is not a satisfactory improvement made in your work, Balchard, drastic measures will need to be taken, regarding your continuing working on this research project.' Radcliffe knocked hard on the bench with his knuckle. '*Drastic measures!*'

Taking the slides to the sink for cleaning, before setting up new ones afresh, Balchard heard Radcliffe clear his throat, in preparation for a statement. 'Tell me that I have been misinformed when I hear that you were seen coming out of one of those disreputable brothel places on Monday. *Am* I misinformed? *Was* Doctor Du Mont mistaken, when he says that he saw you?'

Balchard was caught off guard for a second. Electric fright jarred his inside. If he was found to have ignored the Committee's ruling, he would be finished. His mind raced for escape. 'Must have been someone who looked like me in the dark.' A sudden horror at his gaffe of implying it to have been night-time, when the Professor had not specified it so, had him clattering the slides unduly under the tap.

Clearly not convinced of Balchard's sincerity, Radcliffe

watched him closely through scathing eyes, all the while scratching his chin and fuming silently. On a matter of clinical misdemeanour, he could have crucified the impudent young pup, but on an unfounded allegation of a non-medical issue, he would not sully himself in uncertain dispute. He let the matter go. 'Careful with those slides, Balchard, for goodness sake! At that rate, we'll have no slides left to examine. And those are University property, may I remind you. Not to be thrown about and broken, as you would your own. Break your own glass, if you must, but have respect for the University's equipment. '

'Yes, sir. Sorry, sir.

'I should think so.' Their work was continued in a further heavy silence, broken only by the Professor's exasperated mutterings of incompetent work, resulting in gross wastage of time and material. In the refuge of the silence, Balchard was very much appreciative of his narrow escape. He also noted how Radcliffe had not mentioned, or *questioned*, what Du Mont, *himself*, was doing in that nefarious vicinity, even if he was 'only passing by in a cab'.

It was five days later, while returning on the train from the Army Ordnance range in Salisbury, that Balchard, in light perusal of a provincial newspaper, suddenly froze between turning the pages over, to pull the paper closer. The words leapt up at him:

The Rev. Nathaniel **BLINTOOK**, *pastor of St Ogdburg's, Silbury, was found* **DEAD** *in his churchyard early on Wednesday morning. Reverend Blintook had been found dead, sitting on the* *ground with his back to the church house wall, with an open-eyed expression of joy, 'as if he had just met his Maker', as one witness had put it. There were no signs of foul play. He had not suffered a heart attack. The coroner could not otherwise give a reason for the death, except that it was due to natural causes and most baffling in its instance.*

Balchard lowered the paper slowly, his eyes distantly focused, seemingly staring with devilish glaze at the woman and child opposite. Crumpling the pages up, he threw the newspaper aside with such violence that the nervous couple opposite yearned for another compartment. Back in his room, Balchard took down the Blintook file to append fresh notes, then stopped, numbed in his mind over what to write. Had Blintook *really* seen what he had originally given credence to? Was it possible that more mysterious things *did* move in Heaven than on Earth? Superstitious instinct wrestled with logic. Openly, it was against Balchard's rational reasoning, yet covertly, did not reasoning also say that--? So had Blintook been 'taken' away by Divine decree? In a sense, 'gone', whilst still here in his last few remaining days. To be alive but otherwise so distanced as to render life as an empty shell. Just like his mama. The last thought surprised him, with its intrusion. It occurred to him that up until *then* everything that his mama had planned and provided for him had been for his sake; for his benefit and satisfaction. But after the funeral, things changed. Everything done thenceforth, his being urged to study for the scholarship, for self-betterment, had the surreptitiousness of *removing* him -- of hiding away the desecration of his sinfulness from the eyes of the parish. That his mama had helped him on account of what *others* thought, putting *their* consent and favour before *his*, was a weight that suddenly pressed down on his chest. He had lost her to them. He had lost his mama because of --- *her*. *She* had taken his mama from him.

With his pen suspended in mid-air, Balchard sat staring at the wall, not seeing it, unaware of his surroundings, his mind far away. When his mind came back into the room, a nausea turned his stomach, sending shivers through his limbs. He sought no answer for this. No effort was made to hammer out an explanation on the anvil of reason. Instead, he put his pen down, to press his knuckles into his tightly closed eyes, and leaned forward on his elbows on his desk. He submitted to his anguish, rather than fight against the current, letting it pass through him, like a river of burning lava, until it passed away. If he was reading the pattern of these 'instances' correctly, as they were occurring recently, it was apparent that emotional upset preceded mental confusion and trauma -- the 'dark' period. He waited passively in trepidation for it to come. Without entering one solitary word in the file, Balchard returned it slowly to the shelf, pulled on his coat, and went out.

It was later that afternoon, whilst walking upon Waterloo Bridge, that Balchard was shaken from the daze of his deep thoughts by the barrage of bumping shoulders of passers-by. He subsequently found himself studying the semi-crippled orange-seller woman on the bridge's opposite pavement. Elbowing his way through the crowd, and dodging dangerously between vehicles, he at last stood before the old woman. He studied her for a few moments more before stepping over to the flower girl beside her, to purchase a posy of violets. He proffered them to the old lady. 'For the recovery of your granddaughter, from her recent illness.'

Wide-eyed with surprise, the old lady took the flowers in her hands, as well as in her heart, her wrinkled face breaking into a near toothless smile. 'Thank you kindly, sir.' Surprise gave way to astonishment. ' 'Ere, 'ow did yer know the li'l' granddaught' was ill? 'Ere, -- sir!' She gaped in continued astonishment after the small gentleman, making to cry out again, but he was going off again into the confusion of the bustling river of people. Then he was gone out of her sight, swallowed up in the crowd.

Balchard had hardly been any more clear in understanding his own impulsive action than the old lady had been. Blintook's demise, with its metaphysical implications was still confusing him, giving him strange feelings switching between dark and light sensitivity. He only knew that a feeling had possessed him --- compassion, perhaps? --- and he had followed it, applying himself to the impulse like an inspired dab of paint on the canvas of life, much in contrast to his normally unemotional manner. He had been moved by his insight of the flower lady's situation; without quite understanding how he had gone to buy her flowers. Then he had gone off in a dazed state of mental suspension, merging with the crowd, without being truly part of it, totally isolated from everyone around him.

As far as Balchard could reason, a duel was being waged

within his brain, between opposing personalities, in which his only advantage was his knowing, or thinking he knew the opponent, his so-called lesser devil. But it would be foolish to underestimate the grimness of the struggle. He saw it to be a contention of mammoth intensity, involving the giant trial and testing of wills. If his sanity was slipping -- *as* his sanity was slipping -- would it do so in systematic decline, in accordance with his logical intellect? Would it be a rational orderly madness, or complete chaotic madness? In the changing of his mind into that of another, how much of his original personality would survive? Would any such vestige be *allowed* to remain, to retain its dignity of survival? He winced inwardly at the naive simplicity of Descartes' '*I think, therefore I am*'. So I think, but *what* am I, and what will I *be* in that state of thought? If the thought is insane illusion, am *I* an illusion? Was there any means of foreseeing who it was, what it was, that he was changing into? Was there a strategy for stemming that transition? Did he have an inkling of what action he could take? Or perhaps he must ascertain what it was he *had* to do? It partly shamed him, partly frightened him, to not know the answers; whereas at some other instance, in a more collected state of mind, his intellect would have readily provided a rational solution to the problem. So who was he now, at this exact moment, such that he could not find relief from satisfactory clarity of thought? With the inner confusion being too intangible to grasp and shape into a finite entity, it was easier to envisage any opposing onslaught as coming from outside. He needed a nominal enemy, such as '*them*', for a focus point at which he could direct all his resistant efforts. '*Them*' was everyone and everything outside of him, and hence antagonising him. Perhaps in some deep down recess of that imminent insanity there lurked a cunning Machiavellian foresight of what he was becoming, waiting to welcome him through its door, into its devilish darkness?

CHAPTER 22

London, **November**, **1887**.

'Just as with the pillars of ancient Rome, one need only apply
that initial force of imbalance, and a whole empire collapses
under the weight of its own decadence.' To give added 'weight'
to these words, *agent provocateur* and anarchist, Selik Vlarda,
looked up and around him at the many swaying towers of fish
baskets being hurried to and fro on the heads of the wooden-
hatted Billingsgate Market porters. 'What one would call, I
believe, in your most strange mother tongue, *a push-over*.'
He looked askant, from the towers, in sharp scrutiny of his
companion. 'Would you agree, Mr Balchard?'

'Och, to be sure, to be sure. As sure as me modder was
Oirish and came from Killarney, an' all.' Balchard's words
came out in heavy brogue, thick like the tough tobacco he
was chewing, in keeping with the tough ruffian character
he was pretending to be. It gave him a degree of temporary
relief to escape from the pain of his '*real*' identity by taking
on this role. Even the somewhat hysterical mockery that he
was putting into the part contributed a sense of release, by

allowing him to cast aside the very fetters of society's rigid rules that he had been forced all this time to comply with. *Forced?* Perhaps that was his mistake. Perhaps he should have seen and accepted that he *was* a rebel -- a social rebel. Further to this image, he spat on the head of a cat standing in the way eating a fish, and drove a boot fiercely into its belly, sending it flying up into the air with an agonised squall, to land in a pile of empty baskets.

Vlarda studied the 'Irishman' with a mixture of amusement and initial caution. 'And the father? May one suppose that he too was Irish, to bequeath such a gift to his son?'

Balchard wiped saliva and tobacco flakes from around his unshaven mouth, casting the Turk a warning look. 'You can be supposin' what you loikes, mister, so long as you does it another place and keeps your mouth shut about it, an' so long as Oi gets me moaney, loike we agreed. That was the deal yon bloady Gypsy, Kahamoir, promised me before Oi as much as blinked an Oiye this side o' me sleep this mornin'. Aye, an' wasn't they just the sweetest dreams o' the greenest fields you ever saw this side o' heaven, back in the old country.' Kahamir had, indeed, done a good job as intermediary. Now it was up to Balchard to push the role home, up to its hilt, beyond the mere physical cover of rough demeanour and general dishevelment that matched the roughest scallywags on the waterfront. Unshaven and as black as the oldest wharf beam, he had to play it so that the roughest tide would not wash away his 'tar' of a cover.

Vlarda, having worked with the most wretched of Europe's cut-throat rats, above and below the waterline, knew how

313

to keep his composure at the other's flare of temper. He nodded his standing agreement on the deal. The hot-blooded 'Irishman' calmed down. 'So how was Oi to know me fadder would run off, an' me just the spark of a chicken's egg, an' all? Ah, for to be sure, he was a clever Dan, for didn't me modder always say that he lost all his teeth boitin' a bit off the Blarney-stone. It was oither that, or all that great foightin' in the village pub. Ah, to be sure it was, an' all.' Balchard started punching his palm, not only to echo the mood of his verbal reminiscences, but also as a disguised means of stirring Vlarda's mind and tongue into action on the theme of violence.

Vlarda took the bait. 'I observe your natural zest for action. That is good. Have no fear, it shall come soon. There is much design for the shifting of the slothful beast of burden, lest it should never rise to do its work.' He gazed around him at sprawling skyline of the slumbering City that had long since lain itself down alongside the river, like a dozing animal beside its water-hole, never again to rise from its satisfying recline. In the devious cavern that was his nihilist's mind, Vlarda was fanatically at war with social stagnation, so that any form of rest or order was in itself an accursed impediment to change and improvement by progress. Total disorder and subsequent destruction were the means to incite civil war. And war, itself, was the instrument of change resulting from the reactionary thinking of an established society's resistance to challenging new philosophies that questioned the value of that society's fundamental rules. Looking up at him through dead eyes from their baskets were further taunting examples that blatantly signposted the roaring trade that catered for established tastes of a settled society. Whether it was cod, mackerel, herring, trout or sole, the vacant expressions and very stillness of the fish seemed to nauseate him with the orderliness that they represented. The creeping crustacea and wriggling eels did little to placate him.

Turning away in disgust from them, Vlarda looked at Balchard. 'There is much serious misjudgement in your advice to let a sleeping dog lie down. Such an animal lying in one's path constitutes an obstruction, so impeding one's natural impetus to go forward. The dog must be removed by *force*!' He was emphatic to the point of stabbing a finger hard into the fish-smelling air.

Balchard resisted the impulse to smile, recognising the fervour that typified foreign zealots in their frenzy to make serious political issue out of misinterpreted proverbs. 'And what if the bloady dog *boites*?'

'One must be sure to apply the force so that the dog is made to chase and bite its own tail, so inflicting itself with more pain, more chasing, more madness, to the point that it is finally put down.' Vlarda swung an arm round in a sweeping gesture that indicated fat money-grabbing capitalists, along with fish that ponged to high heaven. 'Your society sleeps the terrible sleep of the palsy. Your pathetic laissez-faire attitude barely credits your social structure with the indolent pulse of the hibernating bear. Even your so-called police preventive measures for curbing the occasional upsurge of civil unrest is laughable from your point of view. You would surely be better to root out the trouble and so rid yourself of it forever, like a bad tooth. But, alas, you cannot even carry out this action which would be of immense self benefit. It is truly pathetic.'

'Doesn't that mean that these troubles can arise again an' again, something loike the continual unrest that you wants, yourself, now?'

'*Fool!* It is the same recurrent action, like a dormant sore awakening in the body from time to time. If that trouble is removed forever, then it is forever in the past, making room for new developments, as forever it must be. That is, until we reach the new world of stateless co-existence without rules, and life without artificial man-imposed parameters.'

'And won't the perfection of being imperfect have then lost its perfection by becoming perfect?' Balchard was plainly trying to 'needle' Vlarda with this tongue-twister.

Vlarda looked at the other in wonder of his odd moments of sparking mental effort. He was not sure if he liked this. He regarded himself as the intellectual, whilst looking upon the 'Irishman' as the instrumental extension of his own superior will and command, like the artist's knife shaping the clay. There was further oddity in that whilst Vlarda was the better attired, and carried a physician's leather bag, his hands and face had the irrevocable peasant's coarseness of skin that denied his right of a higher station. In contrast, Balchard's shabbier clothes did not fully mask the pensive depth of his strangely distant eyes and the blanched cleanliness of his scientist's hands, despite the healing cuts and deliberately dirtied fingernails. Vlarda noted the 'inconsistencies'. 'Your friend, Kahamir, speaks well of you, but can you act with the skill he suggests, when the moment arises, in the face of the adversary?' He looked at one of his own heavily calloused hands and then pointedly at Balchard's hands. 'All is *not* truly revealed in the handshake, contrary to popular belief. You are perhaps a self made poet or scholar? One of the many homespun philosophers that your country forever *claims* to send out across the waters to enlighten the world?' There was as much ridicule as there was indecisive query behind the prying eyes.

'Ah well, now, an' wasn't Oi me modder's cousin's favourite little darlin' boy, now. An' when me poor modder couldn't afford to keep me any more, didn't me auntie take me on as an extra in her bakery shop an' teach me how to count and do clerk work. Ah, to be sure, that was a good loife with me auntie, until those damned English came to the village.'

'You suffered personal oppression at the hands of the English?'

To demonstrate his inborn hatred, Balchard took up a piece of wood and threw it gruffly out into the black water of the river. Stepping up onto a green-moulded mooring post, his thumbs thrust in his pockets, he stood watching the wood fight and leap the crests of the waves thrown up in the wake of a passing steamtug, like a square-shaped salmon in strange waters. The foam-freckled wash floated out from the tug's dark tarred hull to meet the lesser mass at a restless line marked by froth and bobbing debris. Vlarda came up to stand by the bollard, while watching the progress of the white wood outlined against the murky water where it seemed out of place. But was it the *only* thing out of place, he wondered? 'For a man specialising in destruction by explosives, you

317

would appear to nevertheless harbour some constructive thoughts in your quieter self. You are able to hold these two forces together without danger of conflict, Mr Balchard?'

'Are you sayin' that Oi can't do moi job?'

'*Can* you?'

In a whirl of fury, the 'Irishman' jumped down beside Vlarda, jabbing a forefinger angrily into the Turk's chest, at the same time whipping out a knife from nowhere with the other hand. 'Just you be puttin' the doinamoite in this hand, an' Oi'll be givin' you a bigger hole than any you can show me between here an' Finchy McGinty's quarry in Donegal!' In angry ramification of his point, Balchard plunged his blade into the eye of a resplendent skate, to hold the fish out at arm's length. At this, a huge porter came rushing up, brandishing fists that made midgets of the bollards. Giving the porter a wild look, Balchard flashed his teeth and flicked his knife so that the skate flew off to thud into the man's chest with a plop that could have come from his gaping mouth. 'So who says Oi'm wantin' your bloady fish! To be sure, we've got *tadpoles* bigger than that back in Killarney, an' them's the h*uman ones*, an' all, an' all," cried the 'Irishman'.

Although the porter was built like a walking wharf, there was something daunting in the 'Irishman's' insane glare and the glint of the steel blade that made him hold back his aggression. But not everyone was put off by the mad 'Irishman'. Raucous taunts screeched out from above, a second before something slapped Balchard on the shoulder. 'Holy Modder o' Jesus!' cried the 'Irishman', at the sight of the white splattering of bird-dropping on his already dirty coat. All heads turned up at the irate cries, but missed the gull's shadow racing along and off the quay and out over the water.

Smethers' brougham came out of nowhere, as it usually did, to pick Balchard up at the obscure corner of Hogarth's Wharf. As he climbed in, Balchard was surprised to see Sir Basil seated beside Smethers. The Captain noted the surprise, and with a quiet smile at Sir Basil, looked back to Balchard. 'Sir Basil thought it would be interesting if we had a debriefing session out of office, in the field.' Balchard nodded his understanding. He understood, all right. Whenever Smethers or Carter picked him up, it was for the sole purpose of collecting whatever information he had to report. But Sir Basil was here simply to see his circus dog perform before him.

Smethers flicked his cigar. 'Well, Balchard, what have you got for us?' Smethers and Sir Basil listened intently while Balchard gave his account of his meeting with the anarchist, Vlarda. Finishing off his report, Balchard considered putting in 'a piece of his own', purely for the sake of seeing Sir Basil's reaction. 'Apart from his fanatical hunger for violent destruction, the man does seem to possess a most contrasting side of ascetic, virtually monk-like sincerity of thought. Although somewhat naive in his ambition to gain prestige, not through academic or financial achievement, but through manifestation of the aura of his own personal power. His plans he sees as predestined and next to sacred -- a holy crusade, if you wish.'

Smethers blew his smoke up at the carriage roof. 'The man wanted to become a great judge. He was denied the chance to study law at -- where was it -- *Smyrna?*' He looked round at Sir Basil for confirmation. Sir Basil nodded. Smethers turned back to Balchard, taking a draw on his cigar before continuing. 'Anyway, his zeal for revolution, anarchy, whatever you want to call it, comes from the seed of personal bitterness. What he couldn't have, no-one else is allowed to have. I'd put my money on that.' Smethers folded his arms and settled back to enjoy his cigar.

'Indubitably!' said Sir Basil, emerging from his remoteness, in the corner. He leaned forward on his stick, flexing his fingers atop the ivory knob, to give pedantic sustenance to what he had to say. 'It is invariably the way, most surely, that any such revolutionary dissent is founded on personal grudge, deceitfully renamed as political creed. In much the same manner that the lowly church pass-keeper, passed over for promotion, or on the grounds of some other personal *injustice*, suddenly finds enough revelation in new hidden truths, to establish a whole new religion, of which *he* is the divinely inspired new leader. The indignation of being denied personal prestige, reveals to the wounded mind the distorted view that it is a most wicked world -- a world that must be changed -- to accommodate itself in accordance with that now centrally situated twisted mind. Thus, personal grievances find retribution in vainglorious causes that bequeath absolution for the wholesale crime of public destruction and genocide that anarchy carries under its banner.' Sir Basil paused to look at the other two, for some measure of assent.

Smethers looked over his cigar at Balchard, wondering if he saw bits and pieces of what Sir Basil was saying, in *him*.

He wondered further, if Balchard, himself, felt any self-recognition in these words. But Balchard saw no parallel comparison to his own designs. His intentions were more diffuse, flowing along out of sight, not blazingly blatant, like Vlarda's lot.

Sir Basil made to continue, pointing his stick at Balchard, for reference. 'As for this man's "*sincerity*" -- this is the tail-end whisper of conscience, dragging an otherwise perfect social philosophy; the rudder to keep the mind wandering off its moral course. By destroying an evil society, he becomes the new Messiah, the leader -- a person of power. If, alternatively, he *should* be conscious of wrongfulness, then his savage defiance of this renders him the allusion of being above the rules -- that is, personal glorification and prestige.'

'Another little Napoleon, in other words,' cut in Smethers, speaking to the roof, where he blew his smoke.

'Quite,' said Sir Basil, not happy at being interrupted. 'As the Captain most aptly puts it, "another little Napoleon". And all this, the very nectar of those vile gods, bitterness and revenge. Errant uncertainty is thus laid to rest.' Sir Basil tapped his stick on the floor, as final seal to his words. 'Quite frankly, I see all such zealots as a load of hypocrites -- out to get the best for themselves -- like everyone else in society, if one has to be honest. They merely seek the other side of the coin; the very same coin that they so passionately declare to be devoid of value.'

Captain Smethers blew some more smoke to the roof, before turning with a wide grin to Sir Basil. 'All cut and dried -- in a nutshell, then, sir.' Sir Basil frowned at Smethers.

Sometimes the good Captain could act very odd. Smethers blew out another cloud of smoke, this time speaking with a serious tone to the roof. 'But very *dangerous* hypocrites, nevertheless.'

Balchard was remarking on Sir Basil's last words, recalling how on an earlier occasion, also in a brougham, *he* had been contemplating the 'other side of the coin'. But he could not see the remotest similarity between his incentives, and those of the rough-cast Vlarda. He considered his motivations to be justifiable and beyond reproach. They *were, weren't* they?

Smethers knocked on the roof, signalling the driver to stop. He looked straight at Balchard with his disarming no-nonsense smile. Balchard sometimes felt it difficult to hide his mind from that look. Sir Basil, meanwhile, looked away, in rude disinterest, out of the opposite window. In a mock modicum of politeness, Smethers leaned forward to turn the door handle. 'Right, Balchard, you can get off here. Not too far from your hospital place, is it?' Balchard could not restrain his quiet snort of wry amusement at Smethers' hollow concern over the convenience of their dropping him off here. He was being made to get out -- so get out, he *would*. The door closed with its neat click, and the dark carriage and the dark figure parted company in opposite directions, neither party looking back.

When the street had emptied itself of both of them, a new figure appeared, riding a tricycle, stroking a walrus-style moustache, as it stopped to gaze in the direction the carriage had gone. Turning the tricycle round, it headed off in the opposite direction. To follow Balchard.

CHAPTER 23

'What in the name of heavens!' The subject of Guy Du Mont's astonishment strode along the hospital corridor towards him, with its dusty hair standing out wild like an African whirling dervish minus his spear. Or perhaps the Irish navvy's spade would have been a more suitable choice of implement, considering that those wretched Mohammedan mendicants were not civilised enough to wear dirty coats sporting a liberal spattering of bird-shit on their shoulders. The spectacle had certainly turned a number of hospital staff heads, as well as giving George, the porter, reason for a larger than usual scratch of his head as he gazed on in silent wonder.

'Good grief, Balchard, is that really you, or are my senses deceiving me?' said Du Mont. The fishy smell rankled Du Mont's nostrils so that his face contorted in horror. He cringed back a little from the awry figure in front of him. 'But I see and *smell* that I am not mistaken. This *thing* -- this walking cesspit that I am witnessing before me is a real manifestation and not a hallucination; as surely as it has supposedly risen up out of the river bed, bringing half the City's sewage with it, and as surely as it is truly you, Balchard. How *truly*, indeed.'

Du Mont flapped his gloves and shook his head in silent patronising disapproval. 'Young Stolling tells me --- and others do, too --- that you have been acting most irregularly lately, to the point of displaying morbid behaviour symptoms. But *this* --- this, I hadn't expected! *Good Lord*, Balchard, just what do you imagine you are doing? And for that matter, what are you doing *here*; not just now, at this moment, but *here at all*? As much as it pains me to have my profession slighted by you, and as much as it is my misfortune to have to share this hospital's corridors with you, I really have to draw the line at your present mode of conduct as being most dastardly unbecoming for a gentleman and for the profession! I really shall have to report you to the Board, Balchard!'

Balchard did not have any ready explanation that he thought would satisfy Du Mont's repugnance, and so simply continued on his way to the Pathology laboratory, letting the other have his say and wide-eyed stare. At least they both knew where they stood. They always had known, as is usually the case between two so opposed. It was obvious to Balchard that Du Mont was not so much concerned with the infringement of professional and gentlemen's etiquette, as with the elation of ridding his class of a social degenerate.

Balchard stood inside the laboratory doorway, to take in a pensive panoramic view of all the apparatus and materials. He wondered again, like he had been wondering for some time, what it would be like to reconcile himself to a life deprived of all these scientific facilities -- the unique atmosphere, with its chlorinated smell pervading over all. He dismissed the thought, not as an unlikely issue, but as one secondary to the primary issue of getting on with his present work. Balchard was engrossed in his analysis, amidst an assembly of tubes, retorts and burettes, his hair now combed down and his outrageous attire suitably amended behind his rubber apron, when Professor Smelfors made his eventual appearance to seek out, and inspect for himself, the cause of serious rumours. Any malodorous after-effects of the fish market that may have lingered on Balchard's clothes on his arrival were now wholly overcome by the smell of sulphur dioxide, boiling off in the retort of concentrated sulphuric acid and copper turnings, and being led by glass piping into the flask that he was surrounding with ice in a larger jar, for liquefaction of the gas.

Considering the fact that he, himself, had been a bit of a tearaway in his younger days as a student, Professor Smelfors saw nothing fearfully offensive in the young Balchard standing there, getting on with his work and bothering nobody. But Smelfors' word, alas, was carrying less weight with the Board nowadays, by virtue of his coming retirement. The rhythmic mashing of the pancreas tissue under the pestle held Smelfors' attention for some moments, until Balchard put the mortar and pestle down and leaned forward to adjust the zero level of the sodium hydroxide solution in the burette. Dozens of miniature professors reflected in the glassware leaned in as well to share the moment of precision. Satisfied with the level, Balchard turned aside to add several more grams of copper to the retort, at the same time lifting the Bunsen burner to fan the retort's bottom with the flame. Smelfors continued to peer at the burette, his chin tipped up and his pince-nez pushed hard up his nose as he tried with difficulty to focus his eyes on the liquid's level at the zero marking. 'Perhaps a little over the mark, are we not?'

Balchard turned round to see what the other was referring to, but had to pause to yawn before he could make any reply. 'Oi think ---I think not, sir.' Whilst not sure if the Professor had noticed the mistake in accents, Balchard felt the error jar his inside as a sure indication that his usual alertness was slipping, with the overlapping of one character on the other. Almost like the sinister Hyde-over-Jekyll syndrome. But it was not surprising. He was tired after his all-night session in the Shoreditch den of the Turk, Vlarda, discussing the merits and faults of nihilistic tactics as the revolutionary means of freeing man from the suffocating economy of present day politics. It was just as well that the slip of the tongue had occurred here and now, and not there last night, in front of Vlarda's keen eye. Balchard repeated the fact that he disagreed with the Professor, softening his defiance by preoccupying himself with the pouring of 25cc of tartaric acid solution into a conical flask. He added three drops of phenolphthalein as indicator.

'Oh well, in that case, do carry on. I'm sure that your reading is much more reliable than mine. My eyes are not what they used to be.' The old man rubbed his eyes. It was apparent that both men were involved in acute personal circumstances that were getting out of control, with the threat of imminent personal expulsion. They both watched the sodium hydroxide descend in the long glass column, rapidly at first, and then more slowly, as it neared the estimated scale marking. As each hairbreadth scale line slipped up past more slowly, each pendant drop of the solution tore itself away from the tip of the burette with greater reluctance to be the one that caused the change. Balchard shook the flask briskly, between each drop landing in it, so as to accelerate the alkali's diffusion throughout the acid solution. A few more drops, a few more shakes, and then the flask's contents suddenly blushed with a faint pink tinge. Neutralisation. Writing down the burette's scale reading, Balchard then emptied the flask's contents down the sink before washing it out and placing it on the drying rack. He next took up a clean flask to which he began adding a similar volume of acid solution by deft application of a 25cc pipette.

Smelfors, meanwhile, poked and prodded among the test tube samples on the bench, lifting one up, from time to time, for closer inspection. 'Are these the chromosomes? Can you actually see them with the naked eye?'

'A different experiment, entirely, sir.' Balchard's answer was deliberately succinct where he was treading lightly in his early exploratory steps in a relatively new field. Whilst Balchard very much wanted to continue with his analysis, it was evident that Smelfors, in his budding curiosity over the test tubes, was genuinely interested in learning more of the development in this new subject. 'Though not entirely anew in its origin, the subject has of lately come much to light. Perhaps you are familiar, sir, with the early work of Hugo von Mohl, who, some forty five years ago, made the primary observations on these filamentous bodies in the cell nucleus?'

Professor Smelfors smiled and shook his head benignly, amused at the ludicrously mammoth task of his attempting

327

to reach out in recollection of scientific material so far back in his youthful past. 'These threadlike bodies -- they are the 'chromosomes', I presume?'

'Precisely, sir. At least, that is the term that is currently being circulated with much excitement in research circles venturing into that field. From Greek, of course -- *chroma*, for colour, and *soma*, for body.'

'I *am* able to derive the classical root, young man; but do go on.'

'Whilst there are naturally more important fundamental issues to be considered, I am, nevertheless, not sure if I am entirely satisfied with the accuracy of the term.' Balchard paused to turn and position the flask beneath the burette, adding drops of indicator to the acid solution. 'I am of the theory, as of yet unsubstantiated, that the bodies are, in fact, transparent, and not coloured as supposed. It is fairly feasible that the phenomenon of colour arises from the selective absorption of the dyes we initially employ to bring the bodies into view under the microscope.'

The old man's mind marvelled at the leap of a generation in optical advancement, especially considering his own ailment of failing vision. 'Can we really see such minute detail within the *nucleus* of the living cell, *even* with a microscope?'

'It is true that this can sometimes call for more mental perception than actual ocular perception. But this problem can be lessened somewhat by using giant chromosomes found in the salivary gland cells of the *Drosophila melanogaster*, or vinegar-fly.' Balchard reached into a cupboard to take out a beaker full of ice packed round a central test tube. He gave it to the Professor. 'The chromosomal lengths in this insect's salivary gland cells can be something up to as much as four hundred times the length of those in normal cells, as well as being correspondingly thicker. Without question, an easier specimen to facilitate a detailed study.'

Smelfors, eager to witness this breakthrough on the threshold of a new scientific field, pulled the brass microscope over, and opening up a box of slides, prepared to mount them with samples from the test tube.

Balchard hated having to stem the Professor's enthusiasm. 'Ah -- alas, sir, that particular sample hasn't yet been treated with the colouring reagent. Seeking the bodies out without it is hopeless, alas.'

Professor Smelfors was momentarily disappointed, like a child delayed from touching its new toy. His smile returned fairly quickly. 'Oh well, perhaps later, when you have a proper slide mounted. ' He placed the test tube back among the ice. A frown crossed his face. 'And those other 'issues'? You said that there were more important issues to be considered on the subject. Presumably your own motivated interest for research is not merely for want to discriminate between colour and transparency?'

Balchard returned the beaker to the cupboard. 'There is much theory in current circulation that supposes that these bodies do function as the vital information bearers in the progenitive link between parent and offspring. The chain link, so to speak, of the human race; the architectural drawings between the builder and the final buildings; the reason why the human female gives birth to another human and not a rabbit. And not just another human, but one of such duplication of specific characteristics bearing more than coincidental resemblance to that of the parent. Do we know how this is? *Really* know, that is?'

Smelfors sat against the adjacent bench, to smile and whistle, throwing his poor eyes to high heaven. 'Do we now question that one Supreme Authority?'

Balchard turned away to his own bench, in a momentary spur of irritation. 'I question no such *Authority*. I merely seek the facts to put together the mosaic of bricks that comprises but one facet of the final truth.'

'I should imagine that there are many such bricks to be put together before we even have so much as a twinkle in the eye of that facet.'

Balchard turned again, gripped by the zest for his subject. 'As you say, sir, there is a whole universe of facts to be discovered and collated, where the first thought is a mere microcosm. Consider the mechanics whereby one human conveys physical and, indeed -- why not? -- *mental* characteristics to another. One could perhaps pinpoint those factors that contribute to the formation of the criminal mind. Such a step would be a colossal one for the criminologist. Its success would be far-reaching in preventive measures.' Balchard 'pinged' an empty beaker with his finger, to bring his mind down from a purely speculative cloud of the future, to the present ground level of reality. 'Mendel's work, itself, is an irreversible step in that direction, showing in strong outline the principle of systematic relaying of instructions necessary for the continuance of a species from one generation to the next. So much so that our regulation-loving German cousins --- especially Roux and Weismann --- are attributing great importance to the concept. I foresee much advancement in this field over the next decade. But for the present, I am personally swayed to a temptingly strong bridge of inference between the work of Mendel and the functional role of chromosomes.'

'And yet you fear to jump that gap in the 'bridge', lest you should wet yourself in the splash of your falling short?'

'I prefer solid stone to be beneath my feet when crossing water, and forfeit the divine power of walking upon waters to Him possessed of the privilege. Cold rational facts are the keystones supporting my bridges.'

Smelfors put his hands on the bench behind him, to rock himself to and fro slowly in a gentle cradle of distant thought that was spiced with nostalgia. 'If we were to look among the great names of the past, I wonder if we would find more fools than we would find follies carried on the back of those fools. How many of those great minds, had they not possessed the mettle to forge forward with the brainchild through wailing criticism, would have been denied their final honour of immortality mounted on pedestals?' Pushing himself away from the bench, Smelfors straightened up and shook his mind free of sentimental reminiscences of the zealous ideals and energies that had burned in his youth. His sigh was a mixture of regret and uncertainty. 'Whilst not yet fully convinced by your theory, I can positively say that if you have solid faith in an unproven principle, then you must press on and see it through to its end, for the sake of self satisfaction.'

'A paper by Balbiani, on the subject of giant chromosomes,

is being read at the Royal Polytechnic Institution next Thursday, I believe. I shall make a firm point of attending the lecture.' Balchard turned back to the burette to continue with the titration of the acid solution.

'Good; good.' Smelfors hovered over the bench, fidgeting with various pieces to no real purpose, so that it was apparent that something else 'hovered' in his mind. He stole a nervous glance at the young Balchard. 'There isn't *anything else* on your mind, by any chance, that you would wish to talk to me about, *is* there?'

'*Something else?*' Balchard appeared to be too concerned with the drops of alkali plopping into the flask's solution, to have anything else on his mind. Smelfors considered the situation at that very moment to be one of the most unpleasant duties incumbent on a head of department. To encourage social harmony in the department was one thing, but to stamp out r*umoured* discord among staff personnel, especially at his age, was a most distasteful task. 'It's just that a number of allegations -- well, *reports*, rather that allegations -- have been made to me. And, as you can no doubt understand, whilst not being prematurely committed in my judgement either way, it is, nevertheless, my duty, as head of the department, to look into such alleg -- reports. You are coping all right with things otherwise, are you?' Smelfors hid his tentative questioning behind a feigned inspection of random test tubes that had nothing in them to inspect but a few drops of water.

Balchard had nothing to say, peering more closely at the burette's scale for the final reading. After a covert look round at the door for Dr Michaels, and then at the shelves,

Smelfors took some crumpled dockets from his pocket. 'The records for the last two months do show an unusually high incidence of requisitioning of replacements for breakages in the laboratory. Dr Michaels assures me that all is well, and, of course, I'm sure it is. I know that I can take Dr Michaels' word as being most reliable.' He paused to flip through the papers, before looking up at Balchard's back, to give a nervous cough. 'You haven't anything to add to that, have you?'

Balchard turned round to stare at the Professor for a moment, before his eyes darted away to the shelves, finding greater security there among the bottles of chemicals. 'Like yourself, sir, I have great trust in the judgement of Dr Michaels.'

Professor Smelfors stared back for a few seconds more and then snapped out of the situation with a jump of expression that was sheer relief. Stuffing the papers hurriedly back into his pocket, he had a final look around the room, before moving towards the door. 'Splendid, splendid. Do carry on with your work, and don't let me keep you back.'

The door opened at that moment and Dr Michaels entered, a limping confessor-like figure of quiet patience and liberal absolution for all alike.

The Professor held out an arm to him. 'Ah, Dr Michaels, I wonder if I might have a moment of your time, to have a brief word with you.' They went out in a gradual cadence of low voices, leaving Balchard in solitude with his final drops of experiment. His feelings were none too comfortable at the taking of another's false testimony for shield, but for the moment, his greater concern was with the shaking flask. In this nervous moment of thought that marred his concentration, the final drops dripped with new non-restraint into the flask so that the fluid suddenly darkened into a rich red alkali colour. He had overshot the mark this time. Perhaps in more ways than one?

If Smelfors was patiently tolerant of Balchard's possible misconduct in letting it go no further than his careful words of enquiry, Felsham was not so easily mollified, seeing the situation from a different personal perspective. Quite regardless of Smelfors' seniority as Head of Department, he was of the staunch opinion that punitive measures of discipline had to be taken. The incredible report of Balchard's behaviour, relayed to him through Dr Du Mont, had hardened his decision on this. Balchard was summoned to his office. Low voices from behind Felsham's door came to Balchard's ear, sounding like trouble mischievously bubbling in a cauldron, as he raised his hand to knock. He paused for a moment to listen. Unable to make out the words, he knocked hard on the veneered oak panel. Caught like elves in the thick of their connivance, the voices stopped.

As the door suddenly opened wide, Balchard's eyelids closed a fraction, at the angering sight of Du Mont holding the door back in his mockingly ceremonious act of standing aside to let the 'victim' pass on to meet his just desert of doom. The glinting mixture of malice and delight that Balchard saw in Du Mont's face, as he passed, could not have been more abrasive than if he had brushed against a rough stone wall. Drum-rolling Balchard in, with his fingers thrumming on the door edge, Du Mont made no attempt to conceal the malicious intent of his words as he spoke. 'In to get your final marching orders, Balchard?'

Balchard, in return, made no attempt to conceal the hostility in *his* words. 'Damn *you*, Du Mont; damn *you*!'

Du Mont laughed, and with a parting nod to Professor Felsham, he made to leave. 'I'll leave it in your hands.' The loaded remark was followed by Du Mont's quiet laugh as he closed the door behind him. The laughter was louder as he went off along the corridor. Felsham busied himself at his filing cabinet, and then turning round, sifted through papers on his desk. All this in the deliberate drawn-out act of keeping one waiting in a nervous state. Balchard recognised the build-up in a man with much serious thinking on his mind, who had a lot to say. Glancing round the room, at all the established signs of professional accomplishment and stability, Balchard suddenly felt his own security wavering and preparing to take flight. With his sanity tilted by the weight of the occasion pressing down upon him, his past and future raced amok before him, in his mind, while he looked across at Felsham, waiting for the bastard's onslaught.

Felsham sat down heavily behind his desk. He leaned back and raised his chin up to support the best expression of magnificent discontent that he could muster to unnerve Balchard. Whilst Balchard had since spruced up his apparel and general appearance, Felsham still saw a disturbed individual standing in front of him, shifting, fidgeting, and displaying general symptoms of neurotic uncertainty, with its possible release through hysterical outbreak, only just detectable in those burning eyes. Perhaps he had been wrong to place his reliance on Balchard as the man best qualified to assist him with his important research in the Department. But who else was capable of rendering him this assistance, comparable to Balchard's brilliance and expertise? Very much troubled by the dilemma, he put his question to Balchard. '*Well?*'

The atmosphere was heavy with silence, both minds fenced off behind their own personal quandaries. Balchard searched the Professor's face for a message -- for a twitch -- a muscular movement -- a sign of some kind -- anything, to indicate what this was leading up to. He had felt Felsham's wrath many times before; but these spasms always passed over, like small black storm clouds blown away. This was something different. He was mindful of Du Mont's mention of 'final marching orders'. As when one was examining delicate tissues, one had to probe carefully. 'Well *what*, sir?'

Balchard's question caused Felsham's restrained anger to soar. That an educated man of science should revert to such primitive animal form in facial grimace, was an enlightenment of the Darwinian theory of evolution that was currently in circulation. 'You dare ask me 'what'? You dare deny what is an open and obvious outrage? That you should completely disobey the mandate laid down for you by the Disciplinary Committee is outrageous enough, but that you should not have the decency to admit to your wrong-doing is despicable! Totally despicable!' A moment's pause, to regain his gentleman's composure. 'What do you have to say for yourself, Balchard? I take it that you *are* capable of speech? Out with it, man!'

Among all the twisted images milling around in the wallowing mist of Balchard's confused mind, one was of Felsham sitting far away across the room -- his voice bellowing through an open chasm of a mouth, like the circus lion act, banging the desk with his great paws. Balchard did not relish complementing that 'act' by getting his head caught between those great animal teeth. From spluttered mutterings of anger and puzzled questioning passed between the two of them, Balchard learned that he was being hauled up for visiting 'places of gross disrepute', much to the contrary of the Committee's strict ruling. Alarm leapt in Balchard's mind. So Felsham, unlike Radcliffe , had taken seriously, the other night's sighting, by Du Mont, of him coming out of the brothel in Houndsditch? And after him thinking that he had slipped past that one, with Radcliffe ignoring it. But as words babbled and screamed in Balchard's muddled mind, the word 'today' caught his attention, like a guiding horn blast in the fog. Grasping that word, like a raft, to forestall his drowning, Balchard suddenly came to understand that this was all about Du Mont *thinking*, therefore *seeing* him coming in this morning from a whore house, on account of his rag-bag appearance. The ever eager Du Mont, forever ahead of himself, with his gross presumption! Balchard's unexpected outburst of choking laughter only served to further infuriate Felsham.

'Am I to understand that you're now adding impudence to your already disrespectful behaviour? That you should have the impudent audacity to laugh over such behaviour is, frankly, utterly deplorable!

With his mind swimming between anger and relief, Balchard battled to get his words out.

'If there is any instance of impudence to be fathomed from what can only be described as this deep misunderstanding, it is on the sole perpetration of Dr Du Mont and ----' Balchard's voice trailed off, refraining from mentioning Felsham, not wishing to rile him more than he already was.

'You would do well to explain that, Mr Balchard.' But explanations did not fall easily on Felsham's ears. Coming in a nervous flow of disjointed statements that were purely evasive fabrication, Balchard's excuse did not sound wholly convincing. Felsham made this clear with his continual shaking of the head. He needed something more credible to substantiate the reason for Balchard's outlandish behaviour. Balchard's brief relief evaporated, replaced by a caged rat predicament of not being able to reveal the real reason for his weird appearance, without disclosing his connection with Her Majesty's War Office. If he could have spared the mental space of a moment, he would have damned *that* lot as well, for landing him in this difficult position. His inner self squirmed in the panic of indecision, his logic momentarily blocked, just like that laboratory rat, trapped in the maze, not knowing which way to go, which way to turn, to get out. Somewhere amidst his inner confusion, he recalled Smethers' advice of using assertive bluffing to get out of such tight corners. He heard a voice, his own voice, seemingly distant and disconnected, mentioning his 'solicitor taking action against slanderous acts on account of unfounded allegations'. Balchard had no more faith than he had any real certainty in the legal strength of these words, beyond them being a defensive backlash at Felsham's threat of having him dismissed from his post. But it worked. Felsham backed down.

However, the pressure was not off completely. Not accepting his stepping back in defeat that easily, Felsham settled his wrath, if not his spite, by imposing an unduly great work load on Balchard, by way of its tight schedule. The trigeminal myelin axial transections would have to be completed in time for tomorrow's demonstration. The original deadline had been Thursday, three days away. Balchard left the room heavier than he had entered. He had three days work on his shoulders, to be carried out in no more than sixteen hours. That would mean working all night.

With late evening bringing a calmer atmosphere to the laboratory and the hospital in general, through things quieting down, Balchard became more aware of a savage restlessness pulsing through his system. The critical narcotic urge was gripping him, and he had no more cocaine left from Loofer's last supply. Rather than go to the dispensary storeroom, he went along, instead, to Felsham's office. As the Professor's assistant, he knew where he kept his keys and the combination of his safe. While injecting the morphine into the vein, it occurred to him that there was dual purpose in his purloining from Felsham. Not only was he committing personal affront against the old bastard, but there was also the weird thrill of risk, as in his other dangerous work. Perhaps the chance of being caught and shamed over this open felony provided a means of throwing his resentment back at his captors, and hence shift his underlying guilt away from whatever darker deeds were gnawing at his subconscious mind. Was that feasible? He pondered long over this, while pushing the syringe's plunger in.

Just as he was withdrawing the needle from the vein, he stopped suddenly to listen, turning towards the office door. Somebody was coming along the corridor. At this hour? He couldn't imagine who. Dryson? Felsham? George? He could not identify the footsteps. With barely time to react otherwise, he pulled down his sleeve, casting the syringe down upon the desk, beside two jars of methanol preserved specimens. His feeling of alarm transformed to astonishment, still tainted with guilt, when his startled brain registered the dishevelled tramp image in the office doorway as that of his long absent pater.

'Surprised to see me, son?'

'What are *you* doing here?' The false alarm, although subsided, still rang in Balchard's voice, bringing out a mischievous smile on his father's roughened face.

'Maybe you don't want to see me?' An old wisened mind, familiar with the uniquely bristling atmosphere of a misdeed being caught in the act, looked around the office warily. 'So what have you been up to, then, son -- filching the tea money, then, are you? Don't worry, I won't tell on yer.'

Balchard was self conscious of standing too near the needle, 'hidden' as it was beside other scientific objects. To an unscientific eye, it should have been inconspicuous; but in Balchard's mind, in the wake of his guilty act, it stood out like a barge pole. He was afraid that his moving away from it would look guilty to his father's knowing eye and have him rummaging about everywhere to find the 'truant' piece. Just as he had done to him many times when he was a boy. Even though that was a long time ago, he saw his father having the gall to still do that even now. His reserve of controlled voice was not quite enough to remove the feeling of standing naked before his irate pater who was only too ready to take his belt buckle to his lad's buttocks. 'What else, but the usual thing --loads of work. As Professor Felsham's research assistant, and departmental demonstrator, I've been inundated with mountains of departmental administration duties -- and that on top of my own research work .' The words sounded as false as they were to uninterested ears, coming out awkwardly like a mouthful of truant's lies. He shifted nervously, as he saw the quiet refute on the sly face. This not only increased his uneasiness, but also made him, curiously, *angry*. Angry that he could be so made to feel small by this uncouth lout of a pater, when he could all the time handle himself well on a professional basis with other professional gentlemen. Not only here, in the Institute, but in the Metropolitan Police, as well as Her Majesty's War Office. Or was it that other thought that was bothering him? The new thought jarred him. Perhaps he w*asn't* coping well in front of *them*. Perhaps they were all ridiculing him behind his back?

The knowing father shook his head slowly. 'Now don't be givin' me that horse trash, son. I know that look -- I've seen it too often before -- you're up to something' He looked round the room, his experienced eyes searching for mischief of sorts. 'You're filchin', ain't yer!'

Balchard's head moved back slightly in reflexive retreat, as he shook it side to side in denial, like the bad schoolboy caught 'at it', and stepping back from another dose of the buckle. Before he could get his words out, his father waved him quiet. 'Now don't be givin' me that. I knows you for what you are, even if these fancy nancies don't. You're a cheat. You were always up to your cheatin' ways.'

'Don't be stupid!'

'It's you that's bein' stupid, son -- tryin' to hide the likes o' that from me, who knows yer.'

All airs of professional pretence were dropped as they now faced each other openly from the past. 'Yeah, well you *would know* all about cheating, wouldn't you, *pater*!'

The broad smile was a renewal of that paternal lashing: 'Yes, as you well know, it takes one to know one. That scholarship thing, for what it was worth -- I knew things weren't exactly on the level, an' you were up to your tricks in gettin' it, not that I minded -- even if you *was* clever, and I'm not saying you're not. It's just that you always had to cheat to get things you could 'ave got straight with your brain. You always seemed to like doin' wrong on people -- to hurt them -- even your mates -- *know* what I mean. Of course you does, son.'

This last observation stung Balchard, and he sighed pensively, forgetting his father's wounding spiel, to look inside himself for a moment. The father, meanwhile, sidled back, shifting papers about on the desk top, as he began to feel at ease and in his element. He looked at his rebuked son, a devilish frown growing on his face as he readied his next admonishing piece, enjoying the discomfort it was causing the lad, like an insect wriggling on its impaling pin. 'An' there was that business at the university; let's see, what was it now? -- "encroachin' on someone else's intellectual material", was that how they worded it? When they could simply have said you'd tried pinchin' some other geezer's lot.'

'*How did you* -----!' Balchard checked himself from blurting out an inadvertent admission, converting his words to an innocent question: 'How could you possibly know anything about what went on at the university --- you were never there. You never ever showed any interest in anything of my academic progress. You were too busy with *your* lot.'

'Don't you believe it, son. I was always around, somewhere, even if you didn't know -- watching you, askin' about you, from *others*.' A mocking smile prepared his next words: 'You're not the only investigator in town; that sort come ten a penny, they do.'

'But not scientific.'

'*Scientific? Baloney*! Anyhow, I couldn't have been askin' you in person, any more than I could have been there for a plate of cucumber sandwiches and tea proper, with the high and mighty, at your stupid graduation parade what'sit. But I was always around. I wasn't fooled, even if your mother was. How is she, by the way, if you don't mind me askin'?'

'I *do* mind, but she's ---' Balchard fidgeted nervously, '---she's all right.'

A sober silence of a few moments had them each reassessing the other over the situation. The father continued. 'Just like that business with that silly lass; I always knew you were up to no ---' He broke off abruptly, stepping back sharply, at his enraged son seizing up a specimen jar to strike him. Balchard checked himself, once more, putting the jar down slowly as his mercuric rage subsided. The father gave a short laugh, half from being right, half from fright. 'Like I said, son, you were always quick to turn on the violence, to break things an' hurt people; what you couldn't get, you smashed in spite.' He swayed back and splayed an arm around to press home a general point: 'How would it look if I told your bosses, here, that you were going to attack me with that lot, eh?' He pointed at the specimen bottle. 'Dangerous stuff, is it?'

Balchard looked at the methanol fluid in the bottle, and then at his pater's dirty face, smiling icily. 'In your case, it probably *would* be. It's particularly efficient in killing off bacterial growth --- *dirt*, in your language.'

'Well, like I says, it wouldn't look too good, you, in the *medical* profession, attacking people! Could cost you your job, couldn't it?'

'It would just be your word against mine. They would never believe that I would attack my own father.'

'Ah, yes, but how would they *know* I'm your father?' He raised his chin, scratching it slowly to emphasize the challenge of his statement.

A brief frown touched Balchard's face. 'I don't follow you? Of *course* you're my father.'

The father shook his head, like a teacher disappointed that his pupil had not understood the lesson. 'You still haven't got it yet -- and you the clever one. Look, son, you can't fool an old codger like me. I knows a good runner for bettin' when

I sees one -- and I would give you one hundred to one *on*, that you would never have the courage to admit that this old tramp is of your own blood -- your father. That would be too low for you to stoop, you, with your high-minded friends.'

'They're not my *friends!*' Balchard blurted out the remark without understanding why he had done it. Perhaps it was a release from being lectured like this -- and he loathed his father continually addressing him as 'son' -- at this late stage in life. He had never called him anything else but that lowering title. Perhaps it was --?

'*Ah,* -- it's like *that,* is it?' Another slow shake of the sage's head.

'They're my *associates*, if you must be told.'

'Of *course* they is, son, of *course* they is.'

A long silence followed, which said there was truth in what the father has said. Balchard Snr shifted on his feet and rubbed his hands together as a sign of summing up the 'meeting'. 'You're clever, son, so why not do the clever thing, and keep us all happy, and give me what I came for.?'

Balchard's guard immediately fell, no longer needed, now that he knew what his father was after. All the high-flung principles and chastisement flew out the window when the subject of beer money came up. And that was what it was, destitute wretch that his father was. Seeing that his son had now grasped the real issue, the only issue he was really interested in, Balchard Snr made to speed matters up by giving a wheezing cough, followed by some hefty thumps to the chest. 'It's the chest, see. I needs the drink. A good drink keeps it down.'

Having passed the money, like food to a leper, Balchard watched him go out, and waited for his cough to fade down the corridor, before resuming his own serious thoughts. He knew that if his father had been watching from afar all those years, it was only for the purpose of what could be gained in his own interest, and not for any concern over his son's welfare, academic or otherwise. If what his father had said amounted to 'persuasion of a financial nature', he knew that the old bastard would have the gall to carry out his threat, and father and son bleatings be blown! Thinking this over with cold logic, devoid of emotion, like a low Bunsen flame flickering inside him, he weighed up the odds of this becoming a problem in the future. If it should ever constitute a blur on his future horizon, would he have the necessary sang froid to *remove* that 'fleck' from his eye, in spite of it being of his own blood? With his father virtually plundering him, and his mama disowning him, his confusion of mental values was mounting. Here he was, making a career for himself in the embryonic field of forensic analysis, yet he was nevertheless unable, it seemed, to escape from that ever grasping past. Was this a universal rule applicable to all and sundry, or was it some foreboding of fate for him personally?

With the unravelling of metaphysical conundrums having been particularly unsettling of late, he shivered inside, as a weird feeling of nausea came over him. Then the throbbing pain in his head came on again.

It had been occurring more frequently over the weeks, with the duration and intensity increasing each time -- or was it the same pain, only he was becoming weaker and less able to bear it? He leaned on the desk and lowered his head as he thought. He thought of his father's alluding to his childhood tantrums and adolescent violence. Quite remarkable that, in a way, since he had completely forgotten all about those days -- shut off in another world gone by -- in a hitherto closed compartment of his mind. Was it the only thing he had shut off? Perhaps he had shut off more than that? He had quarrelled with *her*. Had he *pushed* her into the river? Qualms of fear, disbelief, guilt, remorse, engulfed him, a swirling melee of all these in frenzied conflict -- none of them coming uppermost to give a much needed stabilising clarity of mind. If there was a way to escape his past, what was it? *What was* it! Oh, how but to flee this dogging spectre!

Tapping the desk with a steel ruler, he wrestled blindly in his mind for an answer. As it came slowly out of its mental mist, he nodded slowly in affirmative. Casting the ruler aside, he strode out of the room, so engrossed in thought, that he forgot to return the morphine to Professor Felsham's safe. The needle still lay on the desk.

CHAPTER 24

The body of Lord Danby was already covered by a white sheet when Balchard entered the deceased's private box in the Adelphi Theatre. Projected out by its brilliant whiteness against the dimness of the auditorium's red velvet, the shrouded form could well have been the ghost of Hamlet's father looking down from castle battlements. Alas, *Midsummer Night's Dream* had been that evening's performance, so snuffing the candle of suspicion in Balchard's mind of any poetic significance between the manner and timing of death and any classical message enacted on stage. Scotland Yard had sent along its representative, Detective Sergeant Dryson, to investigate matters. In his cynical dithering manner, Dryson was bent over, peering and probing to and fro about the box, in mock copy of the technique that he had seen Balchard use, without having a clue of what it was that he was looking for. Balchard, meanwhile, stood stock-still, glancing first at the corpse, hunched forward in its chair, and then looking around him slowly at the 'theatre' of death. Breathing in the atmosphere of the scene of the 'final act', he slowly pulled off his gloves.

Fed up looking for nothing, and his patience thinning, Dryson rose to his feet and turned around, openly annoyed as he now acknowledged Balchard's presence. 'Ah, there you are, Balchard. Thought you'd never turn up. I hope we haven't drawn you away from your cosy all important hospital research-work. But seeing as how you have been somewhat tardy in handing in your last report, we thought that we'd let you have a look in on this one and help put the books in order. That's if you can *spare the time*. No point in having the tax-payer put out good money for '*ancillary work*' if the job's not going to be done. Know what I mean?'

'Indeed I *do*, Detective Sergeant.' Balchard did not bother to elaborate on how he well understood what Dryson was *really* implying, with his glaring open-faced resentment. He felt around in his pocket, to bring out two crumpled sheets of paper. 'And lo and behold, the very document that the Detective Sergeant is seeking.' He held it out for Dryson.

'That the report, then, at long last? Let's see it.' Dryson unfolded the papers with exaggerated fuss and frowned over them. 'What's all this? What do these figures mean -- that diagram, for instance?'

'It means, Detective Sergeant, that the witness could not have seen the victim's face for the first time, in the flash of light created by the exploding bottle. These figures clearly demonstrate that for that amount of alcohol spontaneously igniting and combining with atmospheric oxygen at that distance, Mallory's face would have been outside the radius of the flash. It would have been in the shadow.'

'It may be clear to you, but it's *not* to *me*. Anyway, you're saying that Brown's testimony, that he saw Mallory's face for the very first time, in the flash of the explosion, was pure fabrication? That he must have known him from a previous instance? Is that what you're saying?'

'A most precise logical conclusion, Detective Sergeant, and managed entirely by yourself.'

Dryson's face darkened with anger. 'Don't push me to too far, Balchard! Understand this, Balchard, and understand it well, for your own good. If it wasn't for Superintendent Wraithely's buckling down to the silly whims of the Commissioner's plans of 'modern scientific expansion', embracing the other metropolitan services, I'd have you and your fancy analysis bounced out of here, into the street, before you could say leap-frog. We're of different minds, you and I, working together, sure; but neither of us is fool enough to not see the gap widening between us, if things carry on like this. You're the one who'll suffer, make no mistake. Right? Am I making *my* message clear enough?'

A strange darkness that he did not as yet fully comprehend, passed across Balchard's mind for a chilling second. The throbbing pain started up in his head again. He pulled his steely stare away, at last, from the Detective Sergeant's eyes. 'Shall we proceed, Detective Sergeant?' Balchard put his gloves down on one of the chairs and stepped over to the chair seating the corpse.

Standing on the opposite side of the chair from Balchard, Dryson pulled the sheet from over the head down to the chest. 'Lord Danby in person, though a little bit dead. Eldest son of the Earl of Wexley. Married twice. Rumoured to be contemplating annulment of present marriage with Lady Helena, with intention of securing marital attachment to Lady Rowena, younger daughter of ---'

'Yes, I have read up on your details on the peerage line, Detective Sergeant,' interrupted Balchard, with a reproving glance at the other, while whipping away the sheet completely to throw it down on the floor. It was only fair to see the player to the full in his last part before the final curtain. The *circumstances*, Detective Sergeant, the *circumstances*?'

Dryson rubbed his cheek with his knuckle as if to erase the dry smile that sneaked out in his irritation.. 'That's the funny thing about it. There doesn't seem to be too many circumstances to speak of, to tell the truth. Nobody can say for sure what happened. There were no witnesses to the killing and nobody recalls seeing or hearing anything suspicious that may have had a hand in the matter. And yet the fatal blow was struck, all the same, to the back of the head, just as you can see. Imagine, out here, in full view of hundreds, and nobody saw it. That's the curious one.'

'Intriguing,' murmured Balchard, hovering like a dentist over his patient. The 'patient's partly opened mouth could almost be heard to give that final scream that never came out. Death's two heavy 'shutters' had been pulled down over the eyes to cover what Balchard could imagine to be a frozen stare. He lifted one eyelid for a brief look at the pupil. A gross weight of about sixteen stone had been responsible for holding the body steadfast in the chair against the back-rest, otherwise it would have toppled forward under the impact of the blow, onto the floor. Yet another 'coincidental' factor that had enabled the dastardly act to be carried out without attracting undue attention.

'It must have been a right nail-biter, that's all I can say.'

'Mmmh?' Balchard, down on one knee, was too engrossed in his examination of the wound to take in Dryson's remark in context. Continuing down over the general region of the neck and collar until he was satisfied, he eventually got up slowly, pausing for a few moments thought, before looking up at Dryson. 'You were saying, Detective Sergeant?'

Dryson, with his back to Balchard, was leaning over the low balcony, looking down into the vacuous expanse of the auditorium. It was as if the whole place, despite its being empty, was now, with that uncanny atmosphere of intangible presence peculiar to theatres, looking in on them in their tiny stage up here in the box. 'I'm saying as how it must have been one hell of a good play to hold everybody's attention while somebody steps in here and does the nasties without being seen. Not as much as a flicker of an eyelid.' There was a strong note of annoyance at his poor faith in the public's sense of duty. The blind-eyed reaction of the destitute beggars of Shoreditch was something every policeman came to expect on his regular beat. But this cultured mob were supposed to have some grey matter inside their skulls and so behave responsibly. He wiped his mouth and was about to drop spittle onto the passage below, before thinking better of the temptation and spitting his lot, annoyance included, into an ashtray.

Balchard made a brief examination of the carpet and then stood up. 'Is that how you see it as having happened,

Detective Sergeant? A violent flash of Hamlet's sword that all but one failed to catch?'

'Well, didn't it? I mean, it's feasible, isn't it? You can just see all that lot down there, with their eyes glued to the stage, while what's'isname pops in to deliver the fatal wallop, and Bob's your uncle and it's all over and done with. Like I said, it's possible, isn't it?'

'*Possible* --yes. *Probable* --no. I consider it most unlikely that someone with the brain to contrive such a devilish scheme would throw all caution to the wind with such a crucial factor of risk. While there is the astronomically remote possibility of no-one looking up here at that vital moment, there is, in contrast, the enormously dangerous risk that one individual at least *would* look in this direction. That one pair of eyes would be enough to alert the house and so send the killer to the gallows. In effect, a whole carefully devised plan gone, as you so quaintly put it, in the 'flicker of an eyelid'. No, I see the author of this little private charade commanding a higher echelon of genius and tactics than the crude violence of our common street ruffian who strikes down his victim for a mere few pence.'

'So how *did* it happen, then? ' Dryson took a step forward to assert himself, pointing at the body. 'And let's not be kidding ourselves about this, now. It happened in here as sure as we two are standing here now and as sure as that poor brute is sitting there, dead as a bag of coal. He's been dead a couple of hours or so, because that's what the Doc said when he examined the body. Could have happened any time after the curtain went up. And the attendant remembers showing his poor wretched lordship in here to his seat, so that rules out any silly notion of him being done in elsewhere and dumped here later.' Dryson paused to eye the body critically. 'Besides, I don't think I'd fancy hugging that lot around on my back all on my own. Probably be better with half of B Division from the Yard to do the job properly, without causing a fuss, or giving some sod a ruddy hernia.' He looked from the body to Balchard. '*So*? Any ideas coming out of that head of yours?' Balchard took up his gloves again, tapping his mouth lightly, between pensive bites at the empty fingers. The grin widened on Dryson's face. '*Bitten* off a little more than we can *chew* this time, have we?'

'It is not so much a question of the *amount* one bites off, as the matter of recognising the devious texture of *what* it is that one has bitten off.' Balchard ambled to the box's front, still slapping thoughtfully with the gloves, to look down into the void of empty seats. 'Of a cunning calibre of mind he most certainly is, as surely as he tauntingly carries out his murderous act before our very eyes and so puts *all* of us, as much as *none* of us, as suspect on the 'stage'.'

Dryson leaned over the parapet beside Balchard. 'Yeah, I see what you mean. Much easier with the victim lying on his own parlour floor. That limits the suspects. Here we've got nearly half the blooming Town to stand up in the dock.'

'So on *that*, at least, we are agreed, Detective Sergeant, namely that he was a man who had many bitter enemies?'

'Yes, that at least. We do have our *own* sources of information as well, you know. He apparently was a bit of a right scallywag with the underhand money-lending deals, as sure as he ate caviar by the shovelful, while the poor borrowers hanged themselves for not being able to pay back the interest. In fact, he seems to have had his fingers in every poke as far as shady money deals were concerned. Only, every time that we made a grab, the ruddy pokes were empty. Bit of a womaniser as well. Had his women and then brushed them off like dandruff.' Dryson looked round at the body while touching his own hair self-consciously. 'Mind you, not that he seems to have had *that* problem.'

Balchard returned to the body. 'In that case, one could almost be glad that Society's face has been removed of such a nasty rash of a rogue. So much so that one ponders over the need for further investigation, for the sake of saving further blushing by the more *innocent* parties, however indirectly involved.'

'Yes, well, you can do your 'pondering', Balchard, but I'm a policeman, and as such, I'm not *allowed* to 'ponder'. The Law is the Law, and no-one, but *no-one*, steps outside of it. Not if I can help it. Now you weren't thinking of doing that, by suggesting that I turned a blind eye, were you?' Dryson's eyelids pulled closer slightly, in shrewd scrutiny of Balchard. 'No, somehow I don't think it's that. No, I think it's something else. It's just your round-about way of saying that you can't continue with it because your brains are fuddled. Go on, admit it, you're giving up on the job because you haven't the foggiest notion in hell as to what happened here.'

'The presumption is yours, Detective Sergeant, and a most grossly incorrect one at that, as it happens.'

But Balchard's apparently negative attitude had put the

spark into Dryson, so that he was not so easily quelled in his new confidence as the leader with the ideas. 'Yes, well, the way I see it is easy, Balchard. How about if the bloke was to open that door a little bit, just enough to get in, and creep along the floor on his hands and knees, below the level of the balcony there, and then ---wallop! ---he delivers the blow with his club to the back of the head. What's wrong with that theory, then?'

'I somehow do not envisage a person in such a low-lying position being able to command sufficient strength or leverage to render such a brutal impact to the effect of what we see here.'

'All right, so what about a simple sharp sword jab from just outside the door, then?'

'On the end of a bargepole, perhaps, Detective Sergeant, but not, I fear, by a *simple* sword, to cover that distance.' Dryson's spark of genius waned.

But ideas were not gone completely. 'Well, what about a short-legged dwarf bloke with long arms or a long club?' said a voice behind them.

Dryson looked round angrily at the constable's face peering in round the door. 'Shut up, Evans! *We'll* do the investigating, if you don't mind! Get out!' The head disappeared, returned to its place of duty in the passage outside. The Detective Sergeant's knuckle restarted its rubbing motion on the cheek. He looked down at the floor, toeing the white sheet abstractedly, as if a search under it would help to find an answer. 'Well, he definitely wasn't shot with a gun. That we *do* know. It was one of the first things that I thought of. The idea of a gun being fired from outside in the passage, through a cushion of some sort, to keep the sound of the shot down. But there isn't any sign of a bullet, as far as the Doc was concerned. Not after all *his* poking about.'

'Ah!' Balchard clapped his hands together in obvious delight at this remark. 'It would appear that for once you have employed your observational powers objectively, however accidentally, to use logic as your reasoning instrument. And tell me, Detective Sergeant, did the Doctor also point out the inconsistency of the blood drainage considering the size of the wound and the time -- several hours, I remind you -- that it has had to bleed?'

'No, he didn't. Anyhow, I don't quite follow you.'

'Quite simply, Detective Sergeant, that for a wound of this size, one would expect a greater flow of blood. But here we have a much reduced discharge -- a trickle, in fact -- leaving an overall lesser amount of blood here on the collar and the back. It is as if something has been held up against the back of the head for some time, restricting the outflow of blood.'

'So maybe he put his hand up over the wound before he died.'

'And do you see any sign of blood on the hand, Detective Sergeant? Even so, such a temporary blockage would not have resulted in this effect.'

'No, perhaps not. Which brings us back to square one. What on earth *did* happen?'

Balchard began to put his gloves back on, looking round the box again pensively. But instead of disappointment, like

Dryson's, showing on his face, there was the elated expression of inner excitement. 'What happened here, Detective Sergeant, most surely borders on the realms of the unique. For not only are we confronted by brilliance of tactic, but the material employment of such chicane craft bows to applause on the threshold of a new mode of criminal technique. Truly a *theatrical* performance'

'Yes, well, if you can just give that to me in plain black and white, then maybe some of us will be able to sleep in comfort.' Dryson didn't much care for Balchard's flowery words making light issue of the fact that they had a dead earl on their hands. A whole sixteen stone that would promptly claim first priority on the Commissioner's desk. But he let it go. He had serious police work to see to, without wasting more words fuelling further fancy rhetoric from Balchard. He picked up the sheet, holding it at his chest, ready to throw it over the corpse. Finished, are we?'

Balchard nodded, his mind elsewhere.

'Right.' Casting the sheet none too gently over the deceased, Dryson strode to the door, to yank it open and beckon the constable in from the passage. When the constable came in, Dryson jabbed an arm out in the direction of the corpse. 'Meat wagon!'

'Right, sir.'

Watching the policemen struggling and gasping to put their load onto the stretcher, and move it into the passage, Balchard and Dryson followed at a distance. Going down the stairway, Dryson looked around him at the expressionless faces of the theatre staff. 'Mind you, going by what you said,

Balchard, I don't suppose there'll be much lament, judging by the strength of many a tear that *won't* flow.'

Balchard stopped abruptly, to turn and grip Dryson by the arm. 'Of course! How ingenious! The *strength of a tear*!" He turned away again, muttering to himself in elation of new revelation, whilst descending the next few steps as if he was walking on air.

'Reminded you of something we left out, then, did I? Well don't forget to let me in on it, won't you, Balchard?'

But it was not until they had reached the bottom of the stairs that Balchard turned his attention once more to Dryson. 'Were you aware, Detective Sergeant, that the builders in ancient Cathay used water for breaking up massive boulders, no less? They did, in fact, insert wedges of wood into the cracks of boulders and then would pour water onto the absorbent wood. The wood would subsequently swell up with the added water so giving sufficient leverage to break the boulders. Ingenious, wouldn't you say, Detective Sergeant?' Clearly not caring if Dryson considered the issue to be ingenious or not, Balchard went on ahead, held in his own thoughts.

Dryson stepped after him smartly. 'I'm sure I don't know what you're rattling on about, Balchard, but whatever it is, I wish you would share it with me, so that we can both go and tell my boss, the Commissioner, all about it. You do know that it's your duty, as a public citizen, not to withhold from the police any information vital to an investigation such as this, don't you? If you have as much as an inkling as to what happened upstairs, don't be keeping it to yourself. Just tell me.'

Balchard looked at Dryson with a broad placatory smile that did not hide its mockery. '*Tell you*? But Detective Sergeant, have I not, in fact, just *told you*?'

Dryson's brain was blocked to a standstill, however much it tried. '*Told me*? You haven't told me anything, not unless you call gabbling on about some stupid history lesso----. Here, hold on a second, Balchard. Balchard!'

But Balchard had no more ear for the imbecilic slowness of Dryson, and strode on unheeding, out through the doorway, into the night.

Balchard's troubled mind was not granted refuge in sleep that night. Frightfully bizarre dreams haunted him, their disorderly flow making him toss and turn. *The millwheel turned over and over in the middle of the meadow, to the droning incantation of: "Remember, Adam, that thou art dust, and unto dust thou shalt return". These words from the hollow sounding priest, who was her father. As he tried to approach her grave, his legs began crumbling to dust, forbidding his movement. Suddenly she was the priest, frantically paddling the coffin along in the middle of the river, which was now an ascending staircase, while he hung on to the coffin's side, from the outside. He was frightened of getting into the coffin because it was full to its brim with daffodils. He was terrified of those daffodils, with their vile entwining stalks and the evil black spaces in between staring at him accusingly, judging him with Cyclopean eyes. The daffodils turned to dust, his dust, pouring overboard into him, so that he was sinking. He was drowning.* Erupting in convulsive jerks, he woke up.

The soaking saliva ran down his cheek, from the corner of his mouth. Wiping it away, he looked around himself to regain his bearings. Dim grey light, from another drab dawn, filtered in through grimy window panes, lending no cheer to an even more drab interior. What had once been a stately room was now a dilapidated hovel. Balchard gazed drowsily across the room, at the man leaning into the fireplace, stabbing the ornate Adams wooden mantelpiece with his knife. Watching the sharp point go in and out, again and again, Balchard used the seconds of heavy silence to let the mental vagueness of his surroundings sort itself out.

Levering a splinter of wood out, and throwing it into the fireplace, Vlarda looked round at Balchard. 'So, you are awake now, Mr Balchard.'

'Well, if it's not me, it must be moiself. Oi must have dozed off -- all that drink, an' all, to be sure.'

'It is more than doze, I think; you are in sleep a long time. You do not sleep well.' Another deep thud of steel in wood, and a quick look from piercing eyes. 'You talk much in your sleep, Mr Balchard.' The man's face seemed to hold something more than idle curiosity on its pocked brown surface.

Balchard's hackles were up. It was like having a hand of cards without seeing their faces, nor knowing what cards he had dealt earlier. The Irishman beamed roguishly back. 'So Oi was talkin' loike a headless chicken, was Oi? Just loike moi fadder, an' him the fadder o' many chicks in his woild oats days, an' all. So what was Oi sayin' then, if it wasn't the barley spe-e-akin'?'

Vlarda was not sure if he detected a note of nervousness

behind the cheery verbal blast thrown at him. The glazed look in the Irishman's eyes didn't match the broad smile, which to Vlarda, seemed forced. Was it fear or potential threat, that he saw in them? Like the English would say, the man had too many loose corners to be tied together. Something of an enigma, was Mr Balchard. Vlarda did not fail to consider the possibility of underhanded trickery on the Irishman's part. But he was not into believing his plans to be thwarted. He would not *allow* them to be. He would not even entertain the thought of such a defeatist possibility. That was a purely capitalist weakness. No, whatever the Irishman intended to gain through treacherous double-crossing, if that should be the case, would be outweighed by far, by what he would come to *lose*. As a dedicated nihilist supremely committed in his ideological mission, Vlarda knew that he would cope efficiently with the question of Balchard's trustworthiness, whichever way it should fall. Nothing, but nothing, would interfere with his anarchist campaign. Only a little time would be lost -- that, and a worthless Irish life. Vlarda turned away, to continue his assault on the rococo fire-surround; in his eyes, a capitalist abomination, truly deserving its destruction. 'Mr Balchard says much strange things, as he sleeps.'

'Oh *yes?*' Balchard could barely keep the uneasiness out of his voice this time, as he put forth the question. But Vlarda gave no more response to Balchard, turning all his attention to attacking the wood. Just where *was* the Turk's mind, Balchard wondered, as the anarchist blade was driven relentlessly into the wood, progressively demolishing its original capitalist elegance and structure? Balchard found himself confronted by a sobering reversal of scenarios. In contrast to his natural assumption that he would outwit his foe, he suddenly considered the opposite outcome. What if he were to be 'removed from the field', as Smethers would have put it? In the amazingly philosophical thought of his being rendered stone cold dead and non-existent, he pondered over how things would continue to be run. What would happen if he didn't turn up at the arranged contact point, to meet Carter? Not that he had very much substantial information to relay to Carter. Vlarda was guardedly reticent on the issue of his forthcoming tactics. It was also the stark reality of a possibility that he was simply Smethers' bait, to draw Vlarda out. He didn't put it past Smethers to be using him in full acceptance of the expectancy of his life being lost. The English gentleman hunter sacrificing the life of the tethered goat, to lure the tiger. In overall consideration, then, who would be outwitting whom? Further to these questions, Balchard accepted the stark realisation that he was playfully dwelling on the nothingness, and possible peacefulness thereafter, of his own death.

CHAPTER 25

When Balchard finally reached Duck's Foot Lane through the malt-thick fog, Sam Loofer was opening a tin of curried rabbit and emptying it into the cooking pot. Stirring the dark meat with a wooden spoon, he bade Balchard to sit down on a rickety chair that looked ready to collapse. 'I always likes a late night bite, I does. Don't you, Mr B? Besides, I ain't 'ad as much as a mouthful o' air all day, an' that's nuffin' good in this perishin' weather, I tell yer. Been too busy, I 'as. What with Charlie, an' all. He lumps it again like a pregnant goose, 'e does. Goes an' runs the barrow over some blind beggar of a sod lyin' in the road. Just goes an' breaks the wheel, e' does. Sends all our bleedin' merchandise rollin' all over the Tottenham Court Road, 'e does. You never saw so many 'cripples' suddenly find their legs, to get up an' scarper off with our stuff down that road faster than a nag with a red 'ot poker shoved up its khyber.' Loofer lifted the spoon to clean it by banging it several times on the pot's rim, so that particles of meat flew off, one of them just missing Balchard's face and landing on his sleeve.

Balchard flicked the particle away with his finger. 'Still, you were able to recover part of your merchandise, I see. *None* of which, of course, had ever at any time fallen off the back of a *larger* barrow.' While saying this, Balchard was looking pointedly at the tins of Halford's curried fowl and rabbit stacked three shelves high in the cupboard, in newly burst boxes stamped with Crosse & Blackwell, the well known Soho Square wholesale dealers. Loofer followed Balchard's look with its loaded words and pushed the cupboard door shut. But the door yawned open again, in apparent qualm of conscience, so that Loofer had to ram it shut with a hard thrust of the boot. Emptying a chipped teacup into the wooden sink, he wiped it on the soiled tablecloth and filled it with dark ale from an earthenware jug. Balchard politely declined the offer. Taking out a notebook and pencil, he began writing something down. The last two days had given him ample opportunity to theorise over the Adelphi Theatre murder, so that he was now putting down instructions for Loofer to carry out. The very precise manner of Lord Danby's untimely demise, along with the unique mechanics of application, suggested most strongly that the guilty party had known in advance that his lordship would be attending the theatre that evening. The checking of this, and one other item of paramount importance, would require some considerable leg-work, and this would take time. And time was something Balchard did not have much of to spare, in view of his other pressing engagements with the War Office. He tore the page from the notebook and slid it across the table to Loofer.

While the writing was clearly legible, the meaning of some words was none too explicit to Loofer. Explanation was needed. 'An' yer wants me ter sniff aroun' town for this thingummy what'sit, right, Mr B?' Loofer licked his spoon, while reading the note, to give extra weight to his difficulty in accepting the job. 'Seein' as 'ow I've been kind o' busy these last few days, I don't know if ---'

The bright coins tumbled out of Balchard's hand onto the table in timely remedy for reluctant 'sore feet'. Loofer folded the paper and stuffed it in his waistcoat pocket only a second quicker than he made the coins do a similar disappearing trick. 'Right y'are, Mr B. I'll get on the job faster than you can poke a pickle in a blind flea's ear.' But always one to squeeze a good thing's neck to make it a better thing, Loofer looked round at the darkness outside the window. 'Mind you, with all this perishin' fog ticklin' the old eyeballs an' 'ooter, the goin' can get rough. Know what I mean?'

Balchard rose, pulling on his gloves with a firmness to show that in no way would the hands make another dip into the pockets for more. 'An early start in the morning should suffice, I think.' He stood waiting. Loofer smiled with wicked innocence, feigning a puzzled look at Balchard standing there waiting. He knew perfectly well what Balchard wanted. Balchard leaned forward on the table. 'Haven't we forgotten something?' He pointed at Loofer's waistcoat pocket. 'The money is enough to cover both *that* and -----' Balchard's voice trailed off to let his arched eyebrows carry their innuendo. But there was more than mere reminder lurking beneath those arches, in the double menacing depths of burning eyes.

Loofer's inner glee dissolved, and he rose from his chair, careful to hide his haste. He needed to keep his composure. 'Sure, Mr B. 'Ave it right 'ere, for yer. 'Old on, 'alf a jiff.'

Reaching into a cupboard, it suddenly occurred to Loofer that, of all his many dealings with Balchard, this was the first time that he had ever had his back to him. And there was no-one else here as a witness to his possibly getting the 'atchet! The goose-pimples pricked out on his neck. Rummaging about clumsily until his hand found it, he was glad to turn to face Balchard again and hand over the 'merchandise'.

Pocketing the small bottle of cocaine, Balchard turned and left, taking the room's black atmosphere with him. He was refraining from getting his personal narcotic supply from the Institute's dispensary for the time being. His last effort, just days ago, had narrowly escaped disaster. Only upon his preparing to leave the building, after a tiring all night session, did he miss his syringe, and so recalled leaving it on Felsham's desk, as well as leaving Felsham's safe open. He had just closed it in time.

Loofer leaned over the banister, after the departing Balchard. 'Oh, an' 'ere, Mr B, if yon vicar geezer o' yours is still lookin' for bargains, I can get 'im a grand little winner o' an iron angel, no bother. Mind you, one o' the wings is broken off, but it's still a bargain for fillin' in the odd corner o' the chapel. No? Well 'ow about that key-cuttin' machine you was after, then? I can get you one o' them, no bother. Nothin' wrong with it, 'cept the cutter's a bit blunt, that's all.'

In spite of the fog swarming up from the river and over the Embankment's balustrade, Balchard could still discern the one 'camel' seated on top of another camel. Whilst the lower one was of black cast iron adorning the seat end, the one on top was adorned with its familiar red fez and grey astrakhan coat. Inspector Fieseen Bijali beamed his smile of a million blessings in golden ingots, and the cigarette glow brightened for a second on the end of its ivory holder, just ahead of the large hirsute nostrils. Balchard sat down on the cold iron seat beside the Inspector.

Neither of them was in the mood for a plate of eel soup, sickly green like the fog, and so turned away the disgruntled vendor, who trundled his barrow on along the kerb edge, cursing between each bump of the wheels. Fieseen Bijali spared some of his preoccupation between exhaling smoke and waving away the fog, to give some attention to Balchard. 'The Captain sends his apology, being otherwise detained.

'I see,' said Balchard, with hesitation in his voice that suggested the very opposite.

Fieseen Bijali, in perceiving this very point, allowed himself a deep guttural laugh, without loosening the golden grip on the ivory stalk. 'Ah, but truly another exquisite example of the Englishman's solidity of statement, with its face-saving curtness. You continually say what you do not mean, rather than concede to the defeat of a moment's confusion. One can see how, with a ready salvo of such concise replies to meet the diplomatic fire on every front, your Empire has no fear of lowering its flag. Whilst others hold steadfast over their transgressions by the measure of guns, the British remain so by sleight of tongue.' He waved a hand at the fog, looking round at the river behind them. 'But for the banks on which they stand divided, our two cities are so very much unalike. This fog, for instance

--so cold and confusing, yet reliable in its consistency of occurrence. Just like your evasive words.'

'Better the mist that clears with the dawn, than that which forever dwells in the mind to cloud its judgement,' said Balchard. *And what of that in his own mind?* What Balchard found to be more anomalous than anything so far mentioned was Fieseen Bijali's suffering the weather, here on the Embankment, when it was so obvious that he much preferred the comfort of the luxurious Grand Hotel in Trafalgar Square, where he was staying. The Inspector's dedication to duty was to be measured with care. But for the fact that he and Dryson were both policemen, they were otherwise just like their respective cities, so very much dissimilar in character.

In a hand's flash of gem power rivalling that of the Tower, Fieseen Bijali took out a sealskin wallet and removed from it a fold of paper. He passed the note to Balchard. It was a note confirming that Captain Smethers was unable to keep his rendezvous, being detained elsewhere on special duties, so appointing Fieseen Bijali as impromptu courier in his place. The words and the signature were of the same hand, but that meant nothing, since Balchard had never seen a specimen of Smethers' handwriting. He could only assume that all was well under the circumstances, as stated, and play each card as it was called. Balchard made his report of his last meeting with Vlarda. 'He is particularly influenced in his political fervour by the radical writings of the Russian, Ivan Sergeyevich Turgenev, deceased, and to a lesser degree by some German scholar, a Karl Marx, also now deceased, who once lived here in the City. Whilst the latter speaks of a revolutionary new social order of classless order, it is Turgenev, in his hailing the coming of the complete *disorder* of nothingness, or nihilism, as he so quaintly terms it, who fires the madness of our Turkish friend, Vlarda.'

Fieseen Bijali listened attentively with an inclined head, seemingly weighing up each word by the syllable as if it was gold dust. Not fully understanding the flexibility of English idiom, he frowned at Balchard's classification of Vlarda as their 'friend', when it was clear that he was their enemy. Balchard noted the look, but filed it away in his mind as possibly the key to a disturbingly *different* interpretation. The Inspector leaned in closer, while fussing with the cigarette in its holder. 'And the plans? There has been no specific detailing of Vlarda's intended plan of action, for instance?'

'Specifically, no. However, there is the generalised proposal for a series of trial runs.'

'*Runs? Please?*'

'Sorry; in this case, explosions; spread out over deliberately random locations, so as to defy systematic prediction, with the purpose of causing public outcry in a broad criticism of the police in their mishandling of the situation, so leading to general dissatisfaction and subsequent disorder and chaos.'

Fieseen Bijali paused for an extra long draw on the slender stalk. 'All this he expects from just a number of little bangs? I am wondering if, like a typical Turk, he is being a little over ambitious in expecting too much from too little effort.'

'One must have caution to bear in mind that these are merely the trial efforts.'

'Ah, yes, of course. One infers, therefore, that from these

trials there shall develop larger events --- perhaps the one largest *ultimate event.*'

'My reasoning, precisely.'

There was little more information that Balchard could relay in exact detail, as they conversed for several minutes more, so that the Inspector eventually touched on his personal police subject, as expected. 'And you are sure that there has been no clear rendering of how these activities are to be financed? Where the money comes from, and how it and the explosives are obtained and circulated? No mention of names of contacts along the line, for instance? No mention of whether or not *gold* currency is being used?' For a moment the man's eyes almost glowed brighter than his cigarette. All Balchard could give in answer to the pleading look was a negative nod. They rose at last, to perambulate back slowly in the direction of Fieseen Bijali's more gracious style of living.

While the Inspector busied himself with the fitting of a new cigarette in his holder, Balchard voiced a nagging thought. 'Presumably the Captain was summoned away elsewhere in great urgency, only at the last moment?'

Fieseen Bijali applied the flame and inhaled strongly, to establish a new red glow. 'Correct, as far as I am given to understand. But perhaps *eagerly*, more aptly than urgently, would best describe his swift manner of departure.' There was a faint token twitch of the eye in what Balchard took to be a wink. 'Strictly between the two of us, I rather suspect that the good Captain makes fast his gallop to take up pace with some fine mare that is a beautiful woman. Truly, minds can be universally agreed on this one subject at least, regardless of ideological conflict.' His cigarette appeared to taste all the more satisfying as he dwelt on the thought. Balchard had no great appraisal to offer on the subject.

Suddenly the mist in front of them took on stripes, to give body to four 'Mississippi minstrels' in tall hats, striped trousers and blackened golliwog faces. The pathetic plunking of a banjo and three fiddles was in keeping with the forlorn expressions, so that Fieseen Bijali gestured with a raised arm for them to move on. But the beggar tagging along on their tail was staunch enough to linger on, holding out and rattling his tin cup, while his tiny wire terrier whimpered on his heels. The Inspector made to strike a blow, so that the beggar stepped back promptly out of reach. The dog, however, stood its ground growling, with a mind to sinking its teeth in the Inspector's ankle. An angry kick missed the dog, but aroused the beggar, so that he leaped forward, enraged. ' 'Ere, don't yer bleedin' touch my little Dukey, or I'll 'ave yer, see! Bleedin' Arab!'

Surprised at this uniquely English display of insurrection from the beggar class in protection of a mere animal, Fieseen Bijali could only flick his cigarette ash with disgust in the direction of the beggar, and walk on. Balchard concealed his amusement, clinking a coin into the cup. The Inspector looked round in amazement at this sound of charity, snorting his own personal disdain aloud. 'Back in my country they would be whipped until the bones come out to shine with the sun.'

'Oh, we do have something of the sort here, as well. It's called *work*.'

Behind them, the 'beggar' looked around for his dog, and whistled on it as it sniffed the iron dolphins entwining the lamp standard, before lifting its leg. While he waited on the dog, Carter took the coin, along with the coded message wrapped round it, from the tin cup and put it in his pocket.

CHAPTER 26

The gull screeched out and took off, startled by the head appearing above the cliff edge beside it. Captain Smethers looked up with equal surprise, to follow its flight and then hauled himself up onto the top of the headland, at roughly two hundred feet above the Cornish fishing village. As he stood up, a hefty gust tugged at his leather cap, almost snatching it away, the cold breeze cutting and refreshing. A glance in any direction, and he had travelled miles without restriction. There was nothing there and yet everything was moving, as billions of grass blades frisked about in a sea of green ripples along the broad expanse of the headland. Smethers turned to give a helping hand to the gasping bent figure of Sir Basil, pulling him up onto the level ground. Even between long drawn-out breaths, Sir Basil had a little difficulty in bringing forth his words for a moment. 'Hopefully, Captain, there will be ample reward for all this *hearty* effort.'

'I did warn you that it would be a jolly steep climb up the footpath, sir. Besides, didn't you and my uncle at one time reputedly tame the Alps, supposedly in search of some edelweiss, or whatever?'

Sir Basil thought distantly for a moment on this remark, looking down at the shoreline below them, the sea acknowledging his attention by sending up its foaming cry as it lashed the terra firma. The brief tidal sound was lost amidst the shrieking wind that battered their ears. 'We did, indeed, but that, alas, was on some other somewhat distant shores of youth. As for searching for the *edelweiss*; from what little I can recall, I can only imagine that this was some felicitous fabrication on our part; concocted for the ears of your dearest then aunt -to-be, where your uncle and I had sought after, and found, a much fairer species of 'Alpine Flower' --- *Die Fraulein.*'

'Of course, sir.'

They turned, to move inwards, away from the cliff edge. Isolated on the open plain before them, the house looked smaller than it was, squashed into the ground by the overwhelming urge for flatness between sky and ground. A simple decor of whitewash and black slates gave a maritime air to the building. Whilst the ground floor windows shrunk back in reclusion, the protrusive dormer windows stared out to sea in an endless watch for the enemy. An idyllic retreat for poet or artist, it was otherwise known in exclusive Intelligence circles as the setting that came under the operational codename, SEA HORSE. Whilst there would be no invading Vikings to watch for today, the building would still serve as a vantage point for observing today's demonstration of a naval operation. Or, as Sir Basil had put it earlier: 'an operation *and a half*'.

Aloft, sentinels wearing the house's black and white livery

circled round them in long scrutiny as they approached. The gulls gave out their hoarse warnings and then moved away. Something moved behind a dirty glass window, and had Smethers fingering the .45 Adams revolver in the pocket of his leather coat. Cautioning Sir Basil to stay behind for a moment, Smethers raised the latch softly and eased the door open, to peer inside. The wind rushed past him and banged a door somewhere at the back of the house. Nothing else happened. Only a faint squeaking noise broke the silence from somewhere within, causing him to follow it along the stone flagged passage. There were four doors. One of these had been the false alarm, still moaning backwards and forwards on its rusty hinge, to sigh with relief as Smethers kicked it back into the room. An unmistakable smell of paraffin came from the next room.

The corporal jumped up to salute as Captain Smethers looked in. Down at their feet, a tiny brass paraffin stove continued to hiss, and a tiny brass kettle perched on top of it bubbled on merrily, not at all bothered by the soldiers' silly formalities. 'Saw you coming up the cliff, sir. Thought you would like a cup of tea, sir.'

'Fine. Carry on.'

'Sir!'

Smethers' eyes roamed around the room, but could not see what he was looking for. 'And the rest of our equipment, Corporal?'

The soldier jumped up from the stove again. 'Outside, sir, round the side of the house, out the way of the wind. Thought you'd like it better out there in the sunshine and fresh air, instead o' in here in this rotten dump, sir. I put the stove here 'cause it works better with the flame sheltered from the wind, sir.'

'Good thinking, Corporal. Carry on.'

'Sir!'

Smethers rejoined Sir Basil outside, and they both went round the side of the house to inspect the equipment that was there in the form of two folding chairs and a folding table set up with a wicker food hamper on top of it. Some other equipment pieces in leather casings and straps lay on the grass. Smethers picked up a tubular case, to open it and take out a brass telescope. 'I'll just trot up top a jiffy for a look, sir.'

'You do that. I personally shall have no further strong temptation to follow suit. After that ascent, the only climbing I shall be attempting today will be downhill. I say that most *categorically*!' With that assertive statement, Sir Basil began rummaging in the food hamper for the brandy flask, so that he could replenish what his screaming lungs seemed to have given up for ever and ever.

Inside, in the hall, the stairs beckoned Smethers enter up into the attic. Four three-stair strides and he was up, dry dust conveying the lorn feelings of the attic in full effect. He saw the corporal's fresh footprints in the dust, but nothing else. There was a confusion of shadows, and the sea bird landed on the ledge outside the window. Powerful wings collapsed and lost themselves in the streamlined body of feathers. Stout yellow-scaled legs reminded one of the hidden strength. Smethers went over to the second window to train his telescope on the sea's distant horizon. A quick scan from left to right and back again revealed that nothing had arrived yet. According to schedule, they were already an hour late. But for the fleecy cirrus cloud hurrying on its way to nowhere, there was nothing worth watching that far out at sea. The telescope dipped, drawing its panoramic view inwards, to catch the silent swarm of gulls that had a similar design of descending on the tiny fishing village harbour. Following the birds' motion of circling and alighting on the swaying masts of the small fleet of fishing boats, Smethers moved his inspection down over the wooden vessels and onto the wooden breakwater jetty to which they were moored. The dark-timbered structure grew into a lighter grey stone finger that reached back to join the main quay of the small harbour.

Standing out conspicuously as they ambled idly along the narrow stone walk were three small figures in black coats and tall hats, the austerity of which contrasted sharply with the bright maritime surroundings. Junior civil servants from Whitehall's War Office Department, they had braved the cold to venture out to stare around at the oddities of the fishing community. The rest of their colleagues remained huddled in the sheltered interiors of the two black coaches standing up on the main quay. Everybody was being kept waiting, it seemed. Smethers snapped the telescope shut with a soft click and left it on the window sill, to retire below and leave the attic to its own secrecy. He then instructed the corporal to set up the heliograph apparatus on its tripod and position it just in from the cliff edge, where its signals could be seen from out at sea. After doing that, the corporal's next duty was to keep watch from the upstairs attic window.

Sir Basil added another portion of crab meat pate to his cracker biscuit before looking up as Captain Smethers joined him at the table. 'I gather from your expression that there is nothing to report yet?'

Smethers helped himself to a cup of tea. 'I'm sure it'll turn up soon. Keeping schedules at sea can be something of a sticky wicket, from what I've heard, considering nasty unpredictable turns in the weather, and what not.'

'Oh dear, I do hope that this little jaunt to the seaside is going to reward us with something more substantial than reddened cheeks and salt-laden lungs to take back to our masters in the City.' Removed from the grandiose surroundings of his government office, Sir Basil, seated there in his flapping herring-bone cape and corduroy hat with its flapping brim, now conveyed the comical image of the whimsical grandpapa in the child's nursery book. He bit off another piece of cracker. 'Supposedly one must hold with lateness being the prerogative of the Senior Service. It couldn't be an error in communication, could it?'

'I double checked the cypher myself. There can be no question of an error there. It's just as well Carter went out on field duty early and so reported back to us in time to make arrangements.'

'Carter?'

'You know the one, sir. Corporal Carter, back in the Department at Adelphi Terrace. Our contact man for picking up active field messages from Balchard.'

'Ah, yes, of course, Carter.' Sir Basil frowned. 'But do you mean to say that you did not Make contact with Balchard yourself? I had understood that you had arranged to meet him, yourself?'

'Something of a last minute alteration in plans to test the man's resourcefulness, sir. To see how he would react to a sudden unexpected change in procedure.'

'And?'

'So far, so good. He acted as instructed, by having a written coded version of his report reserved as stand-by, which he passed on to our man, Carter.'

'Why didn't he just tell our man straight out, and so save all this fuss with cyphers and things?'

'He was with someone else at the time, sir.'

'Ah, yes, the light begins to dawn. Our Inspector friend?'

'Precisely, sir.'

'Do we not fully trust Inspector Fieseen Bijali, then?'

'One learns to act with the strictest caution in the field.'

'Agreed, most certainly. I am only a little disappointed in your failure to convey this information to me earlier.'

'Sorry, sir.'

'Now is not the time to be sorry. Rather, one is hopeful that today's operation will be a successful one, and not just an empty fiasco. It *will*, will it not, Captain, since the arrangements are entirely of your choosing?'

'Of course, sir.'

'Splendid. Help yourself to the lobster canapes; absolutely delicious.'

'Thank you, sir, but not just for the moment, if you don't mind.' If Captain Smethers had something to fret over, he made no visible show of it, but simply leaned back in his chair, to look up at the sky that was a faultless cerulean canvass spread out evenly on all sides of the golden disc. The sun blinked as the gulls criss-crossed before it, their shrieks lifting the humans' minds upwards. Smooth leisurely flights carried the gulls up to haughty positions overhead, so that rival fliers hastened to equal the elevation, their wings pumping furiously. All at once the beating stopped and the gulls soared up with an ease that was understood only by them. If only man had wings, or wing-like contraptions, Smethers mused. Would it make his job easier? Different, perhaps. Battalions upon battalions of armed troops sent out on aerial sorties. Even at night, in the blackest darkness, with no land obstacles to impede them. Smethers dismissed the nonsense from his mind and rose to cross over to the cliff edge. As yet there was nothing. Nothing except more confounded birds. Despite their swoops and loops in aerobatic feats of grace calling for applause, the human was no longer interested. Smethers returned to the table, to stab up a generous forkful of lobster, which he ate with only half an appetite.

Luncheon was virtually over with Sir Basil finishing a second portion of rum trifle, so that he was on the point of cutting a fine cigar to accompany his port, when the knocking sounded on the lookout's window above. Smethers was up the stairs and manning the telescope before one could say Jack Tar. To the naked eye, it was just a spiked blob visible after a long stare. But through the telescope it was, to Smethers, the masted brig-rigged iron- clad HMS *Vanguard*, pride of the Navy. Despite his not being a Navy man, himself, Smethers felt honoured at the sight of the powerful 320ft screw-driven vessel with its 7980 tons displacement that weighed under its massive 24ins of wrought iron cladding that gave it its might. The main fire force came from four 16-inch rifled muzzle-loaders each weighing 81 tons and firing 700-pounder shells over a range of 4800 yards. The guns were mounted in turrets of a new swivel-motion design that had 17ins of iron plating and a steel facing that made them as strong as the main 24ins of armour. It was the versatility of this new design of swivel-turret that was being demonstrated today. That, and *something else*.

This 'something else' was anticipated only by an exclusive minority in Intelligence circles, two of whom were Sir Basil and Captain Smethers. Whilst the Admiralty could normally be expected to deal discreetly with its own internal affairs, Sir Basil and Captain Smethers were being privileged with a look-in today, since it was the actual work of their Military Intelligence Department that had first brought the matter to light. It was only after much long discussion that the Admiralty, along with the Home Secretary and the Minister for War, had been finally persuaded by Sir Basil into moving on from initial agreement, to preliminary consideration, and then to promoting the plan to theoretical tactical assessment, and thereafter to agreement for active preparation of the operational stage.

The corporal clattered down the stairs at Smethers' command, to send the message by flashing heliograph that they were ready on shore for the demonstration. HMS *Vanguard* winked back in acknowledgement. Firing would begin in seven minutes countdown. Even Sir Basil, who was not normally aroused by such outside activities, managed to rise to the occasion by expressing a mild degree of excitement at the prospect of witnessing the demonstration. Down on the harbour's main quay, some more figures spilled out of the coaches to watch.

Firing began with puffs of smoke popping out in front of the great muzzles like instant cauliflower, some seconds before the distant dull thuds came to ear, reverberating with secondary background clashing over the water. First one, then another and another and another. Shrill cheers rose up from the harbour, to drown those of the seagulls. Several minutes elapsed while the huge guns were pulled in on ratchet chains, to be reloaded and fired again. But this time the shells whistled away over the sea to plop down into the water in the opposite direction. And this without the ship having turned round, the turrets having turned round, instead. Spirits rose and brandy flasks were duly passed round, both on the quay and up on the cliff top. The corporal didn't receive any share of amenities, but he clapped his cold hands on his arms as a warmer, instead.

The darkened fumes of man's wrath and might gathered steadily in the sky over the battleship as the demonstration continued. Until at last catastrophe decided that enough was enough and laid down its mighty sceptre. At first no-one was sure what one was seeing. Civilian minds witnessing the unfamiliar spectacle of smoke and heavy booming were now presented with what seemed like an inappropriate pouring forth of smoke and a different volume of deep thunderous rumbling, which was altogether confusing. As thick black smoke began to engulf the ship and tiny ribbons of flame streaked up, elated cheers suddenly changed to drones of dismay, like wounded bagpipes, at the realisation that something was wrong. Sir Basil and Captain Smethers exchanged anxious glances for a moment and then the corporal was ordered to signal the distressed ship. No answer came back for what seemed agonisingly long minutes. Then the distant flashing peeped out once more from the depth of the smoke to say that a gun emplacement and its magazine had exploded. There was no clear notion of casualties yet. The cliff top signalled back that immediate help would be sent out from the harbour. Another long silence ensued before HMS *Vanguard* flashed back that it was able to cope with the situation by itself, so that help from the shore was out of the question. No-one from the outside was allowed to see the Senior Service humbled on bended knee.

In the midst of all the messages that passed between ship and shore, there were two words, SEA HORSE, issued by the *Vanguard*, that the corporal had not understood. Sir Basil and Captain Smethers, on the other hand, were able to sigh with relief at this code, knowing that the *entire* operation had been successful. Sir Basil was especially relieved, now that they could pack up their things and return to the City.

paint-work costs. Our pyrotechnic experts did a splendid job in simulating what was *supposed* to be a genuine explosion and fire disaster. In fact, all we saw was harmless smoke charges and carefully arranged breakouts of fire on deck. Secondly, to have aborted the sabotage at its onset would have been to inform the enemy that we have an agent in their camp. Our agent would then be in great danger, as, indeed, would be our plans to thwart the overall plot to topple the country's stability over into a state of chaos.'

Sir Basil paused to press his final point home, with a pedagogic stab of the forefinger into the leather arm-rest. 'No, it was imperative that we played out the charade to its end, down to the very last signals between the shore and the *distressed* ship, so that *all* onlookers would see what they saw as being real. Arrangements were such that amidst the general commotion, one significant code-word would either pass unnoticed, or without undue suspicion on the part of the over-keen observer. This is how seriously sensitive we measure the eye and ear of our '*silly saboteurs*'.'

Still not persuaded, the young man stalled to take a haughty sip of his drink. 'It seems to me that we could have avoided a lot of fuss if we'd just *said* that the explosion had occurred, and let it rest there.'

'But *would* it rest there? Seeing is believing. How often the shrouded whispers of evasive hearsay can breed disbelief like coaxing breaths on the flames of suspicion. If we merely say that the incident occurred, there is the grave possibility that the truth to the contrary will nevertheless leak out to enemy ears, to result in havoc, as I have already said.'

'If you are so concerned with leakages of truth, won't the very crew of the ship itself constitute one such hazard? What of the rogue who had the very gall to plant the bomb on board, in the first place? A Royal Navy seaman in sympathy with, and accepting bribes from, an anarchist movement directed against his own country is something I find to be utterly revolting!' A nervous twirl of the drink in its glass displayed the degree of uneasiness incurred in the Secretary by the thought of this state of affairs.

'Rest assured that one such renegade seaman has since fallen *ill* with some yet unidentified contagion of the maritime strain. For the safety of all other crew members, he has been securely locked away under *quarantine* and strict armed guard, lest the *pestilence* should spread. In similar measure, there is no chance of the crew letting out *rumours*, since all shore leave has been temporarily suspended, with the ship going to a secret location for repairs, after which it will go on a goodwill mission to some foreign port outside the reach of our present adversary.'

'If only I could share your faith in things being so clear-cut and simple, Sir Basil.'

'One can only try.'

'But to play your game we still have to leak it out, with pretentious reluctance, to the press, that we suffered a humiliating naval disaster. Since it *didn't* happen, I see that as a doubly high price to pay.'

Sir Basil nodded sagely with closed eyes. 'But one of the *lesser* evils one learns to choose in preference.'

The Secretary pushed his empty glass away and made

a fuss of checking the time on his watch to air his heavy exasperation. 'I still don't like it, Sir Basil. I really am not happy about this at all. Mark my word, there is going to be a barrage of complaints from the Opposition at Question Time, and I don't see the Minister coming through them wholly unscathed. Heaven knows what will happen if it calls for a division in the Lobby.' He put the watch away, convinced that he now knew the time, with half a dozen re-checks to spare. 'Quite honestly, I can't fathom how you managed to coerce the Admiralty into consenting to your preposterous scheme.'

'In my experience, Viscount Ainsley is a most reasonable man, given to hearing out the wildest of wiles, if you must call them so, where the issue is of national importance. Apart from that, I do believe his grand nephew is soon to gain a footing, by betrothal, in the House of Rothschild, so that financial problems should scarcely darken his brow in the future.' In actual fact, Sir Basil had come up against a formidable wall of resistance in initially trying to persuade Viscount Ainsley to comply with his plan. Only by a hot and cold application of soft cajoling and dire threats had he caused the Sea Lord to relent in his resistance of dishonouring the Service, which was a colossal gesture on his part, even though it was in the service of Her Majesty. Now he was indebted to Viscount Ainsley by a substantial favour that could not be balanced so easily as marrying into a prestigious family of international bankers. To repay the favour could well take the best part of his remaining time in office, which was what, considering its tightrope parameters? Sir Basil felt decidedly old for the moment.

'I can only assume that Viscount Ainsley is getting senile in his old age.' The young man's confidence took a step back as he caught the other's angry glare, and realised the blunder of his remark in remembering that Sir Basil was the Viscount's senior by some seven years or so. 'Begging your pardon, Sir Basil, I really hadn't meant to imply personally that ---' An embarrassing pause melted away, as resurgent youth headed off at a tangent in face-saving diversion. 'I say, who is this agent, anyway? Possibly the Minister can get the PM to arrange a royal mention or presentation in his family's honour. What do you say?'

But Sir Basil gave no spirited reply to this notion, believing in *absolute* discretion.

'Really, Sir Basil, I do believe that you don't even trust *me*!' This gave him the sought-after edge in conversation, so that confidence flooded back as youth's God-given right. 'Anyway, I've got to go now. Must hurry, in fact. Lots of things to sort out with the Minister, before tonight's debate. I can see it being another all-night session, with the lights being turned off long before *it* is.' The young Secretary got up, not without a show of gathering up his ministerial papers with affected importance and tucking them in his leather dispatch case. Official discussion at an end, he looked down at the other with a conciliatory smile. 'Can we expect you for dinner at the weekend, then, Sir Basil? I do believe that 'Bertie' is bringing along his 'Lily' to give a recital. She's shockingly spiffing, I can say. Absolutely. Pity about Lord Danby, though. He was to have played his famous solo piece for us. He was an absolutely fine pianist ---for an amateur, that is.'

'So I have heard. I never really knew the fellow.'

'Really. So there you are, then, like I've been saying; one can get so caught up and overwrought with one's work so as to miss out on the finer points of one's social life. But I say, Sir Basil, if you are leaving, perhaps you would care to share a cab?'

Outside, in the shadows of the club's baroque portal that barred entrance to all but the purest pedigree stock of the country's gentry, there lurked the deeper shadows of an embittered Turkish peasant and a somewhat inebriated 'Irish' navvy. Whilst the 'Irishman' swayed with drink, the Turk swayed slightly with a testing movement of the ominous black mass weighed heavily in his hand. Until a few moments ago, Vlarda had held no preference of target at which to lob his deadly bomb in the brightly lit expanse of St. James's Street; each one of the elegant entrances being enough to incite his loathing at their symbolic atrocity of class division.

However, with this club's privileged hallway throwing out its noble glow from a myriad of sparkling chandelier crystals, the target was chosen. In that instance of hatred, the Turk's fanatical mind had already notched up another devastating blow in the name of nihilism. He emerged from his umbral cover for a better look, in brazen effrontery of the despised blue- blooded ruling class standing before him. It mattered little to him who the two men were, conversing in the hall while capes were put about their shoulders and silk hats and sticks were handed to them by sheep-brained servants who bowed humbly and stepped back from their masters like lowly livestock. He saw not, and cared not, for the faces before him.

He saw only the ritual of class distinction enacted before his blazing eyes, causing his inner rage to flare up rapidly, like the bomb's fuse that he had lit a second before.

Sir Basil and his young companion spared no more than a blink for the dark shape of the beggar skulking on the edge of the street shadows. Vlarda swore and drew back his arm to throw the bomb with its spluttering tongue of sparks. For a fraction of a second, Balchard felt an electrifying sensation of not caring a damn if Sir Basil was blown to pieces -- no qualms of conscience at wiping out two of that sort. A sudden strategic sense of the moment's madness vying with sanity pushed his mental daze aside, and he lurched forward to intervene. The 'Irishman' stepped in to grab the swinging arm in its forward arc. 'For the love o' Jesus, will you be lettin' me have that bloady thing, for to be sure, Oi'm the bomb man here, now. Didn't Oi just do a good job on yon bloady daft boat, an' a clever clockwork bomb it was an' all, to be sure.' In the frenzied tussle that ensued, the bomb heeded neither party, falling, instead, to the ground, seething and spitting amidst the tangle of legs, with no qualms over whose limbs it was going to rip off.

The horror that the infernal thing fizzing away at their feet had but seconds before blowing them to kingdom come caused the two men to freeze in their struggle. Horror screamed in their minds. The fuse suddenly ceased to hiss, announcing that death's door was opening ---NOW!

Balchard booted the bomb up the street, where it exploded in mid-air, throwing them onto their backs, and bringing shy buildings out from the dark in the sudden glare. Windows rattled and shattered, and acrid fumes stung eyes and nostrils. But nobody was hurt. Staggering to his feet, Balchard rubbed his smarting eyes for a second, to peer up at the club entrance. 'Holy St Moichael! Would you be *lo-o-o*-kin' at that, now. All that bloody doinamoite, an' not a bloody hair parted on them bloody English Johnnies heads!' In a burst of anger, he whipped out his knife. 'Well, see here, now, if Oi'll not be havin' their bloody tongues for hatbands, the broighter loikes o' which you never saw on ol' Ma Flaherty's cockerel.' With that fiery utterance, he made to charge up the club steps.

But the gathering of a small army of white-faced servants in the doorway, as well as the piercing '*phe-e-p phe-e-p*' of a police whistle and the heavy clumping of running boots coming from the Jermyn Street end of the street had the Turk pulling the 'Irishman' back by his coat tail. A second scuffle broke out between the two, before they turned and ran off, vanishing as quickly as they had come, round past St. James's Palace into Pall Mall. The policeman paused in the middle of the street, to look up the steps and enquire if anyone was hurt, before continuing his chase in the direction of a dozen pointing fingers. The young Secretary turned to Sir Basil. 'At least we can still rely on the policeman on the beat to do his duty, which, as I have already said, is more than can be said for *some others*.'

Securing the collar chain on his cape, Sir Basil ignored the acid remark, looking up at the sky. 'It looks as if a storm is gathering. I think I shall accept your offer of sharing a cab.'

CHAPTER 28

—

London, December, 1880.

The parks were first to sense the coming of the Yuletide season. A darkening of grey skies came first, followed by leaves twitching to a low sough sifting through them, the green fingers swaying in the rising breezes. Upsurge currents whispered the cry for change across the city, so that plant-growth everywhere was shifting feverishly, nervously, in readiness for the coming. Just as suddenly, a stalling stillness returned. Then down came millions of them. Each with a separate identity, in a swirling motion to answer the clarion call for purity. The snowflakes landed where they were welcome, abandoned by the wind, as it tended to millions more earth-bound passengers. Parks and streets slowly changed colour, like a giant kaleidoscope. The white particles floating down onto soft turf and hard stone, covering greys and greens of the rough and smooth. Only the lamp standards stood out aloof over their territories. Churches, mission halls and soup kitchens all gradually lost their huffy divisions, united at last under the thin blanket covering the city, except where the river and lakes swallowed up the snowflakes without mercy.

But no-one as yet was quite softened to greeting fellow man with peace and goodwill, in spite of the approaching festive season; not when there was still time for a good couple of weeks more of hard graft business. That was partly how Balchard saw it as he trudged from one address to another across the city, in search of new accommodation. His *Times* grew wetter under the falling snow as he crossed off address after address, just short of having his fingers jammed in doors slammed shut by grim-faced landladies who were none too pleased at having the bitter wind bite into their faces. One was either too late to get the vacant rooms, or else the ladies were nervous of taking in dark figures cringing in the night, the face half concealed by collar, the other half by snow. A Bible-thumping evangelist would have remarked on the timely Bethlehem theme of 'no room at the inn'. Balchard could only mutter his annoyance, between blowing on frozen fingers.

That his father had just died meant little to him, other than the compensation of his severing a stigmatic connection with the past. It moved him only in reminding him of the one time, the *only* time, that he had paid a visit, incognito, to that wretched place that had spawned him and spewed him forth, to die-cast him in the plebian mould. Coming down from the large university town, to the miserable insect hole of a hometown that had disowned him in ignominy, had given him a feeling of conquest. Where drabness and desolation now flowered over former respectability, like the weeds and rubble heaps cluttering what had once been dignified doorways.

Thus he had been able to look down in smug satisfaction of superiority. He did not recognise the town, any more than it recognised him, or failed to grant him recognition when it had sent him away in disgrace. He had not felt alone or alienated in that strange town that day. Rather, he had felt an elating sense of freedom -- of his having broken the chains to its shaming memory -- of having wiped away the blemish that was his past. *Or so he had thought then.* But he had since found the past to be continually stalking him, a skulking predator snarling on his heels, its hunger increasing of late.

It was thus through a whirling snow blizzard that Balchard tramped his way uphill, his form bent forward, to the Hampstead town residence of the late Lord Danby. A high spiked wall hid the select dwelling, except at the gateway, where the building leapt out, in bright patches of red sandstone, to penetrate the surrounding grove of snow-sprinkled larches. The trees moved aside so that a forest of twisted Tudor chimney turrets took over, smoking heavily to recover the heat lost through the tall French windows. Where Balchard churned the snow underfoot, he was able to deduce that the large house had reproduced itself in countless little red pieces covering the driveway and scattered up the stairs under the stone portico.

Balchard scraped his boots clean on the iron frame, before pulling on the iron handle at the tradesmen's entrance.

'Mr A Balchard? From Scotland Yard?' The frozen statement rasped out in the way one could only expect from the equally stone-faced butler reading Balchard's letter of authority. After a moment's whispering with someone behind the door, the granite face turned back to the shivering Balchard, to instruct him to go round to the front entrance of the house. This was a disappointment to Balchard. He had especially wanted to enter by the staff door so as to put his questions to the servants in the relative freedom of their working quarters 'below stairs'. Here tongues could often prove to be more loose than they were permitted to be 'upstairs'.

Balchard recognised the unusual act of diverting a tradesman, such as he was, to the *front* of the house as tact in keeping the scandal of murder enquiries from running amok among the unrestrained junior members of the staff. Such restrained silence 'upstairs' had already blocked Dryson's official investigation, so that he had requested permission for Balchard to call upon the house to conduct his own independent line of enquiry. Balchard entered the main hall, brushing under the palms held in the jade grip of two smiling Burmese warriors who rode upon two wider smiling jade dragons. Teak parquets, wider than the raw sienna carpet, and finely veneered wood panelling rising to the ceiling, had that warming effect on one just entered in from the snow. Slightly cooler were the suits of mediaeval armour standing on both sides of the large crest emblazoning the balcony balustrade. '*Semper paratus* -- always ready,' said Balchard quietly, reading from the large shield. It was a motto that was ironically appropriate to the deceased's roguish readiness for seizing up new opportunities by means not entirely befitting the conduct of a gentleman.

Balchard' inside started for a brief instant at the sight of the fair haired Lady Helena, framed in profile against the light of the drawing room window. He was reminded of another *fair lady* for a moment, the shock flooding into his chest. But the woman turned her fair skinned face towards him, to reveal an entirely different person, so that his unease subsided. But the woman had caught his strange startled look, suspended for a lifetime in its fraction of a second, so making him appear even stranger in her eyes. 'Mr Balchard, is it?'

'It is, your ladyship. And most sincerely begging your ladyship's pardon for this intrusion upon so painful an occasion.' Balchard's long absence from the foibles of emotional involvement had seen him through many such 'intrusions'. But it now occurred to him most acutely that his words were no improvement on those of the thespian seized with stage-fright in his opening delivery of lines. To ask himself would be foolish, and he hardly dared re-examine the woman's profile for confirmation of the answer. Yet, for a woman so recently bereaved, there was little sign of grief, her feelings apparently more caught up in her fingers' dithering choice over an open box of chocolates.

There was a third person in the room. So that further introductions were almost as forthcoming as the drawn-out choice of chocolate delicacy. This was Lady Helena's cousin and close companion, Bethany, who, with her sickly complexion and over-sharpness of facial bone, was much in the shadow of her cousin's beauty. But a loquacious tongue compensated for her lack of prettiness. Putting her in the mould of social leech that sucked all that it could from the better endowed, or else destroyed that which it could not have. Balchard wondered if such forbidden fruit could have included the late Lord Danby.

'But what exactly does a *forensic* policeman detective do, I wonder? Does Mr Balchard wear one of those beastly big hats and all those buttons and things and carry a big stick, like all those silly policemen, when he's on duty?' remarked cousin Bethany to her companion, Lady Helena, with a quiet degree of acidity. She also emitted a giggle. But this barely disguised the sarcasm, and her reference to Balchard in the third person almost had him looking under the carpet for the other elusive 'Mr Balchard'.

'I do believe Mr Balchard wears no uniform of such, if any at all, my dear.' At least Lady Danby looked straight into his eyes when she spoke, leaving no doubt as to whom she was referring. Chocolates no longer seemed to be her main interest, unless she had now found one of an even tastier choice.

'Oh dear, does that mean that he goes about his duty indecently clothed, wearing little or no garments at all? How horridly wicked!' The hands held over the mouth, and the body-shaking laughter, suggested that 'horrid' was not the apt choice of word.

Balchard ignored the ridicule. He was more concerned with how to cut through the silly banter to get at the more important issue ant hand. Possibly his moment of calling was untimely. The subject of murder was too gruesome a topic even for close cousins to share in each other's presence, so that perhaps his time could be more gainfully employed 'below stairs', speaking with the staff. Lady Danby dismissed his fears when he put the matter to her, assuring him that he could speak freely on the subject here. There could be little love lost over a man who had been spouse in name only. He had been married more to his wretched banking business affairs, and other affairs that must have included a fair host of harlots stretching far and wide across the city. As well as those that were *not so far away*. For one sharp instant, there was an ice-cool exchange of glances between the two women that was all the more sinister in its aspect of passing between two such '*close* friends'.

Balchard caught the brief look of hostility between them and found it to be singularly feminine in its degree of two-faced tolerance. The female logic escaped him completely, so that it irked him. Moreover, the sight of Lady Helena's generous bosom now rising and falling beneath the tightly drawn silk of her mauve dress, at her upset feelings was unsettling to Balchard. He felt himself possessed by a strange feeling that was not unlike motiveless frustration. Or was it personal resentment inspired by memories from the past? He questioned Lady Danby over her relationship with the late Lord Danby.

'Again, one can hardly be expected to mourn the loss of that which one has never really possessed, can one, Mr Balchard?'

Balchard's mind wavered at the question, rebounding back on him under her soft doe-eyed stare. Its personal implications marred his judgement with secondary interpretations of happenings from the past. He cleared his mind as best he could and proceeded to enquire after the business and social arrangements of Lord Danby over the last few days prior to his death. It only came as half a surprise to Balchard at this stage to realise that his inner bitterness was tracing through in his words, in a faint tone of resentment misdirected at Lady Helena. As it was, Lord Danby's diary for the last few days of his life revealed nothing out of the ordinary. It had been typically crammed with engagements, so having him coming and going, as if seemingly caught in one of those new fashioned circular door things. All those who had needed to know of his activities and specific whereabouts were told so. Those who had no right to the knowledge were denied it. Lady Danby and cousin Bethany, as well as the household staff, had known of his intended attendance at the theatre that evening.

Balchard looked at them thoughtfully. 'Alas, like a clock, the turning hands point at *all* in their passing -- *until it stops.*'

Cousin Bethany released a mocking snort. 'What a silly thing to say.'

'*Silly*, madam?' Balchard's searching stare at the woman suggested that the issue carried by the remark was far from being silly.

Feeling the effect of the long look, the woman twisted her Belgian lace handkerchief in her lap, before turning to her cousin to give a nervous giggle. 'Why, Helena, darling, I do believe the policeman suspects us. Imagine ---*us!*' She clasped her handkerchief to her mouth, to give a good imitation of a laughing horse.

Lady Danby noted that her cousin had said 'us'. One could always rely on that bitch to drag down all those that she could, in the event of her sinking. She turned to look at Balchard, while fondling the cameo brooch on her neck. '*Are* we, in fact, suspect, Mr Balchard?'

'Why, madam, even the guilty party enjoys the privilege of being mere suspect, until proven otherwise. Until then, in the process of eliminating the impossible, it is the common prerogative of all concerned to be no more than *merely* suspect.'

'You make it sound ever so less horrid than it appears, Mr Balchard.' Lady Helena's caressing fingers had wandered down distractedly from the brooch, onto the soft silken chest that rose and fell with a new interest.

Balchard broke the room's heavy atmosphere that he felt was becoming too warm. 'And his lordship's last business appointments, madam?'

'Such a privilege is withheld even from us. To obtain that information, you would have to consult the private secretary. A Mr Goodie, I believe it is. At the City office.'

'The address of which is?'

Miss Bethany could not resist another horse neigh of a giggle. 'Why, my dear Mr Policeman, are you honestly saying that you are totally unaware of Rupert's office in Threadneedle Street? Can you possibly be the one man in the whole of London who doesn't place his precious money in Rupert's hands for *safe-keeping*?'

'Possibly, madam; *possibly*.' Balchard's irritation crept out in the drawn-out accentuation of his words. Miss Bethany was becoming fascinated with the situation, especially the interlocutory rapport between the other two. But a discreet signal passed intuitively from her cousin stressed the acuteness of crowded discomfiture, and the subsequent annoyance building up in Mr Balchard. Heeding the message with some

404

reluctance, cousin Bethany rose to excuse herself and take her leave.

Closing the tall drawing room door behind her departed cousin, Lady Helena came away from it to approach the table and pour out a sherry for Balchard. She held it out high at arm's length to him, so that as he looked at it to take it, he had to look into her eyes immediately in line behind it. 'Is it at all possible that we have perchance met before, Mr Balchard? Even for a fleeting moment's passing, at some beastly dinner, perhaps? I cannot but help sense that you see me from memory --- or as you saw *another*, perhaps?' Balchard could only give an embarrassed negative nod to this, swallowing the sherry with some difficulty. Lady Helena took a step back, joining her hands on her chest, as she examined her man in a new light. 'Was she your heart-felt dearest? Your mistress, perhaps?'

Balchard's collar virtually seemed to want to strangle him. 'It is best, perhaps, that such matters be left to lie peacefully where they rightly belong, in the past.'

She pointed the two index fingers of her joined hands at him in teasing accusation. 'Ah, but *do* they lie peacefully? Is it not better, more peaceful, for them to be released; to fly freely from their prison in the darkest corner of your heart? I think it would be so.'

It did not escape Balchard's notice that her voice was lower and softer with an intimacy which it had not possessed earlier. He also noticed, between nervous sips of sherry, that the door key was no longer in the lock, where it had been minutes before. Since coming away from the door, she had approached nothing else but the table, so it had to be concluded that the key was concealed on her person; up her sleeve at her wrist. Before he could summon the nerve and voice control to say anything on the matter, she turned and went into the adjoining room. That meant that the key was now in there, and to get it, he would have to go in there also. Not sure how to cope with the situation, he sipped some more sherry. What sounded like water pouring into a bath in the next room, caused Balchard some degree of unease. His uneasiness was increased when next she appeared , wearing only scant body -clinging bodice, bloomers and bone-ribbed corset. To Balchard's startled mind, the pink cotton garments were some sizes too small, where the body swelled out in graceful curves at the hips and bosom, and the flesh bulged where the shoulder fabric cut into it, giving two beautifully rounded arms that matched the marble of any Michelangelo, with their pale smoothness.

With hardly as much as a word, or change of expression, she came up to him, and turning her back to him, leaned her head back to ask him, over her shoulder, to unfasten the corset strings. For want of something to do, to occupy his reeling mind, he complied, or at least tried to, finding that his hands had become a fumbling phenomenon of trembling fingers. Much more difficult than holding a simple glass of sherry. No less confounding was her body perfume and the unsettling closeness of her protruding, seemingly proffered, bottom. When she walked away into the room, her bottom, removed of its camouflaging bustle, now rolled with a sensual motion that had his pulse quickening. His relief at her disappearing into the next room was short-lived. When she reappeared a few moments later, the only thing that she wore was her wedding ring. Matching her beautiful flesh were the frescoed loins and groins on the Renaissance ceiling, where gnarled 'acorns' did prouden to 'oaks'.

Balchard's nervous perplexity was total, so that he could only stare, for want of what else to do. But being a woman of breeding, she understood his predicament. She removed the wedding ring, to ease his feeling of guilt. Walking slowly to the table, she stooped to put the ring down, her pendant breasts swinging with the heavy silence of tongueless bells. Their gentle sway matched those of the daffodils in his head, where the solemn peal of *that* distant bell kept in time with the motion. His mind felt to be closing in, in claustrophobic suffocation. Lady Helena was seized by the savage animal instinct of a much frustrated woman. With her suppressed root anger, from her philandering spouse gallivanting around other city 'stables', leaving her in isolation, there was much call for the release of hysterical resentment. This manifested itself with her urge to hunt down her own 'animal', which she now found opportune in Balchard's coming into her boudoir, her 'private chamber'. Pausing for a moment's look at Balchard, she then came up to him, took his unsure hands and clasped them tightly to her breasts as her heart pounded fiercely with mounting excitement. To Balchard, suspended in time for that moment, the door and service bell-cord seemed so very far away.

With her smooth flesh softly caressing his face, he was all at once confused when it suddenly scraped his cheek with the roughness of cold hard carpet. A fuddled brain then realised that his face was pressed against the floor, where he had collapsed in a moment's mental lapse of delirium. After that there was a blurred awareness of her taking him to her bed and slowly undressing him, all the while stroking and caressing him like a wounded pet against her warm silken body. Rolling over on top of her, he stabbed himself up into her fiercely, so that she squealed with wild pleasure at the pain, little realising the burning ferocity of his inner bitterness. Later, much later, when they had rolled aside from each other, onto their backs, breathing heavily, he felt the sweat on his body and face. But the wet around his eyes was different -- a lachrymal solution of sodium chloride and sodium bicarbonate. To be specific -- *tears*. Such was his anguished feeling of cold cynical detachment from his frigidly mechanical carnal act, as to be so clinically precise. There was no place for tender emotion -- only a mixture of anger and shame of betrayal. He had betrayed *her* -- but was this yet *again*?

Hearing his quiet sobbing, she leaned round and raised herself up over him to look into his face. 'Why, you're crying, you poor thing,' she said with motherly concern. She lowered her breast down to his face for him to kiss, while stroking his cheek, then sliding a hand down to his crotch. Pulling her down violently, he buried his weeping face in her breasts. He held her there for a few eternal moments -- perhaps hoping for a miracle -- hoping, perhaps, that he a*lso* might drown in the flood of tears. But Lady Helena wasn't *her*. *Nobody* could ever be h*er*! Nobody could take *her* place! With a furious push he knocked her over onto her back, hurting her, and giving her great fright. Half scrambling, half falling out of bed, Balchard searched frantically among her clothes on the chair for the key to her chamber, to let himself out, all the while ignoring her plaintive cries of injured dignity.

His less than honourable exit from the Danby lordly residence was made less scathing by his being mindful of having more important matters to deal with. Putting the soul-wrenching experience behind him, he stepped forth briskly, a logically minded scientist proceeding once more with his research and investigative work. Back in the laboratory, surrounded by the familiar 'friendly' atmosphere of apparatus and experiments waiting to be arranged, there was much solace to quell his inner unease. In mental flight always, it seemed to him, from the female spectre. Reality was reclaimed when coming in here, where science was profound and straightforward, so that only the exact details required planning. Plans? The question blocked his brain for a second, so that his head swam, and he threw out a hand, to steady himself against the bench. The pain pounded in his head.

'You all right, Adam?' The calming voice of Dr Michaels cutting in, clearing away the darkness. Balchard looked round at Michaels limping quietly into the room. Why had Michaels asked him that, when he was perfectly all right -- apart from this wretched headache? He had been all right, working solidly all day, in fact. *He had, hadn't he?* He closed his eyes, and *she* was there, remonstrating with a cruel scolding finger. He saw Professor Radcliffe terminating his doctoral project, and throwing him out at this morning's meeting. Or was that last week? He opened his eyes. It couldn't have been last week because ----? He couldn't remember if there had been any such meeting at all. Or had he dreamt that? Was it all imaginary? Stark images thrown up, of that which he feared? *Feared?* Dementia praecox * rearing its ugly head? For a fierce instant, he was inclined to tell Dr Michaels to shut up with his consoling words. But he struggled to restrain his inner fury.

*(Dementia praecox -- the earlier, pre-Freudian term for schizophrenia)

CHAPTER 29

The next few days saw the snow turned to a treacherous slush, so that limbs throughout the city skidded, flew and cracked with the syncopation of music hall puppets dancing on the xylophone. Balchard, all the while, sat snugly in the relative warmth of the laboratory, working moodily at his bench. Calibration was required on the possibility of the womb's amniotic fluids constituting a danger through access to the mother's bloodstream, to eventually reach the lung, and give rise to a clot that could upset the heart's rhythm -- perhaps fatally. It was imperative that tests were conducted on the vascular walls. Professor Felsham considered it to be a hare-brained scheme -- a one-in-a-million chance issue not worth pursuing, and came down heavily with criticism on Balchard. He declared Balchard to be losing the threads, and straying from the mainstay objective of his solid serious work -- or what, at one time, *had been* solid serious work. But Balchard ignored Felsham's condemning remarks, working on steadily into his new avenue of research, while at the same time, turning over in his mind, other unrelated matters, one of these being Lord Danby's murder.

As in most inroads to a solution, there are the 'minor' difficulties to be dealt with. A tight- lipped Mr Goodie, in steadfast loyalty to his late master, Lord Danby, had been the living personification of the proverbial difficulty in bleeding a stone. Balchard's initial efforts to extract information from this source had gained him nothing. His questioning had brought out an angry outflow of personal threats. This was followed by a threat to call his solicitor. Balchard tactfully questioned if this would preserve the honour of Lord Danby, any more than it would tarnish it forever in open scandal. The man had subsequently yielded to Balchard's request for details. Such meek-faced co-operation after the initial aggression became clear when one understood that Lord Danby's financial transactions were seldom conducted with a gentleman's code of honour. Many were of a devious underhand cut that made sharks' teeth bend like rubber. Some were on a scale that made the Bank of England's minor transactions rattle like the paltry pence in the blind man's begging bowl.

Just how the 'loyal' Mr Goodie had come to hold so many cards, with such disreputable details, against his master was not fully clear. But their potential purpose was easily inferred as that of the loaded pistol held to the head. That Goodie had intended using this wealth of incriminating material as his insurance in times of pressure from his master did not concern Balchard. Thus he had not pressed the issue. It sufficed that he could surmise on the possible degree of repercussions from those suffering at the foul hands of Lord Danby before his death. But with so many enemies, there was much need for the filtering off of impurities before reaching the solution.

Between straining to examine his filtrate of arterial vascular tissue, and lending half an ear to answering periodic questions thrown at him by a desultory Felsham, a curious thought occurred to Balchard. It was the aspect of Felsham's height, towering over him, as he stood there beside him, looking down critically. Why this relatively unimportant point should claim all his attention, blocking out all else, was puzzling to Balchard. But what was unsettling to him was the fact that it was giving him a weird feeling of inner nausea. It was not Felsham's domineering presence, or the harshness of his criticisms. It was his *height*? Totally irrational. S*he* had not been taller than him, but almost everyone had been. That had made him the focal point of many a jibe. So why did she choose him, the local fool? It did not make sense, from a perspective that he had, rather surprisingly, not hitherto considered. He tried to concentrate his mind back on examining the filtrate. But the inconclusive cluttering in his mind distracted him from that in front of him on the bench. He rose abruptly, to stride over to the window. Staring out without purpose into the street, he no more knew what he was doing standing there, than did Felsham, staring at him, totally puzzled. Unable to bear his restless confusion any longer, Balchard turned and walked, without further word, out of the laboratory.

In his haste to reach the staff cloakroom, to retrieve his syringe and cocaine from his coat, he almost collided with Pilkington-Greeves. 'I say, steady on there, Balchard. Wherever you're going, it'll still be there tomorrow.' But Balchard, in his desperation, had no ear for passing comments, however polite. He did note, however, that it was back to 'Balchard', and not 'Adam'. Rumours, albeit unfounded, did have their effect. As he put the needle to his arm, in the refuge of the water closet, he had the despairing feeling that he might just as well have been injecting water into his system. It would require 'strength' of a different sort to ward off the dark ogre that was battering down his wall of rationality, brick by brick.

It was to an address in Berkeley Street that Balchard walked with an assertive stride the following morning. Standing before the bright blue door, he lifted a broad tweed cuff to wipe away the ridge of hardened snow overhanging the brass professional wall-plate. The remaining rills of moisture ran down the shining surface into the deep inscription of: **Emile Von Sproegel: Dental Surgeon.** Balchard touched his jaw in automatic reflex whilst musing quietly: ' 'Tis an ache of different sorts, I fear, Herr Von Sproegel, that warrants us to call this morning.'

Light entering through the half-moon fanlight above the door was precious to Balchard as he braved the dimness of the narrow hallway to climb the serpentine spiral of wooden stairs. Although there was only one door on the tiny landing, a tinier brass plate on the door again heralded the stairs' arrival at the already announced dental surgery. Inside, the atmosphere was barely less dismal, with an alarming array of ugly steel appliances and 'pointed things' seemingly leaping up at the frightened patient on immediate entrance. Added to this was the disconcerting smell of antiseptic that gave heart to many to turn and run quicker than their stomachs could turn in nausea. Balchard was not affected so.

Emile Von Sproegel's bright red hair spiked out like rusty barbed wire around the oval face peering out from behind two small pebble lenses held in silver wire frames. More surprising was the dexterity with which his hands worked inside the mouth, the stone hard fingers having a feather-light touch. Yet despite the hands being clean and smelling of carbolic, they were much scarred in the manner of one handling something much coarser than that found in the human buccal cavity. They were the hands of the inventor and machinist who handled and fondled his lathes and metals with the same care and attention that the equestrian squire reserved for his stable's best thoroughbreds.

With a mechanical-voiced routine of 'Open wide' and 'Does this hurt?', he made a rapid skilful inspection of Balchard's mouth, plinking and plonking at the teeth with better tuning than the music-hall artiste hammering on his empty bottles. Finished his inspection, he handed Balchard a glass of water and held out an enamel bowl. 'Rinse your mouth out and spit in the bowl, please, Mr Balchard.'

Washing his hands over a small sink in the corner of the room, Von Sproegel then applied a hard-bristled brush with dedicated vigour to his fingernails, in a methodical cleaning action. He spoke over his shoulder in the process. 'You have a fine set of dentures, with nothing to fear for the moment, Mr Balchard. There is a little wearing down of the enamel on the second lower molar -- a pipe, or a pencil it is, you chew, perhaps? -- but this will keep for the time being. You have had the two right lower premolars extracted already, I see. You do not go back to the same doktor?'

'One forever seeks professional improvement.'

'Of course. And your toothache -- it is no longer hurting you, no?'

'No. It was probably just a twinge of my imagination, as one might say.' Balchard affected a 'nervous' smile and shifted in his chair, in the supposed manner of a patient only too relieved to be spared the horror of an extraction.

'Mmm, this is possibly so. Mild neuralgia of the gums can, indeed, sometimes manifest itself from tiredness of the troubled mind. But it is better that you come and see me again in six months time. Yes?'

'I'll try.' The 'patient' spared little haste in rising, to escape the grabbing feeling of the condemned's chair.

Von Sproegel put down his hand towel and crossed the room to commence working a foot-pump that was connected by rubber tubing to a tiny copper apparatus suspended on a wall bracket. Holding his hands to the protruding nozzle on the apparatus, he allowed a fine liquid spray to cover them. Stepping away from the apparatus, he flapped his hands in the air to dry them.

'I see that you are an active disciple of Monsieur Pasteur and your own Doctor Koch, in resorting to the use of carbolic acid antiseptic spray in unending battle against bacterial infection, Herr Von Sproegel. It is tragic that the reactionary minds in this country are so opposed to accepting the need for change demanded by the advancement in scientific research. We do have our own pioneering Doctor Lister in the City, but that, alas, is a minuscule drop in the ocean. For too long we have failed to see the potential enemy beneath the surface, recognising hostile forces only by the colour of their uniforms and flags, and sensing final danger only in openly drawn swords. However, our insidious friend, the bacterium, defies all such martial codes of honour, ravishing whole nations, in multi-millionfold death tolls with its plagues, which no army's armour and artillery can defend against.'

'Ah, so you are a man of science, Mr Balchard?'

'I dabble in such. Analytical chemistry and pathology, mainly.'

'Ah, yes, these are most interesting fields of study.'

'I believe them to be so. And you, yourself, Herr Von Sproegel, do touch upon the science of pneumatics, with no light flare of enthusiasm, I perceive. An honourable field calling for considerable manual aptitude, one might add.'

Von Sproegel threw back his head, a broad smile exploding on his face. 'Ah, yes, you have noticed my work.' He walked round the surgery slowly, touching each one of his shining hand-built scientific pieces with great pride. 'My father was engineer -- *hydraulics* engineer, you understand, in Munchen, or Munich, as you are saying in your language. I learn my craft from him when I was young boy. This is first joy of my life until I have to leave it behind, to study medicine and dentistry at Heidelberg. But even as young student I am still worked in my father's workshop during vacations, until he is died.' He waved a hand around in general indication of all the mechanical devices situated about the surgery. 'Now, perhaps in memorial of him, I continue my work whenever I can.' He stopped, to look with apology at Balchard. 'But perhaps you are not interested so, and I am offending you by keeping you from your business?'

'On the contrary, Herr Von Sproegel, I find the subject to be most compelling. Pray, continue.'

'Then you would like to examine my other modest endeavours in my workshop, yes?'

'Most certainly.'

A door down the short passage from the surgery opened on to a long room of scientific pieces that bespoke of mechanical genius. Machines and tools abounded with seemingly miles of rubber tubing and metal contrivances of all sizes and shapes, to fill all the benches and shelves with a clinical trimness that matched that in the surgery. The subject of care here was not the human patient, but the next invention that one strove to accomplish with the greatest skill that dedicated fingers could render. Von Sproegel's enthusiasm bubbled over profusely in open delight at being able to share his achievements with someone. Balchard looked over the individual pieces, stopping at one in particular. He fingered the copper coiling of the machine. 'Am I mistaken, or do I recognise the compression unit and coils of a cooling system? A *refrigeration* unit, I believe, is the term being currently applied to this new wonder of a principle.'

'Why, yes, it is such a very machine. You are familiar with the principle of refrigeration by collecting, compression and redistribution of a fluid, Mr Balchard?'

'One can appreciate the advantages of preserving various organic cultures and specimens from bacterial putrefaction by maintaining them at low temperatures with ice. However, with the continual need to apply external energy to the unit in order to remove the inner heat, one can only wonder if there is not a less costly method of maintaining low temperatures at an isolated state, separate from the infiltrating heat of the surrounding atmosphere. In the same way, for instance, that sound does not travel through a vacuum. Could we not thus isolate a specimen of a specific temperature in a container that is itself surrounded by a vacuum, so preventing the outflow of that specimen's heat from the container, as much as preventing the inflow of heat to the container from the atmosphere?'

Von Sproegel clapped his hands together in amazement and swore a happy oath in German up at the ceiling. 'But this is -- how do you say? -- *incredible*, Mr Balchard! This is the very principle with which I am now engaged! Look, let me demonstrate.' The man darted to and fro from shelf to shelf about the room like a mad bee, shifting item after item, until he found what he wanted, and came back with a large brass vacuum pump and an even larger steel cylinder. Positioning the cylinder on top of the pump, he connected it by screwing it into the protruding nipple in the centre of the brass piece.

'What we have here, Mr Balchard, is a double-walled container, that is to say, one cylinder contained within another. There are only a few pieces of wire and wood of low conductivity connecting the two cylinders, so reducing the heat exchange between the two, and eventually the atmosphere, to a near zero. It is unfortunate that there is inevitable passage of heat through these connecting parts eventually, but, nevertheless, the temperature of the inner chamber is maintained at a relatively constant level for some considerable time. I will show you.' He worked away feverishly at the pump.

Balchard watched the man's energetic effort for a moment. 'So you foresee a definite purpose for such a design of vacuumised container?'

'But most certainly, Mr Balchard. The enormously significant point is that such appliances could be readily mobile in their usage, independent of the original source of heat. Where one originally had to stay where the fire was to cook foods, one could now carry heated food in these containers and so travel without restriction. The traveller, explorer, soldier, would benefit enormously. Armies could truly march on their stomachs. One could carry all sorts of foods -- solids, liquids, meats, soups, beverages --all sorts of things.'

Balchard glanced at the refrigeration unit and then stared solemnly up into the air as if about to address no-one in particular. 'One could even carry an *icicle*.'

Von Sproegel stopped pumping. The smiling ebullience drained away, to be replaced by a foreboding hard stare through the thick spectacle lenses. A wary hand made a careful adjustment to the silver frame on the bridge of the nose. 'Sorry? I am not understanding you.'

Balchard paused deliberately, toying with a loose bolt lying on the bench, in order to let the full effect of his remark, with its cutting innuendo, sink in. 'I say simply that one could carry an *icicle* in such a container.' He looked at

Von Sproegel, and then gave a pointedly long stare at the refrigeration unit. 'Providing that one first has the facilities for producing such an icicle, one could produce one of a specified size and shape in a mould of one's own making. One could then carry the icicle in a vacuumised container of such convenient dimensions as to be easily concealed beneath one's cloak when *attending the theatre*. At a fitting moment during the performance, one could then load the icicle into the breech of a powerful airgun -- a gentleman's walking stick, of course -- and one could then shoot an unsuspecting individual through the back of the head. One could further rely on the victim's body heat and the heat of the auditorium to melt the ice over a period during which there would be fair chance of the victim being left undisturbed owing to the evening's performance. When the body is eventually found, the very absence of a murder weapon, as well as the apparent *impossibility* of the crime, would serve to baffle the police completely -- and o*thers* momentarily-- so as to isolate the crime from its perpetrator. In short, one could remark lightly that the perpetrator was sealed off from any suspicion in his very own vacuum chamber -- *or so he had believed himself to be.*'

Stepping over to a rack by the door, Balchard began taking out the walking sticks, lifting them up one by one to test them for weight.

Von Sproegel pointed. 'No, not that one. The second one from the left. Yes, *that* is the one.'

'Quite heavy.'

"One point four six kilogrammes, to be precise -- just over

three pounds. Good quality steel, you understand, to give it a muzzle velocity of five hundred and ninety feet per second, and a muzzle energy of five point eight foot pounds. It is a fine piece, no?'

'Impaired only by its misuse, alas.' Balchard put the 'walking stick' back in the rack.

Von Sproegel leaned on the bench with both hands, letting his head sink down in heavy thought. For several seconds he remained so, silent and still, before nodding his head up and down like the soothsayer sadly reconciled to a new conflicting truth. He looked round at Balchard, the trapped appraising the trapper. 'You knew from the beginning? But how?'

'By logical assessment of facts. One plucks not only the shortest straw out from the longest, but also the sheaf and field whence it came.'

Again Von Sproegel nodded his head in new wisdom. 'Ja, I am seeing this precision of mind in someone like yourself, Mr Balchard.' He stood up straight to look Balchard straight in the face. A faint smile nicked the corner of his mouth for the fraction of a second that it took for one scientific mind to recognise and admire the systematic reasoning of another like it. 'And so using this method, you trace the connecting pieces across the 'vacuum'. Ich verstche -- I understand.'

Balchard's inside swelled with appreciation of the other's positive appraisal. 'As you so correctly infer. In the vacuumised system there is eventual flow between the two separated cells through the wrongly supposed 'non-existent connecting materials'. One has but to seek out such links, however low their 'conductivity'.'

Von Sproegel waited, open-faced, for further explanation, enlightenment on another's technique being foremost on his mind, in spite of the overhanging gravity of the situation. Balchard noted that Von Sproegel displayed none of the alarm signals that invariably came close on the heels of the normal criminal's shock of realisation that the trap was sprung. Von Sproegel was accepting the circumstances in his methodical matter of fact manner. Regretting only that 'justice' would now spoil things for many others by bringing the sordid affair out into the open. Considering such close affinity with his own mind, Balchard felt that he owed the other an explanation, even though it meant stepping down in revealing the means of detection. 'Though somewhat painstakingly tedious, the checking of those in the City with access to refrigeration units can be much rewarding. Even if this search provides positive results, the possibility that among these there is but one so mechanically gifted as to *provide one's own* such devices is reward enough. Especially one so able, thereafter, to manufacture the unique means for transporting such an *ice-bullet* to the theatre. The Patent Office, for instance, can often prove to be a veritable gold mine of such information. Particularly so when the Teutonic characteristics of Emile Von Sproegel can be somewhat conspicuous against a background of Anglo-Saxon entries.'

'I see.' Von Sproegel bowed his head at the other's acknowledgement of his work.

'Most demanding was the long list of suspects that required to be narrowed down through elimination by critical factors. From among the many acquaintances of Lord Danby who knew of his engagement at the theatre that evening, one eventually filters out that one with the sole capability of carrying out the final act.' Balchard made no mention of the fact that a good part of the 'leg-work' had been carried out by Sam Loofer.

Von Sproegel walked from shelf to shelf, patting each individual creation. 'Lord Danby was a wicked man -- a most wicked man. What one in this country would perhaps call a cad or a bounder; which in my native land would be considered as not carrying sufficient weight of condemnation. In my tongue, the term befitting such a person would perhaps scorch the decent Englishman's ears.'

'He had a hold over you, this -- *nichtswurdiger*?'

Von Sproegel smiled and bowed again in return for the honour allotted by the other's knowledge of he Germanic tongue in its subtle idiom. 'He had a hold over many. Indeed, are there many over whom he did *not* have a hold? I tell you, Mr Balchard, that society is much improved by the removal of such a vile creature.'

'So one is continually being advised.'

Von Sproegel started to delve into examples of Lord Danby's devious dealings in blackmail that would have eventually rendered the dental practice and other businesses bankrupt. Balchard held up his hand to stop the issuing forth of further sordid details. 'I neither seek nor care for the black images of one's past, but only to clarify and salvage that of the present.'

'And in so doing, you are now come to arrest me, in your true role of policeman, and not as a patient suffering from toothache.'

For once it pleased Balchard to be mistaken for a policeman, since he could thus spare Von Sproegel the indignity of such an imposition. 'One need not fret of any policemen making arrests at this early hour of a fateful morning, Herr Von Sproegel. I come only to say that the light is now focused on your dark deed, and that your next course of action should be of your own volition as would satisfy a gentleman's conscience.' They exchanged courtesy bows and had a final long silent stare at each other before Balchard made to leave, putting down his fee for the dental examination on the surgery desk.

Von Sproegel called out as Balchard opened the surgery door. 'And Herr Balchard --- you will see to that tooth in six months time, ja?'

Balchard noted how Von Sproegel had instinctively fallen back on his native tongue in addressing him as '*Herr* Balchard', and that he had not said 'come back and see *me*'. He nodded without looking back and went out. Going down the stairs slowly and quietly, Balchard paused at the bottom, before opening the outer door to the street. Suddenly from above there came a sharp blast, like that of air exploding from a tube, followed by the sound of something falling. That was followed in turn by the final dull thud of a much heavier mass, like that of a body, collapsing on the floor.

Closing the door softly, Balchard stopped to give the brass plate on the wall a better wipe with his handkerchief, before setting off briskly up the street towards Berkeley Square.

When Balchard eventually arrived back in Montague

Street, he was so steeped in thought over the morning's earlier incident, that he almost failed to notice the triple line marks in the slush outside his own door. Snapping himself out of his thoughts and into the present situation, he turned away from his door and came down the steps to examine the lines just off the pavement. They had come from one end of the street as three parallel lines, and then turned and turned to form a geometrical mesh in the roadway, opposite his door, before going off in the other direction. They were the wheel marks of a lingering tricycle. Balchard looked up the street. There, where the tricycle's back wheels just protruded from around the corner, tending to the mysterious box perched on the vehicle's seat, was the ever intrepid, ever watchful, *Walrus Man*.

Back upstairs in his room, Balchard flopped down into the armchair, ignoring all the work around him. He pushed even the thought of his stalker downstairs out of his mind, to give sole priority to other thoughts haunting him. His brooding mind cast back to *her*. He sifted through what seemed reticent, if not nervous compartments of his memory, shying away from the thought of coming across something he did not wish to know. With *her* father being the local power, and lovingly wrapped round her finger, she could have had all and everything -- and *anyone* she chose. There were more winks and lustful looks thrown at her, than the papillae floating past, anxious to catch the sparkle from her golden hair. And these yearnings were not just from those too old to do else but gaze on through watery eyes, but from the handsomest lads around. So why had she chosen *him*?

The naked body of Lady Helena suddenly intruded upon his thoughts.

Dwelling on its warmth and silken softness for some moments, he transferred the intimacy of that recent experience back to when he had first shared that intimacy with *her*, all that time ago. *He saw her taking him into her for the first time, and his awe at discovering all her sacred parts.* A frown crossed his face at the thought of them lying, united as one, on that soft bed. They had never done it indoors. It had always been outdoors, in the cover of the woods, or in the long grass of the meadows?

Dropping the puzzle for a moment, he rose to find himself a cigar. Lighting it and picking up a beaker for his ash, he returned to the chair. Thinking back once more, he retraced the first pleasure of experiencing the mysterious female body, *with its wondrous rounded form -- exploring its caverns and traversing the silken landscape, to reach the twin rounded hillocks, with their joyous pink pinnacles -- how she had taken him into her warm embrace, sheltering him from the harshness of the outside world. He saw and felt once again, his hands caressing the smooth buttocks, and moving round to discover the heavenly secrecy between the thighs, with their sacred vaginal entrance, where he was allowed to enter with his shy member. Travelling up over the softness of the breasts, along the smooth neck, he looked into that face, with its loving smile. BUT IT WAS THE FACE OF HIS MAMA! And standing beside them was the dark tall, tall, ever so tall figure towering over them, looking down in an exploding thunderclap of black fury. It was his father, catching them together, moulded as one, in their abominable secret incestuous act!*

427

Balchard paused, managing a cool cynical smile, at the thought of Felsham standing over him yesterday. So *that* was why he had been unnerved. Looking up at the ceiling, he took a long draw on his cigar, while thinking calmly in readjustment of new facts, in his controlled scientific manner. He remembered now that he had not been just ten years old, when his father had called his mama a whore, and left. He had been older, *much older*, in his *experience*. But his mind, in its defensive act of disavowal, had displaced his memory back to a non-knowing age of innocence. How very clever. Balchard let his head fall back, to blow his smoke up at the ceiling, while he thought things over slowly, to take in their new significance. He tapped the ash off his cigar into the beaker.

A timid knock sounded on the door, making him wince at its interference. A curious Mrs Wallamsby. 'There's nobody here,' he cried, in his Irish voice, that was not without its menacing note. The floorboards outside squeaked out their retreat. He continued with his recollections. Long-locked floodgates that had just allowed a trickle forth of blocked thoughts before, now suddenly burst open, releasing a great torrent. Long-held secrets flew up at him like bats coming out at last from their darkest caves.

Taking his cigar from his mouth, he sat up straight slowly, to take these in. So he had never partaken of the sexual act with *her*. Never enjoyed that carnal knowledge. All those exciting adventures in the woods and fields -- they had never happened. *She* had never wanted him. In fact, she had never even *liked* him, beyond mere acquaintance as the curiosity that he was in her eyes. All their acts of shared freedom in the open air -- they had never been. They were his mental creations of what he had *wanted* to have, but could *never* have. Their whole 'relationship' was a futile fantasy! He had followed her, pestered her, snatched her photograph from her, spied on her as she swam naked in her father's river.

He stalled in his memories, to recall his father's recent words of how he was apt to resort to violence, if he could not get what he wanted. Yes, he *had* pushed her into the river, when she had shouted angrily at him, telling him to go away. But to kill her had not been his intention. Not at all. He had simply been responding in the only way he could -- in an angry tantrum. Good swimmer that she was, being fully clothed had caused her to perish in the clutches of submerged branches. Even *they* were allowed to have her, where he could not.

That she had been with child, was truly not of his doing. Then he heard her words again, blurted painfully through her face of tears. Words of hatred thrown at her own father! He had bestowed his seed upon his own daughter! Balchard recalled the father not wishing to highlight the circumstances unduly by submitting him to trial. Father and daughter, mother and son. The double irony was --- *interesting*. But it made sense. He saw now, how she had used him, in the times that they had talked, as a violation of her father's rule forbidding her to 'have it' with anyone else -- only with him. Her associating with him, the town's undersized, ugly oddity, was a direct backlash against her father's desecration of her. So her usage of him had been a dilution of her own debasement.

Just like a buffer solution between two opposing chemicals.

Balchard got up to pace nervously, aimlessly, about the room for several moments. Stopping at the side table, he stared for a long while at the medical apparatus and instruments. He sighed and returned to the chair. What thrills of secrecy and defiance of social taboos there may have been between mother and son, before that tempestuous discovery, were gone after the father made his stormy departure from the home forever. Was there then revulsion at his sexual act with his mother? Had he felt guilty at betraying *her*? Or were his feelings for *her*, a betrayal of his mama? Balchard's mind reeled, and he closed his eyes for a moment in confusion. Was he feeling what he felt then, or was he injecting his present feelings into an imagined scenario of how it was then. He bit, instead of inhaling, on the cigar. Whatever it was, he was beleaguered by the female curse.

And then there were the instruments. *That* had frightened him. When that time had come, his mama had expected him, *forced* him, to carry out the horrifying act of abortion on her. The medical books she had already provided, years before, for his studies. Was that a foresight, on her part? Now she provided the instruments. It had puzzled his young naive mind, how she had known what to do, since she had never read his books. Had she come this way before? The question was never ever put to her. Screaming instructions through to his mind, that was numbed with fear and nervousness, she had made him insert the long needles into her, probing into unwelcoming darkness, cold peninsulas of steel, with death dropping off their ends into the crimson waters. Guided through a series of bloody scrapings, he had finally murdered and extracted the foetal body, and thereafter the bloody mash that was the placental attachment tissue. On placing the dead form into a newspaper for disposal later, he had been struck by the remarkable degree to which human semblance was discernible, in spite of the tinyness. *It had been killed because it was small* and *unwanted*. It was a chilling lesson in reflection of his own acute status anxiety syndrome. The whole operation had been revolting, but he had not been sick. His mama had not allowed him to be sick.

For a long time afterwards, his mama had lingered feverishly near death. An unearthly pale aura of death had kept company with her in her illness, for weeks on end, before the unmentionable ailment decided to leave her. Her former cheer and loving smile had never again come through after that. A mere caring, matron-like overseer, had taken her place. But in the midst of all the bloody doings, along with his horror, there had also been the thrill of responsibility in his performing the 'medical act'. That, and the feeling of power over life and death. So he had lost both of them -- his mama, as well as *her*.

None of these revelations, with their controversial implications, gave alarm to Balchard. But he was aware of a weird current of emotion that was akin to ---*what*? He could not specify it precisely at all -- except that it was bringing on that same strange nausea that he had experienced yesterday, in the laboratory. Being unable to apply precise nomenclature to a particular phenomenon was acutely unsettling to Balchard's scientific frame of mind. He got up, to cross the room and look into his cocoa tin. It was empty. Turning round, he lifted a pile of folders off a chair, dropping them noisily on the floor, before sitting down in their place at the side table. His mind numbed and blocked from thinking beyond the moment, he stared unseeing at his lead soldiers, in a frozen quandary of -- *what?* Shadowy abstractions. A grey blankness. Logic clawed at the dark inside of Balchard's mind, seeking out some coherent line of reasoning. Von Sproegel's death, for instance; he had been partly responsible for that. His father's recent passing away must also figure in there somewhere; it was a reflection of the *first* time his father had gone out of his life; on *that* day, when he had towered high over mother and son found 'together'. Mirroring this was the neurotically charged episode with Lady Helena, where the carnal act on the surface seemingly had served as a regressive 'journey' to the deep-down vaults of the subconscious. There was also his scientific preoccupation with whores and needles, and the ever present background of patronising professors forever looming over him, especially Felsham's recent somewhat 'catalytic' effect. Whilst each of these factors may have been insufficient in themselves to trigger off this recollection, nevertheless, he could see them as the contributory pebbles working as a collective whole to cause the climactic landslide of revelation. Intriguing subliminal whisperings, indeed, and in their newly wakened voice plainly calling for axioms anew. Plausible, even, was the theory that a lifetime's denial of one horror -- *her* untimely demise -- was merely the deflective layer covering this newly released, more deeply buried, *real* horror. Social taboo.

A progressive chain reaction, of sorts, of the lower mind? A pattern, or *something*, not wishing to let go? All of these hitherto forbidden facts had come out of a secret compartment of his mind; the 'property' of that 'other person'. That person had sought and lost affection twice, and now he was seeking acceptance of sorts again. Like the cast-out mongrel seeking a new master.

Balchard was vaguely aware of his 'confession' having somehow released pressure somewhere. Like a subterranean trapdoor opening, to let in the gust of clearing wind -- and blow out the phantom bogey man. But his throbbing head pain had not stopped its pounding completely; subdued, yes, but still there with a nagging persistence. He pulled the tray of lead soldiers across. Opening a small paint tin and taking up a brush, he picked up a soldier. A Grenadier of the Russian Imperial Guard, 1709. The little bayonet mounted on the musket needed a touch up of silver.

CHAPTER 30

With December moving into its last weeks, an almost continuous downpour of rain had removed the slush and ice from all but the sorest memories. Hectic dashing about the city in the approaching Christmas rush was made more easy by no longer carrying the risk of fractured limbs. Balchard was very much pressed for time, hurrying between sessions with Radcliffe at the University, while still assisting Scotland Yard, and lending a limb to that department of the War Office, that sought not to ruffle Her Majesty's bustle by way of restricting its distasteful activities to *beneath* Her bustle.

This latter aspect of security may not have been too obvious to the ordinary citizen, where the city seemingly weltered under an onslaught of outrageous bombings. No sooner did a bombing infuriate the public with its vile desecration of some public place, than it was lost amidst the bellowing of street newspaper vendors announcing the latest explosion somewhere else. Little insignificant things, like the murder of a Lord Danby, did not hold the public's interest for long, fading as quickly as the rain could wash the pencilling off the vendors' pavement fly-sheets. The public's anger seethed a lot longer over the Navy's humiliation of having its most worthy vessel scuppered and invalided out of immediate service, much to the taxpayer's pinching of pocket and the politician's dismay. Nor was this public unrest helped any by the agitation arising from armed strikers roaming the City. But at least it had simmered down somewhat, to a shade of November's horror of upheaval from mob rioters about to take over the City, but for the swift iron-handed action of Commissioner, Sir Charles Warren, who had seen fit to deploy a force of constables, Grenadiers and Life Guards totalling just under twelve thousand. At least Her Majesty was 'amused', in that she was conferring on Sir Charles, the Knight Commandership of the Bath. One minor blessing, if it could be counted as such, was that this general preoccupation with this wave of terrorism served to overshadow the Government's embarrassment over its crushing defeat in the municipal by-election in Liverpool.

Unable to hold his agonised gaze on the crucifying headlines for one second longer, Sir Basil crumpled the newspaper's pages together and let it fall onto his desk. Luckily the desk, itself, did not crumple under the mountain of papers piled there in their similar state of undignified dismissal. 'Abbey Mill Pumping Station, it seems, now. That makes how many now? Battersea, Southwark, Knightsbridge, Bethnal Green --- I can't remember the others --- and now this. What are the others, again?'

'A total of eleven bombings to date, sir.' Captain Smethers' calm expression in rendering the grave situation as mere statistics gave Sir Basil reason to stare at him, wondering if he should compliment or criticise.

'*Good grief,* man! *Eleven* bombings! You will forgive me, Captain, if I sound somewhat contrary to our original plan, when I say that I am wondering if we may have overshot our mark.' Hooking his thumbs into his waistcoat pockets, Sir Basil walked over to the window to gaze out at the 180ft needle of stone pointing up into the sky to hallmark an earlier moment of glory in the name of the Empire. A gift from that same country that was giving them headaches now, Cleopatra's Needle had been presented to the British Government by Mehemet Ali in 1819. It had then taken almost another six decades for it to reach this country, and that was not without temporary abandonment in the Bay of Biscay during a storm. Trying to decide if this was a bad omen, or just an attack of morbid spirits before morning tea, Sir Basil sought inner counsel by stroking his long beard in the long silence.

He turned his back to the window. 'As you may not know, I have just been tracked down and routed in a corner by the Home Secretary and Sir Charles Warren together, and needless to say, the two honourable gentlemen were not in the most congenial of moods. Whilst our work normally lies outside the general jurisdiction of the police, it has to be conceded that this situation, with its hue and cry from the public, has developed the furious bubbles of a cauldron of scandal over our handling of War Office issues. Heads are to roll, I am promised most sincerely, if the proper remedial steps are not taken soon.' Sir Basil returned to his desk to reclaim his seat, so that it creaked back dejectedly under his weary weight of office.

Captain Smethers was a little unsettled by Sir Basil's

apparent relinquishing of his standpoint so easily without his usual measure of fire-dragon resistance. 'Wasn't it part of our strategy, sir, to refrain from pulling out the plug prematurely, and to hold back until we had all the fish in the pond, so to speak? It can only be working. With this degree of public unrest, Vlarda's lot can only think that they have us on the run.'

'I am thinking of the athletic gentleman who holds back *too long*, in overestimation of his ability, so that he is unable to close the gap between himself and the leader, and so subsequently loses the race. Our most gracious Sovereign is apt to derive more than mere personal displeasure should we chance to lose *this* race. Would your uniform buttons shine so brightly, Captain, in the Officers' Mess of some God-forsaken speck of an outpost in a remote corner of the Empire?'

Smethers evaded the disquieting thought of such a punitive posting by lifting the newspaper off the desk to tap the front page with his forefinger. 'Balchard *did* say that this Mill job was to be the last dummy run. After that ---' He paused to give a significantly louder tap on the paper. 'The *big bang*.'

'But he has not as yet said where this so-called 'big bang' is to occur?'

'Not yet, but I am about to follow up on that shortly.' Smethers looked at Sir Basil's cannon-ball clock to check the time with his own watch. 'In twenty minutes, to be precise, sir. The good Inspector Fieseen Bijali has requested my presence for a chin-wag at his hotel. His man, Kahamir, does seem to be a regular cornucopia of information, if we are to believe all.'

'And in the meantime, where do you see the final act having its flare?'

'As a stratagem, one can't but help notice the regular pattern of all the bombings being in outlying locations. In fact, whilst the individual point names themselves mean nothing, when joined on a map, they form a rough circle. This strikes me as too much of a coincidence. No, I would venture that these bombings have been placed deliberately at a distance, in order to act as a decoy. Do you follow me, sir?'

'I hardly think that we can classify St James's Street -- outside my club by a hair's-breadth, in fact -- as being distant, Captain.'

'As Balchard informed us, sir, that irregular incident was the result of spontaneous impulse brought on by one of Vlarda's mad moments.' 'So you predict the next bombing as being in the hub of the circle, in the heart of the city?'

'Exactly. And yet ---' A frown furrowed in Captain Smethers' face.

'And yet?'

'There is this one nagging thought.'

'Which is?' Sir Basil felt his inside play him up again with its unkind acids.

'Simply that -- well, in the same way that the bombings have followed a definite pattern for the purpose of misleading us as regards *location*, might they not also be employed to mislead us as regards *method*?'

'I'm afraid you catch my brain none too agile for this morning's mental gymnastic guessing games, Captain. Explain, please.'

'Simply that up until now our growing concern and caution has been for bombs. *Bombs -- blunt, unfocused, impersonal* things used at random in the street, on impersonal things like buildings and public structures, with no pin-pointing of the individual, in spite of incidental injuries inflicted on innocent bystanders. That is, as we have been made to experience up until now, and so expect to experience again. But what if it is *not* so the next time? What if, instead of these impersonal bombs, we have, to throw us off our guard, the personalised b*ullet* or *dagger*?'

'Ah, how astute you are, Captain.' Sir Basil leaned his head back while pulling his fingers down through his beard. 'And the impersonal anarchy replaced by personal assassination.' He looked at the desk clock. 'In which case, I had better not keep you from your meeting with the good Inspector. That clock is six minutes slow, as you may not know.'

'Eight and a half minutes, actually, sir'

'*Eight* and a half!' Sir Basil looked up in surprise at this late discovery, but Captain Smethers had already gone out the door in haste of his urgent appointment.

'What exactly is it I'm supposed to be looking at, then, Balchard? It better be something worthwhile, to drag me all this way.' Detective Sergeant Dryson had a dithering moment of double-eyed winks before deciding which eye to apply to the microscope on the bench in the pathology laboratory. 'I can't see anything. Are you having me on, or something, Balchard?'

Balchard tapped Dryson's fingers with a spatula to guide

them onto the microscope's milled racking knob. 'Perhaps just a small degree of adjustment to accommodate the minute distance that is the difference in focal powers of our eyes, Detective Sergeant. Gently does it, now.'

'It seems worse, now. Gone all black.'

'Turn it the other way, then. *Slowly*. That's it.'

'Ah, that's better. I'm beginning to see something now. There, got it. So what the hell is it, then? Looks like a lump of brick lying in the gutter on a wire frame, or something or other.' Dryson straightened up from the microscope, looking round, more than a little disappointed, at Balchard. 'Is that it, then? The so-called everything and nothing of an eye-boggling wonder that you said was something important that I had to see?'

Balchard tried to keep his patience at this barrage of ignorance over his scientific findings. 'That *lump of brick*, Detective Sergeant, is none other than a grain of dirt lying, not in the *gutter*, as you so quaintly put it, but in the grooved fold of a specimen section from the late Mr Trent's last will and testament. The wire frame effect is the result of chemical staining solutions, derived, I might add, from my own experimental endeavours with vegetable dyes, so bringing out the natural fibres in the parchment, as you see there.'

'So what of it? Why the fuss in asking me here? I'm a busy man, you know, Balchard. I've got a lot of other things to see to, so if there's nothing else to ---'

'The significant point, Detective Sergeant, lies in the presence of the indentations, seen otherwise by you as mere curves, in the fibres, adjacent to the grit particle. These impressions are the result of heavy pressure being brought to bear on the paper's fold, after the paper has been first rubbed in the dirt. A constant pattern of this effect repeated along the fold of the paper gives the overall characteristic of a document that is being made to *look* older than it really is.'

Dryson raised his eyebrows in doubt at this piece of news.

'Having made an extensive study of forgers' materials and methods, let me assure you most emphatically, Detective Sergeant, that this is true. However, if I can only just continue; a careful application of the reagent zinc-chlor-iodine has given a most interesting reaction. See here..' Balchard reached round for a small crucible containing two small pieces of paper. 'Note the same distinctly strong red wine colouration in *both* pieces of paper.'

'Yes, I see it, but what does it mean?'

'It means that both the old document and the brand new writing paper in the nephew's study are of the same linen-cotton fibres. Interesting, at least, wouldn't you say, Detective Sergeant? Furthermore, test drops of sodium hydroxide on the ink of the old paper gives a brown tint, indicating the presence of the constituent dye, aniline. Thus, the ink on the *old* document is the same as that in the inkwell in the nephew's study. But what is of paramount importance, Detective Sergeant, is that aniline was not discovered until 1856, the patent for its being incorporated in inks being granted in 1861, and that is some years *after* the document is purported to have been drawn up! Also significant, but perhaps to a lesser degree, are the tobacco flakes found in the document on its first being withdrawn from the deceased's safe, and the cigarette ash found in the nephew's study. Not only is the ash of the Turkish brand, but the tobacco flakes have the chemical constituents: potassium chloride, lime, magnesia, potash and sand in the ratio of nineteen point three per cent, twenty two point five per cent, nine point two per cent, fourteen point five per cent and one point eight per cent respectively, showing them to be of the Turkish flavour. Demonstrating yet again the strong coincidental common factor between the supposedly aged document and the study of the claimant nephew. Need we proceed any further Detective Sergeant?'

'That's all very well, Balchard, but will it stand up in a Court of Law?'

'Alas, perhaps not, Inspector, but are we both not but mere bloodhounds of the Law? Is it not our function to merely lead the court upon the scent of the criminal act, after which it is the gruesomely heavy duty of those twelve jurors, as wardens of justice, as best we see it, to decide upon the fate of the accused?'

'You could be right, Balchard, but you'll still have to give me something more solid than this to convince my superiors.' Dryson gestured vaguely at the jumbled arrangement of baffling scientific paraphernalia all around him. 'Something in *writing* is what I need.'

'You will find every necessary word entered up in my report of the analysis, Detective Sergeant. And all duly signed at the bottom, as usual, as required.' Balchard handed Dryson the multi-paged report.

Dryson perused the pages without comprehending as

much as a word of the technical material. 'That seems to be in order.'

'So good of *you* to say so, Detective Sergeant.'

Dryson cocked a wary eye at the sarcastic remark, putting the report away in his inside pocket. There was definitely something bugging Balchard. Dryson could see it, almost smell it, it was that thick. Except it was not physical, like that. Not the usual thing, not that there was anything much 'usual' about Balchard. This was -- what? Something *different*. Something about his whole manner just struck him as odd in being out of place from what he had seen before. He was well weathered by Balchard's long-running impudence and his attempts to wind him up with sarcastic proddings. But that was not what this was. In his usual superior-minded brush-offs, Balchard always displayed the sense to hold back from going too far. That caution seemed to have evaporated. The bugger had changed, somehow. It was in his eyes. His expression, his whole attitude, with his words coming out of that frozen face with as much sincerity as a ventriloquist's dummy. He did not seem to give a damn, any longer, about going over the edge. Did he not want his precious 'ancillary' work with the police any more? Maybe he had fallen out with the Old Man back at the Yard. Dryson made a point to check back at the office, to see if there was anything that he had missed out on. 'But you'll still have to be coming down to the Yard to make a personal statement there? And fill us all in with your usual scientific palaver?'

'In that case, if you would care to wait a minute, while I tend to this, Detective Sergeant.'

'Right. But let's not be hanging about too long.'

Balchard set about cleaning and clearing his apparatus on the bench. In the process, he picked up an unfinished report on a chromatography test for his doctoral thesis and threw it off-handedly into the cupboard. While waiting, Dryson searched through his pockets for something. His hardened expression softened to something approaching a smile, as he did so. 'Pity you couldn't have been so smart and found the murderer for that nasty Lord Danby business. You were right, though, about it being an icicle that killed him. Imagine that -- an icicle. Anyway, our Doc agrees with that. But like I always say, there's a mile and a half difference between fancy theories and putting the finger on the murderer at the end of the day. I said it was a tough nut to crack, now, didn't I? But anyhow, we'll track him down in the end, you'll see, mark my word.'

'I eagerly await the day, Detective Sergeant. I most eagerly await *that* day.'

'As it was, all that waiting about for you, hoping that you could uncover something worthwhile on the case, and all to no end, got right up my boss's nose, it did. In fact, it seems that you've been getting up the Commissioner's nose quite a lot recently, Balchard. Not just for this, mind you, but for all these foreigners you seem to be pally with lately. The latest of whom it seems is from across the Nile, no less! A Fried Bean Jelly, for want of a better pronunciation.'

'*Fieseen Bijali*, Detective Sergeant.'

'Yes, well, whatever. At least he's a police inspector, which must go for something, I suppose.'

'Most conciliatory of you, Detective Sergeant.'

'Anyway, there's that, and *other things. Things* that the Old Man won't hardly let out as much as a whisper of to me. Know what I mean? 'Course you do. Talking of which ---' Dryson broke off to remove what he had been looking for from his pocket. He held out the slip of paper, but not without a certain tightness of manner that said it was not being handed over without a touch of conscience. 'I must say that I've had a lot of mixed feelings burning in my guts about giving you this information. I'm relying on you not to be giving me trouble with it, now, what with me looking for my bit of promotion soon.' Dryson paused for an enormous brain-wrenching moment of indecision, before his hand wavered, to finally jerk forward to surrender the paper to Balchard. 'Still, a favour's a favour.'

'Thank you, Detective Sergeant. I sincerely think that *this* will play no part in obstructing your promotion.'

Dryson twisted his face wryly. 'You do try my patience, Balchard.'

'Touche, Detective Sergeant!'

'Anyway, so there we are, then. Like you asked for, that's the list of addresses of all the alien hovels that we're watching, especially in the Shoreditch area, in connection with this bombing business, with a mind to mount raids from our station in Leman Street. *Here*, you're not in with that lot, are you? --- because if you are ---'

'*Detective Sergeant!*' The annoyance in Balchard's voice and eyes matched that in Dryson's. 'As much as I may sometimes walk *alongside* the Law, have you ever -- *really ever* -- known me to walk *against* the Law? Besides, have we both not already said that Fieseen Bijali is a *police* inspector?'

Dryson mellowed for a moment, more in subdued anger, than from satisfaction. Dissatisfaction barked back. 'So who is this bloke, then, police inspector or not? And why is h*e* given the close confidence of special arrangements, when I'm not? It's my town and manor, more than it is his. Strikes me that I'm always the last one to know about these things.' Dryson was clearly not happy about that arrangement.

'Perhaps your Commissioner sees you as the Yard's anchorman in the tug-of-war against crime, Detective Sergeant.'

'Yeah, maybe.' Dryson's disgruntled tone of voice suggested that his mind was a step behind his voice in being convinced that the statement was anywhere near to containing the w*hole* truth. 'So, anyway, what's it all about? Are you going to tell me, now that I've given you the list?'

'Do I not invariably make a point of informing you of my movements and motives in such issues?'

Dryson was not sure what to think about that one for a moment, so that his answer came out with a cautious slowness. 'Y-e-a-h --- I suppose so.'

'Only *suppose*, Detective Sergeant?'

'Oh, all right, then, you *do*.'

'So there we have it, then, Detective Sergeant.'

'Have *what*?' Dryson was no longer sure of what it *was* that he had, or did not have, considering the twist that the conversation had developed. But Balchard was plainly set on enlightening Dryson no further, so that they left the laboratory in virtual silence, with no more words on the matter. Outside in the corridor, Dryson made a final feeble effort at prevailing upon Balchard's taciturn resolve. 'Speaking of foreigners, you'll be interested to know that the Commissioner just signed a deportation order this morning, giving your Indian friends their full marching orders back to old sunny Calcutta. I reckon, personally, that they ought to appreciate that we're doing them a favour by sending them back to all that warm sunshine, instead of keeping them here, in this freezing weather.'

'I rather fancy that the sun rays do bend to the command of our Indian friends *wherever* they may be.'

'Come again?'

Just as they were about to step out into the street, a voice behind them called out after Balchard. It was the young Dr Stolling. 'I say, Balchard --- about that address of gentlemen's rooms in Warwick Street that you mentioned. I do hope that you're not going to be sore, but the truth of the matter is, old boy, that they've been taken by a friend of mine. Richard Wolmsely-Rowe, in fact. You *will* be a sport and understand that I had to help him, won't you, Balchard? We were fags together at Winchester. Can't let the old school down, and all that.'

'I *understand*, believe me.'

'Oh, good. That's jolly sporting of you. You did have me worried, with my mind in a tizzy, for a little while there, I can tell you.'

'Oh well, then, so long as you atoned for a '*little while*', you need fret no longer. Your contrition and absolution are complete as I say it.' There it was again, Dryson noted --

Balchard having a go at his colleagues, with this strange new devil-may-care disregard for their injured feelings, or how they would respond.

Stolling was too relieved to notice Balchard's sarcasm. 'That's all right, then. Anyway, old boy, I considered that I owe you one, so I've been doing a little reading up on that side, myself. It just happens that I think I've come up with another decent place for you.'

Balchard paused at the doorway, to look back at Stolling. 'No need to bother, '*old boy*'. As of now, the quest for a place of decency shall be mine alone.' In a flourishing sweeping motion with his hat in hand, Balchard made a grand cavalier-style low bow, in mocking gesture to the somewhat surprised Stolling. Dryson scratched his cheek, while throwing a meaningful glance at Stolling, before standing aside, and holding the door back, to let 'cavalier' Balchard pass by first in angry exit.

CHAPTER 31

Selik Vlarda stole a serious glance at the gloomy 'Irishman' walking beside him along the gloomy Shoreditch street. The 'Irishman's' morose indrawn mood, by its very absence of holy oaths and fiery Erin wit, had caught Vlarda's attention. It worsened with the pressing presence of sinister shapes closing in around them as they trod the cobbled labyrinth of God -forsaken streets and alleys. Whatever it was that Balchard brooded over, it seemed to smoulder within him, like a volcano in a state of imminent eruption. Or perhaps more aptly, like the dynamite bomb carried in Vlarda's leather bag. He was glad that *he* was holding it, and not Balchard. 'There is something troubling the Irishman on his mind?'

'Whatever is on me moind is for God and God alone, an' Oi'll be thankin' you to leave it there until Oi sees a priest in confession --- Father, Son and Holy Ghost!'

'Ah, but of course, that is the torture of your mind; the silly religion that forbids the taking of lives. You are concerned that tonight we take human lives, instead of useless monarchist statues. Many human lives. This is so, yes?'

The dormant flames of all the ghosts of Erin suddenly

flared up in the other's eyes as he glared at the Turk. 'Loike Oi says, just you be moindin' your lot, an' Oi'll be moindin' moine.' He spat out his wrath, kicking the legs of a destitute form lying sleeping in the foul smelling gutter. After a few more yards of gruff muttering, he climbed down from his hostility. 'Don't you be woarryin' about me not killin' folk. For to be sure, Oi'll not be doin' any extra penance for killin' any doarty English sods. To be sure, Oi saw moi very first blood when Oi was only a dimple of a lad with shorter legs than moi modder's chickens, God bless her soul.' He shuddered inwardly to keep the strain out of his voice in mentioning the maternal.

Vlarda studied the 'Irishman' again, surprised at how different he looked, not just in outer appearance, but in overall character, in his impeccable evening attire, which was their adopted guise for the evening's grand finale of a mission. Unlike an 'Irishman' of his rough background, Balchard seemed remarkably suited to the temporary role of gentleman, the tie and tails fitting him well enough, along with his blanched fingers, that were the mark of a semi-skilled worker, not a labourer. But the pale face was truly worker class, with its suffering of suppression etched across it to a depth that it could not be disguised by any finery of bourgeois festive dress. There was also strange savagery in the face, that was mysteriously his, and his alone, dangerously independent of ideological creed. Was there not just a slight pang of jealousy in the Turk's chest at not owning and controlling this part of the Irishman? Vlarda pushed this critical thought aside with his usual stratagem for concealing chinks in his ideological chain-mail by mounting a counter-attack. 'Make no mistake, Irishman, all these despicable religious rules and rules of social etiquette that you feel bound by in your decadent society are mere artefacts that serve as chains to fetter the multitude of impoverished underdogs forever in servitude of class slavery for the sole benefit of the rich. To escape them completely and forever, the chains must be broken, not merely avoided!'

The 'Irishman' gave a rasping cackle at the long-winded verbiage. 'Is that so, now? You'll not be talkin' through a hole in your hat, now, surely? An' you sayin' such bad things about the Church, an' all. Holy Modder o' Jesus! To be sure, Oi'll not be carin' a donkey's shoite who pulls the bloady lavatory chains, so long as Oi gets me moaney.'

The Turk nodded his head grimly at the foolhardy, but, nevertheless, politically naive 'Irishman'. 'Believe me, you have a lot to learn, in your country's state of political infancy, Irishman. But as you wish, so shall it be -- *for the moment.*'

'To be sure it will, an' all.'

The two walked on, resolved in their political differences, united only in the solid fall of their steps ringing out on the cobble-stones and echoing from the dark mouths of invisible alleys. Sinister foreboding was ever present, looming up to snatch out at them from the ominous dark shapes of buildings leaning in overhead on both sides. Behind his affected front of the non-caring 'Irishman', Balchard *was* gravely concerned. He was deeply worried at the increasing risk of danger that was arising from the escalation of bombings, to present a double-horned threat to the innocent members of the public. The first horn had already seen flying debris from explosions inflict injuries on incidental passers-by, but none of them seriously, as miracles would have it. The second horn was the ugly mood of unrest that this wave of violence was building up between the Metropolitan Police Force and the 'lower' communities of the City. Such strained relations between the two were worsened by the mysterious appearance of leaflets in crude English calling for a people's revolution against the Crown. Thus there was considerable threat of a backlash of retributive purges by the police on the alien quarters of the East End sector of the metropolis. This was the last thing that Sir Basil Effram's people wanted. It reversed the whole purpose of the current mission, which was to prevent important sources of intelligence being removed from the country by enforcement of deportation.

There was also the pain throbbing in Balchard's head.

Hence Balchards' reason for the list of suspect houses and *personae non gratae* given him by Dryson. Raids on these houses could quite easily cause the 'rabbits' to scurry away into deep concealment in other totally unknown 'warrens' from where they could strike another time, in a new wave of unsettling terrorism. However, with Balchard warning them indirectly, their boldness was still intact, so that they were to strike again tonight, and so step unwittingly into the snare. At least, this was how Balchard hoped it would be. All he needed was the opportunity to make it happen so, and there was much want for anxiety in such hope. Added to this, there was the ludicrous danger of them being set upon at any moment by ruffians, on account of their gentlemen's attire, and all their plans being ruined. The gross irony here being that this would be in spite of Balchard and Vlarda carrying enough explosives in the bag to flatten all those in the streets around them.

Suddenly Balchard tensed at the sight of the giant two-headed monster shadow lurking in the alley just ahead of them. A storm lamp shifted so that the 'monster' shifted with it, sliding down the wall to resolve itself into two separate shadows. Sam Loofer stepped out ahead of the trundling wheelbarrow which his mate Charlie was pushing, by himself, as usual, as well as carrying the lamp. Loofer craned in closer for a better look, as Balchard and Vlarda approached. ' 'S'at you, Mr B? 'Bout time, an' all. It's bleedin' cold standin' 'ere with codfish feet waiti----' The words broke off sharply as Balchard drove his fist into Loofer's chin, sending him reeling back against the wall, to slide down onto the ground.

The Turk was instantly ablaze with suspicion. He looked from the crumpled heap of Loofer to Balchard. 'What is the meaning of this, Balchard? Who are they?' Alarm signals flashed in the man's face at the threat of anything interfering with his mission.

'Oi'll show you what it is, so there's no mistakin' it.' With these words, Balchard took out his knife and kneeling over the supine Loofer, stabbed the steel blade in, once, twice, thrice, four times, with grunting satisfaction. '*Bloady -- doarty -- English -- swoine!*' Standing up, he inhaled deeply and let out a long breath of his relief and pleasure at the deed, while fingering the point of the dripping blade and looking down at the still form. 'There now, isn't that a truly grand sight to meet the eyes, an' all.' He turned to the Turk, holding the knife up so that the blood dripped off it between their noses. 'For to be sure, there's no sweeter smell than all the flowers in Killarney, 'cept that of an English swoine's bload on a steel blade.' To press home his rebuff of Vlarda's earlier fancy speech, Balchard took hold of the Turk's cloak and cleaned the blade on the inside, against the red silk.

They looked around them at the other obscure forms huddled against walls and doorways. But nothing stirred or blinked an eye at the killing. Death was as common as lice and pneumonia in this locality's life-style, especially during the dark hours. Only the semi- crippled Charlie showed horror, shuddering violently against the wheelbarrow, with the lamp vibrating in tight clamp against his chest. Seeing no possible danger of incrimination in the terrified face, Balchard and Vlarda strode off swiftly on their more important business.

When their footsteps had faded out of earshot, Charlie plucked up the courage to venture over to the body and hold his lamp over it. He jolted back in fright as the body moved and groaned and then sat up. Loofer put a hand to his jaw to see if it was still in one piece, after Balchard's hefty crack. 'Gawd! That flippin' nutter's a bleedin' lunatic. An' all 'for Queen an' Country', 'e says. What's yer starin' at, you ugly-faced faggot? 'Ere, gimme an 'and up. Gawd, yer looks like yers seen a ghost.'

The shaking Cockney could barely muster his words. 'I dahn't ahnderstahn!'

'Understan'! Don't make me bleedin' laugh. Me 'ead might fall off, from the feel of it. Understan'-- that's a bleedin' whopper of a good 'un comin' from you, that is. 'Bout only thing yer understans is 'ow ter piss on yersel' when we does a job.' Loofer pulled at the hole ripped in his jacket, inflicted by the savage knife thrusts, feeling blood around it. Balchard's. He had cut his own hand to bloody the blade to fool Vlarda. It had been a hair-raising few seconds, that lunatic Balchard's weird bit of play-acting fooling everybody. Some more than others. And for all that, Loofer still wasn't sure. He simply carried out his orders in return for good money. He had been very scared, almost to the point of backing out of the plan, not really trusting the weird Balchard. That bastard was capable of anything in his lunacy. But he respected money, almost more than the safety of his own life, it seemed; and Balchard had made a deal for big money; half now, half later.

Loofer picked up the dead rabbit he had been carrying and swung it round to strike Charlie across the face with it. ' 'Ere, yer bleedin' bag o' goat's dung, 'old this, an' keep an eye on the cart, while I goes fetch a wheelie.' Feeling in his pocket for the note that Mr B had passed to him in the split seconds of their brief 'engagement', Loofer hurried off in search of a cab. If he put a step on it, like Mr B had advised earlier, he was in for a big fat bonus. He broke into a trot at the invigorating thought.

CHAPTER 32

Christmas lanterns hung outside the Bedford Square residence of the Baroness Hoffenmier, the soft red glow playing on the gaily chatting throngs of guests, as they alighted and flowed from their carriages to enter the brilliantly lit doorway. Inside the hall, candlelight and gaslight united in a bright festive glare that shimmered off the regal colonnades flanking the broad stairway, and off the smaller human columns livered in gold braid and silver leggings and wigs, standing lifeless beneath the arches.

But this austerity of white-powdered, white-faced footmen was virtually the only formality. Elsewhere the atmosphere was a pleasantly informal one that tinkled with the sing-song lilt of children's voices rising above the heavier hubbub of adult voices in the background. For as much as the season was that of the child, so also was the party. With ten children of her own, the Baroness was renowned for her overflowing love for 'tiny tots', as she was apt to call all below the age of puberty. Such were her feelings that extravagant parties like this were her continual delight, especially at this time of the year. Thus, along with the brandy, port, cigars and politics at the table, there was also orange juice, fizzy sherbet, chocolate sticks and guessing games, as well. So while the Rt Honourable Liberal MP might wish to sound out the latest policy on the Transvaal development, regarding the Boer situation, from the Prime Minister, the Marquis of Salisbury, he would have to curb his political vent, to take his turn at passing the magic sugar gooseberry, or make way for yet another battalion march of a clockwork soldier.

Passing from room to room, checking everything and everyone, Captain Smethers paused in a doorway to watch Zamberini, the illusionist, remove a long knotted line of coloured flags from Viscountess Evesdale's ear. The children squeaked with delight at this, as did some of the grown-ups. A further wonder of golden balls rolling *up* along the edge of an inclined silk handkerchief held everyone in gasping awe, a quieter degree of which was Captain Smethers' share of attention. Smethers' gaze was interrupted by someone gripping his elbow and pushing a glass of sherry under his nose, to break his preoccupation and replace the empty glass that he held in his hand. 'Well, Smethie, I never imagined that I'd quite see the day when I'd catch your tongue hanging out for this hocus pocus. The dark lewd secret side of you, is it? Here, get that down you.'

Smethers looked round. It was Whynnedyte, his acquaintance from school, and now Private Secretary to the War Minister. 'Oh, hullo, Richard. Thanks.' He took a sip of the drink, only to give a surprised gulp and hold the glass up to the light for inspection, in playfully exaggerated wonder. 'What on earth!'

'Yes, it does have a stronger bouquet than all this rainwater that's being passed around.' To confirm the point, Whynnedyte took another glass of sherry from a passing servant's tray, and taking out his silver flask, poured in the essential additive of gold-tongued cognac. Returning the flask to its secret lair in his pocket, he winked and pointed into the room, at the younger audience watching the magician. 'Not in front of the children.'

Smiling back, Smethers saw the other's behaviour in a slightly different light. Apart from Whynnedyte not caring a damn about bad examples in front of the children, it was an open secret around the clubs that 'Whynny' not only sounded, but drank, like a panting dray horse. Indeed, Smethers could already detect a sibilant slur tickling the edge of the man's words.

Whynnedyte swayed and grinned wickedly over another surreptitious sip at his private elixir. 'Well, Smethie, what's a Hell-fire Club bachelor dog like you doing at an infernal ninny-nanny party, among all these horrible little brute savages, otherwise known as children?'

'Steady on, old man --- and you a loving papa twice over. No, I stand corrected --- it's almost three now, isn't it?'

'*Please* --- don't remind me.'

'By the way, where *is* Juliana? I haven't seen her all evening. She's not unwell, is she?'

'The usual thing. Getting near the time. You know, pains and sickness and all that dreadful sort of thing.' Whynnedyte pulled a long face and took refuge from his ugly thoughts of the female's prenatal struggle, by diving into another mouthful of alcohol.

'That is a pity. Poor Juliana.'

'Nonsense, Smethie, old man. That's their inherited function. Motherhood and all that piffle. Anyway, the doctor has given her some mild tonic to subdue her nervous attacks. Heaven help us when she's in one of those moods. She does wail. My, but how that woman wails. That's the only reason for my being here now -- to get out of her way, with the excuse of looking after that pair of wretched little monsters of mine.' He looked around at the room's 'ah-ing' and 'oh-ing' young audience, and almost jumped with fright at the reminder that his own miserable offspring could be so near, among that lot. 'No, they don't appear to be here. They must be busy demolishing some other part of the house. Thank God that their aunt and nanny are here to keep a rein on them.'

'You make it sound as if I should count my blessings.'

Whynnedyte choked on his drink in exasperation at the utterance. 'Let me tell you, Smethie, old man, that one hasn't an inkling of what true blessings are until one has lost them.'

'Like poor silly old you, no doubt.'

'You have it exactly, old man ---like poor silly old me.' Emptying his glass, Whynnedyte refilled it from his flask, this time not bothering with the sherry for camouflage. He put a hand to Smethers' arm to guide him away from the 'magic room' and its trilling young audience, over to the marble balustrade overlooking the deep stairwell. 'But look here, Smethie, old man, let's talk of other things. It just so happens that I have several little points scraping the old grey matter. You're just the chappie to clear them up for me -- us being old Balliol boys, and all that fudge.' Smethers' hackles instinctively shot up on guard at the cajoling soft talk that the other was now using. He looked around at the other guests for recognition of someone that he could speak to instantly as a polite means of escape. Whether or not Whynnedyte had caught wind of the other's mind for flight, he nevertheless stood facing the balustrade so that Smethers was trapped in the politeness of conversation with his back to the balustrade. 'But as I was saying, Smethie, what on earth is the likes of you *really* doing at a nursery room menagerie like this? Don't think that I haven't noticed the *extras* posted outside and all around us, trying to mix like port and champagne.'

'Extras? What extras? I'm afraid I'm not with you, Richard.'

'Good Lord, man, I know the old bag Baroness is utterly drowning in family riches, but even she can have no real need for all the extra staff we have on duty here tonight, especially outside in the grounds and in the street. One has to be blind to not see them swarming like flies over a treacle cake. *Well?*'

'*Well*, it *is* Christmas-time, after all. The very time when the hidden extra downstairs staff make their appearance up top for seasonal occasions like this. You know what I mean. I'm sure the dear old Baroness can run her household staff efficiently enough without needing *our* service.'

Whynnedyte placed a heavy patronising hand on Smethers' shoulder and leaned in so that two noses were sharing one glass. 'My dear old Smethie, one appreciates how crude animals can be trained to perform tricks in the circus, and all very well, I'm sure. But there is a limit to such things, as in this case. These so-called *extras* that you insist are *staff*, could no more be made to perform the duties of servants and footmen than you could race elephants against thoroughbreds in the Derby!'

The alcohol was having its pickling effect on Whynnedyte's brain, so that Smethers removed the hand from his shoulder and began to shift away. 'It all sounds rather splendid theory, Richard, but we can talk about it later. I want to have a word with Lady Mary over there, so if you'll excuse me for the ---'

'No, no, let me finisssh, old man, let me fishnish.' Whynnedyte pulled himself together and climbed down to a softer manner of approach, to regain the other's approval. 'Look, can't we behave sensibly like two trusting colleagues of our own generation? We both know what it's like confiding with old fuddy-duddies of our elder generation. Lord, I just recently had a gruelling session with your Old Man, Sir Basil, and most surely does one see the camel pass through the eye of the needle more easily than one can get words out of that tight-lipped old fellow. No, no, don't misunderstand me. He's a splendid old chap, and all that, but just a little difficult to pin down in a positive conversation. You would have exactly the same bother with my Old Man, believe me. But we understand each other, don't we? You can tell me what's going on. It's no use denying it. We all know what's going on.'

'I would if I could, Richard.'

'Come on, don't be like that.'

'Like *what?*'

'For heaven's sake, old man, we're *Balliol boys, remember?*'

'So you keep reminding me; who could *forget.*'

'My point precisely, old man, lest some, more than others,

should tend to forget. The fact is, Sir Basil more or less told me everything at his club the other evening. He really had no option to do otherwise as it was, what with our eyebrows being all but singed in the bomb blast. Following that nasty moment, the old gentleman virtually disclosed everything. All I want from you, Smethie, is a simple clarification on the issue. Just that. Is something going to happen tonight? *Here?*'

Smethers was not fooled by the old 'know most, no use hiding the rest' technique of ferreting information, since he knew it was a pack of lies. Sir Basil could not possibly have revealed such details, since the very information had only just come in earlier this evening by Balchard's personal messenger. 'Yes, well, like you just said, Richard, we can't always rely too readily on what the old *fuddy-duddies* tell us.'

Directly on cue to Smethers' mind to escape, two screaming children ran through between them like whistling steam-locomotives gone berserk, causing Whynnedyte to jump back, spilling half his drink. A third child brought up the rear, cantering along astride a brightly painted horse-head stick. An angry Whynnedyte tried landing a smack on the young horseman's ear, but an agile shift of the young head had the clumsy grown-up swiping at nothing but thin air, and spilling the remaining half of his precious drink. A chorus of laughter and soft-voiced rebukes at this hard-handed cruel effort rose from the group of ladies near by, the Baroness, herself, among them.

Smethers did all but run. 'Let's talk about it later, Richard. Tomorrow night, say? Dinner at my club. All right?' As Smethers went to join the ladies, he was there in smiles only, his mind dwelling on what had been unduly touched upon by the fortunately drunk Whynnedyte. News of tonight's 'final act' had only just come in to the office a short time earlier, delivered in person by Balchard's shady associate, Sam Loofer. Up until that point, it had not been known for certain how many others were operating in Vlarda's team of terrorists. But now, it seemed, Balchard had succeeded in wheedling the vital information from the devilish Turk. There were three others, and they would be exploding their bombs tonight at specified times in Portman Square, Cavendish Square and Fitzroy Square. Such activity in these squares was the obvious decoy to draw attention away from what was to happen in *this* square. Police were now positioned, ready to pounce on the anarchists with no more fear of others off the field escaping. There was also to be a bomb exploded at this house tonight; the very mission of Vlarda and Balchard, who supposedly were still on their way, if they were not already here, somewhere.

But Balchard's note had made no mention of any other last minute *ultra* plans, of the sort that now burned in Smethers' worried mind.

He had noticed the blood on Loofer's hands and coat, and had only been half amused by the explanation behind the gory stains. In order to relay his vital information, Balchard had required a trusted messenger to stand by in readiness at a pre-arranged point on a sure route. Loofer had hurried by cab to the Department, so that police and other 'extras' were now in place in and around the house and elsewhere about the city. And yet that persistent point still nagged Smethers' mind. Did Balchard also have this uncanny feeling that something else, beyond the finality of the Turk's bomb, was about to happen? Presumably Balchard had not overpowered Vlarda there and then for fear of frightening off not only the other three bombers, but something more sinister; something that could throw off its cloak of secrecy and step forth out of the shadows at any time, anywhere, into the independent limelight of climactic events.

In fleeting snatches of thought that came to him between the idle chatter around him, Smethers remembered something else. He had noticed on the back of Balchard's note, amidst abstract doodling, a very rough sketch in faint outline of a face, the moustache of which was drawn very heavily so as to give the semblance of a walrus. He also bore in mind that the sketch had been crossed out, so it could be entirely irrelevant.

Most faces were familiar to Smethers in his constant checking of people and movements in and around the house throughout the evening. Only the occasional odd one caused him to ask around politely without arousing suspicions or anxieties. Otherwise, an exchange of glances from one of the 'extra' servants would signal that all was well -- *so far*. Suddenly the humming atmosphere of mixed conversations was broken by a clapping of hands calling for everyone's attention. It was the Baroness telling everyone that young Felicity, her teenage niece, and third eldest child of the Earl of Hartford, was going to sing, accompanied on the piano by young Simon, Marquis of Aylesbury. The tittle-tattle faded and all groups drifted together to flow in a common river into the large mirrored room. Smethers drifted along in the current. With new groupings and positions, he started his checking all over again. In the process, he nodded to the bearded gentleman looking his way whilst engaged in serious discussion with the wife of the Chancellor of the Exchequer. Edward, Prince of Wales, Heir Apparent to the Imperial Crown, nodded back gracefully without an inkling as to whom it was he was bestowing the honour of Royal acknowledgement.

The young niece was well into the second verse of her lively ballad by the time Smethers had completed his survey of the room with enough satisfaction to be able to return his sweeping gaze to the front and give attention to the siren songstress of *Lorelei*. He sucked heavily on his cigar for, as a 'young' niece, she was certainly well developed, coming out in all the right places that interested him more than the silly song. Watching her chest rise and fall with the words, his mind did ungentlemanly things with her dress, whilst caressing the pale skin underneath.

Bloody slashes ripped across her silken neck and shoulders, as glass shards showered her, erupting in from the shattered French window, under the impact of the bag-bomb that came hurtling into the room.

Pandemonium broke out in terrified screams, not all of them female, and the whole room was rushed off its feet, everyone getting nowhere at the same time. Smethers was knocked over backwards in the panic. He had to punch out twice in a desperate struggle to get through to where he had seen the black bag, with its sparkling fuse. The fuse had snaked inside the bag, through a small hole at the top, when Smethers got to it. The bag was securely locked. Snatching the bag up, he ran and smashed his way, backwards, through the French window, out onto the balcony. In the same motion, he swung round and threw the bomb as far as he could out into the foggy square. 'Where the bloody hell are you, Balchard?' Smethers muttered in a lapsed moment of nervous release, while looking into the mist, waiting for the explosion. No explosion came. Balchard, in fact, had 'doctored' the fuse so that it would burn itself out without igniting the 'doinamoite'.

Hearing a scuffling sound from above, Smethers loked up towards the roof. He noticed a rope dangling just off from the balcony edge and snaking up beyond the eave of the building. On the edge of the roof several dark figures appeared to be involved in a bizarre slow waltz motion, most of them holding on to a central struggling one. 'Is that you, Carter?' The fog made it difficult for Smethers to see exactly who it was up on the roof.

'Yes, sir. 'Scuse --a second, sir. Trying to ---'old --- this perishin' bugger ---still.'

'It's all right, Captain Smethers, we have him secured.' The red fez made the identification of Fieseen Bijali easy among the rest of the black clad 'extras'

'Thank you, Inspector. Now if you could all come down, and bring that horrible *thing* with you. As quickly as possible, please.'

Someone must have taken the last words literally, for suddenly, in a frenzied flurry of movement, a dark shape leaped out off the roof edge with a blood-curdling maniacal scream, to plunge downwards, hitting the ground with a sickening dull thud. Everyone stared down in stupefaction, waiting. But dead bodies with broken backs don't usually get up and walk away on their own legs. 'Sorry, sir. Don't know what 'appened there. 'E just sort of got loose an' --well, jumped off by 'imself, sir!' Corporal Carter's apology was accompanied by a balancing sway and slates at his feet racing off into a shattering clink of oblivion in the mist, somewhere near the dead body. Minds reached out to help him regain his balance, lest there was a second 'thumping' disaster.

The red fez bobbed round again. 'Like the Corporal says, Captain, the fool jumped of his own accord. His dedication to a cause, I suppose. The men did their best. We have lost him, alas, but it was no-one's fault.'

'Once again, thank you for your help, Inspector. Now, could you all get yourselves down here, pronto. There'll be plenty of time later for deciding who's to blame for what. And *by God*, it's going to be *somebody*!' Smethers turned to go back inside, and then paused at an afterthought. 'Has anyone seen Mr Balchard?'

Nobody had seen Balchard.

Inside, disorderly cries had subsided to wimpers and snifflings. The niece was being treated for cuts, none of them serious, while an octogenarian great grandpapa was being laid back on a divan and covered with a coat, having complained of chest pains. One not so elderly lady who had collapsed in a faint seemed only to require the refilling of her glass of punch to revitalise her temporarily departed spirit. Fortunately most of the children had been out of the room at the time, and so were none the wiser to the follies of the grown-ups. With initial shock over, and enough strength being mustered to stir limbs, there was a general shift all over the house towards the doors. Those too shaken to walk unaided, relied gratefully on the supporting arm. At least this time the motion was a common one, flowing down the stairs and out of the building, so that Captain Smethers was spared the effort of fighting against the current in his aim to reach the street. All around, nervous eyes glanced about behind nervous chatter to see whose voice would first betray the disbelief in young Captain Smethers' rather weak reassurance that it had all been the sick prank of irresponsible hooligans. Carriages came and went as quickly as they could, the anxious waiting their turn. The Prince of Wales bided his time also, so being spared the ungainly sight of the body being loaded into the police wagon.

Captain Smethers, Fieseen Bijali and the 'extras' waited patiently also, shifting uneasily and looking about for the 'opportunity' to show itself. More carriages drew up and the groups moved a little more inch by inch from the hall and down the steps, Prince Edward among them. As the Prince drew nearer to the bottom, the hilt of a stiletto slid out of a nearby sleeve, into a hand preparing to strike.

The timing and situation as a whole was ideal. A falling body, be it prince or pauper, would not be out of place in a crowd where anyone could be expected to collapse with delayed shock at any moment. A little blood would also not be out of place, considering the circumstances. Ample time to 'run for a doctor', and in so doing, make one's escape. Prince Edward, sometimes loose-living son of the Empress Victoria, came a little further down the steps, and Fieseen

Bijali, sometime Inspector of the Cairo Police, tensed, ready to use the deadly cold steel in his hand.

A sharp metallic click sounded immediately to the rear of Fieseen Bijali. 'Not one inch, Inspector!' said a voice softly from the shadows of the servants' stairs that dipped below the street level. 'Move not an inch of that arm, lest a bullet enters your head. At this distance, miss, I most certainly shall *not*!' Still holding the small revolver out at arm's length, Balchard moved further back into the shadows so that those innocents descending the front steps should not set eyes on him and so be alarmed. 'Now move down slowly, Inspector. *Slowly*, please, and drop the knife backwards, down here. *Gently* now! Splendid. Now stand there, to the side, and let the others pass.'

The others, including the Prince of Wales, passed, to enter their carriages and speed off to the warmth of homes and bosoms of loved ones, or lovers, or mistresses or whatever individual taste was relished most in post-fright. That left the square to its silence and a frustrated Captain Smethers feeling empty-handed without a 'catch'.

Smethers eventually walked over to the Inspector, puzzled by his frozen stance. The Inspector's words were even more puzzling. 'You will now put the handcuffs on me, Captain Smethers, or shall the arrest be the quiet one of a gentleman?' Suspicion exploded into open realisation on Smethers' face, as he peered closer, not fully comprehending the situation. 'I must congratulate you, Captain, both you and Mr Balchard, for your astuteness. Your execution of duty has been truly commendable, beyond anything that I could ever hope to expect from my own officers.'

Smethers was still not fully understanding. 'Why did you change your mind and let it pass? If the opportunity was yours, as it *was*, why didn't you take it and strike His Royal Highness down?'

'But for Mr Balchard, I would have done so.'

'*Balchard?*'

'Why yes, he is holding a gun on me at this very moment. He has already taken my knife, so you needn't worry. I truly think we can drop the formalities now, Mr Balchard.' Fieseen Bijali turned round to look into the darkness of the servants' entrance, while Captain Smethers went down the basement stairs to investigate. He came back holding the knife and giving the Inspector a curious look. 'You've been talking to yourself, Inspector. There's nothing down here but thin air!'

Satisfied that the mission was completed, and the arch-demon removed of his horns, Balchard had melted away once more into the shadows of the night whence he had come. Second only to the surprise that he had been held at gunpoint by 'thin air', a wave of renewed hope for escape came over Fieseen Bijali. He edged away slowly. Smethers' arm shot out, a finger stabbing in the chancing escapist's direction. 'Carter! Get him!' Muttering to himself, Smethers rubbed his cheek with the hilt of the deadly dagger, now rendered harmless, not by himself, as it ought to have been, but by that weird fellow, Balchard, who wasn't even here. 'What a damn funny fellow.' Walking over to study the Inspector face to face, Smethers stood for a moment, taking in the dark Egyptian countenance. He jerked his head, indicating the roof. 'And you *really didn't* push him off?'

'Sorry to disappoint you, Captain, but no, I did not. As your Corporal here will confirm, the fool of a Turk jumped of his own accord. Dedication to a cause, I believe it is called.'

'Bloody stupid, I call it,' muttered Corporal Carter, annoyed at such a fatal slip from his control, and making sure it did not happen a second time by keeping a tight grip on the Inspector's arm.

'And all that was just a front on your part to dampen our suspicion and convince us that you were working with *us*. Or if not fully with *us*, at least not with *them*. Your independent police work of hunting down gold smugglers being your own ruse of a purported personal quest?'

'In your very own words, a jewel of precision, Captain.'

Smethers nodded, not to Fieseen Bijali, or anyone else, but to his own inner self, and walked away towards the house. He spoke over his shoulder at the same time. 'All right, Corporal, you can let the police have him now. We've plenty of time in the morning for interrogation procedures. You can pick him up tomorrow.

'*Me*, sir? *Tomorrow*, sir? Don't I get my Christmas leave, sir? It *starts* tomorrow.'

'*Later*, Carter, later. Now, if you'll just carry on.'

'Right, sir!'

The Inspector called out after the Captain. 'You are not even mildly astonished that I should do this against my country by abetting political unrest? To tarnish my flag, as an Englishman would perhaps poetically put it?'

Smethers turned round. 'One would imagine your flag to be one of untarnishible *gold*. Untarnishible, that is, as our

471

clever Mr Balchard would put it, except when contaminated with chlorine, when it turns *green*. And as we all know, green is the universal flag of *greed*. Good night, Inspector.'

CHAPTER 33

London, January, 1888

Pilkington-Greeves, Guy Du Mont and Professor Smelfors sat in silence in the Professor's study. Only the heavily ticking clock made any sound. Du Mont being too engrossed in his family's stocks and shares in the paper's investment news, while Pilkington-Greeves fidgeted with his watch chain. Professor Smelfors cleared his throat to speak. 'We are decided, are we, gentlemen?' The non response was invitation for Smelfors to press for his plea of a more clement decision. On his way out, with retirement looming up, he had nothing to lose from his outside opinion. Indeed, there would be the subtle satisfaction of being a thorn in the side, when he looked back over his shoulder in sad farewell. 'Professor Radcliffe did say that the University's Awards Board was prepared to consider an amendment of their negative ruling on the thesis, in the case of our shedding some light of a positive opinion on the works. I, myself, find young Balchard's material to be singularly stimulating in particular areas, absolutely brimming with originality of insight and effort that merits an award.'

An infuriated Du Mont cast his paper down on the table. '*Good Lord!* Any fool can contribute *original* material in a thesis. The question is whether or not the contributor is a pig-headed oaf, or someone with decent sense in his stock.' He could not resist a mocking chortle. 'Isn't there some rule of chance which our mathematicians say allows even a *monkey* the opportunity of writing up the entire works of William Shakespeare, provided it is given the time!'

Professor Smelfors was pained at this rather childish outburst by one of his colleagues so bitterly opposed to another. So unbecoming a gentleman, especially of the medical profession. He would have much preferred Du Mont's criticism to have been scientific, and not so emotionally maligned. 'I rather thought that time was somehow divided *against* young Balchard, in his earnest endeavours. And as he *has* pointed out, quite correctly, there is a growing interest in the subject of chromosomes in the European research institutes. Why, only last week there was a lecture and demonstration by the eminent Professor ----'

'*Twaddle!*'

Smelfors was taken aback. 'My dear Du Mont, I can only say that I am most dismayed if such a compliment is the best you can find in yourself for the distinguished Professor Muyens of Geneva!'

'*Balchard.* I meant *Balchard!* The man's a blithering idiot of a charlatan. He makes everything smack of genius by covering it up in obscurities, with no clear thread to follow through for corroboration. Absolute *humbug!*'

'I found some of his work to be fairly interesting, in actual fact,'said Pilkington-Greeves, forgetting the importance of his watchchain. 'Especially his theories pertaining to the factors promoting hereditary criminal tendencies. *Could* be valid, some of it, I suppose.'

Du Mont, surprised that he had been betrayed by what should have been a staunch ally of his own noble station, turned on him. '*Interesting*! Any rubbish can be made to seem *interesting*! Just like that buffoon Darwin, with his educated apes. And where's *his* proof, I ask you? Is that what your own noble family is descended from, Pilkington-Greeves? What *would* the very first Earl of Darwick say to that, I wonder, if he could just hear it? Without a doubt, he'd turn in his proverbial grave. You ought to know better, Pilkington-Greeves.'

Smelfors, heavy with the finality of recording the last words on the issue, lifted his pen and looked to the others. 'So, gentlemen, we are as before? There has been no fundamental change of opinion?' Du Mont reverted to his *Times*, immovable as a rock in his condemnation of Balchard and his sort -- *sort*, rather than station. Smelfors turned to Pilkington-Greeves for hope. His hope was unrewarded. The pen went to paper and scratched out its lasting decree. There was no further need to look up from the paper as he spoke, his voice sounding as weary as the tired metal nib. 'I shall inform the University in due course that there is to be no amendment to their original ruling' That left only one further unpleasant issue. Smelfors cleared his throat. 'As for the matter of his discontinuance of practice at this institute, in the Pathology Department --- *we* are final in our *judgement*?'

He took a brief look at the other two, and then looked back down at his sheet. Professor Felsham had already made his opinion known, in what he believed could only be a foregone conclusion, wasting no more time in attending the meeting, in his hurry to get on with all his research work, now that he had no-one to assist him, as Balchard had done.

Du Mont blurted out, just before the pen touched the paper. 'The man's a downright disgrace to medicine! Why, he as much as retches at the least sign of blood. Shamed old Racliffe's lecture, no less, by erupting in the middle of it and vomiting all the way up the ruddy theatre steps. Damn well nearly ruined my trousers with his filthy swill.'

Professor Smelfors looked up, surprised. 'I heard no mention of this. An exaggeration, surely?'

Pilkington-Greeves was also surprised. 'It's certainly news to me. I always thought that he was substantial enough in *that* aspect of his work.' Pilkington-Greeves suspected that Du Mont was lying, but he kept this to himself.

Du Mont turned away from the others, to sulk in the refuge of his newspaper. 'Everyone is just being polite, that's all.'

'As gentlemen *should* be,' rejoined Professor Smelfors pointedly, entering up a second negative motion on his agenda sheet. Silence, but for the weary clock, reigned once more in the room.

The man was rising to leave Balchard's table just as Dr Michaels entered the public house and came up to join them. Dr Michaels sat down quietly while the man finished his departing piece. 'No, I'm sorry, Mr Balchard, but I've got to change my mind. I must say that I'd expected something a bit different, likes. Nothing personal, but I'd expected a something a bit more on the heavy side that could take care of itself. Know what I mean, likes?'

'Oh, indeed I do, good sir. Indeed I do. And you do not see before you such a muscle-bound creature as may fare for itself in such a time of need? ' Balchard smiled sarcastically while revolving his glass playfully on the stained mahogany table. 'No, I rather fear that Mr Grenfell seeks a beast of brawn with all the slothful accoutrements of the African silver back gorilla, and not the litheness of the cheetah, however well endowed with lightning reflexes, mental, as well as physical. Is that not close to the truth, good sir?'

'Yeah, well, like I says, it's my money. I'm entitled to make my choice of goods before payin' out the cash. That's only fair, now, ain't it?'

'I could never be the one to disagree with you on such a point, good sir. And as such a decision has been made, so be it. But before you take your leave, perhaps you could kindly satisfy my curiosity and tell us what it is that you foresaw as befitting only the hirsute primate of the jungle?'

'*Eh?*'

'The *job*, man, the *job*! What was it you'd wanted me to do for you?'

'Yeah, well, keep your 'air on; no need to lose the rag for nowt. Seems maybe I was right in turnin' you down, if you're goin' to boil the 'ead that easy, mate. Anyway, the fact is I needs a 'heavy' to look after my daughter and escort her to

477

and from her work at the button factory. It's her old boyfriend, see. He's been annoyin' her lately, and he needs shoving' off, if you know what I mean, likes.'

'*Ah*!' Balchard transferred his sarcastic smile from the mahogany table to Dr Michaels. He then looked round at the other man. 'I rather fancy, Mr Grenfell, that your search would best lie in the direction of a good *solid* policeman. Or failing that, in the auspices of a good 'aunt' of a matchmaker who will seek out and provide for the delivery of that most traditional of domestic appliances that is otherwise known as a husband. In the former instance, I can be of some use in providing directions of pursuit; but in the latter instance, I can be of no use whatsoever. As you, yourself, have already declared, Mr Grenfell --- *nothing personal*.'

The man left.

'Something else gone wrong, I take it, Adam?' Dr Michaels leaned round to follow the man's disgruntled departure, before returning his attention to Balchard. 'I must say that you've certainly been having your toll of bad luck lately.'

'One takes it as one does the weather. Four seasons in one day, as typifies the English climate, if one cares to be as philosophical as the music hall comedian.' Balchard's face was as hard as the words were grim.

'Which is more than can be said for others, I suppose.' Dr Michaels' tone of voice did not fully conceal its guilt and he drew imaginary figures in the table's wet beer rings with his finger as further cover of his feelings. He ordered a tankard of ale for himself and some more lighter brew for Balchard. 'Look here, Adam, I really am sorry about you not getting your doctoral thesis accepted by the Awards Board. But that's how it goes, as you well know, old boy. One just has to put that nose to the grindstone and try again, if the urge is there. You'll recall that I did point out some of the weaknesses, if not faults; especially with your extrapolation graphs and other theoretical figures that you never seemed to complete, or have the *time* to complete -- the ideas were there, I grant you -- but the scientific argument and effort to back them up ---?' Dr Michaels threw up a hand at Balchard's grim reaction to this. 'Yes, yes, I know, Adam, you were too busy with your other work, your special *personal* work. You told me many times. But then, maybe that's it. Maybe your place, or vocation, if you want, lies *there*, *outside*, with your forensic investigations, as you call it, and not within the narrow confines of the medical research scientist, in here with us in the institute. Like the good *Testament* says: one can't serve two masters at the same time.' Michaels drew a deep breath and toyed with his tankard before saying his next piece. 'And yet having said that doesn't make me feel any better over the real sore point -- the matter of your mode of resignation from the Department. What can I say, really, except that I'm, well -- sorry.' He shrugged his shoulders with the emptiness that reflected the feebleness of the plea.

'The Committee's request for my resignation came only a short time after my own voluntary design to do so.' Something of a smile somehow managed to release itself after a brief struggle on Balchard's otherwise stern face, so bathing the other in absolution of his sins. But this outward clemency did not match the black storm building up behind Balchard's narrowing eyes.

Dr Michaels let out a sigh of relief. 'I'm glad you're seeing it like that, Adam. As it was, I had to tell them about your condition. Not only because old Smelfors advised it as the best thing for all concerned; but because of the pressure, as you can imagine, from Felsham and Du Mont, as soon as they heard of it. Guy has influential connections, high up. Yours is not the only side he pricks like a thorn. But even so, whichever way you look at it, Adam, it still remains that you are in desperate need of proper medical attention. Your system's intake of cocaine is critical and urgently needs cutting down, if not all at once, then by gradual process. So will you take my advice, if not as your doctor, then as your friend, and call on the specialist that I mentioned? You've got the address. It's in Harley Street. He's an old school chum acquaintance and I can solidly vouch that he's a very decent fellow.'

'I shall keep the matter in mind -- stored among other matters, in its proper order of priority.'

'For God's sake, Adam, be *serious. I'm serious*. Give it a try -- *please*! If only once, at least, as an initial exploratory meeting, to see how you react to the situation. *Will* you?' Balchard nodded solemnly. Dr Michaels once more let out a sigh of relief to release his frustration. 'Thank God for that. Little as it is, I suppose it's the best that one can hope for at this stage, considering circumstances.' He relaxed a little and drank from the pewter tankard. 'Have you solved your problem of new accommodation yet? Stolling told me that you had high hopes of settling the issue with one particular place -- Curzon Street, was it, he said?'

'Indeed, yes. A fine set of gentleman's rooms, without doubt, but a little too costly for one individual's sole pence. However, with a little of the good luck that I am due, I shall chance soon to find a lesser suit, that I can thus better afford, and share with no-one but myself.'

Oh, well, that's good news of some sort, I suppose. It shows your resolve in one thing, at last. Maybe even ----' Dr Michaels broke off to lean close to Balchard and speak in a lower voice. 'I don't know if you've noticed, Adam, but there's a man over there who keeps staring at you all the time. Hardly takes his eyes off our table. Damn rude is the only word I can think of for it. Have you seen him yet? He's the one over on your right with ----'

'With the semblance of a *walrus*,' cut in Balchard. His face had lit up as with sun rays after the blackest of rain clouds, and he laughed, with a strangely sinister tone that Michaels could not place, but which somehow unsettled him inside. 'Indeed, indeed, we *have met* before,' said Balchard, with an air that was somehow distant.

'I'm glad you're taking it so calmly, Adam. But I personally don't see it as the decent behaviour of a gentleman in public. I think I'll go over and give him a piece of my mind.' Balchard tried to reach out for the other's arm, but he was up and away. Dr Michaels stood over the *Walrus Man*. 'Look here, sir, I don't know what the deuce your game is, or what your profession happens to be, but unless you have the bona fide intention of coming across to our table to discuss your business with my colleague and myself, I can only request that you cease to harass us with your unmannerly stare. It just *isn't done* by a decent gentleman. And I'm sure, sir, that you are a decent gentleman at heart.'

The *Walrus Man* looked up, his ample moustache twitching with a mixture of apology and amusement. 'I say, do forgive me. I really must apologise if I've inflicted any inconvenience on you or your colleague. It really has been a point of mine to keep myself at a distance from my subjects, so as not to intrude on their individual privacy. It's all part of my work, you see. Perhaps I can better explain by first introducing myself.' He took out a card and handed it to Dr Michaels. 'My name is ----'

'Samuel Primms, native of the city of Sheffield, where you have yet to complete your studies for a degree in medicine,' came the precision-cut words from behind them. They both looked round in surprise, to see Balchard standing there beaming, with a strange malice in his eyes that seemed totally unrelated to the playful words that he spoke. Balchard continued. 'At present on sabbatical leave, having only recently returned from a voyage as surgeon on board the Swedish whaler, *Tamsil*. And now roaming the streets of the great metropolis, armed with the latest model in silent shutter-release photographic ingenuity --- the Facile f11, I believe.' He tapped the 'ominous' contraption, still wrapped in its camouflage of brown paper, sitting on the table in front of them. 'The very one, unless I am mistaken.'

The moment of amazement was truly Mr Primms', after which he clapped his hands in positive appraisal. 'Why, that's absolutely correct, Mr Balchard. This must surely convince me that you are as you claim to be -- namely, one professing to serve, where others have failed, by the ablest faculty for astute scientific deduction. Yes, I can see you as a forensic analyst for the police and the Home Office.'

Balchard nodded distantly, in cold satisfaction at the recognition of this last truth, his mind plainly elsewhere. Taking out a cigar with one hand and searching in his pockets for a match with the other, he bit off its end with what seemed an intention to inflict the severest pain on it. Between the two 'sages' of the moment, Dr Michaels felt relatively lost. He looked from one to the other for some sort of deliverance.

Balchard saw this, and looking first at Michaels then at Mr Primms, he turned his attention to the cleverly concealed camera on the table. 'A fine specimen of craftsmanship, without question, but for what purposre, I wonder? Perhaps, Mr Primms, you could enlighten both my colleague, Dr Michaels, and myself on the nature of your present work that so calls for such a hidden eye.'

'But of course, Mr Balchard. The truth of the matter is that, what with income being a little on the slump as of lately, I've been inclined to delve into the field of journalism on a freelance basis, to help heap up those pennies again.' He reached out to put an arm over the camera in a gesture of good harmony between two working parts. 'This present project is, in fact, an article on the behaviour patterns of different tradesmen and professional gentlemen. As in your case, Mr Balchard, a professional gentleman, where quite fittingly, my scientific ploy was duly uncovered by your scientific expertise.' Again Balchard nodded in appreciation. But by now his polite manners were solely for the surface. Underneath, his interest had cooled, where his mind passed on to other things. *Just as others had passed over him.* Primms continued. 'Without doubt the camera has helped me considerably in building up a fascinating collection of characters and situation studies. Should my work have constituted a nuisance upon any of my subjects of study at any time, it has been entirely without my knowledge and most certainly without my intention. As I have already said, I have tried most earnestly to keep to the background as best I could so as not to upset anyone.'

'Perhaps it's because Mr Balchard has a sharper eye than most would imagine for noticing the *unnoticeable*, *insignificant*, things in the background --- that's where he's *really in his element*,' quipped Dr Michaels, with a meaningful glance at Balchard.

Balchard ignored the remark and drew thoughtfully on his cigar. 'And do you perhaps foresee society deriving some benefit from this article in the future, Mr Primms?'

'One likes to think that one's efforts will eventually be appreciated and serve some fruitful purpose in the end, however unseemly their beginning. I find the photographs most absorbing. Almost to a magical degree, as timeless stills of the human subjects themselves. Moods and emotive actions captured forever on photographic plates. Investigative types especially, make a most curious study, if you'll pardon the expression. Perhaps your own case most of all, Mr Balchard. Indeed, I am seriously contemplating converting my work into a literary effort, possibly with a vein of the fiction. Who knows, perhaps in years to come I shall become more of the writer than the physician. Like so many of my predecessors who have eventually departed completely from their originally intended gentleman's honourable profession.'

Balchard held up his cigar, blowing on its end to bring out the fierce red glow, wondering on the pain it would cause when applied directly to the human cornea. He turned to smile with acid satisfaction at Dr Michaels. 'It would seem that I am not alone in my plight for changing mounts amidstream in furtherance of the quest for vocational fulfilment.'

'And you would not be offended , Mr Balchard, if I happened to employ my studies of your personal case in such a book in the future? Who knows -- perhaps I could make you famous.'

'On the contrary, Mr Primms, I would deem such an achievement to be an honour. Indeed, perhaps it will be *I* who makes *you* famous with my work.' Balchard took out a professional card and handed it to Primms. 'Perhaps we shall have good reason to meet again, Mr Primms.'

'Quite possibly, Mr Balchard, quite possibly. My card.' Balchard took the card and walked off with Dr Michaels. Just before reaching the door, he turned for a final look at Primms -- Primms the journalist --- Primms the man presenting images to the public. And as demonic clouds unfurled in Balchard's mind, he saw dark images forming. Much darker than those possibly foreseen by Primms. Yes, he saw a definite use for this man, with his journalistic connections.

Suddenly the pain in his head was throbbing with alarmingly high intensity. A rising nausea engulfed him, darkening his vision, as he began to feel faint. He needed oxygen, to get out into the fresh air, to get away from this place -- to anywhere. He desperately needed to escape the piercing intrusion of his sanity that was boring into his brain. With his body burning and his pulse racing, he felt his eardrums near to bursting as the bells once more screamed out their maddening chimes inside his head. A hubbub of voices roared out from gigantic hostile faces all around him, as they watched him fight his way through a copse of chairs that tried to stop him getting to the door. Yet in the midst of this twisting madness, part of him was able to see that this was *another* person inside himself. An *intruder*. Totally alien to that sane self who walked unbending on sane days. Invading through taboo portals, in increasing effort to seize sovereignty of his brain. In the last moments that he retained willpower to resist the other person, he shrank back from visions of the dark deeds the other was intending.

Dr Michaels was at once all around him, having seemingly developed more arms than an octopus, and was helping him out through the door, into the fresh air. Like a fish newly landed, Balchard's brain gasped after its madness, through choking oxygen. As they walked away, the *coup d'etat* was almost over. Balchard's mind was slowly giving way to a new regime of thought. The fearful was gradually subsiding, so that stages of what had to be done now came to him in calm, cold, rational sequence. Mental takeover was all but complete.

'It's certainly feasible and *clever*, Captain -- smacks of double reserve precaution -- Fieseen Bijali working independently of Vlarda, as you say.' Balchard shifted nervously as he sat talking to Captain Smethers' back, waiting for him to come away from the filing cabinet.

'Yes, one has to admit that it really was quite a jolly good means of securing a virtually one hundred per cent security screen over their mission. They obviously reckoned -- the Russians, that is -- that it would allow the Inspector to play his part more convincingly if the Turk was entirely unaware of his alliance, or even of his existence, in the plan. It seems to have worked well. Or at least it almost worked.' Smethers paused for a moment, staring blankly at the wall, thinking how closely the plot had come to within a few feet of succeeding, and what such a horrific act would have meant. He shook off the inside shiver and dipped his head again to continue looking through the files.

'But surely these two worked for different ends, anyway? One for his mercenary gold -- the other for his impassioned suicidal nihilist theory?'

'When stones are thrown in a common direction, one doesn't worry too much about who's throwing them, so long as they serve the common purpose of shattering the enemy's window -- the right hand doesn't know what the left hand is doing. More or less, if you follow me?'

'And all that sort of thing -- I think I get the picture,' replied Balchard gruffly, feeling patronised by Smethers' simplistic examples.

Catching Balchard's agitated tone, Smethers glanced round in sharp reproval before looking back to his files. 'Yes, more or less, with perhaps a special emphasis, however regretfully, on *all that sort of thing*. The gruesome fact is that we're all having to indulge in it to some degree in order to make ends meet and achieve results. However much we may wish to deny it, times are changing, with special significance in the military field. A whole new manual of modus operandi has to be drawn up, as regards the collecting of strategic information. A whole new bag of devious, if not dirty, tricks has to be employed. Which brings me to this.' Smethers held up the file which he had removed from the cabinet. Closing the cabinet drawer, he returned with the file to the table. Before opening the folder, he paused for separate thought. 'Incidentally, the nihilist movement is not so crackpot as one would hope. The movement does seem to be gathering momentum in Europe, with rebellion of the proletariat being more than a mere whisper in the ears of the Crowned Heads. Anyway, back to this.' He opened the folder and began looking through the pages for a few seconds, before reaching out for his teacup as he read. He suddenly looked up, remembering Balchard. 'I'm sorry, would you like some more tea? I see you've finished yours.' Balchard's grimaced shake of the head declining the offer was not fully clear in its message to Smethers. 'I say, Balchard, are you all right?' Balchard's puzzled expression questioned this. 'It's just that you look positively -- well -- *hellish*! And you keep rubbing your head. Are you sure you don't want a drop of the old ---' Smethers was reaching down to a lower drawer for a bottle of brandy. But he was cut off by Balchard's shaking his head and waving this aside as nothing, anxious as he was to learn what new contingency plans Smethers was proposing. 'No? Oh, well.' Smethers dunked his biscuit in his tea and then swore as half of it fell off into the cup. 'The fact is, like I said earlier, we want someone to keep an eye on him and nurture the potential for a good source of intelligence that he could prove to be. To do this, it would be convenient if we could monitor his progress by having someone socially suitable to befriend him and and so milk his confidence,'

'Socially suitable. I see. And that's me? Why *me*, exactly?' Balchard knew perfectly well that it was his working-class background that Smethers considered to be an asset for this assignment. But knowing that the Captain would have some discomfort actually stating this to his face, gentleman that he was, Balchard wanted very much to *see* him suffering that very discomfort. And uncomfortable Smethers *was*. Using the distraction of turning pages as a cover, Smethers tactfully chose his words. 'We know how these people are thinking and, indeed, massing their efforts to topple royalty everywhere, along with the ruling class aristocracy of societies in general -- to replace them with an egalitarian proletariat system. A system where everyone would be equal, and no-one need look further or higher than the self-made man for honour and dignity. At least that's what they're saying for now, from what we can make of intelligence gathered.' Smethers paused for a moment. And unless Balchard solely imagined it, the Captain seemed to duck his head down nearer to his file pages. 'You should be able to slip in with them -- like a duck to water, Balchie, without too great a splash. You've done well for yourself, considering your background -- self-made, self-educated, and so forth. They should take to you without too much suspicion.' Smethers looked up, raising his eyebrows, inviting a response from Balchard. He could see trouble burning in Balchard's face, like a volcano about to release its deep down fury by throwing lava out up top. Suspecting some sort of class conflict to be at the root of Balchard's trouble, Smethers groaned inwardly. It was forever coming across whenever they talked, encroaching on their more important work, and wasting valuable time.

'Looks like it could be a long drawn out affair. *Would* it be? said Balchard.

Relieved to be over the hurdle with Balchard's personal chagrin, born like a cross on his shoulders, the Captain perked up. 'Put bluntly like that -- yes, it probably will be.'

'*How* long?'

Smethers scraped the bristles on his lower lip reflectively for a few seconds. 'That isn't really easy to say at this early stage. Could be for a little while. Could be for a long time. Perhaps a *long, long,* time. I think we can worry about that point when the time comes. Are you game?' Balchard swayed back in his chair, holding his knee and nodding slowly where the mind was not wholly settled. Seeing that more persuasion was needed, Smethers searched for the right cajolery to win Balchard over and wind up the meeting, before the bloody fool backed out. 'That was a brilliant piece of work you carried out for the Department. And the point to remember is that you're contributing this not only to the Department, but in the service of the Crown.' Hollow words, Smethers realised, but he was willing to use anything to get this assignment up and running. He waited, licking his lips. While he waited, he saw anxiety and despair torturing the inner Balchard -- and *something else?*

'And you can trust me not to *wander* -- to not have personal affiliations with the plebeian enemy, *considering my background*?' The sarcasm glowed in Balchard's eyes.

Smethers parried the testing remark with a smile and a little laugh. 'One likes to think that an Englishman of decent education can be trusted to navigate the *correct* course through troubled waters so avoiding *disaster*.'

Balchard noted the replacing of the usual 'decent school' with 'decent education' in a patronising accommodation of his case. He also felt the warning vibrations of Smethers' accentuated words cautioning him against treason. Supposedly the waters could be murky, passing through Traitor's Gate. But behind Smethers' friendly smile lay a remedy of much swifter delivery than incarceration in the Tower with all its entailing political hiccups. Such a clandestine measure required only a reasonable covering cover of darkness and a good spade for out of the way burial. Never known, never seen, never missed.

Smethers slapped the file shut and sat back to look at Balchard, to weigh up his reaction to his advice. 'I should see it as keeping your money on the same horse and sticking with it, win or lose. If you lose, it's only half the pain you'd feel than if you'd changed to a new horse at the last minute, and *it* lost.' Smethers blew out a woeful whistle, picking up the file at the same time, to tap its end on the table. 'Let's face it, as I've just said, the world is changing. New operational techniques, however unsavoury, are becoming more and more incumbent on the job. A small minority has to legislate and perform these duties -- dirty work, if you like -- for the sake of the majority, in the name of national security. Probably at this very moment, as we talk, there are those going about their work in the sewers beneath us, beneath the whole city, in fact, clearing up the mess, *our* mess, and so making things better for us. Everyone benefits in the end. You - me --' Smethers looked pointedly at Queen Victoria's portrait on the wall, '----*everyone*.' He pushed the file across the table for Balchard to inspect. 'At least have a read on the fellow's background. Friedrich Engels. You'll find he's quite an interesting character. In spite of his involvement with his family business, furniture manufacturers, he seems, nevertheless, to have caught the fever of this emerging anti-capitalist movement that this fellow Marx managed to cook up before he died. But Engels has made important communications with him, and so far as we can gather, is engaged in editing and promoting Marx's written works. He's not one to grant friendships easily, any more than popes give private audiences indiscriminately. So I warn you here and now that your task , if you decide to take it up, will not be an easy one. Mind you, if you look upon it from that point of view, that is, as a challenge to your own professional studies, it could well turn out to be your kind of thing, with your work cut out for you. But do first have a browse over his backgtound details and personality assessment before you make up your mind.'

As Balchard turned the pages of the file, a small note fluttered out. 'What's this --- Vladimir Ulyanov? * Russian, I take it?'   *(Later to be known as Vladimir Lenin)

Smethers had leaned forward, frowning, to find out what it was that Balchard had come across, when he suddenly remembered. 'Oh, yes --- *that*. Last minute thing; another

Russian zealot hot on the uptake of this life-with-no-property nonsense that Marx concocted. It does appear to have its dangerously contagious effect, to have influenced him enough to make him want to come over here to see Engels himself. Probably with a mind to spreading the good word over there, among the good Raussian peasants --- a great host of illiterates. He's certainly got a hard task on his hands, if he tries. He's been invited over, courtesy of Herr Engels. And him only a lad; a mere eighteen years old.'

The word 'lad' triggered a new line of images in Balchard's mind, and as he followed them, his mind's eye focused on a distant point in the past. An avalanche of weird feelings fell suddenly upon him, urging him to get up and leave. Chilling tremors passed eerily through him in spite of the room not being cold. With sanity diminishing by the minute, fear of the change mounting within him, and what its ultimate completion would mean, continued to grow and grow. It was becoming uncontrollable. How long could he hold on before control was no longer his? His brain screamed. The room was rapidly becoming claustrophobic, with the walls crushing in on his mind. If he remained seated here, it would suffocate him, squash him, *annihilate* him. Destruction now reared up in his mind, a heaving black monster held back on naught but feeble leash. What last vestiges of sanity he retained made him cringe back in fear from visions most horrific. With his madness fast becoming overwhelming, his remaining sense told him that he could no longer stay in the room, in the company of another human being.

He rose unsteadily to his feet, with his eyes racing all

around the room, settling anywhere but on the man opposite. 'I think my mind is made up.' Again Balchard felt the words come out of his own mouth as if from another person far, far, away.

'Really?' Smethers' lame tone had his expectation balanced on a knife-edge.

'I'll do it.'

'Splendid. Good man. You've done the right thing.' A once more relieved Smethers jumped up and strode swiftly for the filing cabinet, speaking over his shoulder to Balchard. 'If you'll just hang on a second, I'll get the detai -----'

But Balchard, without waiting, had strode out through the doorway, in what seemed a semi hypnotic state. Smethers was about to call him back, but after a moment's better judgement, decided to let him go. He had spent enough time dilly-dallying with a Balchard that seemed to be not all there. He had seemed greatly unsettled and distantly preoccupied on matters not pertaining to their present situation. Smethers had noticed these disturbances in Balchard's behaviour occurring more frequently over the weeks. Had the Department, and he, himself, made a mistake in recruiting Balchard into the operational staff, and indeed, in keeping him on? Smethers slammed the cabinet drawer shut, satisfied in his choice of action. If Balchard *should* become an embarrassment to the Department, making it imperative to 'drop him', then *dropped* he would *be*. Promply and 'invisibly'. In the meantime, he had to summon Carter, to deal with more important matters in hand. Smethers leaned his head out into the small corridor. 'Carter! In here now!' Corporal Carter came into the office to collect new operational rendezvous details for relaying to Balchard. 'Tonight, if you can, Carter.'

'Sir.'

Two nights later, Smethers let Balchard alight from their cab several streets ahead of the place arranged for meeting Engels. That way he could follow slowly, under cover and at a distance, to see that contact was made without any hitches. Watching him go off with Engels and the fervent young Russian, Ulyanov, Smethers saw them as a definitely strange lot. Perhaps suited to each other in their peculiar ways. They were misfits, misguided, if not lost souls --- at variance with their social stations and traditions --- meandering, searching, in choppy waters, like rudderless ships. He had this uncanny feeling that their actions could well have a rocking effect on society. Needless to say, whatever personal 'mischief' Balchard got up to would have to be kept under a lid, away from public scrutiny, the papers, police interference and so forth, for the sake of the country's military security. He directed the cab to turn away, letting them go on their way, tete- a-tete, in heated debate. Their gesticulating hands, especially those of the young Russian, were the only disturbance to the air at *that* moment in time.

Much later that that evening, with business concluded, Balchard left Engels and Ulyanov, to go off into the Bluegate Fields district. The rank smell of human excrement following every turning, as he wandered deeper into the desolate cobble-stoned labyrinth, made it seem like walking along the inside of some gigantic slumbering beast. After some time, Balchard heard the distant voice of what could only be a constable talking to, in turn, what could only be a prostitute. He was asking her for her name. 'What's it ter do wiv you, copper? I ain't done nothink. Maybe yer's wantin' summit yersel', eh?' said a coarse female voice.

'Now don't you be comin' the whorin' tart wi' me, lass, or I'll be runnin' you in.'

'It's Mary.'

'Mary bloomin' what -- *Holy Virgin*?'

'Mary Hunnet, to you, yer great lump o' ---'

'Now be'ave yourself , or I *will* be takin' you in, lass, for obstricting police work.'

'So now yer 'as me name down in yer little book, does I get paid for it, then?'

'None o' your cheek! Go on, 'op it!'

Balchard waited to see if the policeman would go off in the opposite direction. Instead, the heavy footsteps were coming in his direction. As the passing policeman paused and stepped back to look into the dark alley where Balchard was standing, Balchard turned to face into a doorway, pretending to urinate. About to approach the gentleman for a few words of routine checking, the policeman changed his mind and turned away, giving a departing caution over his shoulder to Balchard. 'Mind 'ow you goes, sir --- lots o' thieves an' no-goods 'anging about these streets, 'specially this time o' night. G'night, sir.'

Balchard waited for the footsteps to fade away, before emerging from the alley and going on his way. Several streets on, a dark shape, barely distinguishable as female, detached itself from the shadows, to make a slithering approach to Balchard. Nuzzling her face about his neck in false affection, the woman's roving hand reconnoitred his coat surface for the reassuring wallet bulge that meant a worthwhile customer. 'Are yer a doct'r or summit?' she asked, sparing half an eye for the leather medical bag held firmly by his side.

' "Or summit",' he affirmed avertedly, in a low side murmur. ' "Or summit", ' he repeated.

'Whatcher 'ave in yer bag, then? All them 'orrible cuttin' an' pokin' thingummies? Goin' ter do a bloody 'bort job on some poor lass an' cut 'er bastard bit kid out o' 'er belly, then, are yer?' Peeved by his non-response, she squirmed about inside his limp arms, like a purring cat, cajoling him with her small-talk for a bit of business. 'So 'oo is it, then? Bet I know 'er. Bet it's that fuckin' fartin' cow, Scroggins. She's 'ad it commin' to 'er for long time, she 'as, the bitch. Or maybe it's Polly. It's that Polly, ain't it? Yer can tell me. Go on, tell me.'

The words 'You'll see' failed him, and instead, he heard himself hushing her, whilst tugging her arm and guiding her into the darker recess of a yard entrance.

'What does I call yer, luv?' came the faint whisper, after a pause, from the darkness. Her scream, before its being cut off forever, drowned out all his words but the last.

'----- *daffodils!*'

A moment of heavy breathing followed, before the darkness hissed out its harsh message, slicing the night like his knife's cold blade: ' 'Tis *Jack* I am --- to *this* name will minds more surely harken!'

NB (Whilst Mary Anne '*Polly*' Nichols was the first *known* victim of Jack the Ripper (31 August, 1888), it can never be known how, where, or on whom the Ripper *may possibly* have 'honed' his evil blade as a build-up to those infamously horrendous murders.)